C21

C000244403

28/11/2015		
11/01/2016		

D&P/4261/4.12

Nottinghamshire County Council

Please return / renew by the last date shown.

Published in Great Britain 2013
by Mills & Boon, an imprint of Harlequin (UK) Limited,
Eton House, 18-24 Paradise Road, Richmond, Surrey TW9 1SR

PAYBACK AFFAIRS © by Harlequin Enterprises II B.V./S.à.r.l 2013

Shattered by the CEO, Bound by the Kincaid Baby and *Wed by Deception* were first published in Great Britain by Harlequin (UK) Limited.

Shattered by the CEO © Emilie Rose Cunningham 2008
Bound by the Kincaid Baby © Emilie Rose Cunningham 2008
Wed by Deception © Emilie Rose Cunningham 2008

ISBN: 978 0 263 90569 4
ebook ISBN: 978 1 472 00142 9

05-1013

Harlequin (UK) policy is to use papers that are natural, renewable and recyclable products and made from wood grown in sustainable forests. The logging and manufacturing processes conform to the legal environmental regulations of the country of origin.

Printed and bound in Spain
by Blackprint CPI, Barcelona

Emilie Rose lives in North Carolina with her college sweetheart husband and four sons. Writing is Emilie's third (and hopefully her last) career. She's managed a medical office and run a home day care, neither of which offers half as much satisfaction as plotting happy endings. Her hobbies include quilting, gardening and cooking (especially cheesecake). Her favorite TV shows include *ER, CSI* and Discovery Channel's medical programs. Emilie's a country music fan because she can find an entire book in almost any song.

Letters can be mailed to:
Emilie Rose
PO Box 20145
Raleigh, NC 27619
USA

E-mail: EmilieRoseC@aol.com

SHATTERED
BY THE CEO

BY
EMILIE ROSE

To my parents, who have given so much love
and support even when it wasn't easy.

Mom and Dad, thanks for all you do.

Prologue

"**Y**ou will return to Kincaid Cruise Lines as acting CEO for one full year." The lawyer paused dramatically, his eyes finding Rand Kincaid's over the top of Everett Kincaid's will. "And you will convince Tara Anthony to come back with you as your personal assistant."

The words hit Rand like a bullet, knocking him back in his chair and punching the air from his lungs. "No. *Hell* no."

The lawyer didn't flinch. Years of dealing with Rand's bastard of a father had probably left the man immune to profanity and raised voices.

"Should you refuse, not only will you forfeit your share of your father's estate, but your brother and sister will lose theirs, as well. In fact, if any of you fail in your assigned tasks, then I'm instructed to sell all of Everett's holdings to Mardi Gras Cruising for one dollar. The business, the estate, the investment portfolio."

Son of a bitch. Rand slammed his palms on the table and shot out of his chair. He should have known the old man would find a way to pull his strings—even from the grave. "Mardi Gras is Kincaid's biggest rival, and the CEO is my father's sworn enemy."

"I am aware of that."

Clenching and releasing his fists by his sides, Rand paced the length of the Kincaid Manor dining room. He glanced at his younger brother and sister and saw more than grief and shock in their pale faces. He saw resignation, and in the case of his brother, frustration and suppressed anger.

They expected Rand to walk. The way he had five years ago. The fact that he'd failed to contact Mitch or Nadia or return their calls in the interim had no doubt contributed to their lack of faith in him, but he'd cut all ties because he hadn't wanted to put them in the middle of his war with their father.

Rand struggled to shake off the invisible straight jacket cinching tighter around him. He owed Mitch and Nadia, and not just for abandoning the family business.

He pivoted and refocused on the attorney. "Anyone but her. Not Tara Anthony."

Within three weeks of declaring she loved Rand and wanted to spend the rest of her life with him, the woman had gone after deeper pockets when Rand refused to cough up a wedding ring.

"I'm sorry, Rand. Everett insisted on Ms. Anthony."

His father would. The manipulative despot. He had always coveted whatever Rand had and then he'd taken it by fair means or foul and flaunted his successes like a cat leaves a carcass on the doorstep.

"And if she refuses?" Rand would make sure Tara did.

"Then you'll change her mind. Unless you choose to fail, there is no other option."

Another dead end. Frustration burned like acid in his belly. "I'll contest the will."

The lawyer didn't even blink. "Contesting by any of the three of you immediately results in forfeiture."

Rand struggled with the urge to punch something. His tyrannical father had closed the obvious loopholes before unexpectedly dropping from a heart attack in his latest mistress's bed three days ago. But there had to be a way out, and if there was, Rand would find it.

He planted his fists on the table and leaned toward the attorney. "Richards, you know my father must have been mentally incompetent to demand this."

"He wasn't crazy, Rand," his brother said before Richards could reply. "I'd have known. I worked with him every day. You would have known, too, *if* you'd stuck around." Mitch made no attempt to conceal his anger.

Nadia's head bobbed in agreement. "Dad was impossible, insensitive and immoral. But he wasn't insane."

A volley of curses ricocheted around inside Rand's skull. He straightened and nailed his brother with a hard stare. "Why aren't you protesting? CEO should be your job."

Mitch shrugged, but his jaw looked rapier-sharp. "Dad wanted you."

Rand couldn't contain his snort of disgust.

"That's a first. You were always his favorite and his right-hand man. I was his sparring partner—the one he liked to beat." Not physically, but in every other way. Sports. Business. *Women.* Until his father had taken their competition too far.

Rand looked from his brother to his sister. "This all-for-one garbage is absurd. He spent his life trying to drive us apart."

"And it looks like in death he's trying to bring us together," Nadia replied.

Richards cleared his throat. "Over this past year Everett

realized he'd made some mistakes. He wants the three of you to help him rectify them."

"So he won't eternally rot in hell," Rand muttered. A sense of doom descended on his shoulders. He was trapped. Like a rat in a maze. Exactly how his father liked it.

Whatever game you're playing, old man, I will win this time.

Even if it meant facing Tara again.

He squared his shoulders and looked his brother straight in the eye. "I'll do it. I'll come back to KCL, and I'll make Tara Anthony an offer she can't refuse."

One

The doorbell echoed through the two-story foyer, stopping Tara Anthony in the process of kicking off her shoes. An ivory sandal dangled from her toe.

Tightening her grip on the newel post, she debated ignoring her visitor and then groaned, stabbed her foot back into her shoe and rolled her tense shoulders. Whoever was out there had very likely watched her walk inside thirty seconds ago and knew she was here. As if to prove her point, the bell chimed twice more in quick succession.

No doubt she'd find another developer on the other side of the door, one who wanted to buy her lot, demolish her old house and build a minimansion in its place as had happened with so many of the neighborhood properties. This section of Miami had become an increasingly desirable location lately. But she couldn't sell. She'd promised her mother she'd hold on to the house. Just in case.

Tara pushed back her hair and sighed. She wanted this rotten day to end, and she wasn't up for a pushy sales pitch tonight. But apparently, her hot bath and the pint of Ben & Jerry's she'd planned to have for dinner would have to wait.

Not for long.

Tomorrow she'd buy a bigger No Soliciting sign.

Resolved to deal with her uninvited guest as quickly as possible, she crossed the foyer and yanked open the door. She reeled back in shock at the sight of the tall, broad-shouldered man filling the opening.

"Rand," his name poured from her in a lung-deflating whisper.

An evening breeze ruffled short, straight hair the color of dark chocolate, and his narrowed hazel eyes raked her from head to toe and back.

Emotions tumbled over her like raging river rapids. Shame. Pain. Anger. But something warm and welcoming spurted through her, too. *Love?* Could there be a lingering trace of that misplaced sentiment in her veins?

Surely you aren't still stuck on a man you haven't seen or spoken to in five years?

"May I come in?"

So polite, that deep, rich, goose-bump-raising voice. He hadn't been polite the last time she'd seen him. That day his tone had been cold, cutting and cruel.

You didn't waste any time, did you? You couldn't hook me so you went after deeper pockets. But the joke's on dear ol' dad. He wants you because he thinks I do. But I've already had you, Tara. And finished with you. He's welcome to my leftovers.

The chill that had seeped into her bones that night at Kincaid Manor returned. Wrapping her arms around her chest, she crammed the memories back into their dark closet and focused on the man in front of her.

"What do you want, Rand?"

He looked stiff and perturbed in his perfectly tailored dove-gray suit, white shirt and burgundy raw silk tie, as if he didn't want to be here any more than she wanted him on her front porch. "To discuss my father's final demands."

Everett Kincaid. One of the low points in Tara's life. "I heard he'd passed away. I'm sorry for your loss."

Rand didn't look mournful. "His will involves you."

Everett always had been kind to her, but why would her former boss leave her a bequest? Especially after the way they'd parted. "He left me something?"

Rand's lips flattened into a thin line and his square jaw shifted to an antagonistic angle. "No, but unless you agree to his terms we'll lose everything."

Talk about dramatic. She barely managed not to roll her eyes. And then, puzzled, she frowned. Rand had never been the over-the-top kind. He'd been very straightforward about what he wanted. And what he didn't.

She tucked a curl behind her ear and wondered if he noticed she'd cut her hair or that she'd lost weight since they'd been an item. Or had he slept with so many women that the features blurred together into a homogeneous female form? Had she even left a mark in his memory?

His lousy relationship track record hadn't kept her from falling in love with him five years ago, but back then she'd been young, shy and an impossibly naive twenty-four. She wasn't any of those things anymore. Watching her mother die slowly and painfully had aged Tara what felt like decades.

She should boot Rand and the memories associated with their brief affair right off her property, but curiosity got the better of her. She opened the door farther. "Come in."

His brisk stride carried him past her and straight into the

den. The same cologne he used to wear encircled her like a long-lost friend. A friend who'd stabbed her in the back.

No, that wasn't right. Rand had told her before their first date that he wasn't interested in forever. She was the one who'd broken the rules by getting emotionally involved. But how could she help herself when he'd been everything she'd ever dreamed of in a man? Fun, sexy, intelligent, attentive, gentle, good in bed. Correction. Amazing in bed.

She couldn't help wondering if she could have changed his mind about their future had she kept her mouth shut and let the love and trust sneak up on him. But she'd never know because three months into their affair she'd slipped up after making love and blathered out her feelings for him and her dreams for their future like the besotted twit she'd been.

Her ill-timed words had launched the next Ice Age and the fastest dumping in history. Rand had left her apartment so fast it's a wonder he hadn't burned tracks in her carpet. And then he'd left the country.

A frown line formed between his eyebrows as he examined the room's furnishings. "This looks nothing like your old place."

So he did remember. Her stupid heart skipped erratically. She scanned the room. The traditional furnishings were not the light-and-airy wicker and chintz she'd had in her apartment. "It's my mother's house and it was my grandparents' before it became hers."

His gaze sharpened and shot to the archway leading to the kitchen. "Is your mother at home?"

Tara's heart squeezed with pain and guilt that seemed like they would never end. "She's dead."

"Recently?"

She gave him points for trying to be civil, but she didn't want to discuss her mother with him. The wound was still too raw. "A year ago. But that's not why you're here. Could you get to the point, please? I have plans tonight."

Sad, solo plans, but that was the story of her life these days. Other than a few regrettable exceptions in those lonely months immediately after her mother's death when Tara had needed someone to hold her, someone to keep the loneliness at bay, men had been a nonissue for her since Rand had dumped her. She'd never found the passion or the connection she'd experienced with Rand with another man, nor had she found the solace she'd been seeking on those lonely, regrettable nights. The physical acts with near-strangers had left her feeling emptier and more alone than before, so she'd quit looking.

Tension crackled in the air between them. Rand didn't sit. Neither did she. "Everett's will requires me to return to KCL as CEO—"

"Return? You left Kincaid Cruise Lines? When? Why? The company is your life, your legacy."

"Yes. I left." His expression turned even more formidable. The lines bracketing his mouth carved paths through his five o'clock shadow. She used to love to feel that stubble beneath her fingertips and on her breasts. The memories made her pulse quicken and her skin flush.

"My father insists you come back as my PA for one year."

Rand's shocking revelation made her willing to overlook the fact that he hadn't answered all of her questions. "Me? Why? And why would I want to?"

"If you don't, then Mitch and Nadia will lose their home, their jobs and everything else."

Regret settled heavily in Tara's chest. For three years Nadia had been her friend, probably the closest one Tara had ever had. But a fissure had formed between them when Rand abruptly ended his and Tara's affair, and then Everett's proposition had finished what was left of the relationship. Tara had been so filled with shame and self-loathing she hadn't been able to face Nadia—or any of the Kincaids for that matter—again.

"I don't understand. Why would Everett insist on me returning to my old job? And why now?"

"Who knows what was going through his twisted mind? He has each of us jumping through hoops. He's harassing us from the grave." Bitterness and fury vibrated in Rand's voice.

What had happened to drive the men apart? Rand and his father had always been competitive, but she didn't remember Rand hating Everett. It sounded as if he did now.

"Can't you do something about the will?"

He shook his head. "I had a team of top-notch lawyers go over every word. The will's airtight. I'll pay you ten thousand a month, plus benefits."

Her mouth dropped open. "You're joking."

"No."

That was double what she'd made when she last worked at KCL and more than three times her current salary.

It had taken Tara four months after she'd left Kincaid to find a job. It hadn't been easy without a reference, but she hadn't dared ask for one after the way she'd left without giving notice, without even returning to empty her desk. Her replacement had done that and shipped Tara's belongings to her.

By the time Tara had finally found a position, she'd wiped out her savings, given up her apartment and moved in with her mother. The new job had paid less, but Tara had taken it because of the flexible hours and the opportunity for telecommuting gave her the time she'd needed to care for her mother during the grueling courses of chemotherapy.

Tara definitely planned to leave her current job. Her newly promoted boss was an arrogant, condescending jerk who had decided Tara's "flexible hours" meant she was at his beck and call 24/7. She just hadn't worked up the energy to start looking for a new position yet.

But working with Rand again... Too risky given that tiny flicker of joy she'd experienced earlier. The man had already broken her heart once. She'd have to be a fool to return for a second helping of that kind of agony. She shook her head. "I'm sorry. I'm not interested."

"Fifteen grand a month," he offered without hesitation.

Tara caught her breath at the obscene amount and her knees nearly buckled. Carol Anthony's job as a hairstylist hadn't provided health or life insurance, and Tara had inherited her mother's debts along with her home and possessions. With that kind of money she could pay off the exorbitant medical bills her mother had left behind and stop the increasingly threatening collection notices.

She was more than a little tempted. But why, oh, why did it have to be Rand Kincaid making this offer? "It's not about the money, Rand."

He punched his fists to his hips, shoving his suit coat away from the flat plane of his stomach—a stomach she'd once been free to touch and taste. "Look, we both know you don't give a damn about me. But do it for Nadia and Mitch. They don't deserve to have the rug ripped out from under them. Name your price, Tara."

Tara wavered. Common sense said refuse. But a minuscule, insistent part of her reminded her how good she and Rand had been together. When she'd been with him she'd felt special and important, as if happily-ever-after might actually be possible.

She'd never had time to come to terms with his abrupt ending of their relationship. Before she could sort out her chaotic emotions her mother's persistent cough had been diagnosed as stage-three lung cancer. From that moment through the next few years Tara's life had careened out of control on a roller coaster of hope and despair. Every waking thought had centered on her mother's survival. There had been too many difficult decisions to make and so many fears to face. There hadn't been time to think about her own wants and needs, her broken heart, disappointed dreams or the man who hadn't wanted her.

And then after battling four long, torturous years, her mother had died. Grief and guilt had consumed Tara. Since the funeral she'd been too numb to do anything but go through the motions of daily living. Work. Home. Paying bills.

She'd clung to the status quo like a sailor hung on to a capsized boat, afraid to let go, afraid another crisis would drag her under. Inertia wasn't something she enjoyed, but even one more change seemed like one more than she could handle. That was the only reason Tara could think of to explain why she'd stayed at a job she hated and why she couldn't face boxing up and donating her mother's things or even moving the bedroom furniture her mother had used out of the dining room. She couldn't even open the dining room door.

She chewed the inside of her bottom lip and studied the man in front of her. Was Rand's reappearance in her life a wake-up call? An opportunity to get her life back on track? Hugging herself she stared at the picture of her mother on the mantel.

Live your life without regrets, Tara. Promise me.... Her mother's final words echoed in her head.

Tara had learned two very important lessons as she watched her mother bravely fight and eventually succumb to the disease that had ravaged her body. One was that life shouldn't be filled with regrets for the things you hadn't done. The second was that some things are worth fighting for.

Tara had failed on both accounts.

She hadn't been courageous or unselfish enough to buy her mother more time and maybe even save her life—a fact that would haunt her for eternity.

Second, she'd let Rand walk away. She hadn't fought for him—for *them*. She'd allowed his fear of commitment and his unwillingness to listen to her reasons for turning to his father destroy any chance they might have had for a future together.

Rand watched her silently now with no trace of emotion on his hard-set face, but she was absolutely certain he had felt something for her back then even though he'd denied any emotions deeper than lust. If he hadn't cared, he wouldn't have treated her so well, and she didn't think she'd imagined the quickly masked flash of pain and shock in his eyes that last morning. If his feelings for her hadn't gone deeper than lust, he wouldn't have been hurt by what had appeared to be a betrayal on her part.

Unable to concentrate with his intense stare nailing her in place and compelling her to accept, she turned away. She'd never expected to see Rand Kincaid again, and she could have survived without him in her life. But here he stood in her home. It seemed as if fate were offering her a second chance to make this right—to make *them* right.

Did she dare try?

It would be a huge gamble. She might fail and get her heart shattered all over again, but at least she'd have the satisfaction of knowing she'd given it her best effort.

But how? How could she reach a commitment-phobic man who'd walked away once already? How could she prove to him that good relationships could and did happen?

She peeked at his reflection in the mirror that hung behind the sofa and caught his gaze raking her body. Heat flared in his eyes and kicked her pulse into a faster beat. And then he realized he was under scrutiny and masked his desire. He held her gaze dispassionately, but the raw hunger she'd glimpsed gave her the answer she needed.

She'd start with the one thing that had always been good between them—the sex—and build from there. And this time she wouldn't blurt out her feelings prematurely and scare him away.

Her skin flushed and her heart pounded at the possibility of sleeping with Rand again. She would, ironically, be offering him almost the same deal his father had offered her. Move in, be her partner in *every* way, and she would help him with his problem.

Would Rand have the courage to accept where Tara had failed?

Blinking to break the connection, she wiped her damp hands on her dress, exhaled slowly—shakily—and faced him. "I'll come back to Kincaid on two conditions."

"Name them."

"One, I want a glowing recommendation from you in writing. In advance." If this gamble didn't work out, she didn't want to be forced into another low-paying, dead-end job. She had bills to pay and an obligation to keep this house.

"If I give you the letter now, what's to keep you from walking before the year's up?"

"My word."

He hesitated, his square jaw shifting. "Done. What else?"

Chaos clamored inside her. She licked her dry lips and smoothed her damp hands on her hips again. "You. I want you, Rand. In my life. In my home. In my bed. Exclusively. For that year."

Rand recoiled as if she'd slapped him. "That offer is not on the table."

She fought to conceal her pain.

Did you expect him to be thrilled?

Maybe not thrilled, but something less than appalled would have been nice.

EMILIE ROSE 21

But without their intense physical chemistry on her side, the odds of succeeding in this quest were next to nil. She might as well give up now and save herself the false hopes and heartache. Mentally and physically, she backed away. "Then I can't help you."

His eyes narrowed suspiciously and the gold flecks in his irises glittered dangerously amidst the green. "What is this? Another attempt to get a ring out of me? I've told you before, I don't do commitment."

No, and he never would if she couldn't get past the boundaries he guarded so carefully. Last time he'd never spent an entire night in her bed or even met her mother. If she wanted her plan to succeed, she had to find a way to slip past his defenses and make him a part of her life. But she'd have to be careful. Rand would bolt if he thought she entertained even the faintest hope for wedding bells in their future.

She held his gaze and forced a lackadaisical smile even though her nerves stretched as tightly as piano wires.

"I'm not asking for forever. Just twelve months. You're not so irresistible that every woman wants to marry you, Rand. You and I both know this job is going to take long hours and involve a lot of overnight travel. I already have no social life—and therefore no sex life. Whatever else may have been lacking between us, the sex was always good."

Raw, urgent hunger exploded in his eyes and his chest expanded on a swiftly drawn breath. Her heart missed a beat.

He remembered their passion.

And that subtle reaction gave her hope and the grit to press on. She lifted her chin and squared her shoulders. "When do we start?"

What man in his right mind would refuse sex with a beautiful woman he desired?

He would.

"I can't give you what you want." Rand forced the words through a locked jaw.

Tara lifted a hand and tucked a golden curl behind her ear. Rand clenched his fingers on the memory of how soft her hair had been against his skin and tangled around his hands and wrists. While part of him mourned the long, loose curls, he had to admit the way the chin-length style bared her neck and shoulders was sexy as hell. Professional, but just tousled enough that a man knew she wouldn't mind him messing her up.

"Sex?" Her lips stretched in a tight smile.

"Love." He almost couldn't say the word. He didn't do love. Would never do love.

He was, according to his family, a carbon copy of his father. He'd learned the hard way not to allow himself the luxury of the destructive sentiment.

He'd seen how loving his unfaithful father had destroyed his mother and driven her to take her own life. And Rand had repeated the pattern when he'd broken up with his high school girlfriend before going away to college because he'd wanted to experience all the campus—meaning the female students— had to offer.

He was a selfish bastard, and because of that Serita had swallowed a bunch of pills that night after he'd left her. She'd been luckier than his mother. Someone had found her and called 911 before it was too late. Serita had survived loving a callous Kincaid.

"Ah. This is about what I said that night." Tara ducked her head, but not fast enough to conceal her pink cheeks. And then she lifted her chin and met his gaze. Her eyes were such an intense cobalt-blue that when they'd first met he'd believed them to be colored contacts. He'd been wrong. "I goofed, okay? If you'd hung around long enough for me to apologize and explain that I was lost in the moment—"

"Lost in the moment? You said you loved me, that you wanted to marry me and have my children. You practically named them."

The minute she'd said those words he'd bolted—to protect her from the curse of loving a Kincaid. And he'd worried about her for three solid weeks before returning to find her sneaking out of his father's suite after midnight.

Tara Anthony had played him for a fool and he'd fallen for her innocent act. Never again.

Her color darkened and her gaze bounced away again. "Um, yeah. Sorry about that. But you're…really good in bed."

Once more looking directly at him she added, "We can live here or at your condo. Either place is about the same distance from the office."

Every cell inside him balked. "I'm not playing house with you."

"Then I guess this discussion is over. I'll show you out." Dammit.

Rand snagged her arm when she walked past him, and awareness shot through him on contact with her warm, satiny skin. The electricity between them had been there from the first time he'd shaken her hand on the day she'd signed in as his father's PA. He'd ignored the attraction between them—or tried to—for seven torturous months before saying to hell with it.

It had taken him a month to get Tara to go out with him and another one to get her into bed. Had she been playing him against his father the entire time?

"I no longer own the condo. I live in California."

Her eyebrows lifted and what appeared to be genuine surprise filled her eyes. "I didn't know you'd moved."

That reminded him of her earlier comment. He'd ignored

it before because he thought she was lying. "How could you not know I'd left the company? My departure from KCL had to have caused an upheaval, and my father must have hit the ceiling when I accepted a job with his West Coast competitor less than twenty-four hours after leaving KCL."

"I didn't know because I never returned to the office after…that night."

"The *morning* I caught you leaving my father's bedroom."

Thick lashes descended to shield her eyes. She stubbed a toe into the carpet. "Yes."

The same day he'd told his father to go screw himself because he was through screwing his oldest son. Those were the last words he'd spoken to Everett Kincaid.

"Why did you leave? My father wouldn't marry you, either?"

Her teeth clicked audibly. She jerked her arm free. "To borrow your words, that offer was never on the table. You need to leave, Rand."

He wanted nothing more than to walk out that door and never look back. Her demands were absurd. Was he going to meet them?

Searching for another option, he stared into the eyes he'd once thought guileless—man, he'd been an idiot—and came up empty. For Mitch's and Nadia's sakes he had no choice. Not one his conscience would let him live with. He wouldn't abandon his brother and sister again.

"You won't get anything more than sex from me. No gifts. No rings. No promises. And definitely no children."

Her breath hitched and her eyes rounded when she realized he'd accepted her terms. She blinked and swallowed and then dampened her lips with the pink tip of her tongue.

Hunger for her taste instantly consumed him.

Damn the desire. Damn *her* for making him want her.

Five years ago she'd made him forget every hard lesson

he'd learned. She'd tempted him to break his vow to remain single and unattached.

He wouldn't make the same mistake twice.

Tara Anthony couldn't be trusted, and he was and always would be his father's son. A chip off the old block. A selfish jerk to the core. A man incapable of fidelity.

One who could hurt a woman without a second thought.

A smile wobbled on her mouth. "If you're paying me fifteen thousand dollars a month, then I won't need anything else from you."

He ripped his gaze from her damp lips. "Two weeks. I have to fly home and wrap up loose ends. I'll be back on the sixteenth and our year will begin."

And he hoped like hell he didn't live to regret it.

TWO

"Don't waste my time."

At the sound of his brother's voice Rand set his laptop case on his father's desk and turned toward the door. Mitch had followed him into the large office.

Rand had expected his brother to be glad he'd shown up not ready to pick a fight on Rand's first day on the job. "Excuse me?"

"Don't set up shop here if you're not going to stay the full year. If we're going to lose KCL, then let's make a quick, clean break and get on with our lives. Nadia is going to be miserable stuck in Dallas with nothing to do for twelve months. Don't put her through that if you're going to blow this."

Nadia's portion of the will required her to penthouse-sit and remain unemployed for a year. His sister would go crazy without something to keep her distracted from the memories that haunted her of the husband and child she'd lost.

Just one more reason to curse his old man, the sadistic snake.

"Mitch, I resigned from a job I enjoyed and put my condo on the market. I'm not going to quit. I'm here for the full three-hundred and sixty-five. If we lose KCL, it won't be because *I* failed to do *my* part."

Mitch's disbelief was plain on his face. "Why come back now?"

"Because this time he isn't going to win."

His brother didn't look convinced.

Rand shoved a hand into his pants pocket, withdrew his pocket-knife key chain and flicked it open. The blade flashed silver in the light as he pressed it to his fingertip. With the emotions churning through him he barely felt the prick.

"What in the hell are you doing?" Mitch demanded.

Red oozed from the cut. "You want me to sign in blood?"

"We're not kids anymore, Rand. Blood vows don't cut it. This is business. A multibillion-dollar business in case you've forgotten."

Clearly he wasn't going to erase five years of silence with their old childhood ritual. "I haven't forgotten."

Rand looked around for a tissue and saw nothing usable in his father's Spartan corner office. He dropped his knife with a clatter on the desk and put pressure on the tiny wound with his thumb.

Movement drew his attention to the doorway. Tara, in a pale yellow dress with her gleaming hair scraped back tightly against her skull, stood in the opening. The severe style wasn't unattractive, not with her bone structure, but he missed her golden curls. He shut down that port of thought. Her hair was no concern of his.

Tara's blue gaze traveled from his open knife to the small amount of blood on his fingers, then met his. "I'll find the first-aid kit."

Mitch's gaze tracked her retreat before returning to Rand. "Is she the reason you left?"

"I'm sure Dad spewed his own version of why I quit."

"He said nothing. That's why I'm asking you."

Rand tried to mask his surprise. His father had loved to gloat. "I left because he took our competition too far."

"How so?"

He stonewalled his brother with a look. Sleeping with KCL employees had always been frowned upon. Rand had known better, and to this day he didn't know why he hadn't been able to resist Tara's alluring trap. Since he hadn't been her supervisor, and therefore wouldn't technically be breaking any rules, he'd chosen to ignore company policy.

"What exactly do you want, Mitch? Guarantees? Fine. I guarantee you I'll see this through to the end."

"Why should I believe you? You walked away five years ago without a word. One day you were here. The next you were gone and completely incommunicado. Hell, I didn't even know if you were alive until your name surfaced on the letterhead of our competition." Mitch's eyes narrowed. "Rumor had it you'd run away with Tara."

Apparently the rumor mill hadn't known Tara was two-timing him with his father. "You should know better than to listen to rumors."

"C'mon, Rand. You and Tara disappeared on the same day."

Tara's gasp drew Rand's attention to the door. Her wide-eyed expression indicated she'd overheard. She searched his face as if seeking confirmation of Mitch's statement.

So she hadn't been lying. *About that.* She really hadn't known he'd left KCL.

"I—I have the first-aid kit. Let me see your cut," Tara said when he neither confirmed nor denied Mitch's statement. Her heels tapped out a brisk beat as she crossed the marble floor.

She set a small plastic box on the desk, opened it and extracted the necessary items, then held out her hand.

Rand cursed himself for being a fool. Why had he thought he could walk back in here and have things be the same—specifically his formerly close relationship with his brother? He regretted that casualty more than any other, but he'd sowed those bitter seeds with his silence, and now he'd have to harvest the crop of resentment.

He laid the back of his hand in Tara's palm and discovered that some things hadn't changed. Even knowing she was a liar didn't stop that same old zing from ripping through his veins. Her familiar sultry, spicy fragrance filled his lungs as she bent over her task. He welcomed the distracting sting of disinfectant as she gently cleaned the nick.

"Should I have the staff prepare your old suite of rooms at the house?" Mitch asked.

Rand's living arrangements were only going to add fuel to the rumors. Was that Tara's plan? Did she think she could use gossip to force him into a commitment? If so, she'd be disappointed.

Rand met Tara's gaze then his brother's. "I have a place lined up. Besides, you already have company."

Mitch's part of the will required him to play daddy to a child from one of their father's affairs, a one-year-old half brother Rand hadn't known existed until Richards handed out inheritance assignments. The boy and his guardian had moved into Kincaid Manor. Rand had yet to meet the kid. But in his opinion, the boy was better off not having Everett Kincaid in his life.

Tara quickly and efficiently bandaged Rand's finger, then released his hand and packed away her first-aid supplies without mentioning their cohabitation. If she planned to use it as leverage, then why hadn't she informed Mitch?

"Human resources has the first candidate for the director of shared services position downstairs. Which one of you is conducting the final interviews?" she asked.

"Show him or her to the conference room," Rand directed and looked at Mitch. "Meet me there in five. You know Nadia's current duties better than I do, and you'll be better able to gauge which applicant can handle them. But I'm sitting in. The COO should join us, too."

"There is no chief operating officer. Dad eliminated the position when you left."

Rand banked the information to deal with later. No doubt that action had launched its own series of rumors. "Then we'll handle the interviews together. As a team."

Mitch remained motionless for a full ten seconds, his gaze direct and hard. Rand held his brother's challenging stare and once again cursed his father for putting Rand in what should have been Mitch's job. As chief financial officer, his brother was the logical choice if the COO position had been eliminated—even if Rand had been raised to be CEO of KCL and had the experience of the top job with the competition. Mitch nodded and left Rand's office. Tara turned to follow him.

"Tara." She paused then looked at Rand. He lifted his hand to indicate the bandage. "Thanks."

"You're welcome." She bit her lip and shifted on her sandaled feet. "Did you leave because of me?"

The pain in her voice slipped between his ribs quicker than his pen knife had pricked his finger. He hardened himself to the wounded shadows in her eyes.

She was a damned good actress. Too bad her talent was wasted on him.

"You were merely the straw that broke this camel's back. You and my father deserved each other."

She flinched. "But I—"

"What, Tara?" he barked when she didn't continue.

Her chin and gaze fell. "Nothing."

"Good. Because the subject of the past is closed. Clear?"

Her shoulders snapped straight. "Yes, sir. Anything else?"

Rand scanned his father's—and now his—domain. He'd always hated this office. With its architectural glass-and-chrome desk, the bare, cold marble floors and the glass walls overlooking Biscayne Bay, the room looked more like a trophy case than a workspace. An empty trophy case. He eyed his father's metal mesh ergonomic chair with disgust. The old man's motto—"a real executive never looks like he's working"—rang in Rand's ears.

Not Rand's management style.

"Get me some furniture. Desk. File cabinets. Shelves. Tables. Wood, for godsakes. This pane of glass is useless. I want a decent chair—leather—rugs on the floor and comfortable visitor seating that doesn't look like acrylic urinals. And send the IT team up to connect my laptop to the company network. My father may have refused to work with a computer, but I won't work without one."

"Yes, sir." Her words snapped as sharp as a salute.

"I need hard copies of the press releases for the past five years, a current financial statement and a list of KCL's officers and division heads within the hour. That's all for now."

She pivoted sharply and headed for the doorway, but then stopped and faced him again without speaking.

"Spit it out, Tara."

"When are you moving in?"

Ah, yes, the other part of this ridiculous farce. Why had she demanded sex and cohabitation? What did she expect to gain if not a rich husband? He didn't buy her too-busy-to-date story. A woman who looked like Tara wouldn't lack dates or sexual partners if she wanted them.

But this time the scheming witch would fail.

"Tonight." Damned if the hunger for her didn't hit him hard in the gut. He desired her and he resented the hell out of her ability to yank his strings. "I want my own bedroom."

"But—"

"You'll get laid, Tara. But I won't sleep in your bed, hold you afterward or pretend we're a happy couple. I'm living under your roof because you've given me no choice. Don't forget that. Not for one second. I certainly won't."

She paled, nodded and quickly left him, driving home the fact that he really was a chip off the old block.

A real son of a bitch.

The voices in the KCL cafeteria petered out as soon as Tara entered. Heads turned and she found herself under the scrutiny of more than a hundred pairs of eyes.

She recognized a few familiar faces scattered among a sea of new ones and forced a smile. The buzz of conversation suddenly resumed. Apparently the employees who'd tapped into the gossip grapevine felt duty-bound to update those who hadn't.

Mitch's words replayed in her head. *You and Tara disappeared on the same day.*

She hadn't known. She'd deliberately sought a job outside the travel industry and had skipped the business and travel sections of the newspaper so she wouldn't hear talk about the Kincaids. She hadn't even read Everett's obituary. And now she and Rand were returning to KCL on the same day and working together. Tongues would wag for sure—especially if word of their living arrangements leaked out. That was one part of the plan she hadn't thought through.

Chilling doubt crept over her. Had she made a mistake?

No. When she'd been with Rand, he'd made her feel special, as though he couldn't get enough of her or wait to see

her again. She'd felt the same way about him. He'd been a part
of her life that had been carefree, happy and fun. Her life was
none of those things now. She was tired of being alone and
she wanted to feel connected again.

She only hoped those old feelings were still there, waiting
to be nurtured back to life. From the quiver of awareness she
experienced each time he was near, she had to believe that was
the case. And today for the first time in ages she'd awoken
looking forward to the day instead of counting the hours until
it ended.

She crossed the bright and spacious cafeteria, and headed
toward the food line. Kincaid's had always pampered its employees with first-rate amenities. Tara had loved working here.

Despite rumors from the business community to the
contrary, she'd always believed Everett Kincaid to be a decent
guy. Her former boss had offered her the gentle affection
she'd never received from her own absentee father. When her
mother was diagnosed it had seemed natural to seek Everett's
advice. He'd offered a solution. Move in. Let him take care
of everything. But the idea of sleeping with him when she still
loved his son…

She pushed down the icky feeling and reminded herself
Everett had been lonely and looking for companionship and
a woman who didn't have her sights set on being the next Mrs.
Everett Kincaid. Tara had been a logical choice. They worked
well together and respected each other. And Tara had needed
the kind of financial help only someone with Everett's deep
pockets could afford.

But Tara ultimately hadn't had the stomach to accept his
offer, and she hated herself for being weak when her mother
needed her. Weak where Rand had been strong.

The hum of conversation died again as Tara picked up a
tray and silverware. She glanced over her shoulder toward the

entrance and saw Rand. Almost as one the other employees' gazes bounced from him to her and back again, like spectators of a tennis match waiting to see the next shot.

He spotted her and stalked in her direction. Tara's appetite fled, but she went through the motions of ordering shrimp scampi, grilled asparagus and rice pilaf even though her antennae were attuned to his approach. She calmly said hello to a few of the familiar line staff as if her heart weren't beating at twice its normal rate.

"My desk is gone," Rand said from close behind her—too close for a boss-employee relationship. She could feel his body heat and smell his crisp Lacoste cologne. Her mouth dried.

Conscious of their audience, she neutralized her expression, put a few inches between them then turned and met his gaze. "I had your office emptied while you were conducting interviews. Your new desk, along with everything else you requested, will be delivered at two. IT has your laptop."

"Good."

She gaped at him. Years of bottling up her emotions bubbled over. "*Good?* I worked miracles and all you can say is *good?*"

One dark eyebrow lifted at her vehemence. Okay, so maybe she'd been soft-spoken and eager to please when they'd dated before, and according to her mother, Tara had always had a tendency to avoid conflict and confrontation. But Tara wasn't the same starry-eyed girl Rand used to know—the one who'd been overawed at being pulled from the reservations center downstairs and moved to the executive suite on the top floor. Wrangling with her mother's multitude of doctors had given her a backbone.

"Thank you for being so efficient, Ms. Anthony," he said in a voice heavily laden with sarcasm.

She turned her back on him, but out of sight didn't mean out of mind in this case. Rand shadowed her through the line, his presence following her like a heat lamp.

When they reached the cashier he extended his arm past her, offering his company ID, which acted as both identification and debit card. "Put both meals on my account."

"You don't have to buy my lunch," Tara protested.

"I'm buying. Deal with it."

The cashier swiped his card without arguing.

Rand followed Tara to an empty table and sat beside her—close beside her. A prickle of uneasiness crept up her neck. "What are you doing?"

"This is what you wanted, isn't it? For everyone to see us together? Did it wound your pride when I dumped you, Tara?"

She searched his hard face for a remnant of the charmer she'd fallen for but found none. Back then she'd heard him described as gorgeous yet soulless, but she hadn't believed it for one minute. She'd seen his love for Nadia and Mitch and felt his passion for her in bed.

Had he changed that much? Probably not. The Rand she remembered hadn't been under as much stress as he was now. He'd recently lost his father, moved clear across the country and taken over KCL. Anyone would be cranky under those circumstances. She'd cut him a little slack.

"No one knew about our affair then, Rand, and no one has to know now."

"People knew. My father knew. And I'm sure human resources will spread the news that you and I both listed the same home address."

Another oversight. She hadn't thought about HR. "Your father had ways of finding out all kinds of information."

"He had spies."

"Oh, please. You didn't used to be so melodramatic. Everett

was a nice guy. People talked to him and he listened. Everyone except his competitors loved him."

"They loved him because he bought their affection," he said bitterly.

"That's not true. They loved him because he cared. KCL is a perfect example. Headquarters has trained chefs to prepare four-star-restaurant-quality foods at below cost prices, onsite child care, a medical center and a gym with personal trainers and dieticians on staff. And most of the company's employees could never afford to take a cruise on any of KCL's ships if it weren't for Everett's policy of deeply discounting employee rates."

She unrolled her cloth napkin and placed her silverware beside her plate even though the idea of eating repulsed her at the moment. Rand's proximity kept her nerves and her stomach tied in knots.

"Your father's ideology of a strong connection between work, family life and vacation time results in tight friendships with co-workers and a supportive community atmosphere. People like working here. They liked working for him."

With pity in his eyes, Rand shook his head. "He had you completely fooled. My father never did anything out of the goodness of his heart. There was always an ulterior motive and a price tag attached.

"FYI, Tara, it's cheaper to provide all the goods and services you mentioned, thereby keeping morale high and turnover and absenteeism low, than it is to repeatedly train new employees or waste money hiring temps who don't know the job."

What he said made a sick kind of sense. "You've become very cynical."

"Not cynical. Realistic. I was CEO of Wayfarer Cruise Lines for five years. I know what I'm talking about because I implemented the same programs myself and reaped the same rewards. Trust me, it's all about the bottom line." He picked up his knife and cut into his thick, juicy, medium-rare steak. "I knew my father. Better than you apparently."

If she believed Rand's account that Everett always had an eye toward benefiting himself, then she would have to seriously consider what Rand had said that morning when he'd caught her fleeing Everett's suite. Rand had claimed Everett was using her as a pawn in a game against his oldest son.

But she couldn't swallow that harsh tale because it would mean she'd completely misjudged the man she'd worked for, a man she'd admired and respected. A man she'd *almost* slept with. Never mind that Everett's proposition had totally shocked her. She was convinced he'd offered his protection and financial assistance because he genuinely cared for her and needed a full-time hostess. And he'd promised to pay for her mother to have the best oncologists available because he didn't want Tara to worry.

Right?

But a small part of her wanted to believe Rand, because it made Tara's inability to become Everett's mistress a smidgeon easier to swallow.

"This is your room."

Rand followed Tara into a decent-sized square room and set the two suitcases he'd brought in beside the queen-size bed. Not bad. More homey than a hotel, but nothing like his luxurious high-rise condo or the palatial Kincaid Manor. The double window was a plus.

Tara crossed the room and hung the garment bag she'd carried in from his Porsche in the closet. "This is the biggest bedroom. You can redecorate with more masculine colors if you want. With only Mom and me here, I'm afraid everything is pretty feminine."

He wouldn't be here long enough for the Monet decor to bother him. He hoped that once Tara realized she wasn't going to snag him she'd give up on her absurd scheme and let him get his own place. "Your father wasn't around?"

"He disappeared when I was seven."

Surprised, he looked at her. "You never told me that."

She stared at the beige carpet. "I, um, guess I didn't want to bore you. And you really never asked about my family."

An intentional oversight. Their relationship had been action-packed and tightly focused on their strong sexual attraction. He'd always been careful about revealing anything that Tara might inadvertently share with his father, and that meant avoiding personal topics. "Your parents were divorced?"

He wished his had been. And then maybe his father wouldn't have driven his mother to drink and suicide. Her death had been ruled an accident. But Rand knew better. He knew, and he should have found a way to prevent it.

"It's hard to divorce a man who's not here."

"He's dead?"

She shrugged and turned away to fluff a pillow. "I don't know. When I say he disappeared, I mean he literally disappeared. He left for work one morning and never came back. No one ever found his body or his car, and we never heard from him again. Mom and I moved into this house with my grandparents. It's where my mother lived when she met my father."

Sympathy slipped under his skin. He hardened himself to the unwanted emotion. Was Tara telling the truth or yanking his chain? He didn't know what to believe anymore. He'd believed her when she said she loved him. But then she'd turned to Everett days later, proving to Rand that his judgment concerning Tara was faulty.

He shook off the sting of betrayal.

"We stayed because Mom wanted him to be able to find us."

He stared in disbelief. "She thought he'd come back after twenty-odd years?"

She shrugged. "If he'd been injured or had amnesia or something, he might."

"Do you believe that?"

Her gaze broke away. She smoothed a hand over the bedspread. "I don't know. But Mom asked me to keep the house just in case, so I will."

He couldn't argue with illogical logic. "Bathroom?"

"Through there." She pointed to a door.

"Internet hookup?"

"Anywhere in the house. I installed a wireless network when I moved in. My mother was—wasn't well. I needed to be able to work wherever she needed me." The strong emotional undercurrents in her voice warned him to change the topic or get embroiled in an emotional tar pit he'd rather avoid.

Five years ago he'd been enthralled by Tara, now he felt entrapped. Last time he'd wined and dined her and swept her off her feet. This time he wasn't going to waste the effort. "Your room?"

"Across the hall."

"Show me."

She pivoted and crossed the caramel-colored carpet. Rand followed a few steps behind. His gaze dropped to her butt. She'd lost weight since they were together. He'd enjoyed her generous curves before, but this leaner version had its own appeal. Not that it mattered how attractively she baited her trap. He wasn't biting her hook.

A maple queen-size four-poster bed took up most of the space. His blood heated and need clenched like a fist in his groin. He didn't want to want her, dammit. But, to borrow a cliché, he'd made his bed and he'd have to lie in it. With Tara.

Consider it a job.

He'd had worse jobs than pleasuring an attractive woman. His father had made sure of that by making Rand work his way up from the bottom of the cruise line ranks. Not so for Mitch or Nadia. His siblings had never had to work in the bowels of a KCL ship or spend months sleeping in a window-less cabin.

Looking uneasy, Tara hugged herself and faced him.

Might as well get started.

He grasped her upper arms, hauled her close and slammed his mouth over hers. The initial contact with her warm, silky lips hit him like a runaway barge, rocking him off balance. And then the familiar taste, scent and softness of her flooded him with heat, desire and memories. He ruthlessly suppressed all three and focused on the mechanics of the embrace.

He sliced his tongue through her lips, taking, pillaging, trying to force a response and get the task done as quickly as possible.

Tara stood woodenly in his arms for several seconds while his tongue twined with the slickness of hers, then she shud-dered and shoved against his chest. He let her go and she backed away, covering her lips with two fingers.

What exactly did she want from him? She'd said sex. For a year. He'd give her exactly what she demanded. Nothing more. Nothing less. If she didn't like it, that was her problem.

He reached for his tie, loosened it then started on his shirt buttons.

Her wide gaze fastened on his chest. "Wh-what are you doing?"

"I'm going to *do* you. Isn't that why I'm here?"

She bit her lip. "Maybe we should wait."

He paused in the act of yanking his shirttail free. "Until after dinner?"

"Until we've…become reacquainted."

Her nipples tented her dress in little peaks, her breaths

came quick and shallow, and the pulse in her neck fluttered wildly. Desire pinked her cheeks.

"You want me—whether or not you're willing to admit it." And as much as he hated it, he wanted her. Physically.

It's a trap. Keep the hell away from her.

Not an option.

He closed the distance between them. "You made this deal, Tara, and I'm ready to deliver my end of it."

"I-if I wanted sex with a stranger, I'd drive to the beach and find one."

The idea of Tara with some other guy irked him. She was twenty-nine. Of course she'd had other lovers.

Including his father. He shoved down the disgust and dragged his fingertips down the smooth skin of her arm. He relished her shiver.

"But we're not strangers, are we?"

She jerked away. "I'll start dinner."

She tried to step around him. He blocked her path. "So you're calling the shots. I perform on command. Like a trained dog. Or a gigolo."

She gulped and briefly closed her eyes. "I had hoped the desire would be mutual. Like it was before."

"Before you slept with my father?"

She frowned. "I told you I didn't sleep with Everett."

"You forget, Tara, I know what you look like after you've been screwed. Your mussed hair, smudged makeup and the hickey you had on your neck that night, told the tale."

She sighed and shook her head. "Believe what you will."

The vulnerability in her expression nearly sucked him in. She lifted a trembling hand to brush back a loosened strand of hair. "We used to be good together, Rand. Don't you want that again?"

Did he want to be a gullible fool again? Hell no.

Given her betrayal and the Kincaid men's history with women, cutting her loose had been his only option. "I don't repeat my mistakes."

She flinched. "I never considered us a mistake."

He had to keep her happy or risk having her walk out before the end of the required year. He didn't know what game Tara was playing. She hadn't asked for romance when she'd brokered this bargain, but apparently she required a measure of pandering before they hit the sheets.

Fine. If she wanted seduction she'd get it. But that was all she'd get. She wouldn't get his heart this time.

Three

The hair on the back of Tara's neck rose. She didn't have to turn to know Rand stood behind her. Close behind her.

She'd been so engrossed in her reading she hadn't heard him return from Tuesday morning's round of interviews. He must have slipped in through the back door of his office.

He planted a big hand on either side of her blotter, trapping her against the desk between charcoal-colored suit-clad arms. Even with the back of her chair separating their bodies she could feel the heat radiating from him and smell his delicious scent.

She swallowed to ease the sudden dryness of her mouth. "Can I do something for you?"

"No."

"Then why are you breathing down my neck?"

"I'm reading over your shoulder." His breath stirred her hair and something inside her fluttered to life like a butterfly wiggling to get free of its cocoon.

"I'll send you the link to the company newspaper archives, and then you can read at your computer between interviews. Better yet, you can wait for my notes—the ones you asked me to make." She pushed her chair back, forcing him to move or have his wing-tipped toes run over.

"But reading over your shoulder is more fun." Rand stepped aside, leaned against the corner of her U-shaped workstation and smiled.

That familiar slow, seductive smile made her stomach flip. She studied the fit form beneath his tailored suit, his crisp white shirt and his neatly knotted black-and-gray striped silk tie. There was a difference in his body language today, one she couldn't decipher. It made her uneasy.

He was up to something. She could see the cool assessment in his eyes and behind that false smile. She'd sensed that same calculation in his kiss last night—a kiss that had been all technique and no emotion. If there had been even a trace of genuine passion in his embrace, she would have made love with him. She needed to be held that badly.

God, she was pitiful.

But the thought of having Rand "do her," as he'd said, repulsed her. She wanted him to make love with her because he desired her. Not because he had to perform.

If it weren't for the fire sometimes making the gold flecks glimmer among the green in his hazel eyes, she'd wonder if he found the prospect of making love with her as abhorrent as she had the idea of intimacy with his father.

If only she hadn't…

Live your life without regrets, Tara. Promise me.

She stiffened her spine. "If you need something to do, Rand, then go write my recommendation letter."

"It's written."

"I'd like a copy."

He eased upright and leisurely strolled into his office as if they didn't have a packed schedule for the day. She'd never known Rand to leisurely do anything…except explore her body. Heat prickled beneath her skin at the rush of memories and desire.

She narrowed her gaze on his broad shoulders and shifted in her chair to relieve the tension seeping through her.

Getting rid of him had been far too easy. His behavior confused her. Five years ago she'd loved Rand's focus and intensity. When he'd been at work he'd been all business, but when they were together and away from the office he'd been equally single-minded in his attention to her and his dedication to having fun.

Today he was muddying the waters, and she didn't know what to make of it.

She checked his appointment book. He had ten minutes before his next interview. With Nadia out of the office for twelve months fulfilling her part of Everett's will, Rand and Mitch had to hire her replacement soon. None of the pre-screened candidates human resources had sent up yesterday had seemed a good fit.

Tara turned back to her monitor and tried to concentrate on the words without much luck. Rand had asked her to list any pertinent happenings at KCL during their absence. She'd thought the company newsletters would be a good place to start. Instead, what she'd found—or rather what she *hadn't* found—disturbed her.

Rand returned, once more blocking her escape from her desk. "What's the problem?"

"Our departures from KCL are never mentioned in the first year's worth of company newsletters after we left. That's unusual. When someone leaves there's always a brief note stating years of service, company awards and such—unless the employee was fired. I don't like the idea of my co-workers believing I was fired. You shouldn't, either. It will make it difficult to gain their trust."

"My father was never one to offer excuses, explanations or apologies." Rand bent over her desk and scrawled his signature on a piece of KCL letterhead. He slid it across the glossy surface.

Tara took it, but didn't read past the header. "This is postdated."

"You think I'd hand you the ammunition to waltz out of here prematurely? If you quit early, we lose everything."

Which went back to their main problem. He didn't trust her. Had he ever? Tara sat back in her seat with a sigh. "I gave you my word I wouldn't leave, and I signed an employment contract. Don't you trust anyone, Rand? Anyone at all?"

"I know when to protect my own interests. Or in this case, Mitch's and Nadia's." He hitched a hip on her desk, invading her space with a long, lean knife-creased trouser-encased thigh. "Arrange a cocktail party for the executives of each of the brands by the end of the week. Plan to attend as my date."

"Is that wise? Us dating openly, I mean."

"I need a hostess, and you're the one who insisted on exclusivity."

So she had. And she'd occasionally provided the same service for Everett. Was that why her former boss had believed she'd be open to a more intimate relationship? "At Kincaid Manor?"

"Anywhere but there."

"Your father always—"

"I'm not my father. I don't need to flaunt my wealth or have a woman half my age on my arm to make me feel like a man. And I won't be taken in by a pretty face or a good lay. You'll do well to remember that."

She gasped at his rude comment. Was he trying to rattle her? If so, it was working. "Are you deliberately being obnoxious so I'll release you from your part of our agreement?"

He reached out and traced her jaw. Her pulse stumbled erratically beneath the slow drag of his fingertip.

"Why would I do that, Tara, when as you said, the sex between us was always good?"

Her mouth dried and her palms moistened. Arousal streamed through her. But suspicion dammed her response. She scooted her chair out of his reach. What was he trying to pull? First he'd flat-out refused to be her lover and then he'd accepted reluctantly. And now he was trying to seduce her?

His about-face didn't ring true, then she realized why. There wasn't any passion in his eyes despite his comment on their sex life. Rand was cold and distant—the way he'd been the day he'd climbed from her bed and broken her heart, and the day he'd caught her leaving his father's bedroom.

He wasn't at all someone she wanted to be intimate with. Not like this.

She didn't doubt he could make her ache for him even with this emotionless seduction. He'd always been a skilled lover. But perfect technique wasn't what she wanted. She wanted the unbridled passion they'd shared in the past, and it looked like she'd have to fight for it.

He glanced at his watch and stood. "We're going out to dinner tonight. Wear something sexy and low-cut if you want to get me in the mood."

He pivoted on his heel and stalked into his office.

Aghast, Tara stared after him. And then anger blasted through her. He'd just thrown down the gauntlet.

If she wanted to get him in the mood?

Oh, she'd get him in the mood all right. In fact, she wasn't going to be happy until she'd shattered Rand Kincaid's icy control and won back the man who'd given her the happiest days of her life.

Tara knew the minute her eyes met Rand's that her decision to fight dirty was the right one.

Tiny bubbles of excitement effervesced in her veins as she descended the stairs to where Rand waited by the front door. She could feel the heat from his unblinking appraisal warming her skin and her core. She forced her fingers from the newel post and indicated her dress with what she hoped looked more like a casual flip than a nervous flail. "Look familiar?"

"You expect me to remember your clothing?"

Oh, he remembered all right. His tight voice, flaring nostrils and the color slashed across his cheekbones gave it away. Those telltale signs made the hour she'd spent taking in the cocktail dress two sizes worth every second. Thank God for her grandmother's sewing lessons and her ancient sewing machine because Tara hadn't had the time, money or necessity to shop for evening wear since Rand had dumped her.

"I wore this dress the night we first made love," she told him anyway.

His lips flattened and his shoulders stiffened, but he remained silent.

"I fixed the tear. You know, from when you ripped the dress off of me in your foyer." His gaze dropped to her bodice as if seeking the mend, and hunger hardened his face. Her nipples tightened in response. Did he remember she hadn't worn a bra that night? Could he tell she wasn't now?

"Are you ready to go?" he asked tightly.

For the first time in years she felt alive and eager instead of numb. When he looked at her that way—as if he wanted to strip her and take her where she stood—she believed her plan to make him fall in love with her could actually work.

"Oh, I'm ready." She added a quick, mischievous smile to the words even though her stomach had twisted into a cork-screw of nerves. "Are you?"

She didn't mean for dinner. The desire burning in those hazel eyes told her the ashes of Rand's desire were far from cold.

And she had every intention of fanning the flames.

Even at the risk of getting burned.

He'd underestimated his opponent.

And that was exactly how he had to classify Tara from now on, Rand decided as he followed her out of the humid Miami air and into the cool, darkened house. She wanted something from him, and as with any business deal, he'd concede some points but not all. That way everyone left the bartering table satisfied.

Grace in victory wasn't a concept he'd learned from his father. Everett Kincaid had relished crushing and humiliating his adversaries. Rand preferred to allow his competitors to walk away beaten but not broken. Defeated, but not destroyed. In the tight-knit, almost incestuous cruise industry no one knew when they'd have to work for or with a previous foe again. Burning bridges wasn't smart business.

Time to seal this deal.

Moonlight shone through the living room windows, glinting off Tara's loose curls like moonbeams on rippling water split by a ship's bow. Before she could turn on the lamp he intercepted her hand and carried it to his chest. Her breath caught audibly.

She'd been leading him around by his libido for most of the evening, starting with a dress that brought back memories hot enough to cauterize his veins, followed by brushing up against him on the restaurant's dance floor until he was so hard he could barely walk back to their table.

She was good, *very* good, at luring a man into her trap.

It was time to regain control of the situation. He relaxed his clenched jaw and slowly reeled her in. His heart pounded out a hard-driving rock tempo beneath her palm. Snaking an arm around her waist, he brought her body flush against his. Hot, urgent desire pulsed through him.

Sex. Physical hunger. That's all this is.

And he could control that.

"Ran—"

He smothered her words with his mouth, stole them from her tongue with his. He didn't want to talk. Didn't want to be distracted from the job ahead.

She tasted of the tiramisu she'd had for dessert mixed with a hint of the sweet wine she'd sipped throughout dinner.

And Tara. She tasted like Tara.

Damn the memories he couldn't erase.

Her fingers fisted on his chest, but her resistance lasted only seconds before her body relaxed and curved into his, molding her soft breasts against a rib cage that felt so tight he could barely inhale.

He still wanted her even after she'd betrayed him, and the knowledge burned like sea water in a fresh gash.

Rand shut down his emotions and focused on his actions— actions guaranteed to seduce the woman in his arms. He swept a hand down her back, splayed his fingers over her butt and pressed her against his raging hard-on. Her quickly snatched breath dragged the air from his lungs.

Skimming his hands from Tara's hips to her waist to her shoulders and then finally her breasts, he mapped her new shape while he devoured her mouth. Hardened nipples teased his palms as he cupped and caressed her.

She broke the kiss to gasp for breath, and he dipped to sample the warm spot beneath her ear. Her skin was fragrant and satiny beneath his lips, tender and tempting against his tongue. Memories battered him. He bulldozed them back.

She shivered and drove her hands beneath his suit coat. Short nails raked parallel to his spine, inciting his own involuntary shudder.

Tara leaned away and stared up at him with her lips damp and swollen, and her breasts rising and falling rapidly beneath her low, rounded neckline. She pushed off his jacket.

He searched her face looking for signs of the conniving woman he knew her to be, but the shadows obscured his view. He grasped her waist and swung her into the moonlight. Dense lashes curtained her eyes.

She reached for the side zip of her dress, the one he hadn't been able to find five years ago. The sound ripped the silence, then she dipped her shoulders, first one and then the other. The black fabric floated to the floor with a swish, leaving her bare except for a tiny pair of black panties and her stiletto heels.

He gritted his teeth to hold back a groan. He even remembered her shoes. Or more accurately, he remembered doing her in those shoes. And nothing else. More than once.

Damn.

Heat and pressure built inside him until he felt like a Molotov cocktail—ready to blow with the slightest spark. He inhaled so deeply, so quickly, his lungs nearly exploded. Releasing the air in a slow, controlled hiss, he fisted his hands and fought the need to take her hard and fast where they stood.

Tara had been curvy and beautiful before, but now… Now she looked incredible. The curves were still there, only tighter, sexier. The moonlight caressed her breasts, the indentation of her waist, her hips, her legs. Oh, yeah, she'd definitely come well-armed for this mission.

He reached for his tie.

"Let me." She nudged his hands aside. Her fingers teased his neck with butterfly-light brushes as she loosened the knot, then she pulled the tie free like a slithering silk snake. She dropped it and started on his buttons. The roar of his pulse nearly deafened him.

Once she had his shirt opened, she closed the gap between them and strung a line of feather-light kisses along his collarbone. Rockets of fire shot to his groin. He ground his teeth together. She eased the cloth from his shoulders and licked the skin covering the pulse jackhammering in his neck. And then she nipped him and he nearly lost it. His fingers convulsed at her waist.

For godsakes, pull it together. It hasn't been that long since you've gotten laid.

Sweat beaded his brow and upper lip. He was hanging onto his control by his fingertips, and if he didn't take this upstairs, he was going to make an unforgivable mistake. Sex without protection.

He would never tie himself permanently to a woman. Or a child. He couldn't risk failing, either.

He tossed his shirt aside, swept her into his arms and headed for the stairs. But even within his grasp she didn't abandon her assault on his senses. She smelled good. Spicy. Sultry. Like sex.

Her arms looped around his neck, crushing her bare breasts to his chest, and the tip of her tongue traced his ear. Hot. Wet. She blew on the damp flesh. The effect was anything but cooling. A groan he couldn't contain barreled up from his lungs.

Tara had learned some new tricks since their breakup. Wondering who'd taught her made Rand's stomach churn like a concrete mixer.

In her room he stood her beside the bed. A small table lamp with a Tiffany shade cast a dappled puddle of Technicolor lights on the spread. One yank sent the covers flying to the foot of the mattress.

"Condoms." His voice sounded strangled.

She folded her hands demurely in front of her waist as if she were self-conscious. But he knew better. She'd demanded this charade. And that took balls. "In the drawer."

He pulled the knob she indicated with a glance, located the box and ripped it open. Extracting a ribbon of protection, he tore one packet free and tossed it onto the bed.

"Lose the panties. Keep the shoes."

A quiet laugh bubbled from her and a sexy smile tilted her lips. She looked up at him through her thick lashes and desire bolted through him, as jagged and searing as lightning.

He cursed silently. He'd said the same words to her in the past. Back when he was foolish enough to believe she was his every fantasy come to life. Back when he'd believed he could play with fire and not get burned.

Before she'd screwed—

Don't go there.

But the chilling thought brought him a measure of restraint. He wasn't going to think about…her other partners. Not here. Not now. It didn't matter whether she'd had one other lover or a dozen. He'd dumped her. Not his concern.

So why did the idea ride his back like a cheap wool shirt?

Get on with it. Give her what she wants until she begs for mercy.

She wiggled the lacy triangle over her hips and ankles then reclined on the bed with one knee bent. His gaze raked over her. Damp red lips, slightly parted. Taupe nipples tightly puckered on full, round breasts. The slight curve of her belly. An untamed tangle of golden curls. And legs…Tara had always had the most amazing legs. Long. Sleek. Toned. Her best weapon.

Her shoes—definitely do me shoes—were a reminder why he was here and what she'd demanded of him.

He reached for his belt with surprisingly unsteady hands. What was his problem? This wasn't his first trip to the sheets.

She watched his every move through slumberous eyes. His zipper rasped. He shoved his pants and boxers to the floor then had to sit down to remove the shoes and socks he'd forgotten.

She rattled him. He took a sobering gulp of air.

The mattress shifted beneath him. A whisper of warm, moist breath was his only warning before her lips brushed his nape. He snapped to rigid attention. Above and below the waist.

She cupped his shoulders then stroked downward as if she were reacquainting herself with the feel of his back, hips and buttocks. She hugged him from behind, aligning her hot naked curves against him. Her breasts burned his skin and her hands splayed over his lower abdomen. His muscles contracted, bunching with need beneath the soft scrape of her nails. Her thumb swept across his engorged tip, catching a slick droplet and rubbing it in.

A sharp stab of hunger had him sucking a swift breath. He bent to tackle his socks and shoes. Finally, he kicked both aside, then he turned and tumbled Tara back onto the pillows. He couldn't let her set the pace. Couldn't let her push his buttons. Couldn't let her make him lose control. Couldn't let her make him forget why he was here.

Do the job.

He kissed her on the lips. Hard. Fast. And then he worked his way lower. His tongue found and circled one nipple while his hand found the other. He plucked, sucked, rolled and licked until she squirmed beneath him and panted his name. Navigating south, he drew a damp line to her navel and then lower. Her fragrance went straight to his head. Both of them.

Every muscle in his body tensed. It took him a full ten seconds before he could think again. He found her swollen flesh. Smelled her. Tasted her. Laved her. Sucked her.

Too good. Too familiar. Too much.

He traced her slick entrance with his fingers and then plunged deep. Her hips arched. She dug her fingers into his hair and whispered his name. Using knowledge he thought he'd lost, knowledge he *should* have lost, dammit, he drove her relentlessly toward a climax with his mouth and hands.

Moments later orgasm broke over her, convulsing her body, contracting her internal muscles around his fingers. Her low, shuddery moan had him grasping himself with his free hand and damming the eruption about to happen.

He clenched his teeth until the white-hot haze ebbed.

What in the hell? He'd almost lost it. And he wasn't even inside her. He hadn't come prematurely since his teens. His *early* teens. And he'd almost—

He shook off the unsettling thought. Tara had always had that effect on him. She'd always made him want to rush. Going slow with her had been a challenge every time.

He grabbed the condom and shoved it on. And then he grasped Tara's buttocks, lifted her hips and drove deep into the wet, tight glove of her body. Buried to the hilt, he froze, locked his muscles and fought for control as sensation scorched a lava trail up his spine.

She's a job, dammit. Do her. Screw her. Forget her.

But she didn't feel like a job. She felt hot and slick and soft and so damned good. The fingers she dragged down his back sent sparks skipping down his vertebrae.

"Rand, don't stop. Please." She wiggled impatiently and clutched his waist. His brain short-circuited and his nerves crackled like downed power lines. He withdrew and surged in harder, faster.

Do her, screw her, forget her, he silently chanted with each thrust.

He tried to focus on the mechanics. His arms and legs trembled with the effort to hold back. His lungs burned. And then he made a mistake. He looked into her deep blue, passion-darkened eyes, and the hunger on her flushed face sucked him into a black hole of need. She cried out and her body quaked as another climax rippled through her.

Did she come like that with him?

The rogue thought slammed his libido like a submerged iceberg, stilling his movements, sinking his desire. Struggling to fill his deflated lungs and ban the repulsive image from his mind, Rand pulled away and sat on the edge of the bed with his elbows on his knees and his head clasped between his hands.

Damn. Damn. Damn. He couldn't do this.

When he had a measure of control he turned and looked at Tara, at her flushed face and her heavy-lidded eyes.

"Good for you?" He bit out the words.

"Yes," she said on an exhalation. Her brow furrowed. She rolled to her side and reached for him. "But—"

He shot to his feet before she could touch him and gathered his discarded clothing. "Then good night."

"But, Rand, you didn't—"

He slammed the bedroom door, cutting off her words.

No. He hadn't. But he'd come close.

Too damned close to forgetting why he was here.

Blackmail. His father's. Tara's.

And he'd almost forgotten who he was, what was at stake and that she'd lied to him before.

And that was a mistake he couldn't afford to make.

Four

Why had Rand left without finishing? Tara wondered as she swiped on her mascara Wednesday morning.

He'd been lost in the passion with her. She was sure of it. She'd felt his heat, his hardness, the rapid slamming of his heart and the trembling as he tried to slow his pace. And then he'd just…stopped.

Had she done something to repulse him?

Her idea of getting closer to Rand by getting *closer* to Rand had failed. Sex hadn't brought them together. It had driven them further apart, and now her emotions about last night were a tangled mess. He'd given her exactly what she asked for, but despite the climaxes, she wasn't satisfied. Physically or emotionally. In fact, she felt a bit…icky.

Not that the sex hadn't been good up until he'd walked out. But making love was supposed to be about *two* people. Not one. She needed more than just a superficial encounter.

She needed to know she mattered to someone.

In her experience Rand had never been the cuddle-until-morning type, but in the past he'd held her afterward at least until their pulses slowed and sometimes until she'd fallen asleep. But this time he'd—

She stopped midthought and stared at her reflection as realization dawned. She'd done it again. She'd let him walk away without demanding an explanation. Why?

Because she was afraid of what he might say.

The sobering reminder that she lacked courage when it counted chilled her. She'd learned the hard way that being a coward and taking the easy way out left too much room for regret. And hadn't she vowed not to do that again? If she wanted to make this relationship work, then she'd have to find the courage to ask what went wrong.

No more avoiding conflict. No matter how much she preferred not to make waves.

She put away her makeup and left her bedroom determined to ask difficult questions and possibly receive hard-to-hear criticisms. She paused in the hallway to gather her nerve and silence settled over her like a heavy, smothering quilt. An old, familiar emptiness filled the house. Rand wasn't here. She knew it even before she tapped on his door and didn't get a response.

Nonetheless she turned the knob and pushed open the panel. He'd made his bed. No discarded clothing littered the floor and no personal belongings cluttered the furniture surfaces. Only a lingering trace of his cologne hinted at his occupancy.

Desire and disappointment, relief and regret mingled in her belly. Since Rand had apparently left the house before she'd awoken for the second morning in a row, she'd have to ask her questions at the office. Not the ideal place for awkward morning-after encounters or private conversations.

Had he planned it that way? Was leaving before sunrise his way of keeping the walls between them intact?

She left his room and went downstairs. Last night's black silk dress draped the back of the rocking chair instead of lying puddled on the floor where she'd dropped it. Only Rand could have put it there.

She entered the kitchen. Like yesterday, Rand hadn't left any signs of his passing through. There weren't any breakfast dishes cluttering the sink or drain board, and the coffeepot stood cool and empty. If not for the slight tenderness between her legs, she'd believe she'd dreamed up his reappearance in her life.

She forced herself to eat a yogurt and drink a glass of juice even though hunger was the last thing on her mind. Her stomach churned over the encounter to come. She had to confront Rand and find out why he'd held back and why he'd left her. And then she'd find a way to make the next time better. For both of them.

Unfortunately, the pre-rush-hour drive to Kincaid Cruise Lines' towering waterfront building overlooking Biscayne Bay and the Port of Miami remained uneventful, giving Tara plenty of time to think about all the ways this affair could go wrong. By the time she pulled in to her assigned parking space her nerves had tied themselves into knots a Boy Scout would envy.

The security guard waved her through and then the glass elevator whisked her all too swiftly up the outside of the building to the top floor. Even the amazing view of the bay and the boats couldn't distract her from the encounter ahead.

She entered her office—the same one she'd used when she'd been Everett's PA. She was going backward, in many respects, to move forward. And yet nothing was the same. Especially not her.

The click of computer keys and rustle of paper carried

through Rand's open office door, affecting her pulse like a starting gun and sending it racing. She stashed her purse in a drawer, took a bracing breath and gathered her courage before crossing to the doorway.

"There are eight brands under the KCL umbrella," Rand said without looking up from his laptop. "All are profitable except the Rendezvous Line. Reserve the first available balcony cabin for us on a three- or four-day cruise. I want to see for myself why those bookings are down when that price point is the fastest growing market for our competitors."

From the look of his rolled-back shirt cuffs and the two to-go cups from a nearby coffee shop chain shoved toward the corner of his desk, he'd been here a while. "Us?"

His hazel eyes lifted and met hers coolly as if he hadn't been in her bed and inside her body last night. Unease prickled her scalp. Had sleeping with her meant nothing to him?

"It's primarily a couple's cruise. I don't want any fanfare or special treatment. I want to travel as an average Joe, not the company CEO."

The idea of taking a romantic cruise with Rand made her pulse flutter and warmth pool beneath her skin, but his all-business face erected barriers larger than the Rocky Mountains between them. She had to get past those barriers. If sex wouldn't do it, what would?

"I'll make the reservations in my name and through a travel agency if that will help with anonymity," she offered and he nodded.

"Give me the dates when you have them." His gaze returned to the computer screen, dismissing her.

Determined to get the awkward conversation over with before the rest of KCL's employees arrived or she chickened out, she tangled her fingers and approached his desk. "Rand, about last night—"

His jaw turned rigid and his head snapped up, corking her questions. His eyes met hers before slowly raking over her as if he were visually stripping away the red sleeveless dress and matching bolero jacket she'd worn to boost her confidence. His pupils expanded and her heart shuddered.

"What do you want, Tara? A roll on the company couch?"

Her breath caught and heat arrowed through her belly. A tumble of confusing emotions rumbled through her. She glanced at the leather sofa that had been delivered Monday along with the rest of the office furniture then back at Rand. Was he serious about sex in the office? Did she want him to be?

And how could she possibly desire him when he was being this cold and distant? Was she that needy?

He calmly checked his watch. "Mitch will be here in five minutes. You'll have to wait until tonight. Unless you want him to join us. I wouldn't want you to miss out on one of the Kincaid men."

His insolence left her speechless. Fury flooded her until she thought the dam on her temper would burst.

The slam of his office door made Rand wince.

He'd never deliberately humiliated an employee—or anyone for that matter. Humiliation had been his father's specialty. Rand knew firsthand. And he didn't like it.

But for a moment he'd seen an earnest and tender look in Tara's eyes that convinced him she wanted to make more out of last night than there was. He'd had to snuff that notion fast.

Last night… He shook his head. Last night he'd come too close for comfort to losing his head and forgetting what was at stake. Too close to forgetting she'd taken him in once before with her passion-glazed eyes and words of love.

Still, he'd been a bastard. Just like his old man.

Before he could rise to find her and apologize the door flew open and Tara stormed back through. She marched toward him with her fists clenched by her sides and angry red streaks marking her cheekbones.

Would she punch him? He deserved it.

She stopped in front of his desk, her body trembling. "I know what you're doing. You're trying to get out of your part of our deal with your rude, crass comment. But don't forget for one moment who loses if I quit. I just left one obnoxious boss. I will not tolerate another one. The only reason I'm not already cleaning out my desk is because I gave you my word and because Nadia and Mitch can't help it if their brother is sometimes a jerk. But if you make one more nasty remark like that, Rand Kincaid, I'll revoke my promise and I'll walk. And *you* will fail your brother and sister. Do you understand?"

Taken aback, he stared at the woman in front of him. The Tara he remembered had been soothing, soft-spoken and amenable. He'd never seen this assertive, untamed side of her before. The spark in her eyes and the strength in her spine looked more like the woman he knew her to be—one who could profess her undying love for one man then sleep with his father as soon as that man was out of town.

"I'm sorry, Tara. I was out of line."

Some of the starch seeped from her shoulders. She capped off her tirade by ducking her head and looking embarrassed. Her blush was so damned endearing and convincing, he almost wanted to circle the desk and hug her. And that wouldn't do. He couldn't fall for her trickery again.

"Completely out of line." She turned and left, brushing past Mitch on his way in with a brisk, "Good morning, Mitch."

"Hello, Tara." His brother stared after her then shut the door. "Lover's spat?"

"Explain that remark."

"You're shacking up with Tara."

The gossip grapevine thrived at KCL, and this time it had broken speed records. This was only his third day as CEO.

Rand clamped a hand across the sudden snarl of tension at the base of his skull. If he was going to keep KCL employees and the public from losing trust in the company after the change in leadership, he needed credibility. As Tara had already pointed out, a cloud of suspicion hung over their unexplained departures five years ago. Sleeping with his PA wasn't going to help matters. "Where did you hear it?"

"My PA picked it up in the cafeteria this morning." Mitch folded his arms. "So you did leave with Tara."

"No. I moved to California alone. But I am living in her home now."

"Rekindling the old romance?"

"There is no romance."

He considered telling Mitch about Tara's ultimatum, but confessing he'd become a pawn in Tara's game was as infuriating as it was frustrating. And arousing.

He hated that she'd backed him into a corner and turned him into her personal gigolo. Hated that, despite all he knew about her, she still had the power to make him want her. And he definitely hated the way his pulse had jackhammered and his blood had rushed below his belt the minute he'd heard her in the outer office this morning.

His sleep last night and his concentration this morning had been shot to hell because her breathy cries kept echoing through his head.

"Am I going to have to clean up after you the way I am after Dad?"

Mitch's reminder of their father's inability to be faithful to his wife or any other woman was exactly what Rand needed to hear to get his head back in gear. Even if Tara tried to sucker

him into a long-term relationship, Rand didn't have the staying power to make it last.

Like father, like son.

"How is it going with Dad's little brat and his guardian?
What was the tenacious aunt's name again?" Rand asked.

"It's going fine. Her name is Carly. But we're talking about
you." Mitch lowered himself into one of the sleek leather visitor
chairs stationed in front of Rand's wide mahogany desk.

Tara had indeed worked miracles on this formerly sterile
space. Besides the office paraphernalia he'd requested, she'd
added plants, art that actually looked like something recog-
nizable and a sofa long enough for him to stretch out on if he
had to pull an all-nighter in the office. An oversize ottoman
doubled as a coffee table and a foot stool. And the wooden
cabinet/shelf combo against the wall concealed a refrigerator.

Rand tossed his pen on his desk. "I can handle my own
affairs."

"Why did you leave, Rand? The truth this time. No BS.
And don't deny Tara's involvement. Your reaction to her name
at the reading of the will and the tension between you when
I walked in proves she was part of it."

Rand debated redirecting the discussion to the résumés on
his desk, but Mitch wore a familiar stubborn look on his face
that said he wasn't going to be diverted. His brother had a right
to his questions, and he needed assurances that Rand wouldn't
let him down this time.

And as much as Rand hated revealing the truth, Mitch
needed to keep a wary eye on Tara. If she was looking for a
rich husband, Mitch was just as likely a target. His jab about
Tara missing out on one of the Kincaid men had hit a little
too close to the mark. The idea gave Rand heartburn.

"When I returned from auditing the Mediterranean line five
years ago, I caught Tara leaving Dad's suite."

Mitch swore. "Not again."

"Yes, again." Tara hadn't been the first of Rand's lovers to end up in his father's bed, but she had been the only one Rand had given a damn about.

Had Everett pursued Tara or had Tara done the chasing? Either was a betrayal, but which was the most egregious? Tara's, Rand decided, because he expected no less from his father.

Rand stood and crossed to the windows to stare out at the blue-green water thirty stories below. "I was sick of his games, sick of him coveting everything and everyone I possessed. I didn't want to put you or Nadia in the middle. So I left."

"I was always in the middle, Rand, like a referee in a prize fight. But Tara was fair territory. You'd dumped her. Hell, I even considered asking her out. You have to admit she's smart and easy on the eyes."

Every muscle in Rand's body clenched. He spun and faced his brother with his fists ready. The challenge on Mitch's face dared him to argue. Rand couldn't. The moment he'd ended his affair with Tara he'd lost whatever temporary claim he had on her. Having no ties to her had been his choice. And it had been the right decision—the only decision—given the Kincaid history with women.

So why had seeing her with his father sucker punched him? And why did the idea of Tara with Mitch make him want to hit something?

Because she'd claimed she loved you.

And for a split second that night in her bed five years ago when she'd been spinning her fairy tale, Rand had believed her, and he'd wanted the life she'd described. Until he'd remembered who he was. *What* he was. A bastard who let people down. Just like his old man. He'd remembered what loving Everett Kincaid had done to his mother, and what loving Rand had done to Serita. He'd known he couldn't risk that with Tara.

And then he had recalled how his mother had told him she loved him minutes before peeling out in his father's prized '69 Jaguar XKE and plowing it into a tree at a hundred miles per hour. He'd remembered that Serita had called him on the phone and said the same words either right before or right after swallowing a bottle of pills. Had she intended those to be her final words?

But the joke had been on him. While he'd been agonizing over whether or not to risk loving Tara and letting her love him, Tara had moved on.

"Chasing Tara would have been a waste of time anyway," Mitch said, interrupting Rand's thoughts. "She still had it bad for you."

"Not so bad if she turned to Dad three weeks after we broke up."

"Whatever. Being second string to my big brother was a position I was tired of playing. I wasn't going after your girl." Mitch's bitterness came through loud and clear.

"She wasn't mine and you were never second string. You were the golden child who could do no wrong."

For a moment Mitch stared silently then he shook his head. "Why do you think Dad pushed you so hard, Rand? It was because he knew I idolized my big brother, and I'd have to raise my game to keep up with the standards you set. And you always aimed for perfection."

An invisible band tightened around Rand's chest. Mitch had idolized him and Rand had let him down by walking out and hauling himself to the other side of the country to nurse his wounded ego. "He yanked both our chains."

Mitch nodded. "Dad was a master manipulator. He had ways of getting what he wanted from each of us. He pushed and goaded you because you thrived on the competition. He was more devious with me because I never let him know when he'd pushed my buttons."

Rand cursed. How had he missed that?

Because you were too busy butting heads with the ol' man and too busy blaming him for being such an ass your mother would rather be dead than married to him.

And too busy hating yourself for being just like him. Selfish. Self-absorbed. Unable to love a woman the way she deserved to be loved.

Mitch stood. "It's against company policy to fraternize with a direct subordinate. Tara was as out of bounds for Dad then as she is for you now. Don't set us up for a sexual harassment law suit."

His brother would crack a rib laughing if he knew the price for Tara's participation was stud service. Rand ignored the rebuke and asked, "Since when did our father play by the rules?"

Mitch's gaze shifted to the trio of potted trees Tara had positioned in the corner to keep the late afternoon sun's blinding rays from creating a glare on Rand's computer screen. "Yeah."

The tone of that single word sent a prickle of unease creeping up the back of Rand's neck. "Is there something you're not telling me, Mitch?"

"I have everything under control. You need to make sure this thing between you and Tara doesn't turn sour. If you piss her off and she leaves before the end of the year—"

"She won't." He'd do everything in his power to make sure she didn't. He hated someone else holding the cards, calling the shots and controlling the outcomes. That wasn't his style. He liked having the upper hand. But the ridiculous terms of the will had him handcuffed, and for the time being Tara held the key. "At the end of the year KCL will be yours and Nadia's."

"What about you?"

For the first time in his life, Rand realized he didn't have a long-term plan. He hadn't thought beyond fulfilling his duty and not letting his father screw Nadia and Mitch out of their inheritance. He hadn't thought beyond beating his father at his own game.

Would there be a place for him at KCL?

Did he want to spend the rest of his life walking in his father's shoes?

He didn't have the answers.

"We'll table that discussion for now. We have work to do. I want Nadia's replacement chosen by the end of business today." He tapped the résumés on his desk. "One of these applicants has every quality we're looking for—if she survives the interview."

Mitch looked ready to argue, but Rand preempted him by pressing the speaker button. "Tara, please send the first candidate through to the boardroom."

"Yes, sir." Her snippy reply told him his apology hadn't totally placated her. He shouldn't care. He'd done what he had to do to make sure she knew she wouldn't fool him this time.

Tara Anthony was a complication he didn't need. Come hell, high water or hurt feelings he would keep his objectivity. Emotional distance was the key to surviving this year of playing house with a woman determined to land herself a rich husband.

He had plenty of practice with meaningless, no-strings sex. It was the only kind he'd ever allowed himself to have. He never got sucked in to his lovers' lives. They came together, satisfied each other's physical needs, then went their separate ways when the chemistry burned out.

This affair wouldn't be any different. He wouldn't let it.

"Waiting up for me?"

Rand's hard voice startled Tara. She pressed a hand over

her jolted heart and spun around. He stood in the open door of the dining room—the door she'd kept firmly closed for a year. His narrowed eyes pinned her in place.

"You startled me." Belatedly she remembered her tears and quickly turned back to her boxes.

"Tara?"

Ignoring the question in his voice, she swiped her face then snatched up the packaging tape and concentrated on stretching a long, sticky strip across the box's flaps. "I thought you were working late. You said it would take you half the night to go through the information I compiled on each of KCL's brands' executives, and you wanted to be familiar with each employee's history before the cocktail party tomorrow night."

He'd told—no, *ordered*—her to eat dinner without him and not to wait up. After the way he'd hurt her feelings and angered her with his nasty remark this morning, she'd been happy to have time alone. She hadn't even been able to escape him at lunch because he'd insisted she join him, Mitch and Julie, the newly hired director of shared services, for lunch at a South Beach Thai restaurant.

Her plan to regain what she and Rand had once had was on shaky ground because she couldn't get past his anger and distrust. She'd lost hope this morning after their ugly confrontation, and she needed to regroup and rethink her plan.

Maybe…maybe this new bitter version of Rand wasn't a man she could love.

Her fingers tightened on the tape dispenser and the serrated edge dug into her flesh. Exhaling, she made a conscious effort to relax her grip before she drew blood.

She could hear the sound of Rand's footsteps cross the hardwood floor. He stopped just behind her right shoulder. His scent and warmth reached out to her, and she had to fight the urge to turn and lay her head against his chest. Tonight had been hard, like saying goodbye to her mother all over again. But she'd known it would be. That's why she'd avoided this task so long.

"Why are you packing? You can't leave. You signed a contract."

"I'm packing up my mother's things. It's something I should have done a long time ago."

She chanced a peek at him from under her lashes. His green and gold eyes searched her face, then scanned the room, taking in the portable toilet, wheelchair and walker and the bedroom suite from Tara's old apartment.

When her mother could no longer climb the stairs, Tara had done her best to make her comfortable in this makeshift bedroom. Her mom had gone downhill fast in her last six months. She'd barely left this room except to be wheeled to doctors' appointments. She'd spent most of her time in Tara's wicker rocking chair in front of the bay window overlooking the back garden.

"She was handicapped?"

"She was dying. Lung cancer. Too many years of smoking." His impenetrable mask softened a little. "I'm sorry."

"Me, too. But it's time to move on. She wouldn't want me to keep this stuff when it could benefit someone else. It would have been cheaper to rent the medical equipment instead of buying it, but renting seemed like…" Her throat closed, burned. She stopped, swallowed, inhaled and then tried again. "Renting seemed like admitting it would only be a matter of time before I had to turn it back in. I wasn't ready…to give up."

He studied her long and hard, then glanced at the door and rocked on the balls of his feet as if he wanted to leave. Instead he sank back on his heels, shoved his hands in his pockets and inhaled deeply. "You never mentioned her illness when we were together."

"She hadn't been diagnosed then. That came…after…us." One moment Tara had been wallowing in heartache and woe-is-me, and the next her world had turned upside down.

Rand had been working overseas when she'd received the news, and with the ugly way he'd ended things, calling him hadn't been an option.

Forget it. There is no us. We have no future. I won't marry you or father your children. It was sex, Tara. Nothing more.

She'd had no one to turn to except the doctors, whose faces and prognoses had been grim. Panic had set in. She'd been so afraid of losing her mother and of the misery, surgeries and chemo her mother had ahead of her. The day after Tara had found out, she'd broken down in her office at KCL. Everett had whisked her to Kincaid Manor, where she'd poured out her fears.

And then Tara had failed her mother by refusing the one lifeline they'd been offered. Shame scalded her cheeks and weighted her shoulders.

She pushed back the pain and checked her watch. After ten. "I didn't realize it was so late. Have you eaten? I could fix something."

"I ate. Did you?" He indicated the boxes stacked in the corner with a nod. "Looks like you've been at this for a while."

"I…no, I haven't eaten. I…couldn't."

"You have to eat, Tara."

Her stomach seconded his opinion by growling loudly. "I'll grab something later. I'm almost finished."

She lifted another empty box from the floor to the mattress.

Rand laid his warm palm over the back of her hand, stilling her movements. "Take a break."

Her pulse did a quickstep, but despite her body's involuntary reaction, the idea of being intimate with him after what he'd said earlier today about sharing her with Mitch repelled her. As she suspected he'd intended his comment to.

She swallowed the lump in her throat. "I, um…don't need you tonight. So you can…go to bed. Good night."

His gaze held hers for a long moment. "Despite six months working in a ship's galley, I'm not a whiz in the kitchen. But I won't poison you. I'll scramble some eggs and make toast."

Why was he being nice after being so hateful this morning? She couldn't understand him. She bent her head and flicked a fingernail on the box flap. "You don't have to cook for me."

"Tara." He waited until she looked at him. His jaw shifted as if he were grinding his teeth. "You won't be any good to me tomorrow if you don't fuel up tonight."

She snapped her shoulders back. So much for believing his compassion was altruistic. "I'll manage."

"Is that how you lost the weight? By starving yourself? Get your butt in the kitchen," he ordered, then yanked the box from her hand.

She held her ground. "Why are you doing this?"

"Because I don't want you to be a liability."

"You don't want me period." She grimaced and bit her lip. She hadn't meant to let that slip. So much for holding onto her pride.

He caught her chin with his fingers before she could duck again. "I don't want to want you. That's a whole different story. Now get in there and sit down. I'll help you pack after you eat. Two of us will knock it out faster than one."

Emotion squeezed her chest and stung her eyes at this un-expected glimpse of the man she'd fallen for five years ago. Rand had always claimed to be hard-hearted and self-serving, but she'd seen past the facade to the man he'd tried so hard to hide. He might be a ruthless businessman, but no matter how many times he denied it, Rand Kincaid cared about others.

She studied his face. His lips were so close, his eyes so intense. He'd been a gentle and unselfish lover who'd coaxed her past her shyness and taught her about pleasure, about her own body. A less generous man wouldn't have bothered. She wanted to cradle his stubble-shadowed jaw and hurl herself in his arms.

Tonight proved the man she remembered, the one she'd loved, was still in there. Somewhere. All she had to do was draw him out.

Her waning hopes rebounded. All wasn't lost. And to borrow another of Tara's famous last words, tomorrow was another day.

And this time she wasn't giving up without a fight.

Five

"Could you hold me? Just for a minute?"

Tara's quiet question turned the dining room colder than a ship's freezer. Rand's muscles froze and his brain screamed, *No. Hell no. Don't fall for her tricks.*

But over the past hour of packing her mother's belongings she'd confused the hell out of him. Had she really been fighting to hide her tears and quivering bottom lip from him, or had she been giving the performance of a lifetime, letting him see just enough bogus pain to suck him in? Because her quiet, solitary grief had been so convincing she'd almost choked *him* up.

If she was really hurting and not acting, then a simple hug wasn't too much to ask. From anyone other than him.

But he owed her. She'd busted her butt at the office, doing more work in three days than most assistants could accomplish in three weeks. She hadn't complained once about the staggering workload involved in getting him up-to-date on the company, the twelve-hour days or the lack of breaks. She'd simply had snacks and drinks sent up from the cafeteria.

He flexed his fingers, knowing what he needed to do, what he *ought* to do, and dreading it. He opened his arms. Tara fell against him. The soft thud of her body hit him like a freight train. He reluctantly encircled her with his arms. Reminding himself this could be an act to lure him into her trap, he tried hard to stay detached, tried to ignore her scent, her softness, her heat.

But indifference was nearly impossible when he could feel her breaths hitching, could feel the tension in her rigid body as she fought to maintain control. Or faked it.

Warmth seeped through his shirt. Tears. The dampness spread across his chest and her body trembled against his.

He didn't do crying women.

This was exactly the kind of emotionally charged situation he avoided with his lovers. Normally he'd have been long gone by now. Watching Tara hug a sweater or a book or some other trinket to her chest and then carefully sort each item into boxes had brought back memories he'd rather not revisit. Memories of the Kincaid staff packing away his mother's possessions after her death.

Rand had wanted to keep his mother's favorite scarf, the one that smelled like her. His father had ripped it from Rand's hands with a terse, "What are you, a pansy-boy? Go to your room."

All Rand had wanted was a tangible memory of his mother. Hell, he'd been fourteen and drowning in the guilt of not being able to keep her from driving. Rand had known his mother was drunk and angry with his father about another woman. He'd known because she'd always ranted to Rand when his father screwed around.

Confidant wasn't a good role for a kid, and Rand blamed his selfish, immoral ass of a father for putting him in that unenviable position. But Rand hadn't argued. He'd been terrified his father would find out his role in not preventing his mother's death and kick him out.

By the time Rand had been allowed out of his room every trace of his mother had been removed from the house. Not even Nadia had been allowed to keep any of their mother's things.

He stuffed down the memories and sat on the mattress of the mechanical hospital-style bed, pulling Tara between his thighs. Every effort had been made to turn this room into a comfortable bedroom, but not even Tara's old headboard bolted to the wall could make this anything less than it was. An invalid's room.

He recognized the furniture from his affair with Tara, and memories flooded him. Memories of hot sex and of the playful bondage games involving that headboard. Memories that made him granite hard.

He shifted, hoping Tara would pull it together and break up the snuggle party. "You okay?"

She nodded and sniffed. And moved closer. Close enough that her hair tickled his chin and her scent filled his lungs. Close enough that her breasts pressed his chest and her mound nudged his inner thigh. Her heat burned him. And turned him on.

He moved to ease the pressure against his growing erection by leaning back on the pillows propped against the headboard and stretching out his leg. But Tara crawled into the bed with him and settled beside him. Her hips and legs aligned with his, and she rested her cheek on his chest. She wiggled even closer, reminding him she'd always been the cuddly type.

She was the only lover he'd ever lingered with, but in limited doses. More was risky.

So was this.

He wanted up. And out. Of this room. Of this house. Of this state.

This wasn't part of their agreement. He couldn't trust her. The hardening flesh beneath his fly reminded him he couldn't trust himself, either.

"It's like sa-saying goo-goodbye again," she whispered brokenly before he could turn his thoughts into action and peel her off. "It's just so…ha-hard." The raw pain in her voice sounded genuine.

But then he'd been taken in by Tara's lies before.

Rand awkwardly patted her back, but said nothing. He didn't want to encourage any tearful reminiscences.

Tara's little gasping breaths eventually slowed and the fist on his chest relaxed. The tension eased from her body on a long sigh and she sank like a dead weight on his left shoulder.

Had she fallen asleep?

Oh, hell. Why hadn't he run the minute she'd turned those big blue wounded eyes on him?

Why hadn't he gone to bed earlier when she'd told him to instead of insisting she eat?

His arm tingled with pins and needles and started going numb. He stared at the dining room ceiling, at the chandelier hanging on a shortened chain above the bed.

He should wake her or at the very least dump her on her pink sheets and leave her.

But he remained immobile. He'd give her a few more minutes. If she was exhausted, it was because he'd worked her flat out this week. Once she rested she'd have more control over her messy emotions and be less likely to have another meltdown.

If the meltdown was real.

She might be looking for a rich guy to make her future easier, but the contradictions between gold digger, hard worker and a woman who grieved for her mother nagged him like a puzzle with a missing piece.

Minutes ticked past. He didn't know how many because he couldn't see his watch and there were no clocks in the room. His lids grew heavy. He rested his chin on her crown and let the flowery scent of her shampoo fill his nostrils with every breath. She still used the same brand. It pissed him off that he recognized it.

Getting caught up in a woman's Hallmark moments screwed with his detachment.

But he owed Tara tonight. Just tonight. For going above and beyond the call of duty. For giving KCL a year of her life. If she continued at the pace she'd been working, she'd be a bargain—even at the outlandish salary he was paying her.

But he had to make damn sure he didn't make a fool of himself over her again.

"It's 5:00 a.m. Why are you up?" Rand growled from the kitchen entry Thursday morning.

Startled, Tara looked up from the newspaper. "Good morning. If you're determined to get an early start every day, then I might as well join you. We can carpool and conserve gas."

Judging by his scowl that was the last thing he wanted to hear from her. "You won't get overtime for going in early."

She shrugged. "I didn't ask for it. I made *huevos rancheros.* Is that still your favorite?"

Not that they'd ever had breakfast together. Rand had never hung around long enough. But he'd mentioned it once. Funny how she'd remembered, but back then she'd hung on his every word.

His jaw shifted. "I told you, no playing house."

Was he cranky because they'd spent half the night in her mother's bed? When a bad dream had jolted Tara awake shortly after three she'd been shocked to find herself in Rand's arms. He'd released her, risen without a word and gone upstairs as if he couldn't get away from her fast enough.

"It's just breakfast, Rand. Eat and drink your coffee and then we can go. I'll fill you in on the arrangements for to-night's cocktail and dinner party on the way to the office."

"I'll take breakfast to go. You can fill me in later—when you come in at nine."

"I haven't come in later than eight one single day this week and you know it." She couldn't help pointing out that fact. "But have it your way. The resealable containers are in the cabinet to the left of the dishwasher, and the disposable forks are in the bottom drawer."

After filling a travel mug with coffee and packing the *huevos rancheros,* he paused by the table and scowled down at her. "If you think this sharing-and-morning-coffee routine is what I want, you're mistaken. You're better off sticking to the sex. At least I enjoyed that."

The old Tara would have let that comment pass, but the new Tara was turning over a new leaf. She was stronger and bolder now. Strong and bold enough to fight for what she wanted, and last night only reinforced her belief that Rand Kincaid was the man she wanted.

"But you didn't enjoy it. Why is that?"

His chin snapped up. "Because I couldn't help wondering if you'd cried out my father's name when you came the way you did mine."

She flinched at the unexpected lash of pain. "How many times do I have to tell you? I didn't sleep with Everett."

"You also claim you lied when you said you loved me and wanted to have my children. Why should I believe you're not lying now?"

She opened her mouth and closed it again. He had a point. She hated that he believed she'd slept with his father, but nothing she said was going to change Rand's mind. He had to come to that realization himself. And when he did, he'd realize how selfish she'd been. Her refusal to become Everett's partner in exchange for top-notch oncologists' care could very well have cost her mother her life.

Would Rand hate her for being weak? Because she certainly hated herself.

She sighed. "I'm not lying."

"Truth seems to be a fluctuating commodity with you. I'll see you at the office. Thanks for the breakfast and coffee. But tomorrow, don't bother."

"Any idea which heads will roll?"

Tara turned toward the familiar, raspy female voice. "Hello, Patricia."

Patricia Pottsmith had been head of human resources when Tara had originally joined KCL seven years ago. She'd been a cutthroat and ambitious manager back then, and her current position as vice president of the Rendezvous line implied that hadn't changed. She'd moved up the ladder quickly. Tara suspected it was because Patricia didn't mind who she stepped on.

"How about a little insider info for an old friend? A new broom always sweeps clean. Who is Rand going to fire?"

Tara didn't bother to point out they had never been friends. "Even if I knew Rand's plans I wouldn't reveal confidential information."

"I hired you and recommended you as Everett's PA." Patricia's haughty tone implied Tara owed her.

"I'm sorry. You'll have to get what you want from Rand. He'll be calling in each brand's management team for meetings starting Monday."

"Well, at least *your* job is secure. For as long as Rand's interest lasts, that is."

The bottom dropped out of Tara's stomach. "Excuse me?"

"Sleeping with the boss has its perks. I don't hold that against you, Tara. I've done it myself."

Tara tried to hide her distress and shock. Distress that she and Rand had become the hot topic. Shock that Patricia might have slept with Everett. Tara wondered again if she'd misjudged her boss. "Do the other executives believe I slept with Rand to get this job?"

Patricia rolled a narrow shoulder. "It's common knowledge that you never filled out a new application, interviewed or underwent a criminal background check and drug test. HR didn't hire you. You've been wasting away at a backwater small business since you left KCL, and yet you waltz back into one of the most sought after positions in the company—a company that prides itself on promoting from within."

To know this supposedly confidential information Patricia must have used and abused her HR connections. Tara scanned the group of sixteen men and women—the presidents and vice presidents of each line—who'd gathered in the glitzy private hotel dining room for cocktails and dinner. Their snide appraisals made her want to run.

The joy over an event well-planned and discovery of the perfect cocktail dress in a tiny boutique during a mad lunch-hour shopping dash drained away. Suddenly, her black jersey off-the-shoulder dress felt sleazy instead of subtly sexy. The garment exposed more cleavage than she was used to revealing. Not that the dress was daring by most people's—or Miami's—standards, but it was by Tara's.

She wanted a sweater. Or an overcoat.

And she wished Rand were here. But an international call about a problem at an Italian port had detained him as they were leaving her house. She'd driven herself and he planned to follow as soon as he could.

As if her thoughts had conjured him, Rand strode through the doorway. He wore a black dinner jacket over a white collarless shirt and black, sharply creased pants.

The years in California had been good for him. He'd always been confident, but he seemed even more so now. He dominated the room by simply being here, and it wasn't because of his position. It was the air of command he radiated. Conversations stalled and heads turned.

He scanned the room and his attention locked on her. He stopped in his tracks. His gaze slowly raked her from head to toe and back. At any other time his heated look would have made her shiver with awareness and pleasure. But not tonight. Not knowing that others thought she'd sold herself to get this job.

Yes, she was sleeping with Rand, but not because of work. It was because she thought they might be perfect life partners not convenient temporary bedmates.

"Excuse me, Patricia." Tara forced herself to move toward Rand. Her unsteady legs had nothing to do with the obscenely high heels she'd bought to go with the knee-length dress with a longer hem in the back that swished flirtatiously as she walked.

She stopped a circumspect yard away from him. "I've had the bartender serve drinks and appetizers. We're not far behind schedule. You'll still have time to mingle. All I need is a sign from you when you're ready for dinner to be served."

His eyes narrowed. "What's wrong?"

Had her tone given away her agitation? She made a conscious effort to blank her face. "They're waiting to see who you're going to fire. Let me get your drink."

He grabbed her elbow. "Tara."

She tugged but he didn't release her. His long, warm fingers held tight. She could feel the eyes of the executives on them. "Don't. Don't touch me. Not here. Please."

He frowned at her then shifted to stand between her and their guests, turning his back to the room and blocking her view of the executives and theirs of her. "I'll ask again. What's wrong?"

She hesitated, but if Rand was concerned with his credibility as CEO then he needed to know. "They know we're living together, and they think I slept with you to get this job."

His lips flattened into a thin line. "You knew sharing an address would cause problems."

"Yes... No. I didn't think it through. I didn't expect... animosity."

"You want me to move out?" His eyes searched hers.

If she wanted a chance with Rand, it was now or never. This opportunity wouldn't come again. She'd lived through watching her mother fade more with each passing day. She could handle a little gossip.

Live your life without regrets, Tara.

Lifting her chin, she squared her shoulders. "No."

"Then you have to suck it up and deal with their attitudes. You and I know the truth. We're both profiting from this situation." He waited until she nodded, then faced his employees. "Thank you for coming. I know you have questions. I'll answer as many of those as I can tonight. But first I want to thank Tara. She's put her life on hold this year for KCL.

"I recruited her and bribed her to return as part of the transition team because my father always claimed she was the best PA he'd ever had. In four short days, I've learned that if anything, he underestimated her worth. Tara has already become an invaluable asset to me. I place a great deal of trust in her opinions."

With a few words Rand implied the employees had better respect her, or else. After his gentleness last night, his support now was enough to make her eyes sting. She blinked to hold back the tears. She'd had to be strong for her mother for so long. Having someone stand up for her made her throat tighten.

No wonder she'd fallen in love with Rand five years ago.

"Most of you are familiar faces," Rand continued. "I look forward to getting to know the rest of you and learning how you believe you can increase sales in your brand. We have issues to address, and we will be making adjustments this year. But for the most part, KCL is on the right course. Your input is and will always be welcome. I have an open door policy, but if at any time you can't reach me, you can take your concerns to Tara and trust that she will relay *everything* you say to me. We work as a team."

Tara saw Patricia Pottsmith stiffen.

Rand turned to Tara. "I'll take that drink now."

She smiled at him and nodded. He'd called them a team. He couldn't possibly know how badly she wanted that to be true in every sense of the word or how hard she planned to work to make it happen. And every ounce of kindness he showed her only made her more determined to recapture the passion of their past.

Tara tapped on Rand's closed bedroom door.

Seconds passed, but he didn't answer. She knew he was here because she'd heard him come upstairs while she was removing her makeup.

Was he avoiding her? The evening had gone nicely for the most part. There had been some tension, but Rand had handled it well. And she wanted to tell him that.

She rapped again, harder this time. She was on the verge of returning to her room when the door flew open. A dripping Rand stood on the other side. Water streamed from his hair, cascading over his bare, broad shoulders and trickling through the dark curls on his chest and belly to be absorbed by the mauve towel encircling his hips. The dark hairs on his legs clung to his tanned flesh.

She jerked her gaze from his bare feet to his eyes. He looked annoyed, but that didn't stop hunger from swirling in her midsection. Not even the feminine, colored towel could lessen his masculine appeal. Bubbles clung to his neck behind his left ear. Shampoo suds?

She hugged her robe tighter around her waist, fisting her fingers in the fabric and fighting the urge to brush the bubbles away. "I—I'm sorry. I didn't realize you were in the shower."

"What do you want, Tara? A command performance?"

She flinched. "N-no. I wanted to thank you for tonight, for backing me. And I wanted to tell you that you handled the executives' anxiety better than Everett would have."

His jaw shifted and his eyes narrowed. "Thanks. Good night."

He pivoted and stalked back into the room without closing the door.

Don't let him walk away this time.

She followed him, admiring the wide, droplet-spattered V of his torso and watching as he grabbed another towel from the bathroom rail and briskly scrubbed the moisture from his hair and skin. The muscles of his back and arms flexed with his movements and her body responded by generating heat in her belly and her skin. "But you didn't have to lie, Rand."

He met her gaze in the mirror. "I don't lie."

"I meant about Everett saying I was the best PA he'd had."

"That was the truth. My father thought you could do no wrong."

"Really?" That meant a lot because she had tried very hard not to disappoint him after he'd taken a chance on pulling her from reservations.

She smiled and Rand turned to scowl at her. He scowled a lot these days. She didn't remember him doing so in the past...except for that last morning.

She cleared her throat. "Well...anyway, thanks for telling me and for your other compliments. And thank you for last night."

He shrugged one shoulder. "It was nothing."

"It wasn't *nothing* to me." She closed the distance between them and rose on tiptoe to brush a quick thank-you kiss on his cheek. But something went amiss the minute her palm encountered the steamy, damp flesh of his naked chest.

Rand sucked in a sharp breath. His hand gripped her waist, and he turned his head. Their lips met. Brushed. Clung. Separated.

Surprised by the sensual impact of what she'd intended as a friendly peck, Tara eased back and tried to catch her breath. His heart pounded heavily beneath her hand, racing almost as fast as hers. The gold flecks in his hazel eyes glittered and his pupils expanded with desire. An answering need swelled within her.

Moisture flooded her mouth. She gulped it down and gave in to temptation to reach up for the stray suds. She stroked them down his neck and across his collarbone, not stopping until her hands rested side by side on his chest.

She licked her lips. "I didn't come in here for this."

But that didn't mean she didn't want it. Want *him*.

Live your life without regrets.

Sliding her hands to his shoulders, she rose again and covered his mouth with hers. Rand didn't pull away, nor did he do anything to aid her. He stood as still as a statue. But so much warmer. Hotter.

Her pulse stuttered like the woodpecker that sometimes woke her by pecking on the gutter outside her bedroom. She sipped from Rand's mouth and then traced his lips with her tongue.

An almost inaudible sound rumbled deep in his throat. The fingers at her waist tightened. But he didn't push her away.

In their past relationship she'd never been bold enough to

take the initiative with him, but back then she'd been inexperienced and unsure.

She tasted him, sweeping the soft inner flesh of his lips and his slick teeth, and then she leaned in to him. His saunalike heat soaked through her thin gown and robe, scorching her breasts and abdomen and making her ache deep in her core.

Only Rand could melt her with nothing more than a kiss. Only Rand could banish the emptiness and loneliness clawing at her. She wanted him like she'd never wanted any other man. Showing him seemed…important somehow.

She lifted her head and sank back on her heels, then glided her hands over his chest, across the hard nubs of his tiny nipples and the sparse curls covering his pectorals. She traced the hairline leading to the towel with a feather-light caress. His skin goose-bumped and his stomach muscles contracted beneath her fingertips. His indrawn breath hissed.

She'd always loved touching him, pleasuring him, making this man who seemed so in control ninety-nine percent of the time lose it. He'd taught her how. In fact, he'd taught her everything she knew about making love, but she'd always been tentative and afraid of doing something wrong. In the end she had, but it had been her words, not her actions, that drove him away.

Leaning in, she painted a wet circle around one nipple and then the other. She grasped the towel on his hips for balance, sliding her fingers behind the damp barrier. The knot loosened. She tugged and the covering dropped to the floor, revealing his thick erection.

He wanted her. Wanted this. The undeniable proof stood between them.

Encircling his smooth shaft with one hand, she cupped him with the other and tested his length, his silkiness. His muscles turned rigid, the tendons of his face and neck strained.

She circled the satiny head with her thumb the way she knew he liked and relished his groan.

"Tara—"

"Shh. Let me." She sank to her knees and licked him from base to tip.

He jammed his fingers into her hair so swiftly she expected him to yank her away. But he didn't. Parting her lips, she took as much of him into her mouth as she could, stroking him, loving him. His texture. His taste. His response. Each growl and hiss and pulse rewarded her efforts.

She dragged one hand down a rock-hard thigh and skimmed it around to cup his clenched buttocks. Her tongue swirled around him and the fingers in her hair trembled. Each little quake teased her scalp and heated her core. She smiled and deepened her kiss, knowing he liked what she was doing.

Rand swore.

"Tara." He ground out her name in a command, a warning, a plea.

She dragged her short nails up and down the back of his thigh. The tremors spread to his legs. His toes curled into the rug.

She remembered his erogenous zones, the spots that made Rand shudder, and she shamelessly reacquainted herself with each one, lingering until his back bowed and his fingers fisted. He tried to pull away, but she cinched her arms around him and wouldn't let him go. And then he roared out his pleasure.

Moments later his hands fell heavily to her shoulders, then he cupped her face and urged her to stand. She rose slowly, kissing a path from his hipbone to his sternum, his collarbone, his jaw and finally his mouth.

Rand's arms banded around her, crushing her body to his as he kissed her so fiercely she grew dizzy and had to break away to gasp for breath. His hazel eyes burned into hers and his nostrils flared with each inhalation.

Happy that she could give him as much pleasure as he'd given her two nights ago, she smiled and traced a finger along his jaw. As long as they had this explosive chemistry between them, she had a chance to revive and improve on their past relationship.

"Thank you for being there for me." Her words came out choppy with emotion. It had been so long since she'd had someone to lean on. But she wasn't going to turn on the waterworks in front of him again. She'd done enough of that last night.

She wiggled free and made a beeline for the door.

"What was that about?" Rand's harsh voice stopped her before she could escape. Tara looked at him over her shoulder. Suspicion clouded his eyes, and it tore her heart. Why couldn't he trust her?

"I wanted to make you feel good."

The flush of passion had faded from his face and his lips made a thin, straight line. "What do you expect in return?"

She shook her head. "Nothing."

"Right." Disbelief stretched out the word. He closed the distance between them until he loomed over her. "You want me. I can see it in your eyes and the color of your cheeks. Your nipples are hard. I'll bet you're wet, Tara."

"Without a doubt."

He lifted his hand and grasped her shoulder. His thumb covered the racing pulse at the base of her neck. She shivered.

"I didn't say I wasn't aroused, Rand. I said I didn't expect anything from you tonight."

"But you wouldn't say no." The razor-sharp edge had returned to his voice. He dragged a finger to her breast, bumped over a tightened nipple, bisected her belly and grazed the sensitive area between her thighs.

Desire clenched her womb. But Rand seemed angry instead

of turned on and his anger wasn't what she craved. The gold flecks in his irises glittered, but not with hunger. This wasn't the same man she'd lost her heart to. This Rand was harder, less trusting and less charming.

What had made him that way?

"I wouldn't say no if I thought you wanted me right now. But you don't. And I don't want you back in my bed until you want to be there." Backing him into a corner and demanding sex had only thickened the walls between them. She had to give him space.

His eyes narrowed to slits. "What game are you playing?"

"No game." She stepped away although part of her ached to stay, to find sexual pleasure with him even though she knew she'd regret it later. "Good night, Rand. I'll see you in the morning."

She slipped through the door and into her room.

Gaining his trust would be difficult, but if she couldn't do that, then she'd never win his heart. Five years ago she hadn't been up to the task, but today she was older, wiser, stronger and more determined. She wasn't going to rush this time. She had a full year to accomplish her goal.

She wanted the man she'd fallen in love with back, and then she'd win him over.

Because this time nothing less than everything Rand Kincaid had to offer would be enough.

Six

The sudden roar of an engine broke Rand's concentration Saturday evening.

He looked over his laptop screen and out the window beyond the desk he'd set up in his bedroom, and spotted Tara with a red lawnmower on the back lawn. A floppy straw hat covered her hair and face, but her skimpy bathing-suit top and *short* shorts did a piss-poor job of covering her from her shoulders to the white sneakers on her feet. His gaze cruised past the curves of her breasts to her midriff and long legs and back up again. His pulse quickened.

He forced his attention back to the spreadsheet, but the numbers might as well have been encrypted. He shoved the pages away. So much for the financial report. His brain had been hijacked by his libido.

Again.

The entire week had been a challenge. Tara was everything

he'd said at the executives' dinner and more. Smart. Efficient. Productive. She seemed to anticipate his needs even before he recognized them.

She was also a distraction. Her scent lingered in his office long after she left, and he heard every movement she made on the other side of the wall dividing her workspace from his. He'd never had trouble blocking out his previous PAs' voices, but at this rate his open door policy was in danger of becoming the closed door variety.

She'd played him with the oldest trick in the book Thursday night. Seduction. And it pissed him off. Heat steamed from his pores and his body switched to red alert at the mental replay of her hot, wet mouth pulling a response from him. One he'd wanted to deny but couldn't.

Cursing his inability to block the images from his memory, he closed his laptop, and gave in to the temptation to look at her again.

What was it about Tara Anthony that made him ignore rules and good sense?

Tara swiped a hand across her forehead, driving Rand's gaze to the outside thermometer hanging by the back gate in the flower-flooded garden. Eighty-eight degrees. He drummed his fingers on the desk.

He'd been cloistered in his bedroom working for most of the day. And he wanted to stay here, avoiding Tara, avoiding the sexual craving her proximity caused, avoiding the memory of her talented, lying mouth. Avoiding the relationship he wanted no part of but she seemed insistent on forcing.

But his conscience wouldn't let him, and he couldn't concentrate with her making all that racket. He shot out of his chair, headed downstairs and plowed open the back door. He slammed into a humid wall of heat the second he hit the patio.

Tracking the engine noise, he stepped off the hot flag-

stones and around a hedge of tall green shrubs loaded with
pink blooms and buzzing bees, and jerked to a halt when he
spotted Tara bent at the waist with one hand on the mower
handle. The curve of her backside pointed in his direction, and
her shorts rode up to expose paler crescents of flesh beneath
the ragged hem.

His muscles seized and his eyes gorged. A burn unrelated
to the evening sun baked his skin. He fisted his hands by his
side against the urge to trace those untanned curves. Most
women hated tan lines, but he loved them. That pale flesh sig-
nified something taboo, an area meant to be concealed.

Tara scooped up a yellow ball, straightened then tossed the
toy over the six-foot wooden privacy fence separating her
yard from her neighbor's. She resumed mowing, her long,
lean leg muscles flexing with each stride.

"Tara." She either didn't hear him or ignored him. "Tara,"
he shouted.

She spun around so abruptly the noisy engine died. "What?"

The closer he got to her, the drier his mouth became. Her
blue underwire top cupped and lifted her breasts like lingerie
or his hands would, and her denim shorts were so old and
faded it was a wonder they hadn't split at the seams when she'd
bent over. On second thoughts, they hadn't torn because they
were too large and barely clung to her hips. The waistband
gaped to reveal her navel. Frayed bits of bleached fabric
danced along the tops of her thighs in the slight evening breeze.
A sheen of sweat glistened on her body, and a rivulet ran from
between her breasts to disappear behind her loose waistband.

One tug and Tara's denim cutoffs would be tatters. Rand's
fingers twitched. He swallowed, but the gesture did nothing
to wet his dry mouth or douse the fire behind his fly. Neither
did his gulps of suntan-oil-and-fresh-cut-grass-scented air.

"Why don't you have a lawn service?" The unwanted attraction pissed him off and his anger came through in his clipped words.

She shrugged, removed her hat and wiped her forehead with her forearm. "Too expensive."

"Not with the salary I'm paying you."

"That money is earmarked for something else."

"What?"

She shifted and the shorts slid south a fraction of an inch. Another wiggle of her hips and they'd hit the grass.

Was she wearing panties?

Was prancing around out here in her skimpy clothing part of her hook-a-husband plan?

As if she'd guessed his thoughts, she hitched up her pants. "Most of it's going toward my mother's medical bills. If I don't get them paid off soon the creditors are going to put a lien on the house."

"The house she wanted you to keep."

"Yes."

"Just in case your father came looking for her," he said, repeating her ridiculous story. "What kind of woman loves a man who walks out on her?"

"The kind who vowed to love, honor and cherish until death parted them. We never had proof that my father died. Mom kept her vow."

So had his mother, he realized. The sobering thought knocked Rand back a step. His mother had loved her jackass of a husband despite his repeated infidelities.

Tara sighed. "Rand, did you need something? Because I'd like to get this finished before the forecasted thunderstorms roll in."

As if to reinforce her point, thunder rumbled in the distance. Sweat glued the fabric of his polo shirt to his torso. "I'll hire a landscaping crew and have them onsite first thing Monday. You don't have to do this."

She shook her head. "Yes, I do. The yard is something my mother and I always worked on together. I need to do this. For her. For me."

Crap. Another Hallmark moment.

It was bad enough that pictures littered the flat surfaces in the house—pictures of the happy kind of childhood Rand and his siblings hadn't had. Pictures of the kind of life Tara had told him she wanted five years ago. With him.

Face it. She lied about loving you and you fell for it. Get over it and move on.

Curses ricocheted around his skull and every instinct told him to retreat inside and get back to work. She was sucking him into suburbia and into a relationship against his will.

He did not want to share her home, her chores or her life. But he could hardly sit inside in the air-conditioning while Tara toiled away in the summer heat. He wasn't a freeloader.

And since you're not paying your way with sex—

Dammit. He wasn't pissed off that she hadn't approached him since the night she'd blown his…mind. He didn't want to be her gigolo.

"How can I help?" The words clawed their way up his throat.

She tilted her head and considered him for several seconds. "If you'll mow, I'll handle the Weed Eater."

Rand studied the machine. He knew nothing about lawnmowers or mowing grass. Kincaid Manor had always employed a team of gardeners. Since moving out of the family house more than a decade ago, he'd lived in high-rise urban condos surrounded by concrete. If there had been any plants in his complexes, he hadn't noticed them.

But he'd spent one summer working in the engine room of a 160,000-ton cruise ship. He could handle one small push mower. "Okay."

Tara's gaze drifted over his shirt and khaki pants. She did

that often—looked him over from top to bottom. And his body reacted predictably. Every time. He resented the ease with which she pushed his buttons when no other woman's come-hither looks did a thing for him—unless he allowed it. Fighting the unwanted response, he shoved his hands in his pockets.

"You'll need to change first. You'll roast in long pants." Without waiting for his reply she walked away.

His gaze remained riveted to the sway of her behind until she disappeared into the shed that looked like a small chalet in the back corner of the property. Cursing silently, Rand returned to his bedroom, changed into an old sleeveless T-shirt, gym shorts and running shoes and went back outside.

Even before he finished reading the instructions printed on the machine's handle, he'd sweated through his shirt. He peeled off the soggy, clingy cotton and tossed it onto the patio, then bent and pulled the mower's cord. The motor sputtered but didn't start. He cursed and tried again. Another sputter. Another curse.

A slender leg entered his peripheral vision. He tracked that sleek, lightly tanned skin upward, past a shapely thigh, a hip, the indenture of her waist and the swell of her breast. Tara stood beside him carrying a Weed Eater and wearing safety goggles on her brim-shadowed face. She looked like a model from the pages of a handyman's sexy calendar—the kind a guy would hide in his gym locker or his garage. Any red-blooded male would want to roll in the grass with her in that getup.

"Have you ever used a lawnmower?" she asked, her eyes raking over his bare chest.

"No. But I can handle it," he said through clenched teeth.

She smiled and squeezed the two handles together. "Safety feature. If you let go and the handles separate, the mower shuts off. Now pull the cord."

He did, conscious of her nearly naked body beside him and

of those blue eyes tracking his every move. The engine roared to life. He fastened his fingers around the vibrating bar. Tara nodded and leaned forward until her breast bumped his elbow and her lips touched his ear. Fire sparked in Rand's groin. His hand slipped and silence once again descended on the yard as the engine died.

She dropped back on her heels. "Stick to the grass and stay out of the flower beds. I'll get the hard to reach stuff."

And then she sashayed away, leaving him to master the machine. She fired up the Weed Eater. The alluring play of muscles beneath her skin as she whirred her way along the fence enclosing the yard held him captive. She hadn't had those muscles five years ago. He knew, because there wasn't an inch of her he hadn't explored. With his hands. His lips. His tongue.

Rand blinked and pivoted away from her distracting presence. He restarted the mower and shoved it forward, focusing on plowing straight lines through the thick emerald carpet of grass. If he didn't pay attention, he'd probably cut off his foot.

The contradictions in Tara's behavior nagged him as he worked. She still drove the same car she'd owned when they dated. She wore old clothing better suited to a rag bag, did her own yard work and paid her mother's bills.

He glanced once more at the woman who'd blackmailed him into being her house and bedmate. Had he been wrong about Tara in the past?

No, dammit. He'd seen her coming out of his father's bedroom with a hickey on her neck, a flushed face and messed-up clothing. Regardless of what lie she'd concocted, she'd been intimate with his father.

Add in that she hadn't accepted the KCL job until Rand offered a salary that was quadruple the industry standard and agreed to play house, and it was clear Tara Anthony was up to something. The question was what?

She had to be looking for a sugar daddy.

But she wouldn't find one in him.

For Mitch's and Nadia's sakes Rand would be smarter this time around. Because he had a hell of a lot more to lose.

"Good morning, Rand."

Tara caught the almost imperceptible hitch in Rand's step and the brief flash of surprise in his eyes when he turned the corner into their office suite and realized she'd beaten him to work Monday morning.

Mouth tight, he nodded and resumed his course. He had to pass her desk to get to his office. "You're in early."

He'd hibernated in his room for most of the weekend. She'd barely seen him except for the time he'd mowed her grass Saturday evening. They couldn't build a relationship that way.

He looked delicious in a taupe suit and light blue shirt. A fresh tan from that hour of yard work darkened his lean face, and the memory of how he'd looked shirtless and sweaty made her temperature spike.

She rose. His pace faltered again as his hazel eyes roved over her new wraparound dress. She loved the way the fuchsia fabric hugged her breasts and waist and floated just above her knees. But she loved his nostril-flaring reaction even more.

Working primarily from home since she'd left KCL meant she had an extremely limited professional wardrobe. Most of that was too big. She'd spent Sunday afternoon shopping because she needed both work and cruise wear. By the time she'd returned from the outlet mall last night Rand's door had been securely shut. He'd left a note in the kitchen telling her he'd already eaten dinner.

He snapped his head forward and stalked toward his inner sanctum, but not before Tara noted the appreciative expansion of his pupils. Encouraged, she gathered her notepad and followed him.

"We have a ton of stuff to get through before we leave for the cruise on Friday. The first brand's most recent financials are waiting on your desk, and the president and VP are due at eight-thirty."

Four more nights and she'd have him all to herself…along with 2800 people on the ship, that is. She almost danced in her new d'Orsay pumps with anticipation.

Rand stopped so quickly she plowed into his back. His heat and scent enfolded her, but she righted herself and smoothed the spot where her pen had touched his suit coat, checking for a stain. None. Good.

He stiffened and stepped out of reach. "What is that?"

She tracked his gaze and stated the obvious, "A coffee-pot. When you're not using it the roll-down door will conceal it."

He turned his thin-lipped frown from the new addition on the shelving unit to her. "Where did it come from? And why is it here?"

"I picked it up this morning at your favorite coffee shop, along with a pound of freshly ground beans. The pot has a timer. I'll set it up so your coffee will be ready each morning when you arrive, and since you insist on leaving home without breakfast, I'm having it delivered from the KCL cafeteria every day at eight because you're cranky when you're hungry."

Her announcement earned her a darker scowl.

"I've chosen this week's menu, but you're welcome to make adjustments if you like. Here are the chef's suggestions for next week after we return from our cruise. Of course, I didn't tell him why we'd be out of the office since that would defeat the purpose of an incognito inspection."

She offered him the list of choices. When one of his hands

clenched the handles of his leather laptop bag and the other remained fisted by his side, she put the paper in his in-box.

"Tara—"

"You're welcome," she interrupted. She'd learned by his growls that he didn't like her doing things for him such as his laundry or preparing meals and leaving them in the refrigerator. But she had to cook and clean for herself. Doing so for one more wasn't a bother. In fact, after a year of silence and solitude she liked having someone else to look after.

She crossed to the pot and filled a mug, which she then set on his blotter. "I've already dealt with most of your e-mail, but I flagged a couple for your attention. Do you need anything else before you tackle your in-box?"

She could almost hear him grinding his teeth as he opened his bag and withdrew his computer. "No."

"I'll bring in your breakfast as soon as it's brought up, and I'll let you know when the first management team arrives."

She turned on her heel and retreated to her office.

"Tara, it won't work."

She pivoted and examined his hard face. "What won't?"

"Buttering me up."

She frowned. "*Buttering you up* implies I want something."

He closed the distance between them in two long strides, not stopping until he was so close she could see the gleam on his freshly shaven jaw and smell his cologne and a hint of mint toothpaste. "You're after a wedding ring."

Her breath caught and her heart skipped. He didn't know that for sure. He was only guessing. What would he do if she confirmed his suspicions? He couldn't fire her without jeopardizing his part of the will. But he might fortify the walls barricading his heart, and she had a formidable battle on her hands already.

"I'm after a mutually satisfying relationship. That's it."

And it was everything. Five years ago he'd been her playmate and her bedmate. She wanted both back. And she wanted more. Much more.

His intense gaze made her want to squirm, but she'd told nothing but the truth.

"I don't believe you."

"Well…that's certainly honest. My mother always claimed trust was built on actions, not words. So I guess I'll have to prove to you that I'm not after anything that you won't willingly give."

The trick was convincing him to give willingly.

Tara had given Rand space this past week and he'd used it to avoid her. That ended now.

Excitement and anticipation quickened her pulse and dampened her skin late Friday afternoon. She had three nights at sea with Rand to look forward to. Three nights and four days of sharing a cabin. And a bed.

She could hardly wait. The Miami-to-the-Bahamas Rendezvous trip would be her first cruise and her first real vacation in six years, but neither was the main attraction. The man ahead of her held that honor. She wanted to get Rand to relax with her, to leave the world of work, tailored suits and tightly knotted ties behind. His current navy twill pants, white polo shirt and baseball cap were a good start.

She followed him into their assigned cabin, mimicking his moves of inspecting the closet and the tiny lavatory, which contained a sink, toilet and compact shower/bath stall. Definitely not large enough for two.

Reserving a middle-of-the-road cabin—not the cheapest, nor one of the luxury suites—had seemed the best way to blend in. The room was smaller than she'd expected. But then what did she know about cruising? Nothing. And the cabin's limited size could work to her advantage. There was literally nowhere for Rand to hide.

Besides the bed, there was a love seat, two tiny bedside tables and coffee table, as well as a wall unit with drawers, a minifridge and a television quietly playing a show about the proper use of life jackets. Seeing those life jackets in the center of the bed reminded her that she'd soon be out of her depth. In more ways than one.

Rand set his cap on a shelf, snapped off the TV and inspected the narrow rectangular space with his hands on his hips. He crossed the carpet and slid open the glass door. Warm sea-scented air flooded the air-conditioned room. Tara joined him on a private balcony about the size of a single bed and looked over the railing. Lifeboats hung from the sides of the ship just below their balconies.

The theme song from *Titanic* launched in her brain. But even that chilling intrusion couldn't dampen her enthusiasm. She wanted to bounce and giggle. Instead, she trailed Rand back inside. He didn't look happy.

"Is there a problem?"

His gaze landed on the bed they'd soon be sharing before returning to hers. "The room is clean, uncluttered and suitably equipped for the price point. The textiles could be fresher."

He seemed more tense than usual despite his casual attire. "Are you worried about being out of the office? Mitch's PA assured me your brother could handle everything until Tuesday when we return."

"I'm sure he can."

"Rand? Are you okay?"

He looked at her, his gaze running over the flirty strapless apricot sundress that left her shoulders and most of her legs bare. "Why wouldn't I be?"

"You tell me." She tilted her head and her new dangly gold

earrings tapped the sensitive spot on her neck—the one that drove her wild when Rand grazed the skin with his teeth. She couldn't wait for him to do it again, and if this trip went according to plan, he'd do so often.

She'd dreamed about strolling hand in hand on the beaches during the day and on the deck by moonlight, quiet dinners and sharing his bed.

They hadn't been intimate since that night she'd pleasured him. Instead of spending quality time together this past week they'd had an endless series of meetings with the executive staff during the day, and he'd spent evenings in his bedroom working on his laptop. They probably hadn't had two hours total of private face time since Monday morning. That didn't mean she hadn't been aware of his every movement both at home and work.

She was counting on the forced togetherness of the cruise making it impossible for him to keep his distance. "I've never cruised before. I can't wait for you to show me the ropes."

Cruising wouldn't be the only first she'd shared with him, but telling a commitment-phobic man she'd been a virgin before they'd slept together that first night hadn't seemed like a good idea at the time. She was pretty sure the revelation would have ended not only their evening but also their relationship.

His eyes narrowed. "Aren't you the one who claimed the discounted rates made cruising affordable?"

"I've never had anyone to go with." Except him. "My mother was afraid of the water and Nadia wasn't interested." She dug in to her carry-on and pulled out the cruise materials. "We need to sign up for our shore excursions."

His frown deepened. "I'm here to work, not play. You're here as camouflage. You're on your own except for the lifeboat drill and dinners where we'll need to present ourselves as a couple. Do whatever you want. Go ashore. Use the spa. KCL will cover your expenses. *Reasonable* expenses. No jewelry. No designer clothing."

Taken aback by the rapid unraveling of her plans, she struggled to regroup. If she didn't change his mind, their romantic getaway would be a solitary vacation. She'd been alone enough since her mother died. "But…how will you find out the reasons bookings are down if you don't do the full cruise experience?"

"I know what to look for."

"I could help."

"If this is your first cruise, then you won't recognize substandard issues."

He had a point. "You could teach me."

"Tara—"

"What about the welcoming party?"

"I need to check the ship and the chaos of castoff is the best time."

His hard gaze pinned her in place. She scrambled for a valid reason to be with him.

"Do you really want to tip your hand and let them know you're here on our first day? I mean, I realize the check-in associate saw your name, but you had on your hat and your passport still lists a California address. I don't think she recognized you or made the connection to KCL. We should stick together. You said yourself we'll draw less attention as a couple."

His lips thinned in irritation. "Fine. But don't expect to play inseparable newlyweds throughout the cruise."

Newlyweds. The word sent her temperature skyrocketing. Her gaze bounced to the bed, then back to Rand's face. The banked heat in his eyes made her shiver, and the obvious fact that he wanted her kept her going.

She licked her dry lips. She would soon have him exactly

where she wanted him, but could she make him happy to be there? Could she make him yearn to share her bed the way he used to?

That was the mission she intended to accomplish over the next three nights.

Seven

Rand slid his key card into the lock. He'd deliberately stayed out well past midnight to avoid sharing the domesticated get-ready-for-bed routine.

As soon as he crossed the threshold a sense of confinement doubled his pulse rate, constricted his lungs and pushed sweat from his pores. He'd spent months at sea working all over KCL ships and in almost every capacity and slept in cabins barely large enough to turn around in. Three nights of sharing a balcony cabin wouldn't be a problem.

If his roommate were anyone else.

His claustrophobic reaction had nothing to do with the dimensions of the room, and everything to do with the woman he'd left in the bar hours earlier. But even though the comedian onstage had been entertaining, Rand had needed to get away from Tara's laugh. It brought back too many memories—memories of a time when he'd let his guard down.

He eased the door closed and entered the unlit room as silently as possible. Would she be waiting up for him? Or had she gone to bed?

Bed. The heavy throb of his heart echoed a yard lower.

He searched the mattress in the darkness. The white terry-cloth elephant sitting in the center of the spread was the bed's only occupant. Rand had spent nine months between his junior and senior years of college working as a cabin steward. Back then he'd known how to form a dozen different animals from rolled and folded bath towels.

As his eyes adjusted to the lack of light he noted the empty lavatory and his suitcase sitting on the love seat. He stopped in his tracks. Empty bed. Empty chair. No Tara. Another possibility snagged him like a briar ripping along his skin.

The Rendezvous brand primarily targeted couples, but there were always singles on board. Had Tara given up on landing him and lingered in the bar to hook a more willing victim?

An uncomfortable burn settled in his stomach. He scanned the deserted cabin once more. The fluttering bottom corner of the curtain caught his eye and pulled him forward. He pushed back the panel and found Tara sitting on the balcony. She hadn't bothered to turn on the light.

That wasn't relief filling his lungs. The sea air simply made it easier to breathe. He shoved the sliding glass door open the rest of the way. "Seasick?"

She lifted her face. Moonlight washed her cheeks. She'd removed her makeup, but not her dress. From his vantage point above her, the strapless bodice revealed a tempting shadow of cleavage, and then the ocean breeze caught her zigzag hem, drawing his gaze from her sexy sandals to an arousing length of sleek thighs. "No."

"Then why aren't you in bed?"

"I forgot my nightgown."

Her reply hit him like a kick in the crotch, propelling the air from his lungs. Did she think he was stupid enough to fall for that? "How convenient."

She winced at his sarcasm. "Our luggage wasn't delivered until almost nine. By the time I unpacked and realized I'd left my nightie in the dryer, the gift shop had closed. Can I borrow a T-shirt tonight? Unless you don't mind if I sleep naked."

The lower half of his anatomy responded with resounding approval. Luckily, his brain kicked in. Tara had always been good at making her lies sound believable. Too bad he hadn't known that then. But he made a mental note that the luggage had been delivered late. "I'll get a shirt."

She rose. "Thank you."

He backed inside and headed for his luggage. Two flicks later it opened. He withdrew a white T-shirt and handed it over.

"Thanks. I'll only be a minute." Tara crossed the shadowy cabin quickly and disappeared into the bathroom. The door closed.

Something about watching her pad across a bedroom hit him like a double shot of espresso. Sleep would be a long time coming.

Rand eyed the bed and debated stripping to his boxers and getting under the covers before she returned. Stripping…the way Tara was currently on the other side of that wall. He gritted his teeth against another below-the-belt pulse of arousal.

Moments later the door opened. Tara returned, leaving the lavatory light on. Despite the extra-tall size, his shirt only covered her to the tops of her thighs, leaving a mouthwatering amount of leg bare. Even in the moonlight he could make out the shape and jiggle of her breasts beneath the loose white fabric as she hung her dress in the closet. When she turned toward the bed he saw the raised texture of her erect nipples and silently swore.

Was she wearing anything at all under there? Or would he be able to slide his hand beneath the cotton and cup her bare bottom?

You're not cupping anything.

"Which side?" she asked.

It took a few seconds for his brain to engage and figure out she meant which side of the bed. "I don't care."

She picked up the elephant and smiled. "Isn't he adorable?"

"The more creative the animals, the better you'll tip your steward at the end of the voyage."

She stuck her tongue out. "Spoilsport."

The childish gesture reminded him how much fun he'd had with her before she'd betrayed him. Few Florida residents hadn't visited the proliferation of theme parks and tourist traps dotting the state like mushrooms. But oddly enough neither she nor he had. They'd spent a lot of their time visiting amusement parks and acting like kids during the day and igniting the sheets like very naughty adults at night. Screaming on roller-coaster rides or in passion made it easy to avoid personal topics, and playing tourist with Tara had been like having the childhood he and his siblings hadn't had.

She'd been one of the few people he'd been able to relax with. More fool him.

She carefully set the towel creature on the shelf before lifting the covers on the far side of the bed and climbing between the sheets. "Bathroom's all yours."

Her comment jarred him into action. He retrieved his shaving kit and the essentials and retreated to the head. After brushing his teeth he donned clean boxers and sat on the closed toilet lid. How long would it take her to fall asleep? He gave her ten additional minutes before snapping off the light and easing open the door.

She must have gotten up and closed the curtains. He wanted them open, but didn't want to wake her with the noise.

He couldn't see anything in the pitch-black room, but he could hear Tara's breathing coming slow, even and deep as he approached the bed. He slid between the sheets and lay stiffly, flat on his back. He folded his hands behind his head and stared at the ceiling he could barely make out, dreading the sleepless night ahead. Dreaded lying beside Tara. Wanting her. His sex thickened and ached—a problem any sane man would have handled in the shower.

No, a sane man would take the sex she offered without second thoughts.

But Rand knew how skillfully she'd cast her net last time, how easily she'd suckered him into wanting more than a casual fling despite his vow to never marry, have children or let a woman depend on him.

Tara's breathing altered. She rolled over and snuggled up to him. One silky smooth leg bent and rested on his thigh. Her hand splayed over his sternum. He ground his teeth until his jaw hurt. And then her hand shifted. Downward. Her burning touch skimmed over his bare skin and came to rest just above his navel. His heart slammed against his ribs. Another half inch and she'd encounter the evidence of his horniness, which even now stretched toward her hand.

Was she asleep or playing him? He'd bet his Porsche 911 Carrera S Cabriolet it was the latter.

Why are you denying yourself? She used you last time. It's time for reimbursement. With interest.

Good point.

He wanted her and he'd take what she offered. Forewarned was forearmed, or so the cliché claimed. As for her falling in love with him… Impossible. For that to happen she'd have to be a different kind of woman. One who didn't profess her love for one man and then screw his father days later.

Rand covered her hand with his and guided it lower until

her palm rested over his engorged flesh. The thin knit of his boxers offered no protection from the scalding heat of her touch and his erection jerked in response. A reflex. Nothing more.

Tara's breath hitched. Her fingers twitched, and then tension invaded her lax muscles. Either she'd been asleep and he'd woken her or she was damned good at faking it.

And with Tara Anthony he couldn't trust his judgment to know the difference.

Waking with a handful of Rand was nothing short of a dream or a fantasy.

Tara tried to focus her rousing brain and figure out what was going on. Her fingers curled around thick, cotton-covered steel. Oh, yes. Definitely Rand. She inhaled a shaky breath and his familiar scent confirmed the identification. His palm covered the back of her hand, anchoring it in place.

She tipped back her head, but she couldn't see his features in the inky room. "What—?"

"It's just sex," he rasped in a low, husky voice that made her insides sizzle with sexual excitement.

"Okay." *For now.* She tested his length and his breath hissed.

He rolled her onto her back. One hair-roughened leg separated hers and pinned her in place. His big, hot hand released hers to stroke from her thigh to beneath her borrowed T-shirt. His palm coasted over her panties, her waist and covered her breast. Sure. Fast. Impatient. He found her nipple like a heat-seeking missile and tweaked it until she squirmed with need.

"I won't marry you."

She bit her lip. She hadn't expected winning him back to be easy. But this was a gamble she had to take. A gamble with risks. "I didn't ask you to."

His mouth took hers, his tongue plunged, dueled, stroked.

He devoured her as if his control had snapped, as if he couldn't get enough of her. And that was exactly what she wanted.

She didn't know what had brought on this change of heart, but she wasn't about to argue. She wanted this, wanted Rand. She needed to be consumed by his passion.

She smoothed her hands down the warm supple skin of his back and over his buttocks. The muscles contracted beneath her caress. She dragged her nails back up his spine in a feather-light scrape the way she knew he liked and savored his shudder. He wouldn't react to her touch so easily if he didn't desire her.

He fisted the hem of the T-shirt and ripped it over her head. She wished she could see his face when he looked at her, but she could only sense his eyes on her when he braced himself on one straight arm above her.

His fingers curled over her panties and snatched them past her ankles. That same hand skimmed back up her legs and found her wetness with unwavering accuracy. She started at the electrifying jolt of arousal. He bent and took her nipple into his hot mouth.

His fingers and tongue swirled simultaneously and everything inside her turned liquid, molten. He wasn't gentle, but she didn't want him to be. Pleasure blossomed within her, bowing her back and pouring out of her mouth in a low moan. Tara tangled her fingers in his hair and held him to her breast as relentless waves of pleasure pounded her.

She'd missed this. Missed *him*. His touch, the hungry tugs of his mouth and the steam of his breath on her skin felt so good. Better than anything or anyone she'd tried and failed to find since he'd left her.

The snarling knot of need twisted tighter and tighter, but she wasn't ready to unravel yet, wasn't ready to have this heady hunger satiated. She wanted to savor the rush of sensations, so she fought off her climax. Fought and failed.

Against her will, release snapped through her muscles and whirled through her core, leaving the tickling, tingling sensation in her toes that only Rand could deliver.

Before she could catch her breath he lifted his head. "Where are the condoms?"

With her body still quivering, she rolled to her side and opened the drawer, saying a silent prayer of thanks that she'd been optimistic and prepared. Her fingers closed around a plastic packet. She lay back. He'd removed his briefs and his thick erection strained against her thigh for attention.

Rand took the condom from her, leaving her hands free to map his taut frame as he dealt with the protection. Her senses seemed heightened to his textures, his scent, his heat. She shaped the mounds of his pectorals, thumbed his tiny hard nipples, traced the ridged muscles of his abdomen, his appendix scar, and finally combed her fingers through the tangle of curls at the root of his arousal.

When she reached lower he swore, grabbed her wrists and pinned them to the pillow beside her head. He shifted until his rock-hard thighs spread hers. His thick shaft nudged her entrance. Eager to receive him, Tara lifted her hips and Rand slid deep in one long, slow thrust. He felt so right buried deep inside her, as if a missing part had finally been found and returned.

The darkness intensified the sounds of his harsh breathing, the feel of his hard, hot body plunging into hers again and again, and the unique aroma of his skin and their sex. Wanting to touch him, she struggled against the hands holding her captive, but Rand held fast.

His back arched. He found her mouth for one brief, voracious, breath-stealing kiss and then his mouth grazed her jaw. He nipped her earlobe, her neck. Each gentle love bite shot bolts of desire straight to her core, arousing her more than she'd ever thought possible. She nuzzled his temple, his brow.

"Rand, please," she begged and struggled to free her hands. She needed to hold him, to pleasure him the way he did her, to show him how good this was. How good *they* were. Together. This wasn't just sex. It was tenderness and sharing.

He answered by shifting both of her hands to one of his. His weight held her in place as his other hand shifted to her breast. He buffed her distended flesh with his thumb, sparking a response deep inside her, and then he bisected her breasts, her belly and found her center. He plied her with precision until her breaths came in pants and her muscles knotted. Orgasm whipped through her once more, causing her body to spasm and his name to explode from her lips.

He muffled his answering growl against her neck, sending the vibration straight down her spine. And then he stilled above her except for the bellows of his chest pressing and withdrawing from hers. The cabin fell silent except for their gasping breaths and the thunder of her pulse in her ears.

He released her hands, but before she could wrap her arms around him he slid to her side and rolled onto his back, throwing a forearm across his face.

Satisfaction engulfed her. *This* was what they used to share. *This* is what she'd missed when he said goodbye. *This* is why she couldn't sleep with Everett.

Because she still loved Rand.

She twisted to her side and laid a palm on his sweat-slick chest over the whorls of hair covering his racing heart, then she leaned in to press a kiss to his skin.

He stiffened and bolted upright, dodging her lips and dislodging her hand. He rose and headed for the bathroom. The door closed and the lock clicked, dimming her rosy glow. The shower turned on and her euphoria sank like an anchor.

That was not how she'd wanted their evening to end.

She may have taken a giant step forward in having him want to make love to her, but she'd taken two steps back. He'd literally locked her out.

Fun for one just didn't have the same kick as sharing new experiences.

Tara turned in her snorkeling gear, gathered her towel and beach bag and trudged barefoot through the sand between the cabanas selling drinks, souvenirs and beach supplies toward the barbecue area of Crescent Key, Kincaid Cruise Line's tiny private island and the cruise's first stop.

She would have enjoyed exploring the brightly colored reef and fish so much more with Rand by her side. But he'd been gone when she'd awoken this morning. After years of listening for her mother, Tara had considered herself a light sleeper, but apparently she wasn't easily roused after two off-the-Richter-scale orgasms. She'd never heard Rand get up or leave.

"Hey, are you solo?" a blond guy about Tara's age called out as he jogged up beside her. He was good-looking in a toothy, preppy kind of way.

"Yes." Not by choice.

"Me, too. I'm Joe. I was in your snorkeling group."

She hadn't noticed. "I'm Tara."

"Where are you headed next?"

"Lunch and then the Jet Ski Zone. I have a couple of hours before my lesson."

"Same here. Mind if I tag along?"

She wished Rand would look at her with the kind of interest Joe showed. But Rand might not even see the new bikini she'd bought with him in mind. And she didn't want to give Joe the wrong idea. "I don't think—"

He held up his hands and backed a step. "Not putting the moves on you or anything. Unless you're interested, that is.

It's just that this place is really geared for couples, and my travel buddies have split. We were supposed to meet for lunch, but I haven't spotted them yet."

"I'm with someone. He stayed onboard." And then an idea hit her. "Travel buddies?"

"There are six of us in three cabins. We were fraternity brothers at UVA, and we've met every summer since graduation for a cruise vacation. This is our fifth." He nodded to someone behind her. Tara turned and saw another guy about the same age headed in their direction. He wore the same kind of overlong swim trunks—board shorts, she'd heard them called.

"Is that one of your friends?"

"Yeah."

"This is my first cruise, and I have a lot to learn. Would you and your friends be willing to answer a few questions over lunch? I'll buy the first round of drinks."

"You've got yourself a deal, Tara."

Tara had lied. But the question was, when?

Rand strode through the sand, searching left and right for Tara. Had she lied when she said she loved him? Or lied when she said she didn't?

Because last night she'd made love like she meant it.

He hadn't seen it in her eyes. But he'd felt it in her touch. Tasted it in her kiss. Heard it in the way she sighed his name.

Like she had before she'd betrayed him.

Was it a betrayal?

She'd said she loved him.

But you dumped her and told her to find another man— one who could give her what she needed.

But not his father. Anybody but him. She'd known how much Everett Kincaid liked to stick it to his oldest son.

Or had she? Rand's gait faltered. He couldn't remember discussing his strained relationship with his father with her.

You're making excuses for her.

Damn. Damn. Damn. She'd gotten to him. Again.

But if she was starting to care about him, then he had to nip those feelings in the bud. Before it was too late. He couldn't afford to let Tara get close or convince herself she loved him, because he couldn't live with another woman's death or near-death on his conscience.

Cursing his weakness for Tara and his stupidity for craving her body and her company, he scanned the cabanas, beaches and tables. How hard could it be to find one curly-haired blonde on a small island with no roads and no exit other than the tender that had brought her over? Crescent Key had been named for its shape. KCL had posted different excursion sites in and around the island. If he followed the curve long enough he'd find Tara.

The hot sand seeped into his sandals and the sun toasted his bare back. He'd dressed in swim trunks—like a tourist—as camouflage, but it had been a long time since he'd been comfortable in such casual clothing. Five years, to be exact. He'd spent every day since leaving Miami trying to get Wayfarer Cruise Lines ahead of KCL.

Trying to beat Everett Kincaid at his own game.

A laugh stopped Rand in his tracks. Tara's laugh. He pivoted and followed the sound around a tiki-hut bar and found her at an umbrella-covered table surrounded by a group of six guys. Twenty-somethings. Closer to her age than Rand's thirty-five. Empty plates, beer bottles, drink cups and a couple of half-filled bowls of chips and salsa littered the picnic table.

The burn in his gut caught him off guard. Indigestion? Probably. He'd speak to the ship's chef.

Or was he jealous? Couldn't be. To be jealous he'd have to have feelings for Tara beyond the anger that festered inside

him at her manipulativeness. Feelings beyond the respect for
her work. Beyond lust for her body.

Her black bikini left her back almost completely bare.

"Tara."

She startled at the bark of her name and twisted around on
the bench seat. "Rand. Hi."

Was that a guilty flush on her cheeks? Could she be audi-
tioning potential lovers when she'd left his bed only hours ago?

He planted a hand on her shoulder and nodded to her male
harem. "Gentlemen. Rand Kincaid. Kincaid Cruise Lines. I
hope you don't mind if I steal my assistant."

It wasn't a question.

He noted Tara's widened eyes, and then one of the guys
laughed and grinned at Tara. "You work for the cruise line?
That explains all the questions."

Tara's shoulder shrugged beneath Rand's hand. He looked
down to see her nose—now sporting a fresh dusting of
freckles—wrinkle. "Sorry for the secrecy. But it really is my
first cruise, and I know very little about what's out there. I appreciate you giving me your thoughts on the comparisons
between KCL vacations and our competitors'."

She tucked a pen into the spirals of a little pink notebook. Rand recalled Tara had always carried a notebook in
her purse. She was a big fan of note taking. Had been even
back when she'd worked for his father. A breeze ruffled the
pages—pages filled with her small neat handwriting. Handwriting not formatted like addresses or phone numbers.

Working? She'd been *working?* Didn't she realize each of
these guys eyed her as if she were a tender and juicy filet
mignon and they couldn't wait to take a bite? And given the
mouthwatering cleavage he could see from his position above
her, Rand couldn't blame them.

She rose and gathered her belongings. He let his hand fall
from her shoulder.

"I guess this means you'll have to skip your first Jet Ski ride," one of the guys said and scowled at Rand. "That sucks. She wanted to learn."

Tara bit her lip, and disappointment flashed across her face. "I guess so. But I am supposed to be working. It was nice meeting you. Thanks again for your help."

"Thanks for the drinks," a blond guy replied. "Maybe we'll see you at the luau tonight. Save a dance for me."

"I'll see what I can do, Joe." Tara waved and looked questioningly at Rand.

He grasped her elbow and led her to the opposite side of the tiki hut from the devouring eyes of her fan club. "You were working?"

"Yes, and I have some really good info for you. But why did you blow your cover?"

Good question. He didn't like the answer. He *had* been jealous. Dammit. More fool him. "You've never ridden a Jet Ski?"

"No."

A smart man would head back to the ship and put some clothes on the woman. His gaze raked over her lightly tanned skin, savoring the swell of her breasts in the bikini top, the curve of her waist and the dip of her navel above a tiny skirted bottom. And then there were her legs.

The rush of blood to his groin annoyed the hell out of him. He grabbed her hand and towed her behind him. "Let's go."

"The boat's the other way."

"Ship," he corrected automatically. "But the Jet Skis are this way."

"But—"

"You want lessons. You'll get lessons. From me." And he'd be damned if she'd be dancing with the frat boy later.

Eight

The hard thighs clamped around Tara's and the firm hands grasping her ribs just below her breasts should have made her feel relaxed and comfortable. But they had the opposite effect.

She held her breath as the Jet Ski shot over the crest of a wave and splashed down again. Exhilaration made her pulse race, intensifying her other senses to the tang of salt on her lips, the warmth of the sun on her skin and the tease of wind in her hair. The vibration of the machine beneath her and the feel of the man behind her made her…well, hot in a way that the sea water spraying over her skin couldn't cool.

A horn sounded, signaling the end of their hour on the personal watercraft. Disappointment sagged through her. She wasn't ready to go in, wasn't ready to share the man or the machine with other people on the tiny island or go back to work. She could happily ride for hours longer in the aquamarine-blue water with Rand's arms and legs wrapped around her.

As if he sensed her reluctance to return Rand transferred his hands from her torso to flank hers on the handlebars. She instantly missed the heat of his palms. He throttled them down and made a wide U-turn toward shore. She couldn't believe he'd let her drive, but he'd insisted she learn.

She leaned back against him to catch her breath. Despite the life jackets separating their bodies, she couldn't be more conscious of every hard, muscular inch of him behind her and the strong arms bracketing her.

"That was fun," she shouted over the engine's rumble as she tilted her head back onto his shoulder. "And we survived without Jaws coming up to eat us."

"You're not out of the water yet," Rand growled in her ear, then sank his teeth into her neck in a love bite.

She squealed and squirmed then twisted on the wide, cushioned seat she straddled to look at Rand. The wicked grin on his tanned face made her breath hitch and her heart squeeze. *This* was the man she'd fallen in love with. The one who played as hard as he worked.

Her laughter died and her smile wobbled. "Thank you. That was great."

His smile faded and tension invaded his features. Her reflection stared back at her from his mirrored sunglasses, but she'd bet if she could see his eyes, she'd see the barriers drop back in place, as well. "You're welcome."

He guided the craft into the cove, where they would be anchored for the next group, and fell in line behind a dozen other riders.

She faced forward again and burrowed deeper into the arms surrounding her. "But you really blew your cover when you flashed your KCL ID and commandeered a ride when you weren't registered for the excursion."

He shrugged against her back. "The attendant probably

won't talk to anyone on the ship, but it doesn't matter if he does. I've seen what I needed to see."

Her breath snagged. Did that mean they'd leave the cruise early? She didn't want to fly back to Miami from Nassau tomorrow. She wasn't ready. She wanted her three nights. "Like what?"

"That's strictly need-to-know information."

She bristled. "We're a team. You said so."

"And KCL is an information sieve."

"I'm not part of the gossip mill. I never was."

An employee came forward to anchor their ride, temporarily stilling her protest. Rand climbed off and waded toward shore. Tara followed, collected her beach bag and towel and stomped after him. He led her to the closest bar and bought a couple of bottles of water using his cruise ID/charge card/room key.

Glancing longingly at an unoccupied hammock as they passed, Tara followed him toward an empty pair of lounge chairs tucked beneath a shade tree. She dumped her stuff beside the chair and sat. Maybe she could nap in a hammock later. The ship wouldn't sail until after tonight's luau. They had hours left on the island. Unless Rand had a helicopter swoop in and take them home. She knew Everett had some-times done that because she'd arranged the flights.

She accepted the bottle he offered. "Rand, how can I help you if you keep me out of the loop?"

He glanced pointedly at the guests in nearby chairs. "You can help by remembering this is a confidential investigation."

His abrupt tone made her hackles rise. She gritted her teeth and sipped her water. Trust. It all went back to trust—or the lack thereof. She hadn't earned his. Yet. But she would.

She set her water aside and dug a bottle of sunscreen out of her bag. She'd been good about slathering it on, but her fair skin could only handle so much sun and most of the excursion activities were held out in the open. The cloudless cerulean skies might be good for business, but not for her pale complexion. Rand, on the other hand, had already darkened several shades.

The urge to press herself against his warm, tanned skin gnawed at her. "I don't suppose I can talk you in to hula lessons later?"

"If you insist." No smile accompanied his words. The fun, playful guy had vanished. Rand set his water on the table between them and rose. He snatched the lotion bottle out of her hands and made a circular motion with one finger. Tara turned her back. A shiver she couldn't suppress rippled over her in anticipation of his hands on her skin.

Rand straddled the chaise behind her. His legs flanked hers as they had on the Jet Ski, but this time without touching. She regretted the scant distance.

She heard the snick of the cap, smelled the coconut-scented sunscreen and then his hands settled on her shoulders. The lotion was cool, but his hands quickly warmed the cream *and her* as he slicked it over her back, arms and shoulders.

His fingers dipped beneath the edge of her bikini bottom just above her buttocks and her breath stalled then quickened. He dragged a finger along the elastic. "You're burning here."

Her breasts tightened and her core heated. She considered leaning back against his chest so he could reach her front, but the other sun-worshippers were too close. Instead, she gave in to the temptation to stroke his hot sun-baked, bare thighs. The wiry hairs tickled her palms and his muscles turned rock-hard beneath her hands.

He caught her wrists and returned her hands to her lap, then dropped the sunscreen bottle between her legs. Disappointment slid through her.

"You can do the rest." His voice sounded huskier than usual.

She twisted to look at his face, but he rose and stalked back to his chair. He was always putting distance between them. However, the ridge in his trunks as he eased onto the lounger told her what she needed to know. Touching her hadn't left him unaffected. Good.

She was tempted to suggest they return to the ship and the privacy of their cabin to try and alleviate their mutual hunger, but she'd seen a side of Rand today that she'd begun to fear had vanished forever. She was determined to lure the fun-loving man out again.

"Want me to do your back?" Her palms tingled in antici-pation.

"No." That hard, bitten-off response carried the sting of re-jection, but she'd made too much progress in the past hour to give up so easily.

"I bet you know all the good hiding places on the island," she prompted.

He gulped his water instead of replying.

"We could find one."

She couldn't see behind his glasses, but his sudden still-ness, the flare of his nostrils and the thin white line forming around his mouth was hard to miss. "You're the one who said we have a confidence issue with KCL employees. Getting caught banging my PA in the lighthouse won't improve it."

She flinched at the crude statement, but acknowledged he had a point. Her gaze shifted to the black-and-white diamond-patterned lighthouse looming over the island. Too bad. She would have liked a private tour of the tall structure…and anything else Rand had to offer behind the thick, sturdy walls.

Forcing her eyes back to Rand she decided to aim for a less sensitive subject. "It must have been fun having an island as a playground when you were growing up. Did you and Nadia and Mitch come here often?"

"It wasn't a playground. When we came, we came to work."

"Doing what?" Other than telling her he'd worked onboard several ships, he'd never given her details.

"Mitch worked watercraft. Jet Skis, parasailing. Nadia taught snorkeling and kayaking."

She waited for him to expand. He didn't. "What did you do?"

"Food prep. Trash detail. Maintenance. Dad always gave me the hottest, dirtiest jobs. The only time I had a job with tips was when I worked as a cabin steward. He liked the idea of me cleaning toilets."

That didn't sound like the Everett she'd known. "Why would he do that?"

"He said if I wanted to run KCL I needed to have an intimate knowledge of the underbelly. He did his best to make sure I got it."

Rand's bitterness brought a lump to her throat. "I'm sorry."

His lips compressed even more. "I'm not. I understand my workforce the way few CEOs do. My father did his best to break me, but in the end he did me a favor."

Tara stared aghast. She'd known Everett could be ruthless with his competitors. But had he been as merciless with his own children? Apparently so.

How could the man Rand described be the same one who'd treated her so well? Had she been so blinded by the excitement of being transferred to the top floor that she'd seen everything through rose-colored glasses?

Maybe even her relationship with Rand.

Doubts made her stomach churn.

No. No. She had loved Rand.

Hadn't she?

Although she had to admit, she'd learned more about him

in the past ten days than she'd learned in the months they'd known each other before. Rand Kincaid was far more complex than the gorgeous, charming guy who'd swept her off her feet, shown her a good time and taught her about the pleasures of sex. But she knew now he'd barely let her scratch the surface.

Shaking her head, she lay back on her chair and pulled the brim of her hat over her face. How could she have believed herself in love with a man she'd barely known?

Because *this* Rand had depth and character and integrity that the younger man she remembered had never displayed.

And he was much more attractive.

"Must be nice to get a paid vacation less than two weeks after starting a new job."

Mitch's bitter comment pulled Tara's attention away from the papers spewing out of the printer Monday afternoon. She swiveled her desk chair and saw him entering her office with a long, confident stride very similar to his brother's.

She'd never had a problem with Mitch when she worked for KCL last time. In fact, she'd considered him the peacemaker in many of the disagreements between Rand and Everett. But ever since she'd returned he'd been cool.

"Back off, Mitch," Rand said from his open door before Tara could reply. "If you have a problem with the way my staff or I operate, then you come to me."

The brothers faced off, each with his hands clenched by his sides. Their stances and profiles were so similar. They shared the same tall frames, broad shoulders, thick dark brows, straight noses and stubborn chins. Tara had never noticed the similarities before.

"You skipped out without saying a word." Mitch's voice carried an undercurrent Tara couldn't fathom.

"Your PA knew we were going out of town, and she

knew when we'd be back. If she didn't inform you, that's your problem."

"She didn't know where you'd gone and you didn't answer your cell phone. Hell, for all I knew you'd headed back to California." He and Rand exchanged another long, silent look.

"I was out of cell range."

"A vacation violates the terms of the will."

"Then it's a good thing Tara and I weren't on vacation. We were working on KCL business," Rand said in a lowered tone. "I couldn't reveal our plans without raising a flag."

Any remnants of the man who'd shared her cabin and her bed each night of the cruise had vanished the moment they'd stepped ashore this morning.

Rand had indeed danced with her at the luau and made love to her every night of the cruise, but it was as if he didn't want to make love, yet couldn't help himself. And as he'd stated at the beginning of their agreement, he hadn't held her afterward or played happy couple. Each time he'd risen from the bed immediately after his climax, even before their breathing slowed or the sweat dried on their skin. He'd retreated to the bathroom, then returned to lie on his side of the mattress.

The contradiction between mind-melting passion and the detached man on the opposite side of the bed had been disconcerting to say the least. They'd been together. But apart. Far, far apart.

Once they'd reached her home he'd barely allowed them time to drop off their luggage and change into work clothes before heading into the office. He was all business this afternoon, from his tightly knotted navy tie to his polished cognac-colored wingtips. She wasn't sure if she should consider today's carpooling as a sign of progress or just a way for him to guarantee she'd be at her desk and ready to work when he needed something from her. Like the data she'd printed out.

"What were you working on that you couldn't do it here?" Mitch asked.

Rand glanced at Tara. "Have the switchboard pick up the calls and bring your notebook and the spreadsheets into my office."

He turned on his heel and headed for the inner sanctum, closely followed by Mitch. "Dammit, Rand, what's going on?"

Surprised, but happy to be included after he'd shut her out on the island, Tara did as Rand instructed and joined them. She needed a machete to cut through the tense silence in the room.

"Close the door," Rand ordered and Tara did. He jerked his head, indicating she sit in the visitor chair beside Mitch's. "We took a three-night trip on the *Abalone*. Tell him what you found, Tara."

"Whoa. Hold it. You voluntarily went on a cruise? You hate cruising."

Tara's shocked gaze shot from Mitch's to Rand's face. Rand hated cruising? He'd never said anything. And how could he hate traveling on a ship with as much experience as he'd had?

"Necessity." He nodded for Tara to go ahead.

Smothering the questions bouncing around her brain, she flipped open her notebook. "I interviewed about three dozen customers while onboard, but a group of six men who've taken five different destination cruises with Rendezvous over the past five years gave me the most information. They're single, but fit the target age and income demographic of the brand. They said in the past two years the quality and quantity of the food had dropped off noticeably, and the alcoholic drinks appeared to be watered down. They're seriously considering switching to another cruise line for next year's trip."

Rand extended his hand. Tara passed him the spreadsheets. One tanned finger skated down the columns and then stopped. "Two years ago Rendezvous requested and received four-point-six million for refurbishing. From what I saw onboard, none of the textiles has been replaced in ten years. The carpets, drapes and bedspreads are worn and faded. The towels are thin. Not threadbare, but close. I saw chipped dishes in the stacks every time I ate at one of the buffets."

The boat was shabbily decorated? That's what he hadn't wanted to tell her?

His hazel gaze drilled Mitch. "Where did that money go if not into the ships?"

"I have no clue without checking the ledgers."

"Tara will access those for us and print copies. I want you to go over them with a magnifying glass *at home.* I'll do the same. And we need to check every other ship in the brand, because the *Abalone* sure as hell hasn't been refurbished."

Mitch's eyes narrowed. "You think someone is skimming?"

Tara's stomach plunged. Rand suspected embezzlement. And he thought she'd tell the guilty party? Why would he think…

Because you told him you'd lied.

But he'd decided to trust her now. That's what mattered.

Rand's gaze shifted to Tara then back to his brother. "Until we see the other ships and the books I won't know for sure. But it looks that way. And you can thank Tara for pointing us in the right direction. If she hadn't targeted the repeat customers with her questions, we'd never have known where to start looking."

Pleasure and pride bloomed inside her at his praise.

Rand gave her another long, intense look. "This conversation stays in this room. Mitch, I don't even want your PA to get a whiff of it. Not with the way the KCL gossip factory works. If someone is embezzling from KCL, then we don't want to tip them off and give them time to abscond or cover their tracks."

Mitch leaned forward, bracing his elbows on the arms of the chair. "What's the plan?"

"I want every Rendezvous ship inspected for improvements as it comes to port. Since each cruise originates in Miami that's something we can handle without fanfare."

Mitch nodded.

"And with Nadia in Dallas, that means you and I will have to do the legwork because I'm not trusting this to anyone else."

Tara jotted notes and reminders to reschedule appointments set around docking times. She glanced at Rand. "You might want to spot-check the other brands, as well, to cover your investigation."

Both men's gazes focused on her. She shrugged. "My mother loved mysteries. I read a lot of them to her when she was…ill. There were always red herrings to keep from giving away the true villain."

Rand nodded. "Good point, Tara."

She basked in his approval.

"You have to love the devious way a woman's mind works," Mitch added. Tara fought a wince at the jab, and Rand scowled at him.

"Can we have a minute?" Mitch asked Rand and tilted his head toward Tara.

Rand suspected he knew where his brother's train of thought was headed, but he had to hear him out. "Sure. Tara, would you get me a list of the ships' arrival times and dates for the next quarter?"

Mitch didn't speak again until after the door closed behind Tara. "You're trusting *her?*"

After what he'd revealed to Mitch two weeks ago, Rand understood his brother's skepticism. "In this, I am."

"Man, you're screwing her again, aren't you? Are you in love with her again, too?"

The muscles in Rand's back snapped tight. "I was never in love with Tara."

"Bull. Last time Nadia and I took bets on how long you would hold out before you decided to risk the Kincaid Curse and marry the woman."

Rand rose and paced to the window. He stared out at the port, at all that open space but the sense of confinement remained. "Do I look that stupid? Loving a Kincaid is bad news. Besides our parents' lousy marriage, neither you, Nadia or I have had one good relationship between us."

"Nadia came close."

Hands on his hips, he faced his brother. "Yeah, and that turned out great. Her husband and the baby she carried were killed leaving the wedding reception. Have you talked to her?"

"No. I keep meaning to call."

"I'll call her tonight. Tell her what's going on. See if she has any input."

"Terms of the will say she can't work."

"What kind of crazy, manipulative crap is that? She has to stay unemployed and house-sit for a year?"

Mitch shrugged. "Dad wasn't crazy, Rand, despite what you think. And after his first stroke—"

Shock rippled over him. "Stroke? What stroke?"

"The one he had eleven months ago. It was mild. The doctors fixed him up with some clot-busting miracle drug, and he had almost no lingering effects. Didn't even miss a day of work."

"Why didn't you call me?"

"He ordered us not to. He wanted you to come back on your own."

"Crawl back, you mean." Even when facing death his father hadn't wanted him around. Nice to know.

Mitch shook his head. "Believe it or not, I think he respected you more for leaving than he would have if you'd stayed. He kept tabs on Wayfarer. And you."

The claustrophobic sensation intensified. "He should have kept tabs on Rendezvous."

"As CFO, that was my job."

"You don't have access to the full scope of paperwork. The CEO's office does. But we both know Dad was never a hands-on manager. We will get to the bottom of this, Mitch. If I accomplish nothing else this year, I will straighten out the mess he left behind."

"Just don't make a bigger one of your own with your PA. And for godsakes don't knock her up like Dad did that Corbin woman."

"I won't. Fifty more weeks, and then Tara and I are done."

Never mind that Tara brought him more satisfaction in bed and out than any other woman. Their relationship was about sex. Nothing more. Nothing less.

And it was temporary. He couldn't let it be anything else.

"Take a break." Rand's voice interrupted Tara's concentration.

"What?"

"That's the third time you've massaged your neck in the last ten minutes."

She lowered her hand to the kitchen table where they'd spread the Rendezvous data she'd printed out and blinked her gritty eyes. Hours of poring over columns of numbers had given her a headache, and it was getting more difficult to focus. "Sorry."

"It's tedious, mind-numbing work and we're both tired." He stood and stretched, mesmerizing Tara with his lithe, powerful body.

Arousal and renewed energy rushed through her. "I'll make coffee."

"No. It's late. We need to go to bed. This can wait until tomorrow." He turned and walked into the den.

Tara rose on surprisingly unsteady legs. Would he sleep with her tonight? Onboard the ship Rand had shared her bed because he had to. Here he had his own room. Should she invite and/or entice him? Or see what happened?

The old Tara would have waited for him to make the first move. What would the new Tara do?

"Is this your mother?" he called from the den before she could make a decision or formulate a plan.

Tara joined him. He held the picture from the mantel in his hand. "Yes."

"You have her hair."

She reached up self-consciously and touched a curl that had slipped free from her tightly pulled-back style. "No. She has mine. I had it cut and made into a wig for her."

His head snapped in her direction. He searched her hair and face through narrowed eyes. "You can do that?"

"Yes. There are several companies that make custom wigs. It's not cheap, but it was worth every penny. It made her less self-conscious about going out after she lost her hair."

"She had chemotherapy?"

Her throat clogged. She nodded. "Several courses. It was brutal."

He replaced the frame without taking his gaze from hers. "When did you find out?"

"About?"

"Her diagnosis."

"Twenty days after you left for Europe."

His jaw shifted. "And you told my father."

"I— Yes. I couldn't help it…I kind of lost it one day in the office." Embarrassment warmed her cheeks.

"The bastard," Rand spat out. He pivoted sharply and paced to stand at the window overlooking the backyard. She hadn't drawn the curtains yet and fireflies flickered in the darkness.

Rand's spine looked as straight and rigid as steel. His hands fisted and released by his side.

"What do you mean?"

He turned and she caught her breath at the suppressed fury in his eyes. "My father's forte was finding a woman's weak spot and exploiting it."

"I don't think that's what he—"

He closed the distance between them in three swift strides, caught her shoulders and gave her a gentle shake. "Open your eyes, dammit. He was a sorry, no good, conniving son of a bitch. And you are too smart to be this stupid about him."

Tara reeled back at his vehemence. She'd never seen Rand this furious or out of control. "I—I only know what I saw and how Everett treated me."

Her reply seemed to anger him further. His jaw muscles bunched and his lips disappeared into a thin line. He released her and backed away. "I have to make a call. Good night."

He pivoted and left the room. She listened to him ascend the stairs, then his door thumped shut. That answered her question about whether they'd sleep together tonight.

Her thoughts whirred crazily. Her last encounter with Rand five years ago tumbled through her head. *The joke's on dear ol' Dad. He wants you because he thinks I do.*

Was Rand right, or was his view colored by his bitterness toward Everett? Surely Everett wouldn't have used her to score one on Rand? But father and son had been extremely competitive.

On autopilot, Tara returned to the kitchen, piled the Rendezvous reports into a neat stack and slid them into a manila envelope, but making order of the papers did nothing toward organizing her thoughts. She sank into a chair and propped her forehead on her palms.

She hated that everything she'd learned since Rand's return made her question her judgment. Before Rand had come back into her life she'd known right from wrong. Her mother had died. It was Tara's fault. She'd stood by and done nothing when a potential life-saving solution had been offered.

But now...now she didn't know what to think. About her former boss. About her own intelligence.

What had Rand said in the cafeteria that day? Something about Everett never doing anything out of the goodness of his heart and always having a price tag attached. Was it true?

She replayed her last encounter with Everett, searching for clues she'd missed.

Rand will never marry you, my dear. He won't come back for you or help you through this. Let me help, Tara. Let me make everything all right. I'll hire the best oncologists money can buy. Your mother will have top-notch medical care, and I promise, together you and I will minimize her suffering as much as possible.

All I ask in return is that you move in to Kincaid Manor. I need a hostess and a partner. I'm lonely, Tara. But I won't risk all I've worked for, all I've created in building Kincaid Cruise Lines, by marrying again. We are a good team at work, and we can be on a personal level, as well.

I swear I'll stand by you throughout this ordeal. Tara, let me take care of you. Let me take care of everything.

His concern had sounded genuine, and his confession of loneliness had been touching. He'd made his proposition sound so simple and attractive. She'd been surprised but also shamelessly tempted. Not because she was attracted to Everett, but because she'd liked and respected him and believed he wouldn't hurt her already damaged heart even more.

And it wasn't as if she were a shy virgin looking for a man to replace Rand. In fact, she'd sworn off falling in love again.

Everett was only asking for sex and companionship. For her mother's sake Tara should have been able to deliver both.

While she'd debated Everett had draped an arm around her shoulders and pulled her into a fatherly embrace. She'd needed to lean on someone so badly that she hadn't pulled away. Overwhelmed and afraid, she'd wanted to let him take care of everything, and she'd finally whispered okay.

Everett had kissed her on the forehead, on the temple and then on the mouth. She'd held it together until he'd touched her, and then she'd shuddered not with passion but in revulsion. And she'd pushed him away.

Rand had left her, but even if she'd never see him again, the idea of becoming intimate with his father when she'd still loved Rand had made her want to throw up.

In a flash of insight, she'd discovered her Achilles' heel. She'd believed herself willing to do anything to save her mother. But she'd been wrong. She selfishly clung to the only thing of value she had left. Her body. And her mother had paid the price.

If Rand couldn't forgive her for turning to his father, then he'd never forgive her for standing by and letting her mother die. Rand Kincaid respected strength and he abhorred weakness. Sleeping with her proved he'd go to any lengths for the ones he loved.

And Tara had let her mother down.

Nine

Would a selfish bitch cut her hair and have it made into a wig for her mother?

It's just hair. It grows back.

But hadn't Nadia freaked when she'd come out of her coma after the accident and discovered the doctor had shaved her head for brain surgery?

Logical or not, women were possessive of their hair.

But Tara hadn't been.

Rand snapped his cell phone closed when Nadia didn't answer, and turned to stare at his closed bedroom door.

Tara Anthony confused him. The evidence didn't add up.

Would a mercenary tramp take a job far below her salary level and qualifications to stay home and nurse her ailing parent? Tara was too smart to waste her brain in a third-rate small business. From the belated update he'd had her add to her personnel file he knew she must have been bored out of her mind with her previous job.

And yet she'd stuck it out for years.

Would a gold digger stick around for Mitch's and Nadia's sakes when he, Rand admitted, had been an ass? He'd be the first to acknowledge that between his anger toward his father and Tara, his frustration over the tension with Mitch and his worry over his sister and KCL, he'd been a lousy boss. His Wayfarer PA would have been horrified by his behavior. And she would have quit. On the first day. But Tara had put up with his bad attitude.

The Tara he'd known before would have retreated when he barked. She would have left him alone when he hurled insults. But his distancing techniques had failed. This new Tara stood her ground.

Five years ago she'd been a pretty face, a good time. Today she had a new strength and insight he couldn't help but admire. Had her trials with her mother brought about the change?

Had she fooled him with an innocent act five years ago and this backbone of steel was her true character? Or was she fooling him now?

Proof Rand had seen with his own eyes labeled her a gold digger. She'd been coming out of his father's bedroom late at night and had a fresh hickey on her neck, dammit. The buttons of her shirt had been misaligned, which meant at some point they had been unbuttoned.

Why sleep with his father if not for financial gain? Yes, Tara genuinely seemed to have admired his father. *How could any woman be that naive?* But surely her feelings couldn't have run deeper for a man who'd been twice her age? Not unless she'd been looking for a father figure since her father was nowhere to be found.

Her current bargain of shacking up, plus an exorbitant

salary, reinforced the money angle. Could she be hedging her bets? Trying to hook a rich husband but filling her coffers in case she failed to snag him?

Did she really intend to use her salary to pay off her mother's medical bills? Judging by the worn furnishing of the house and her old car and clothing, she certainly wasn't wasting her money on luxuries.

He shoved a hand through his hair in frustration and paced in front of the window. He didn't have the answers and not knowing frustrated the hell out of him.

Just like the Rendezvous books, something in this scenario didn't add up. Something was off-kilter and he couldn't put his finger on what.

Had he made a mistake? Had he misjudged Tara?

If so, when? Then? Or now?

Since he'd moved in Tara had worked as long and hard as he did—longer actually, because she'd done his laundry and cooked for him, despite his demands that she not. In fact, she'd done everything she could to make him comfortable both here and at the office, and he'd given nothing in return except rude remarks, a hard time and mechanical sex.

Even mechanical sex is good with Tara.

He shut down that thought, ignored the involuntary leap of his pulse and stared at the blackened panes.

She mowed her own grass, for godsakes, and had refused his offers to hire a landscaping crew and a housekeeper. If she were looking for Easy Street, she should have jumped on both offers.

Was it all a ruse to lure him into her snare?

As Rand had told Tara downstairs his father specialized in exploiting weaknesses. Could that be what happened? Had his father swooped in on Tara and taken advantage when she didn't stand a chance of resisting? It was beginning to look that way.

A naive girl, as Rand had believed Tara to be five years ago, wouldn't stand a chance against a master manipulator like Everett Kincaid.

Maybe Tara wasn't a greedy fortune hunter.

Maybe she'd been as much of a victim of his father's machinations as the rest of them.

Yeah, and maybe she's taking you for a ride.

Rand's gut told him to trust the earnestness and the pain he saw in those big, blue eyes. And his gut wasn't often wrong. But the consequences of misjudging were too high. For him. For KCL. For Tara.

It all boiled down to whether or not he could forgive her for sleeping with the enemy.

And tonight, that answer was no.

One of them had misjudged Everett. The question was, who?

And the only way Tara could find out was to get to know Rand on a deeper level than the superficial one he'd offered her five years ago. Even if that meant tracking Rand down and battering in the doors he kept closing in her face.

Rand surfaced in the shallow end of the Olympic-size pool located in the health club on the first floor of KCL. His chest rose and fell rapidly from his exertions. Water plastered his dark hair to his skull and streamed down his body like a lover's caress. With his eyes still closed he shook his head, slinging water across her legs.

"Why do you hate cruising?"

His eyes flew open then narrowed. He swiped a hand down his face. She'd been in a chair poolside for the past twenty minutes, watching the sole occupant of the pool slice through the water at a punishing pace, but he must not have noticed. "You're early."

"I thought you'd come in to get started on the Rendezvous requisition lists before any of the other employees arrived. I came in to pull them up for you. When I couldn't find you upstairs, the security guard told me you were down here."

"I needed a workout." Rand planted his hands on the tile edge and heaved himself out of the water in a glistening display of rippling muscle.

Tara's mouth dried and other parts of her moistened even more than the balmy humidity of the indoor pool area mandated. Her gaze fell to the wet, black swim trunks clinging to and clearly outlining his masculinity. A sliver of untanned skin at his waistband made her yearn to reach out and trace the pale line. With her tongue. Once upon a time she'd been welcome to do exactly that.

She blinked and lifted her gaze back to his face. After only three nights of sleeping with him by her side she'd missed him last night. Missed the sound of his breathing and his warm presence beside her beneath the covers. But it was more than just a means to ending the loneliness that had consumed her since she'd lost her mother. She'd missed Rand.

"Why do you hate cruising?" she repeated.

He reached for the towel in the chair beside hers and dragged it over his skin. "Does it matter?"

"It does to me."

He hesitated and shifted his gaze to the mural of leaping dolphins on the far wall. "When I worked onboard I always had the least desirable accommodations. The ones my father refused to inflict on a crew member. Usually a small interior cabin in the noisiest part of the ship. No porthole. I rarely saw the horizon unless I made a point to walk the decks between shifts."

"That sounds like solitary confinement."

"An apt description."

Pieces of the Rand Kincaid puzzle clicked together and she

didn't like the picture forming. Had she known Everett Kincaid at all? She added another mental tick in the "no" column.

"During our cruise you only returned to the cabin to sleep or change clothes. And you always kept the drapes open."

His hard gaze returned to hers. "Is there a point to your chatter?"

"I thought you were avoiding being alone with me."

"I was."

She winced. "You rearranged the furniture at the office and at home so your desks face the window, and you won't let me close the blinds in your office even when the afternoon sun glares on your computer screen."

Now she knew why and her heart squeezed. The plants she'd added to block the late afternoon rays wouldn't cure this problem.

Rand remained silent. His muscles corded with tension. "We have an early meeting to prepare for."

She ignored his attempt to derail the conversation. "You're claustrophobic. Because of Everett. Because of what he did to you."

"I am not claustrophobic. I ride in elevators every day."

This man who hated weakness had one of his own—one he refused to acknowledge even to himself.

Even though his body language discouraged sympathy, she couldn't help but offer it. If anybody ever needed to be held, Rand did. Regardless of his still damp body, she moved forward and wrapped her arms around him.

He stiffened. "Tara—"

She tilted back her head so she could see his face and he could see hers. He needed to know she didn't think less of him because he wasn't perfect. "I don't know what Everett hoped to gain by treating you that way. But it was wrong."

He dropped the towel in the chair and caught her shoulders. But instead of pushing her away he stared into her eyes for long, silent seconds. His eyes probed hers as if he were trying to see inside her. And then he bent and covered her mouth with his. The kiss wasn't hard or seductive or even hungry like the ones they'd shared before. This one was gentle, tender and so soft that tears pricked behind her eyelids.

He slowly lifted his head, his lips clinging to hers for precious seconds.

A door opened behind her and a pair of KCL employees entered, breaking whatever connection she and Rand had just made. He lowered his hands and stepped away. "I'll be upstairs in ten minutes. Order breakfast. We'll eat together."

Feeling as if the blinders had been ripped from her eyes, Tara headed upstairs. Rand had good reason to hate his father.

Tara was beginning to hate him, too. Because Everett Kincaid had a cruel side she'd never suspected.

"How are you?" Rand said into his cell phone as he leaned back in his office chair late Tuesday afternoon.

"So you do remember how to use a phone. Nice to know. I'm fine. How are you, big brother?"

The sarcasm in Nadia's voice hit its target. She hadn't forgiven him for five years of neglect. "Nadia, I couldn't call."

"I know you couldn't call Mitch because he might mention it to Dad, but you could have called me, Rand."

"I knew Mitch would look out for you."

"I didn't want to talk to Mitch. I wanted to talk to you. You could have at least let me know you were okay."

Despite their six-year age difference Rand and Nadia had been close before he left Miami. She'd never gone to their father with her problems. She'd come to Rand. His refusal to return her calls after he'd abandoned KCL had closed that door. But he'd known breaking that connection was the only way to protect her from their father's scheming machinations to get back at his oldest son.

He massaged the stiff back of his neck. "I'm worried about you. You've been down there a month. Alone."

"I'm fine, and despite a surplus of my own boring company and my shrink's too-frequent calls, I'm not suicidal. *Yet.*"

Alarm blasted through him. He bolted upright. "I'm coming to Dallas."

"I'm kidding. Don't screw up this stupid will clause because of me. I'm fine. Really. I'm not Mom. I'm not going to kill myself."

A chill raced over him. There were some things they had never discussed. Their mother's death was one of them. His gaze shot to the open door between his office and Tara's. He rose, crossed the room and closed it. "What are you talking about?"

Silence greeted him. His mother's and Serita's faces flashed like strobe lights in his mind.

"Nadia, talk to me."

"You didn't know?" she asked in a quiet, tentative tone.

A sick feeling churned in his stomach. "Know what?"

"That mom was…unstable."

"You were only eight when Mom died. You don't know what you're talking about."

"Dad told me. After Lucas…"

The lying son of a bitch. Rand fought to keep his fury out of his voice. "After Lucas and your baby died."

"Yes. I'm sorry, Rand. I thought you knew. Everybody said you were the closest to Mom. After…my accident Dad sent me to a shrink. He was afraid Mom's illness ran in the family and that I wouldn't be able to deal with losing Lucas and our baby. At Dad's insistence I've been seeing a shrink monthly ever since. I guess that's one thing I won't miss now that Dad's gone. I can finally get out of therapy."

Her laugh sounded hollow.

The pain in his jaw made Rand unclench his teeth. "Our mother's only problem was him. The lying, cheating jerk she married."

More silence. "No, Rand, Mom was manic depressive with a touch of paranoia thrown in. I know because after the accident the doctors tested me every which way but Sunday to make sure I wasn't the same. When I realized they were giving me a mental health exam I clammed up and refused to answer any more questions until they leveled with me. Dad allowed them to tell me about Mom."

Rand closed his eyes and pinched the bridge of his nose. Denial steamed through every pore. "That sounds like some of Dad's usual manipulative bull."

"It's not. According to the doctor Mom was fine when she stayed on her meds, but sometimes she'd become convinced Dad was trying to control her by drugging her and she'd go off them."

If that were true, then it explained some of his mother's erratic behavior. Most of the time she'd be a happy and normal mom, other times she'd be a clingy and morose woman who tearfully railed about her husband's sins to her oldest son. Had her conviction that her husband was cheating on her been paranoia or fact? His father had certainly tomcatted around since her death.

"I'm sorry if I tainted your memories of Mom."

"You didn't. I knew—" He swallowed. After years of secrecy, it was time to come clean. "I knew hitting the tree wasn't an accident. I didn't realize anyone else knew."

"I suspect that's because to Dad appearances were everything. Like that stupid portrait hanging in the living room at Kincaid Manor, we always had to look and act like the perfect family. And Rand, from the conversations I've overheard over the years, Dad knew. I think he might have paid someone to make sure the police reports said 'accident,' but I'm not sure. You know how he was. He always refused to discuss anything with me."

"Bribing someone and refusing to admit it sounds like him." Rand shoved a hand through his hair and paced. "I should have stopped her that night, Nadia. I knew Mom was drunk and upset over Dad's latest bimbo. I should have taken the keys to all the cars to bed with me. Not just her keys."

Nadia's gasp carried down the line as clearly as if she'd been in the room beside him. "How can you blame yourself? Rand, you were *fourteen*. And she was determined. If you'd stopped her that night then there would have been another night."

"No. I could have stopped her," he repeated.

"God, I hate doing this," she muttered almost inaudibly. "Do you know how many times she tried to kill herself?"

Rand's heart slammed hard against his ribs. His fingernails dug into his palms. "She tried more than once?"

"Yes. Do you remember the vacations she'd go on alone?"

Everything seemed to slow to a crawl, even the KCL ship he could see departing port via Government Cut moved in slow motion.

Memories flashed through his mind. *Your father thinks I need time away. I think he just wants me out of the house so he can entertain his girlfriend.*

He wiped a hand down his face. "Yes."

"Apparently, those were inpatient treatments."

"You don't know that. You were too young. It started before you were out of diapers."

"I know what my doctors told me."

A fist closed in his gut. He should have known. "I should have done something."

"Rand, listen to yourself. You were the kid. She was the adult. She was supposed to be responsible for you. Not the other way around. And since Mom apparently wasn't capable, we had Mrs. Duncan."

Mrs. Duncan, the housekeeper/guard dog who, as far as he knew, still ruled Kincaid Manor. "If I'd told Dad—"

"God, Rand Kincaid, you are just like him."

Not what he wanted to hear.

"You want to control the world. Well, you can't."

Rand bristled at the words she practically shouted at him, but before he could object, Nadia continued, "Look, I know you probably won't believe this, but Dad loved Mom, and he did everything within his power to keep her from hurting herself. I don't think he cheated on her."

No, Rand didn't believe it. Not after hearing his mother's tearful rants. He'd borne the guilt over his mother's death for so long he couldn't shirk it that easily, and he didn't want to trust this new information. "I repeat, you can't know that. You were only a kid."

"Maybe I don't have the memories of Mom that you have, but I know firsthand that Dad was almost obsessive about making sure we were mentally tougher than she was. I dealt with his smothering watchdog approach after my accident. I know that was ten years after Mom's death, but still, the protective trait was there."

His father had an obsession over their mental health? Was that why he'd tested Rand at every turn? Or had Everett Kincaid pushed his oldest son because the Kincaid patriarch was a twisted tyrant? Rand would never know. The only one with the answers had been cremated and had his ashes scattered in the Gulf Stream.

"I want to talk to Mom's doctors. Give me their names."

"You can't. They're dead. But mine has Mom's medical records and I've read them. That's how I know about every conversation Dad had with her doctor and every hospitalization. They're all documented. I can get a copy for you if you insist."

The story was too far from what he'd believed for years for him to swallow it so easily. "Her doctor shared confidential records?"

"I convinced my shrink that I needed to be informed and educated so I'd know what behaviors to look for if I started slipping."

Fear raced up his spine like an electric current, and the back of his neck prickled. "Is that likely? You slipping?"

"No, Rand, I'm okay. Really, truly okay. We all are. I just needed to understand why sometimes my mother loved me and sometimes she couldn't seem to stand the sight of me."

A crushing sensation settled on his chest. Why hadn't they had this discussion years ago? "I know what you mean."

"And while I'm rocking your world, I guess I should tell you Dad admitted 'Uncle Robert' was really a pediatric shrink, and he came around to make sure we were okay after Mom died and that we hadn't inherited her illness. As you said, I was only eight, so I barely remember him, but you probably do."

Rand recalled the gray-haired man who'd come to dinner often over a period of months and asked a lot of questions. Rand had believed it was because their father's friend was genuinely interested in the Kincaid siblings' comings and goings—more so than their own father, who'd usually remained mute and steely-eyed during the long meals.

"The one Dad said was a friend from college." And now that Rand thought about it, the guy was pretty old to be one of their father's classmates.

"Yes, he's the one. Now can we switch to a less morose subject? Like how is my replacement working out?"

Rand had more questions. And he would ask them. Another

time. After he'd digested this series of bombshells. Nadia's revelations had tilted his whole world on its axis and jeopardized everything he thought he knew.

"Julie's good, Nadia. But we have another problem." His new leather chair creaked as he sat at his desk and pulled the data Tara had gathered forward.

He outlined the investigation and his suspicions. For several moments the discussion focused on areas Nadia suggested he examine more closely. She spoke so fast Rand hoped he could decipher his hastily written notes later.

And then she paused. "I can hear by the way you talk about Tara that you're falling for her again."

His pen stabbed a hole in the legal pad. "You're mistaken."

He didn't do love and the idea of letting Tara love him scared the hell out of him.

"Please don't hurt her again, Rand. She's deserves better than the way you treated her last time."

He bit his tongue on telling Nadia exactly what her friend had done.

"You know I can't risk anything permanent with her. Not with my track record."

"You mean Serita?"

"Yes."

"Call her, Rand. Get Serita's side of the story. I think you'll be surprised at what she has to say about that night."

He balked. "I don't want to reopen old wounds."

"Trust me on this. You need to call her."

This morning Tara had tried to get into his head with her nonsense about claustrophobia, and now Nadia wanted to probe his psyche. Not his idea of fun.

He ended his discussion with Nadia and sat staring at the phone number she'd given him as if it were a coiled snake. His mind grappled with the possibility that his mother's death might not have been his fault and that his father might not have been the most unfaithful ass east of the Mississippi.

If he'd been wrong about those—and he wasn't convinced he was—then what else might he be wrong about?

It had taken Rand twenty-four hours to admit Nadia was right. Until he resolved his past it would govern his future.

He reached for the phone and punched in Serita's number with an unsteady hand. Dread weighted his gut like ballast.

"Serita's zoo."

The familiar cheerful voice hit him like a sucker punch, knocking the words from his tongue.

"Hello? Anyone there?"

He could hear children in the background. He cleared his throat. "Serita, it's Rand Kincaid."

"Oh, my gosh. Rand. How are you? Did you know the reunion committee—of which I'm in charge—has been searching high and low for you?"

"No. I've been in California until recently. Serita, I…need to know how you are."

"How long do you have?" She laughed. "Let's see. I'm married. Billy and I have three little hellions, hence the Serita's zoo greeting, and we live outside Kissimmee." She paused. "But that's not what you're asking. Is it?"

"I need to know about that night."

"It wasn't your fault, Rand. Nadia always said— Oops."

His sister's suggestion to call suddenly made sense. "You've kept in touch with Nadia?"

"She's the class agent for her year. I am for ours. And class representatives talk. Okay, here's the abbreviated version. I faked a suicide attempt because I was ticked off with my parents. All of my friends were going away to college and my overprotective parents wouldn't let me. And being a drama queen, I reacted by doing the one thing guaranteed to make my folks crack down even tighter. Dumb, huh? And of course, I am paying now because my oldest daughter is just like me."

Faked. Stunned, he leaned back in his chair.

"Rand? You did the right thing in breaking up with me. We were too young to get serious, and I was way too immature. Besides, if I'd married you, I never would have met Billy. And he's the one I was meant to be with. He's my Prince Charming."

He heard satisfaction and happiness in Serita's voice, and a load of guilt lifted from his shoulders. "I'm glad you're okay."

"Oh, buggers. Little Billy's splashing in the potty again. Gotta go. Keep in touch. And I expect to see you at the next reunion. No excuses."

The dial tone sounded.

Rand stared at the receiver and slowly cradled it. The one-two punch of his telephone conversations with Serita and Nadia left him reeling but also feeling lighter than he had in decades. He hadn't been the cause of Serita's self-destructive behavior, and according to Nadia, the blame for his mother's death couldn't be laid at his door, either.

That left Tara. If she'd been a victim of his father's machinations, could he blame her? Look how the SOB had made Rand jump through hoops, and Rand was no naive pushover.

Forgiveness no longer seemed too much to ask.

It was time to take a chance on a relationship with Tara. He wasn't thinking marriage or even long-term. His head wasn't ready to take that leap yet, but for the first time in his life, the possibility of a relationship measured in weeks or months instead of hours or days, was there. And Tara had proven through standing by her mother and by not taking any crap from Rand that she was strong enough to handle whatever the future held.

He shut down his computer and locked away the notes on

his exchange with Nadia. Anticipation seeped into his blood-stream. Anticipation of an evening with Tara.

Showing Tara a good time had always resulted in a good time for him. She'd been the one who'd helped him defuse the tension when the battles with his father had become too much. And she'd done it again in the past two weeks. With the Jet Ski ride, the stupid hula lessons and even letting him mow her grass.

He shot to his feet, crossed the room and yanked open his door. "Grab your stuff and let's go."

Tara startled and glanced at her watch. "It's barely five."

"We're leaving. Lock up."

"Let me pack the confidential files to work on tonight."

"No. No work tonight."

Her confusion over his deviation from the norm of working almost around the clock showed in her puckered brow and the teeth pinching her bottom lip. "Did you decide to turn every-thing over to a forensic accountant like we discussed?"

"Not yet."

She shut down her computer, locked away the files and re-trieved her purse.

"Where are we going?" she asked as she rose.

"Home. To bed."

Her eyes went wide and her purse slipped from her fingers and bounced off her shoe. Rand bent, snatched it up and handed it to her. Heat pooled in his groin. He planned to make love to Tara tonight without holding back. It was time. Hell, past time. "Ready?"

"Yes."

Hope flared in her big, blue eyes, and for the first time, Rand didn't feel an urgent need to crush it with caustic words.

Ten

Had she imagined the look in Rand's eyes?

By the time she and Rand had made the twenty-five-minute drive to her house in his Porsche convertible Tara had convinced herself she'd made a mistake. The roar of the wind and the sounds of traffic during the ride had made conversation difficult. She had no barometer to measure his strange mood.

Her legs trembled as she traversed the sidewalk leading to her front door. She lifted a trembling hand to smooth her windblown hair. He caught it, pulled her behind the bougainvillea screening her front porch from the street and backed her against the porch post. His hands cupped her face, holding her while he studied her as if memorizing her features. His thumbs skated over her cheekbones.

Anticipation tempered with desire and something softer, warmer and sweeter than anything she'd ever seen from Rand before simmered in his eyes.

No. She hadn't made a mistake.

Her heart skipped erratically. Hope filled her chest and bathed her with a heat far stronger than the summer sun's evening glow. She dampened her lips and his eyes tracked the movement.

He bent his head and touched his lips to hers in a kiss so gentle, so fleeting, she sighed.

"Let's take this inside."

The gravelly timbre of his voice whipped her hormones into a frenzy. Whatever had come over him, she liked it, and she wasn't about to argue.

Rand unlocked the door, ushered her over the threshold and then reengaged the lock with a quick flick of his wrist. Without a word he laced his fingers through hers and led her upstairs to her bedroom. Her pulse raced, and it had nothing to do with his swift ascent of the stairs.

In her room he shrugged out of his suit coat and tossed it on a chair, and then he took her purse and sent it in the same direction.

"Rand?" She kept waiting for one of his barbs—the ones she'd finally figured out he used to push her away whenever she got too close.

He lifted his hands and removed the pins from her hair, dropping them on the bedside table. When he finished, he finger-combed her curls. "I like it short."

"Thank you?"

"It's sexy. Makes it easy for me to do this." He buried his face in her neck. His five o'clock shadow pricked deliciously beneath her ear, contrasting with the soft touch of his lips, the erotic scrape of his teeth along her tendon and the slick heat of his tongue.

She shivered and hooked her fingers over his belt for balance. He found her zipper and lowered it. Cool air dusted her spine. And then he straightened and pulled her fuchsia sheath dress over her head, leaving her in the matching fuchsia bikini-panty-and-bra set she'd bought specifically with him in mind. The flare of his nostrils and his expanding pupils told her he liked the semi-sheer lace. Her dress landed somewhere near the chair, but his eyes never left her and hers never left his.

His hands clasped her hips and his thumbs caressed the sensitive skin beneath her navel. Goose bumps lifted her skin.

She covered his hands. "Rand, what's going on?"

He looked deep into her eyes. "We're going to do something that's overdue. We're going to make love in your bed. All night long."

Her breath stalled in her chest and the blood drained from her head. She felt wobbly and weak. He'd said *make love* instead of *have sex* or, even worse, *do her.*

Did that mean what she thought it meant? She was afraid to let herself hope. She'd hoped for miracles before, with Rand, with her mother, and she'd been the loser both times.

Tara's bold, new courage deserted her. She couldn't ask for clarification. Because his reply could be the answer to her prayers. Or the end of her dreams. But she could show him what she wanted him to mean.

She reached up, curled her fingers around his neck and brought his lips to hers. He took her mouth in a hot, hungry kiss, raking his hands up and down her bare back, and she poured every ounce of feeling she had into her response.

A flick of his fingers loosened her bra. When he broke the kiss and pulled back slightly to remove it she shoved her hands between them and tackled the buttons of his shirt. Concentrating on the task wasn't easy with his hands shaping her breasts and buffing the sensitive tips. Once she had his shirt open and his shirttails free, she burrowed herself against his skin, absorbing his heat and relishing the tickle of his chest hair on her tightly beaded nipples.

Rand released her long enough to deal with his cuffs and then he removed his shirt. His gaze devoured her, her breasts, her panties, her legs, her face. She'd waited years to see that look of pure, unrestrained passion aimed at her from those hazel eyes.

She loosened his leather belt buckle and his pants and eagerly shoved the fabric down his thighs. His hands mimicked her actions, skimming her panties over her hips. The lace pooled at her ankles. She kicked her sandals and panties out of the way, and stood naked before him in the bright sunlight streaming through the windows. She suddenly felt self-conscious and crossed her arms. Each time they'd made love the room had either been dimly lit or dark.

"Don't. You look beautiful. You were gorgeous before, but now…" He pursed his lips and let out a silent whistle. "Stunning."

She basked in the words, but even more so in the approval and hunger in his eyes. This was what she'd wanted from him five years ago when he'd swept her off her feet and what she wanted even more now. And with every passing second she wanted to believe in miracles.

He sat on the mattress to remove his shoes. Tara quickly knelt in front of him and took over the task. Her fingers trembled, but as soon as the wingtips, socks and pants were history she rose, eager to hold him, to be as close to him as she possibly could be.

Instead of standing, Rand grasped her waist and pulled her between his legs to lave her breast with his tongue. She shifted impatiently as he circled, grazed, sucked and caressed, but he wouldn't be rushed. One big hand splayed across her bottom, alternately kneading her flesh and caressing her crevice. The other combed through her curls, found her slickness and stroked, igniting the desire smoldering low in her belly.

She tangled her fingers in his hair, then shaped his brow, cheekbones, stubbled jaw and strong neck while he worked magic with his hands and mouth. The tremors started deep within her. She didn't want to peak alone this time. She wanted to share that moment with Rand, for she truly would be making love.

She dug her nails into his broad shoulders, wiggled free of his embrace and opened the nightstand drawer. After locating a condom she knelt again to roll it over his hard, smooth flesh. His hands dug into the edge of the mattress. His chest and his penis expanded. His scent—part arousal, part Rand—filled her senses.

And then he bolted to his feet, pulling her with him and into his arms. The heat of his body scalded her and his caressing hands lit trails of fire over her skin. His kisses devoured her with sweeps and swirls of his tongue and left her with a head-spinning shortage of oxygen. She clung to him, stroked him, his shoulders, his back, his buttocks, his upper thighs— every supple, taut inch within reach.

She couldn't get enough of him and the feeling seemed mutual. There was a desperate edge to his hunger that she didn't understand, but her body responded in kind. And when his thigh thrust between hers, she welcomed the pressure, curled her fingers into his waist and her moan poured into his mouth.

He lifted his head, ripped back the covers and swept her into his arms to lay her in the center of the mattress. Tara eagerly opened her arms. He settled in the cradle of her legs and paused for precious heart-pounding moments on the brink of joining them.

His gaze locked with hers and he slowly filled her until she was so full emotion nearly burst from her. She ached to blurt out her feelings, to release the floodgates on the words of love waiting on the tip of her tongue. But the last time she'd done that she'd driven him away. And she couldn't risk that now.

Biting her tongue, she let her touch do the talking, silently whispering the words with each caress, every kiss, each tilt of her hips as she took him deeper into her core and into her soul. Into her heart.

She immersed herself in the heat of his skin, the power of his body and the taste of him. With each passing second she loved him more. And she started to believe in a future with Rand.

Each powerful thrust increased the tension inside her and every withdrawal left her gasping and aching for his return. She wrapped her arms and legs around him, holding him close and trying to get closer still.

And then release showered over her, tightening and releasing her muscles, tingling her toes and her flesh and stealing her breath. Rand stiffened in her arms and threw back his head. His face contorted with pleasure as he joined her.

Several pounding heartbeats later his eyes opened and found hers again. He lowered slowly, reverently, to kiss her brow, her nose, her mouth. Sliding to her side, he pulled her into his arms and held her tightly, in a way he hadn't before. He nuzzled her temple, stroked her back. Every gentle caress made her feel cherished and loved in a way she never had. Her breathing eventually returned to normal and the moisture on her skin evaporated. She braced herself for his departure, but he didn't pull away.

This was exactly how she wanted her relationship with Rand to be. The passion. The spontaneity. The connection. They'd had the first two last time around, and this time she wanted them all. This union had shown her what could be and it was so much more satisfying than the sex they'd had on the cruise.

Rand leaned back, separating their upper bodies only far enough to meet her gaze. She was certain her love shone in her eyes. There was no possible way to contain it and she didn't even try. Happiness bubbled within her and she couldn't stop a broad smile.

He cupped her cheek. "I know why you did it. And I don't blame you."

Confused, Tara blinked. "Did what?"

Revulsion flickered across Rand's face so quickly she almost missed it. But she hadn't. And that glimpse sent a frisson over her. Her smile faded and her muscles tensed.

"Slept with my father."

Her heart stuttered and her heated body chilled. "I told you I never slept with Everett."

"It's okay, Tara. I forgive you."

Tara scrambled out of his arms and out of the bed. "You can't forgive me for something I didn't do."

He sat up. The sheet fell away to reveal every inch of him. "You don't have to be ashamed. We can put it behind us and forget it ever happened. It's okay. I understand."

"No. You don't. You don't have a clue what happened that night."

"You don't have to lie."

Her dream of a future with Rand gave a last gasp and died. She closed her eyes and let her head fall back as she realized her mistake. She hadn't earned his trust now or then. Both times she'd rushed the relationship, counting on the physical bond leading his heart into an emotional commitment. She'd given him everything—her body and her heart—before he was ready to accept them.

He didn't trust her. And he probably never would. Nothing she could say would convince him she hadn't betrayed him.

Feeling exposed, she ducked into the bathroom, snatched her robe off the hook on the back of the door and shoved her arms into the sleeves. Her hands fumbled so badly it took three tries to tie the slippery satiny sash.

Rand stood by the bed when she returned. Naked. Powerful.

"Without trust, Rand, you have nothing. And that's what we have. Nothing." She'd gambled and she'd lost. A sob built in her chest. She fought to contain it, gulping it back, but it only rose again. She forced calming air through her nose and into her lungs, but it hurt. Everything hurt. It hurt to think, to stand here and look at the beautiful bronzed body of the man she'd wanted to share her life, her home and her heart with.

And it nearly crushed her to admit defeat. But this was a battle she couldn't win.

"Get out. Out of my room. Out of my house."

Rand stiffened and a muscle in his jaw ticked. "What about KCL and the terms of my father's will?"

The question carved another chunk out of her heart. His first concern wasn't about her or them, but about the business.

"That you'd even have to ask only proves my point. You don't know me at all. I'm going to take a shower. When I get out, I want you to be gone."

A gurgle of noise jolted Rand awake.

Bleary-eyed, he tracked the sound to the coffeepot. Set on timer. By Tara.

Tara.

Why in the hell couldn't she admit she'd made a mistake and been led astray by his father? Rand could live with mistakes, but not with lies. Dishonesty was a deal breaker.

Focusing on his anger and trying to ignore the strange ache in his chest and the hammers pounding in his head, he swung his legs off the leather sofa, planted his feet on the rug Tara had chosen and scrubbed his hands up his face and through his hair.

If what Nadia had said was true, he wasn't to blame for their mother's death. But he'd sure as hell cost them their inheritance by trying to force a confession out of Tara.

Could he live with that failure?

No.

But his sleep-deprived brain refused to cough up an acceptable alternative. Once he had a pot of coffee onboard to counteract the two hours of sleep he'd had, he was going to come up with a strategy to fix the situation.

If he could.

Not *if*, dammit. He would.

The only way to hold on to KCL, Kincaid Manor and his father's hefty investment portfolio was to convince Tara to stay on as his PA. Not an easy feat since he'd called her a liar in bed.

Could he work with a liar?

For Nadia's and Mitch's sakes he'd find a way. But personally, he and Tara were finished. Unless she came clean.

She cared about him. He'd seen it in her eyes, felt it in her touch, tasted it on her lips. They made a good team. In the office and out of it. Why ruin a successful relationship when he was offering forgiveness? What did she have to gain by lying?

The questions nagged him because Tara's actions weren't logical. But he didn't have the answers.

He stood and tried to stretch the kinks from his spine. Outside the wall of windows the sun rose over the bay and the Atlantic beyond Government Cut, the channel used by KCL ships. He could have gone to a hotel or to Kincaid Manor last night, but he'd needed time alone to think and something to occupy his mind. What better than the Rendezvous puzzle?

He'd stayed up most of the night, poring over the documents Tara had compiled and reading the notes she'd jotted in the margins. After comparing her findings with Nadia's suggestions he'd spotted a clear trail that should eventually lead to who'd been embezzling from KCL.

He wanted to run his theory by Tara. Without her to share his hypothesis the discovery lacked the punch he usually felt before closing a deal. She'd become an important part of his team.

But Tara wasn't here.

Needing a cold shower to clear his head and wash the grit from his eyes, he made his way to the en suite bathroom. Once again, Tara's touch reminded him of what he'd lost because of her stubborn refusal to confess. She'd stocked his private bath with everything he could possibly need, from toothpaste to razors to clean towels and even an unopened bottle of his cologne. He wouldn't even need to fetch his shaving kit from his car.

Extracting the clean suit, shirt and tie she'd insisted he keep in the closet Rand stripped, showered, shaved and dressed. He paused in front of the mirror, tightened the knot of his tie and squared his shoulders.

He'd made Tara an offer she couldn't refuse once before. He'd do it again. And if her demands were unreasonable he'd sic the legal department on her. She'd signed an employment contract and he'd hold her to it.

He stepped out of the bathroom, picked up the mug that Tara had selected. A sound in the outer office stilled his hand before he could pour the brew. He glanced at his watch. Eight. No one should be here this early. And since Tara had kept the confidential documents locked in her desk, whoever was out there was breaching security.

Luckily, he'd had a duplicate key to her desk and the documents were in his office now. He stealthily crossed to the open door and jerked to a halt.

Tara. She bent over her desk, depositing her purse in the drawer.

A rush of something warm and soothing and energizing and…*good* that he couldn't identify suffused him. He tamped down the unacceptable flood of emotions. She'd probably come to clean out her desk. The signed letter of recommendation he'd written would make leaving easier—until he involved the legal team.

An ugly thought snuck up on him. Had she asked for that letter because she planned to leave him in the lurch all along to get even for him dumping her years ago?

Vindictiveness didn't seem to be Tara's style.

"I didn't expect to see you today."

She startled and turned a pale face in his direction. Despite heavier than usual makeup, bruised circles shadowed the area beneath her eyes. "I gave you my word I'd see this year through. But we're boss/employee from now on and that's it."

His thoughts exactly. So why did he experience a sudden and irritating jab of dissatisfaction? "You're not quitting?"

"Not unless you fire me."

He'd take the reprieve any way he could get it. It meant one less battle he had to win. "I need you to finish the year."

The urge to sink his fingers into the soft golden curls she hadn't bothered to scrape back this morning and kiss her in gratitude wasn't welcome. He'd sworn off getting personal with her this time around. Her lips were off-limits.

"Your car was in the parking garage. How did you get here?"

"I took a taxi." She sat in her chair and booted up her computer as if last night hadn't happened. But her cool tone, her steel-beam-straight spine and her tense features implied anger. What did she have to be angry about? He was the one who'd been wronged.

Did she feel ashamed and guilty for turning to his father? He understood guilt. He'd lived with it for two decades. But he'd offered to wipe the slate clean. All she had to do was admit—

His thoughts stopped dead in the water like a ship running aground. He backtracked over last night's words. She'd said that if he had to ask her intentions toward KCL, he didn't know her. She'd promised him a year. And here she was.

Would a woman who kept her promises lie?

Once again, the facts didn't add up. But if Tara hadn't lied… No, she had. He'd seen the proof. "Tara—"

"The Rendezvous file isn't in my drawer," she interrupted. "Do you have it?"

"Yes. But—"

"I wasn't finished with my calculations. May I have it back?"

"Not yet." Determined to make sense of her illogical behavior, he planted a hand on each side of her U-shaped workstation, blocking her in. "Tara—"

"What in the hell is going on?" Mitch demanded from the doorway. "Security says you slept in your office last night."

Frustrated by the interruption, Rand peeled his gaze from the surprise in Tara's eyes to his brother. "What of it?"

"Did you?"

He straightened. "Yes."

Mitch looked ready to explode. But anger couldn't cover the worry in his brother's eyes as he looked from Rand to Tara and back. "Could I speak to you privately?"

Rand stared at Tara, who swiveled her chair, turned her back on him and picked up the phone. She was back onboard as his PA, and he wasn't going to screw that up. She wanted business only? Fine. He couldn't agree more.

Liar.

He'd miss her, he admitted reluctantly. He'd miss trying to follow the sharp and sometimes convoluted way her mind worked. He'd miss playing with her. Having sex with her.

He'd never before had an intimate encounter as satisfying as he'd had last night. Ever. His blood heated and headed south of his belt. All he had to do was recall the end of the evening to derail his hormones.

"Hold my calls." He led Mitch into the office and shut the door. "I talked to Nadia yesterday."

"What's going on?"

"She claims she's fine."

"That's not what I meant and you know it. With you and Tara."

His molars clamped together. "None of your business."

"It's my business if you're going to screw up. I warned you not to let your personal relationship cause problems. Did you?"

"She's here, isn't she?"

"You slept in your office and your car is loaded with suitcases. Either she threw you out or you moved out."

Not something he'd confirm or deny.

"Do you want to move in to the manor?"

"You have a full house. I'll find a place. Can we talk KCL business? Or is this a social club?" Even before Mitch's shoulders snapped back and his chin thrust forward, Rand regretted his harsh words. He rubbed his throbbing temple, then filled his coffee mug and a second one for Mitch, hoping caffeine would nix his headache.

He pointed at the papers he'd left spread across the coffee table/ottoman when he'd finally given up and closed his eyes last night. Correction. This morning. "Have a seat and take a look. Nadia gave me a list of places to check records. I put those calculations together with Tara's, and we have a warm trail to turn over to a forensic accountant."

He strode to the windows and stared out at the water while he sipped his coffee. Behind him he heard the shuffle of papers and the clicking of calculator keys as Mitch went over the entries. If only the situation with Tara was as easy to comprehend as the columns of fabricated numbers. But no such luck. Rand had his work cut out for him. Keeping Tara happy. Keeping her here. Defining new boundaries. Controlling his hormones.

Good thing he enjoyed a challenge.

"These are Tara's notes?" Mitch asked ten minutes later.

Rand turned. "Yes."

"She's good. Too smart to be a PA."

Pride filled Rand. Pride he didn't have a right to feel. He couldn't take any credit for Tara's intelligence. "I noticed."

"Too smart to fall for Dad's crap."

"Maybe." He scrubbed his free hand across his nape. Yet another clue that didn't fit. As he'd read through Tara's notes last night he kept asking himself one question. How had his father lured her into the trap? Whatever the bait, it had to have been good. Good enough to lie for. What could Tara be hiding?

"Any chance you misinterpreted what you saw that night?"

A question he'd asked himself a hundred times. "Seeing is believing."

"Unless it's an illusion."

An option he hadn't considered. The hairs on the back of his neck prickled. "You think Dad set me up?"

"It's a possibility, given your history. There was nothing he liked better than testing your limits. Problem is, until the day you walked, you never broke. He'd see that as a challenge."

A test or a betrayal? The only ones who knew the truth were a dead man and the woman in the outer office.

Eleven

She'd rather be alone than with a man who didn't trust her, Tara told herself as she shut down her computer Friday evening.

But being right didn't mean she didn't hurt.

If not for the teamwork she and Rand had shared before their argument, she'd never give a second thought to the change in atmosphere of recent weeks. To anyone else Rand probably seemed like the perfect boss. Cool, detached and impersonal. He'd spoken to her only when necessary. But she'd felt him watching her on too many occasions to count. Watching and waiting. For what, she didn't know.

Not having humiliated herself by blurting out her feelings for Rand when they'd made love that night three *l-o-n-g* weeks ago was cold comfort when she crawled into bed alone each night.

Work. Home. Paying bills. She was right back where she'd started from before Rand Kincaid reentered her life. The only difference was that now she had a job that challenged her and money to pay off her debts to go with her freshly broken heart.

She picked up her pen and made an *X* over the date. Keeping a promise had never been more difficult, and each day she marked off on the calendar was a bittersweet one. Another day with the man she loved meant one day less until she'd leave him.

The light went out on her phone as Rand ended his call. "Tara, get in here."

She caught her breath at the sound of his voice and her pulse did that stupid little tripping thing. Again. Would she ever stop loving him?

She rose, smoothed her hands down her hips, picked up her notepad and blanked her expression.

Mitch stood as she entered Rand's office. "Quite the sleuth, aren't you?"

She kept her gaze on him rather than look at Rand because each time she looked into those hazel eyes her heart splintered a new crack. "I'm sorry?"

"The money trail. You enjoyed tracking it."

She shrugged. "If you let me sniff around long enough, I usually find what I'm looking for. It comes from reading all those mysteries to my mother."

Mitch walked toward the door, but paused with his hand on the frame. "It's a shame everyone isn't that bright."

The door closed behind him, leaving her no choice but to face Rand, who stood behind his desk. In general, she avoided looking directly at him by never looking higher than the knot of his tie. Not easy considering they worked nine to ten hours together most days. But she didn't want him reading her heart-break on her face.

She braced herself and lifted her gaze. He needed a haircut. The dark chocolate-colored strands hung over his white collar.

And he could use a shave, too. Five o'clock shadow darkened his jaw and upper lip. The combination of shaggy hair and stubbled jaw made him look too sexy for words. He'd discarded his suit coat, loosened his tie and rolled up his shirtsleeves.

Silence stretched between them until she thought her nerves would snap. She fought the urge to fidget under his steady stare. "What did he mean by *everyone isn't that bright?*"

"That you've put together all the clues. Using your data the forensic accountant found the embezzlement trail leading not only to Patricia Pottsmith, but also implicating Donald Green, her boss and the president of Rendezvous. The arrest warrants are being served downstairs under Mitch's supervision as we speak."

The news only mildly surprised her. Patricia had always looked out for number one.

Rand came around his desk, crossed to the sofa and indicated she join him.

Tara sat at the far end and fiddled with the pen tucked in the spiral wire of her notebook. If she sat any closer, she'd have to smell him. Too late. The air-conditioning kicked on, carrying a whiff of his cologne to tease her senses. Need rose within her. Need she had every intention of ignoring for the next ten and a half months.

Maybe by the end of the year he'd trust her….

Stop it. You are not going to get your hopes up and dashed again.

"What tipped you off?" Rand asked, making her look at him. She saw triumph in his eyes, but also a glint of something she couldn't identify.

"Patricia said something at the cocktail party about sleeping with her boss. Originally, I thought she meant Everett, but then I tapped in to the KCL gossip grapevine and found out she and Donald often travel together unrelated to KCL business."

"Good job."

His praise hit her like a sunbeam, showering her with warmth. "It's what you paid me to do."

"No, Tara. You went beyond the call of duty on this one. And when we've finished with our year as boss and PA, Mitch and I want you to stay on at KCL."

She bit her lip and hesitated. "Are you staying?"

"Yes."

She wouldn't be able to bear seeing him in the halls or cafeteria. "I don't think—"

"We're creating an assistant director of shared services position for you. You'd get to work with Nadia and track expenditures within each of the brands."

A job and opportunity she'd jump at under any other circumstances.

"It's a promotion," he added when she remained silent.

"Thank you for your confidence in my abilities, but I'll have to pass."

Disappointment flickered across his face.

She wrapped both hands around her notepad and prepared to stand. "Is that all?"

"No." He shifted closer on the sofa, took the notebook from her and tossed it on the ottoman/coffee table. His hands enfolded hers, making her breath hitch and her heart stutter. "I want you to tell me what happened that night."

"Which night?" She knew exactly which one he meant. Her stomach churned.

"The night you *didn't* sleep with my father."

Her lungs refused to function. She finally managed to wheeze in a breath despite the sarcophaguslike constriction of her rib cage. "You believe me?"

"Yes. And I'm the one Mitch is claiming isn't too bright. All the clues have been right in front of me. And I couldn't put them together. You were with my father. But you didn't sleep with him. I get that now. There's not a greedy or selfish bone in your body. The Tara Anthony I know does the right thing, not the easy thing. Like taking a dead-end job so she can make her mother's last months easier and keeping a house because her mother asked her to even though a developer would pay you far in excess of its value to sell.

"Why were you there, Tara? What did my father hold over you to force you into a position where he could take advantage of you?"

If she told him he'd probably despise her for letting her mother die. But she'd already lost him. What did it matter?

"I didn't sleep with Everett that night, Rand. But I wish I had."

"What?" He sat back, his hands fisting by his sides. She could see him fighting to stay calm. But his shock or disgust or whatever you called it was only to be expected.

"Your father offered me a way to possibly save my mother's life. He said he'd take care of her and get her the best oncologist care money could buy if I'd move into Kincaid Manor and become his partner in every way."

He shot to his feet, fury radiating from every clenched muscle in his body. "He used your dying mother to bribe you to become his *mistress?* Damnation, he's sunk to a new low."

She shook her head. But the doubts nagged like a splinter under her skin. "He was lonely. He needed a hostess. And he wanted to help me."

"Tara, he was trying to screw *me* by screwing *you.*"

She flinched. Crudely put. But was it true? She didn't know what to believe anymore. She'd heard so much conflicting information about Everett. And much of it pointed to Everett not being the nice guy she'd believed. How could she have read him so wrong? Look at the deplorable way he'd treated his own son.

She decided she might as well tell Rand the whole pitiful tale so he'd understand why she couldn't accept the plum job he'd offered. "I accepted his proposition, but in the end I couldn't follow through. Because I loved you. I had some crazy, romantic notion that one day you'd come back for me. Dumb. Huh?"

Humiliation burned her cheeks.

She'd waited for Rand like her mother had waited for her father. Tara wondered if that made her loyal or just stupid.

Rand dragged in a slow breath. "You loved me. You weren't lying that night I left you. The first time."

"No. But I lied and said I didn't to try to win you back because I knew you'd refuse my terms if you knew I'd never gotten over you. It was never just about sex for me, Rand. I wanted a chance to make us work. My mother's last words were 'Live your life without regrets.' And I had two. Not fighting for us. And not doing everything I possibly could to help her."

She looked at her hands. "If I'd slept with Everett, I could have bought my mother more time or possibly even saved her life. But I was selfish and I was a coward. It was just sex and I should have been able to do it. That kind of cowardice isn't something you could possibly understand since you were willing to do anything for the ones you loved. Even sleep with me."

He sighed, and it was such a deep, heartfelt sound she had to look at him. "You mean I prostituted myself and you didn't."

"No! You were strong where I was weak. I respect your strength and your sacrifice."

He sat beside her again, closer this time so that his thigh and shoulder brushed hers. "You weren't the coward, Tara. I was. I let you go twice because I was afraid of what could happen if I loved you and let you down.

"My mother committed suicide. I always believed it was because my father was a faithless SOB. And I blamed myself for not finding a way to stop her. I've always been told I was just like my father, a chip off the old block. And when my high school girlfriend ate a bottle of pills after I broke up with her, it reinforced that point. I was a selfish bastard. But I've since learned that my mother's death probably wasn't my father's fault, and it wasn't mine. Serita's faked suicide attempt wasn't, either. But I didn't know that then."

Horrified, she shook her head. "Rand. I would never—"

He covered her mouth with his palm. The warmth of his skin stilled her lips. His other hand cupped her shoulder, holding her in place.

"Let me finish before we're interrupted. I only have about ten minutes before Mitch gets back, and I don't want to share this—*you*—with him.

"I thought I was doing the right thing five years ago by walking away from what we had. I thought I was protecting you. What I didn't factor into the equation was you. You're strong and smart. Too smart to hurt yourself. And you have too much integrity to sleep your way onto Easy Street."

He transferred the hand covering her mouth to her shoulder. "I came back from Europe early to ask my father why he cheated on my mother. I needed to know why he couldn't be faithful. Because after three weeks of trying to forget you, I couldn't. I didn't want to repeat his mistakes by hurting you. I was in love with you, Tara, but I was afraid of what Mitch and I have always called the Kincaid Curse. We Kincaids have a hard time keeping the ones we love."

Surprise rendered her speechless. He'd loved her?

"I've fallen in love with you again. And don't want to lose you."

The emotion and the sincerity in his unwavering gaze made her eyes sting and her throat burn. "You have?"

"Yes. Back then I loved your naivete, your generous spirit, your trusting nature. I loved that you made me forget the stress of the job and showed me how to have fun. Now I love all those things and more. I love your inner strength, your ability to sniff out a crime and your loyalty to my father, Nadia, Mitch and even me despite the fact that I've been a blind idiot and an ass a good part of the time.

"It was because I loved you then that seeing you with my father was such a kick in the teeth. All I could see was that after saying you loved me, you'd turned to the one man I refused to share with. I wasn't rational that night. I was hurt. And I reacted by striking back instead of listening.

"But striking back cost me my family. It cost me KCL. It cost me you. These weeks without you have been hell."

"I've been here every day."

He shook his head. "Not the same. You're physically here and you're giving one hundred percent to your job. But you're not mine. I miss us. I miss you. The apartment I'm living in isn't the only thing that's empty. I am. And I would do anything—*anything*—to get another chance at winning your heart."

Tears welled in her eyes. She blinked them back. But she couldn't crush the hope welling in her chest. "You don't hate me for failing my mother?"

His fingers tightened on her shoulders. "Tara, your mother waited a lifetime for the man she loved to return. What would she have said if you'd told her about my father's offer?"

She swallowed and looked away. "She would have been horrified."

"You had a slim chance of prolonging her life. But would she have wanted to live with the burden of knowing what price you'd paid?"

Her tears spilled over, burning trails down her cheeks, and her chin quivered as she compressed her lips to hold back a sob. She shook her head. "No. She would have hated that."

He swept her tears away with his thumbs and tilted her face until she looked him in the eye. "You didn't let her down, Tara, and you weren't a coward. You held out for what you and she believed in and you continued her legacy of being true to your heart. It would serve me right if I've killed your love and you dumped me. I wouldn't blame you if you walked out. On me and your job. I can survive without KCL. I did it for five years. But I don't want to go another day without waking up beside you."

He dropped to his knee in front of the sofa. "Marry me, Tara. Let me be that man for you, the one you love for eternity. Tell me how to make that happen and I'll do it. Whatever it takes."

Joy bubbled over in a laugh. She cradled his face in her palms and leaned forward to brush a gentle kiss over his lips. "You just did. Yes, Rand, I'll marry you."

She hurled herself into his arms. Rand rose, carrying her with him and lifting her off her feet until they stood hip to hip and heart to heart. He kissed her softly, reverently, and then lifted his head.

Tara smiled up at him. "I am just like my mother. I love you, Rand Kincaid. I always have. And I don't ever intend to stop."

"And I'll be right here beside you, loving you back."

Epilogue

Ten months later

Rand accepted Everett Kincaid's letter from the attorney. He wasn't looking forward to hearing from the dead.

"If you have any questions, please call," Richards said, then left the office.

Rand joined Tara on the leather sofa in his office. She reached for his hand and gave him an encouraging squeeze before passing him the letter opener.

"Do you want to be alone to read this?" Tara asked.

"No. You're part of this. I want you here."

Tara snuggled closer, wrapping her arms around his waist and resting her cheek on his shoulder as he sliced open the envelope. If she noticed his hands were less than steady as he unfolded the sheets written in his father's handwriting she didn't mention it.

He angled the letter so she could read along with him.

Dear Son,

If you're reading this, then you've fulfilled the terms of my will, and you're still at KCL with Tara by your side. And I've gone to wherever it is manipulative old men go when time runs out.

The competition between us drove us apart, but it also made you stronger. I tested you at every turn. I had my reasons. Good ones. You'll have to take my word on that. And you passed every test.

Tara passed her test, too. Five years ago she was in a tight spot and needed money. I offered to be her protector if she'd betray her feelings for you. She refused. Can't say the same for the other women I thought might eventually become my daughter-in-law. I tested them. They failed.

I'm sorry that you had to witness that night and Tara's test. I realize it made you hate me more than you already did. Worse, it drove you and Tara apart. That was never my intention.

For what it's worth, I never cheated on your mother. Wasn't even tempted. I worshipped the ground Mary Elizabeth walked on. But until you feel that kind of love you won't know what I mean. If my plan worked the way I intended, you've found it with Tara by now. She's the right one, son, and the only one worthy of you.

I've watched you since you left my shadow, Rand. You are a man who can stand on his own merits, one who didn't climb the ladder of success due to nepotism. You've earned the right to be CEO of Kincaid Cruise Lines the hard way, and I have no doubt you'll be a better one than I ever was.

I've never said it to your face, and now it's too late, but I'll tell you anyhow.

I love you, son. You've made me proud.

Your father,

Everett Kincaid

He'd waited his entire life to hear those words.

A wad of emotion rose in Rand's throat and nearly choked him. Tara's arms tightened around him. He tilted his head to rest his cheek on her crown and closed his eyes while he struggled to gather his composure.

The letter answered so many questions.

He didn't have to explain about his mother's illness. Tara knew the whole story because it was something she'd needed to know before taking a chance on him. The doctor swore the chances of their children inheriting his mother's illness were slim and Tara had been willing to risk the gamble.

But Tara didn't know about the past women his father had lured away.

He straightened and found empathy and understanding in her damp blue eyes. "He used to steal my girlfriends and then tell me about it in graphic detail. I thought he was just a greedy, sadistic, dirty old man."

"I think you saw what Everett wanted you to see."

"Maybe. But he was wrong. I never wanted to marry any of those other women. Never even considered it. Until you. You're the only one who made me willing to risk the Kincaid Curse."

She smiled. "It makes me feel better to know Everett wasn't really interested in getting me into bed. I can even respect him for looking out for your interests. But I especially like that he plotted to get us back together."

"I owe him for that." Rand kissed her brow. Sharing Tara's home and waking beside her every morning for the past ten months had been a jolt. A pleasant one. And it was a luxury he would never take for granted. "Now that our year's up why don't we take a belated honeymoon? Maybe an extended Hawaiian cruise? Or Polynesia?"

"You hate cruising."

"What better way to get over cabin claustrophobia than by

having a very good reason to stay locked away? You and a bed." He flashed her a naughty grin.

Her face softened. She covered his hand. The sunlight streaming through the office windows flashed on the wedding and engagement rings he'd slipped on her finger six months ago during a private ceremony in the garden she and her mother had nurtured together.

She curled her fingers over his and carried his hand to her stomach. He caressed her, letting her warmth seep through his skin and into his veins. Desire flared within him. Hot. Intense. Predictable. But always new and exciting. The woman got to him without even trying, and it wouldn't be the first time the leather sofa had been used for something besides sitting.

"Maybe we'd better wait on that cruise for a year or two. I'm already a little queasy."

Confused, he frowned. And then the happiness glowing in her eyes hit him like a runaway barge. "You're pregnant?"

Tara beamed, blushed and nodded. "Apparently that night we, um…worked late…" She patted the leather cushion.

The night they'd been too impatient to look for a condom.

Contentment like nothing he'd ever experienced expanded inside him. Rand yanked Tara into his arms and kissed her, but he was grinning so hard it wasn't much of a kiss.

Thanks to his father, he and Tara had a second chance. And Rand wasn't going to let the old man down.

A chuckle rumbled up from his chest. "I wonder what Dad would think about his grandchild being conceived in his office?"

Tara wrinkled her nose. "Knowing Everett, I'm sure he'd find a way to take credit for it."

* * * * *

BOUND BY
THE KINCAID BABY

BY
EMILIE ROSE

To friends found when we're not looking.
Sometimes they are the ones who show us
a new and better perspective.

Prologue

"Consider it done," Mitch Kincaid said Sunday afternoon to the trio gathered around the Kincaid Manor dining-room table for the reading of his father's will.

"Don't make it sound easy. Nothing involving a woman ever is," his older brother, Rand, warned.

"Hey!" their younger sister, Nadia, protested.

Richards, the attorney, looked over his half-glasses at Mitch. "The child is your half brother and stands to inherit one quarter of your father's estate. When billions of dollars are involved, unforeseen complications often arise."

"Let me get this straight. I'm supposed to bring my father's illegitimate son home to Kincaid Manor and keep him here for one year," Mitch summarized the absurd scenario Richards had read moments ago. It didn't sound any better now than it had then.

"That is correct. And if you fail to complete your task, you will also fail to inherit your share of Everett's estate." Richards paused to scan the three legitimate Kincaid offspring. "You all will. And everything Everett possessed will be sold to Kincaid Cruise Line's chief rival for one dollar."

Billions in assets and investments down the toilet. Fifty ships. Five more on order. Eight branded cruise lines under the Kincaid umbrella. Sixty thousand employees. All resting on Mitch's shoulders.

He tried to shrug off the crushing weight. Kincaid Cruise Lines wasn't just his job; it was his life, his wife, his mistress, his child. He wasn't like his brother, who, if not for their father's unexpected death three days ago, wouldn't be in Miami now. Rand had walked away from the family and the business five years ago without looking back.

Mitch wouldn't let KCL go without a fight. That meant not only did he have to accomplish his assigned task, but also he had to make damned sure each of his siblings held up their end of the inheritance obligations, too. Or lose everything.

Not gonna happen. Not on my watch.

He made a conscious effort to relax the hands he'd fisted. "What happens to the kid when the year is up?"

"That depends on who you want controlling his fortune until he reaches twenty-one. You or his aunt," Richards replied.

"Not the aunt," Mitch replied without hesitation and turned to his brother and sister. They hadn't been privy to the latest complication of their father's life or the cleanup detail Mitch had screwed up. No doubt that was why their father had assigned him babysitting duty. Punishment.

"The boy's mother is dead and her twin sister is the kid's guardian. I'm betting Carly Corbin is identical to her greedy, conniving twin in more than looks. She's young and single. She'll want to dump the kid. If she doesn't, I'll convince her."

"How?" Rand asked.

"Money. I've never met a woman who didn't have a price." His comment elicited another indignant squawk from Nadia.

"Dad instructed me to pay the boy's mother a hundred grand to have an abortion—an abortion she obviously never had and managed to conceal from us or we wouldn't be having this conversation."

Mitch's first mistake had been to trust the woman when she'd accepted the money. He should have ensured she'd done what she'd been paid to do whether or not he'd approved of his father's plan.

Rand's eyes narrowed. "You're sure the little bastard is Dad's?"

Mitch nodded. "A DNA test confirmed it."

A familiar hard knot returned to Mitch's chest. Their father had received the test results just days before the child's mother had been killed in a hit-and-run accident while crossing the street. The driver and car responsible hadn't been found.

He hoped like hell his father hadn't had a part in the woman's death. But Everett Kincaid had never liked playing by any rules other than his own. No one knew that better than Mitch—his father's right-hand man.

Nadia nervously tapped her nails on the table, anxious no doubt to hear her inheritance requirement. "Ignoring your incredibly sexist remarks and assuming Ms. Corbin hands over—what is our brother's name?" She glanced at her copy of the will. "Rhett. Oh, I get it. Ever-*Rhett*. After Dad. Cute. What do you know about taking care of a one-year-old?"

Mitch knew more than Nadia thought. But he wasn't going there. Ever again. "I don't need to know anything. I'll hire a nanny. The manor's large enough I'll never have to see the brat."

He aligned his pen beside the thick pile of pages constituting the will. "I'll have him installed in the nursery by the end of the month. Before year's end, I'll have guardianship and the aunt will be history. Bank on it."

One

A pricey pewter-colored SUV blocked Carly's driveway Monday evening.

She maneuvered the stroller around the big bumper and glanced at her house. The setting sun's slanted rays revealed an equally expensive-looking man on her porch swing. If he was the dishwasher repairman she'd called this morning, then she seriously needed to consider changing occupations because appliance repair paid better than physical therapy.

He rose as she turned up the walk, unfolding a tall and broad-shouldered frame beneath a black suit and pale yellow shirt and knotted black patterned tie. Short dark hair swept back from his forehead, and as she drew nearer she noticed the intense green eyes set beneath thick eyebrows in a gorgeous face. The kind of face that could launch a thousand sexual fantasies.

Despite the oppressive June heat and Miami humidity, he looked fresh from the boardroom while she dripped with sweat. And he had the successful and affluent thing going for him which meant he was probably one of Marlene's men.

Sadness slammed Carly like a rogue wave and sucked at her footsteps, tugging her into a riptide of grief. Maybe he didn't know Marlene was…

Carly swallowed the lump rising in her throat.

Gone. Her twin was *gone*. Forever. And all Carly had left of Marlene was her sister's precious baby boy.

She blinked at the sting of tears. When her vision cleared, she registered that this guy was young. Early thirties. Her sister had preferred wealthy men, specifically wealthy *older* men. Like Everett Kincaid. Rhett's daddy.

As if her nephew knew Carly was thinking about the father he'd never met and now never would meet, Rhett let loose a string of one-year-old babble.

God, she loved him. He was so darned adorable she wanted to snatch him up and hug him until he squealed. Hug him like she'd never hugged her own daughter. She tamped down that disturbing thought.

Rhett would get his cuddle, but first she had to deal with her visitor. "Can I help you?"

"Carly Corbin?" His voice was deep, polished, clipped. He descended the porch stairs to join her on the sidewalk and his eyes raked over her, making her conscious of her faded, skimpy running shorts, sweat-dampened T-shirt and stringy ponytail.

She had to tip her head back to look into his face. "Who's asking?"

"I'm Mitch Kincaid."

Anger flashed through Carly. So this was the jerk who'd done everything he could to break up her sister and Everett and who'd later tried to bully Marlene into having an abortion. It was because of his pestering that Marlene had given up her luxury apartment and moved in with Carly.

She'd heard about Everett's older children from Marlene.

Fear expanded in her chest, crowding out the anger. God help her if the Kincaids ever found out about Marlene's plot to snare Everett. Carly was terrified they would use it to take Rhett from her.

But they won't find out. You burned Marlene's journal. Nobody but you knows and you're not telling.

She dampened her suddenly dry lips. "And?"

"I'm here to meet…my brother. Is that him?" His narrowed gaze swept Rhett from his shock of baby-fine dark hair to his drool-covered grinning face to his chubby knees and double-knotted sneakers.

"Half brother," she corrected. "And, yes. This is Rhett."

Mitch's surprise-widened eyes found hers. "He looks like a Kincaid."

"Did you think Marlene lied?"

"DNA proved she didn't." His bitter tone indicated displeasure over that circumstance. "May I come in?"

Carly truly believed in close-knit family ties and wanted those for Rhett, but something was off here. Rhett's handsome half brother hadn't squatted down to the child's level or even spoken to him directly. That made her uneasy.

"Maybe another time. I need to feed Rhett, give him his bath and get him ready for bed."

"It's about Rhett's inheritance."

She bit her lip. Marlene hadn't had life insurance. At twenty-eight, she hadn't believed she needed it. Neither of them had. Carly made a decent salary, but the burial costs, child care and car and house payments consumed most of her income. She didn't know how she'd sock money away for Rhett's college education. "Everett provided for him?"

Kincaid's sexy full lips flattened and his eyes hardened. "Conditionally."

"Up. Up." Rhett held up his arms and squirmed to get out of the stroller.

Carly unbuckled him and lifted his warm, wiggly little body against hers. She held him tight and savored his sweet baby smell. "What do you mean conditionally?"

"Perhaps we could discuss my father's will while you feed the boy."

The boy. Kincaid hadn't even made eye contact with *the boy.*

Carly wanted Rhett to have everything a growing child needed, and she'd like for him to get to know his half siblings—in case something ever happened to her. Marlene's death had been a shocking and sudden reminder that bad and unexpected things did happen. That meant she had to deal with Rhett's handsome half brother sooner or later. Might as well get it over with.

"Okay. But I'm warning you now that you need to shuck your designer suit jacket."

"*I'm* not going to feed him."

She ought to make him. Just for fun. She fought a smile and lost. "If you're in the same room, you need to be dressed for feeding time. It gets messy."

The intense green gaze locked on her face for several seconds, and his eyes met and held hers. Something deep inside Carly tingled. She squashed the fizzy feeling, pivoted quickly and jogged up the stairs. Her hand wasn't quite steady as she unlocked the front door, then gestured for him to follow her inside.

He'd removed his coat while she wasn't looking, and even though she'd told him to, now she wished he hadn't. Those wide shoulders hadn't been an illusion created by an excellent tailor. She'd bet he had washboard abs under that shirt and long, corded muscles beneath his knife-edged creased trousers. She worked with enough athletes to recognize and admire peak physical conditioning when she saw it.

She led the way through the house, leaving her unwanted guest to shut the door and follow. Or not. In the kitchen she washed Rhett's hands, strapped him into his high chair and poured a sprinkling of Cheerios on his tray to keep him occupied while she prepared his dinner.

She retrieved a sippy cup of milk and a couple of bottles of water from the fridge. Politeness demanded she offer her "guest" a drink and she did so ungraciously by plunking a bottle down on the counter in silent offering to the man who took up far too much space in her kitchen. She twisted the cap off her own. After chugging half the icy liquid, she pulled out a cutting board and started Rhett's dinner.

"So talk." She kept a wary eye on Kincaid.

He transferred the unopened water bottle from one long-fingered hand to the other and back again like a metronome. "Rhett will inherit one-quarter share of my—our—father's estate."

The knife slipped from her grip and hit the stainless sink with a loud clank. Everett Kincaid had been a billionaire. Anyone who read the newspaper knew that. Kincaid Cruise Lines was a huge firm that for years had been voted one of the top five places in the country to work.

"You're kidding me."

"No." That bitten out word carried hidden nuances Carly couldn't begin to decipher.

Maybe Everett wasn't the lecherous miser Carly thought him to be if he'd made arrangements for his son. She retrieved the knife, rinsed it and then focused on cutting bite-size pieces of bananas, grapes and cheese without severing a digit. "Go on."

"The condition is that Rhett must reside in Kincaid Manor for one full year to claim his share."

It took a second for that to sink in. And when it did, her heart slammed against her chest and her nerves snarled.

Feeling as if she'd swallowed a bucket of wet sand, she swung around to face Mitch Kincaid. "You want to take him from me."

"I'll make it worth your while."

She blinked and shook her head. "I don't understand."

"I'll pay you one hundred thousand dollars for your trouble. The same amount my father paid your sister to have an abortion."

No. Carly sucked a quick breath. Marlene had done a few questionable things over the years, but Carly couldn't believe her sister would stoop so low as to accept money for an abortion and then not have one. Besides, Marlene had been thrilled about her pregnancy and overjoyed at Rhett's birth. She would never have considered ending it.

But then Carly remembered Marlene's plan to coerce Everett into marriage and she wasn't as certain Mitch was lying as she'd like to be. That notebook had revealed an unattractive side of her sister that Carly hadn't known existed.

"Marlene didn't have that kind of money."

"I have proof she did. She lived with you for the last fifteen months of her life. You had to have seen evidence of her windfall." The last word dripped sarcasm. "You probably even benefited from it."

Indignant, she snapped erect. "I did not. And I don't know about any money."

Rhett pounded on his tray, jerking Carly back to the present. She numbly carried him his food.

Mitch Kincaid had to be lying. If Marlene had taken the money, then what had she done with it? She certainly hadn't spent it. Her living expenses after she quit her job as an air hostess for a corporate jet service had been negligible because, as Mitch pointed out, Marlene had moved in with Carly. Afterward the formerly sociable Corbin sister had rarely left the house until after Rhett's birth. She'd claimed it was because she was heartbroken over Everett's betrayal and his refusal to acknowledge his child.

Could Marlene have taken the money and used it for

hospital bills? Carly made a mental note to ask the attorney how one went about tracing things like that.

"I don't believe you, and I'm not loaning this child to you."

"I'm not asking to borrow him. I'm offering to take over as his guardian. You'll be free to go about your life unencumbered."

Déjà vu. Her heart clenched in horror and a chill enveloped her. The words sounded eerily similar to those she'd heard twelve years ago. She fought the urge to pull Rhett from his chair and hold him close.

"I love Rhett. I don't consider him an encumbrance. And my sister wanted *me* to raise him."

"As a struggling single parent?"

"If necessary."

"C'mon, Carly, you're young, single and attractive. Why would you want to be saddled with someone else's brat?"

Her brain snagged on *attractive,* but repudiated *brat.* Then she recalled how scraggly she looked after a five-mile run. Clearly Kincaid was willing to say whatever it took to get what he wanted.

"I was there when Rhett was born, when he cut his first tooth, said his first word and took his first step. God willing, I'll be there for every other milestone. I'm not giving him up."

"I can offer the boy more than you can." His supercilious gaze encompassed her outdated kitchen.

"My house may not be up to Kincaid standards, but it's safe and childproofed and full of love. I have a huge fenced backyard." She hated that she sounded defensive. She had nothing to prove to this jerk.

"What does a physical therapist make these days? Sixty, seventy grand a year?"

He knew what she did and how much she made. The knowledge sent a prickle of apprehension over her. How did he know? "None of your busin—"

"That's nothing compared to the roughly one point two-five billion Rhett will inherit if he comes with me."

"Billion?" she squeaked.

"Not in cash. Most of the assets aren't liquid," he clarified. "Either he moves in with me or he gets nothing."

Light-headed and growing queasier by the second, Carly sank into a chair. How could she deprive her nephew of the inheritance he so rightly deserved, one that would set him up so that he'd never want for anything?

But how could she let him go?

She couldn't. Carly had promised Marlene that if anything happened to her, she'd raise Rhett and love him—love him the way she'd never been allowed to love her own daughter.

Mitch Kincaid wasn't offering love. Other than that first searching glance, he'd barely looked at Rhett and had yet to touch him.

She took a deep breath and tried to think logically. Marlene had yearned for Everett to acknowledge his son, and now, better late than never, he had. Maybe there was a way to make this work. "I need to speak to my attorney. And I'll need a copy of the will."

Kincaid's mouth tightened with impatience. "We have a limited amount of time to implement my father's terms, Ms. Corbin. What will it take? Five hundred thousand for your trouble?"

At first she thought he was joking, then realized from the hard glint in his eyes and the harsh angle of his jaw that he was serious. Carly gaped at him. He honestly wanted to buy her nephew. Worse, he thought she'd sell Rhett. The idea infuriated her.

No wonder Marlene had called Everett's son a dirty, conniving rat bastard.

"You're out of your mind. You can't buy and sell people."

"A million?" He ignored her comment and extracted a

checkbook and pen from the jacket draped over his arm as if writing a million-dollar check was no big deal.

She rose on shaky legs. "Rhett isn't for sale, Mr. Kincaid. You need to leave."

Rhett chose that moment to cackle with glee and squish bananas through his fingers. And then the little urchin clutched fistfuls of his hair, moussing the silky strands with the banana mush. "Unless you'd like to help with cleanup."

Kincaid backed away as if a sewage spill threatened his polished shoes. He reached into his coat pocket again and this time withdrew a business card that he laid on the counter next to his unopened water. "I'll have a copy of the will couriered over immediately. Talk to your lawyer tomorrow and call me."

He turned on his heel. Brisk footsteps retreated, then the front door opened and closed.

Carly looked at her adorable nephew and her chest ached. "Oh, Rhett. What are we going to do? I can't lose you."

She dampened a washcloth and attacked his messy hands and face. "But you deserve a share of your daddy's estate. And I'm going to see that you get it."

"I'm sorry to interrupt," Marie, Mitch's personal assistant, said from the boardroom entrance, "but there's a Carly Corbin downstairs insisting on seeing you. She doesn't have an appointment."

About time.

"Show her to my office." After Marie left, Mitch stood and looked down the table at his brother. "Three days. It took her three days to cave. The question is how much is this little bastard going to cost us? I'll be back."

Rand waved him on. "Take your time. I'll handle the next applicant for Nadia's position and then grab lunch."

The damned will had left Mitch with an interminable number of complications. His sister had been banished to

Dallas to house-sit as required by her inheritance clause. Her sudden absence only increased his workload. He had to find her temporary replacement, and he had his brother's help whether he wanted it or not, thanks to dear ol' dad making Rand CEO instead of Mitch. That irritated Mitch like a sliver of glass stuck in his foot.

Rand had abandoned the business. Hell, his brother hadn't even spoken to anyone in the family in five years. Five years during which Mitch had busted his ass to prove he was worthy of taking the reins of KCL when his father retired.

But Dad had wanted Rand back and in charge.

Mitch entered his office through the connecting door to the boardroom. Before he could sit down Marie showed in his guest.

Carly barely acknowledged his presence with a brief nod before her wide brown eyes gazed past him to scan the thirty-foot wall of windows and the view of Biscayne Bay behind him.

He stiffened. Women didn't overlook him. It wasn't conceit to admit that his wealth wasn't his only asset. But Carly didn't seem interested in his face or body. Ignoring the jab to his pride, he took advantage of her inattention to assess her.

Her features weren't classically beautiful. But close enough. Her breasts were decent. Neither too big nor too small. Probably real. She wore a bubble gum-pink tracksuit with black stripes down the length of her legs. Killer legs, he recalled from their last meeting. Too bad she'd covered them today. Getting another look would have been a nice bonus to closing the deal.

Overall, Carly was nice-looking. Not traffic-stopping. But interesting. Until she smiled. That smile of hers could melt bricks. She wasn't smiling today.

Since she was an identical twin, he could see why his father had been attracted to her sister. But damnation, couldn't the man have practiced safe sex after preaching about it for decades? Or had Marlene Corbin had something to do with the birth control failure? Mitch would bet money on it. His father had made a number of mistakes, but he hadn't been stupid.

Carly's gaze finally returned to Mitch. A weird paralysis seized his lungs. He fought it off. "Do we have a deal, Ms. Corbin?"

"Rhett can move into Kincaid Manor," she stated matter-of-factly.

Victory surged through him. He pulled his checkbook from his interior coat pocket. "Excell—"

"But only if I come with him."

His fingers contracted around his pen. "Excuse me?"

"You exude about as much warmth as dry ice, Kincaid. Children need more than that."

His spine went rigid at the insult. "I know how to handle kids."

"Really? Because I didn't see evidence of that the other day. You didn't even try to make a connection with your brother."

"Half brother, as you pointed out. There wasn't time."

"Eye contact and a smile only take a second."

She had him there. "And your price?"

"I don't want your money."

Yeah, like he believed that. What game was she playing? "What of your home? You'll leave it vacant?"

"I can rent it for enough to cover the mortgage."

Her plan shouldn't have surprised him. In his experience, women were always looking for a free ride. In Carly's case, Kincaid Manor would be like a spa vacation compared to the in-need-of-renovation structure she inhabited. "Your presence isn't required."

"Rhett stays with me, his guardian. And since my attorney says you only had thirty days from the reading of the will to begin fulfilling your part of your father's demands or forfeit your inheritance, you're going to have to come to terms with the package deal sooner rather than later."

Nineteen of those days had passed. Days during which Mitch had employed two teams of lawyers to try to find a loophole in the will. When they'd failed, he'd spent more time hiring a nanny and trying to find out what he could about Carly Corbin. If Carly hadn't come to him by tomorrow, he would have gone after her.

"I would imagine you have my number since you have everything else." She backed toward the door.

"Carly, how much do you want?" He signed a blank check and then slid it and his pen across the desk. "You fill in the amount. Whatever you feel is fair."

Without even glancing at the pen and check, she observed him as if he were three-day-old July roadkill. "You just don't get it, do you, Kincaid?"

He linked his hands behind his back, hoping to appear casual instead of frustrated and irritated and damn near desperate. "Then perhaps you'll enlighten me."

"This isn't about money. It's about a little boy and what's best for him. It's always about doing what's best for the child. *Always*. In this case, you're not it."

"The boy will lack for nothing."

"Materially. And his name is Rhett."

Mitch struggled to rein in his temper, but his entire head grew hot. "*Rhett* will have the best of care."

Angry color stained Carly's cheeks and sparked in her eyes, making her look even more attractive. She approached his desk, planted her hands on the polished surface and leaned toward him. "Who will hold him when he's cranky? Who'll kiss his boo-boos and rock him when he has a nightmare? Who will tell him about his mother? And who will make sure he knows he was loved and w-wanted?"

The slight crack in her voice nailed him in the gut. She'd just lost her sister, and even if Marlene had been a mercenary, manipulative bitch, apparently Carly had cared for her. Maybe giving up the boy wouldn't be completely painless. But like ripping off a bandage, the discomfort wouldn't last long.

Being the middle child meant Mitch had learned the art of negotiation in the cradle. If he didn't compromise, he'd lose the brat. "I have employed a highly qualified nanny. I'm not trying to cut you out of his life completely. We'll arrange visitation."

"A nanny? You're going to *pay* someone to love him?" Her indignant tone and humorless laugh didn't bode well. Gold fragments glinted in her dark irises. "Is money your answer to everything?"

"There's nothing wrong with nannies. My siblings and I were raised by a series of competent—"

Her snort cut him off. "Now I get it. No wonder you're such a robot."

He flinched at her insult.

Leaving the check untouched on his desk, she marched to the door and paused with her hand on the knob. "That's my offer, Kincaid. Take it or leave it. You get both of us or neither of us. You can pursue this in court with a whole platoon of lawyers if you want, but considering your father allegedly paid my sister an obscene amount of money to abort, and you and your siblings are driven by potential monetary gains, no judge in his right mind will ever award you custody of Rhett even if you are an almighty Kincaid. And that's *if* you can get the case heard before your thirty days are up. Because rest assured, if you sue for custody, I will delay you in every way possible."

Her ponytail swung out parallel to the floor as she pivoted abruptly and slammed the door behind her.

Mitch swore. It didn't help that she was right. His attorneys had told him the same thing. He'd counted on her being as greedy as her sister and wanting fast cash.

Instead, he had no doubt Carly Corbin was in it to milk him for the long haul. And he had no choice but to accede to her absurd demands.

But he had every intention of winning this battle and he'd do whatever it took to come out on top.

"There's no place like home," Carly muttered under her breath. "There's certainly no place like this one."

She stood in the circular driveway Saturday morning staring up at the expansive ivory-stone facade of Kincaid Manor. The place looked like a castle that had been yanked out of the English countryside and dropped into a Miami gated community.

She'd had to stop and give her name at a guardhouse to get into the neighborhood, and then talk to a disembodied voice at a second set of elaborate iron gates. Those gates had glided shut behind her, locking her inside the Kincaid compound the moment her car had passed through.

Sunlight glinted off a multitude of windows on a steeply roofed two-story structure the length of your average strip mall. Shrubbery pruned to the nth degree surrounded the foundation and fenced the sidewalk as if intended to keep visitors from straying onto the perfectly manicured emerald lawn.

Not exactly ideal for a growing boy whose only speeds were asleep and wide open, but Carly's attorney had instructed her to make nice and play along while they explored their legal options. For Rhett's sake, she could put up with just about anything.

Hours after she'd left the KCL offices, Mitch had called, "invited" her to stay and given her directions to Kincaid Manor. Carly had immediately sat down and developed a step-by-step plan to bond the Kincaid offspring. She'd work on Mitch first, then she'd tackle his brother, Rand.

"Let's hope the palace is childproofed, buddy."

Rhett squirmed in her arms and babbled a reply. She set him down and herded him toward the porch. He toddled away with a childish giggle.

The imposing lead-glass front door opened, framing Mitch Kincaid. How appropriate. The lord of the manor had deigned to oversee their arrival. But he didn't step out to greet them. He waited, arms folded, while she helped Rhett scramble up the stairs on his hands and knees.

Even though it was the weekend, Mitch wore a suit—this one stark black with a blinding white shirt and a ruby tie. Did the man ever unwind?

Mitch barely glanced at Rhett. "You brought your things?"

Before she could stop him, Rhett bolted across the porch and wrapped his little arms around his half brother's thigh. Her nephew never met a stranger.

Mitch stiffened.

Was that a flash of panic Carly detected in his eyes? Of course not. Who would be scared of an adorable child? She must have mistaken annoyance for fear.

Rhett grasped two chubby fists in the immaculate fabric of Mitch's trousers and bounced, demanding, "Up. Up. Pig me up."

Step one in getting these two to know each other: Mitch might as well learn from the get-go that once Rhett started that song and dance, it wouldn't end until he got what he wanted.

"My minivan's loaded. I wanted to get Rhett settled before I started schlepping our luggage."

"Ingrid," Mitch spoke over his shoulder. "Take the boy to the nursery while I show Ms. Corbin to her suite."

A stacked and stunning blonde in snug hipster jeans and an even tighter, belly-showing T-shirt appeared behind him. The hand she placed on Mitch's lean waist as she ducked around him in the wide doorway was far too familiar for an employee, and her long acrylic nails were likely to put someone's eye out. "Come on, little Brett."

"Rhett," Carly corrected automatically and stepped between the woman and Rhett at the same time Mitch shifted.

Carly and Mitch collided. Her hip ended up aligned with

his rock-hard thigh and her shoulder pressed the equally firm wall of his chest. She inhaled sharply, and Mitch's cologne filled her nose. A flood of warmth and awareness swept through her. She stomped on the unwanted response and focused on the problem. *The other problem.* "Who are you?"

The blonde tossed her long hair over her shoulder and smiled intimately at Mitch before replying, "I'm Rhett's nanny."

With a face and body like that, I'll just bet you are.

Carly glared at Mitch, then bent to pry Rhett's stubby fingers from the lord of the manor's pants. Mitch's muscles contracted beneath her touch as she maneuvered. She could feel body heat radiating through the summer-weight fabric, and it almost scorched her. And being at eye level with his crotch was…distracting to say the least.

She finally freed her wiggly nephew and scooped him up. "I told you Rhett didn't need a nanny."

"Who will watch him while you're working? Or do you intend to quit your job and live off my largesse?" The superior way he intoned the words and looked down at her, as if he expected her to freeload off him, set her teeth on edge.

"I'm not quitting my job. I'll watch Rhett when I'm here, and when I'm at work Lucy, his regular day-care provider, will watch him."

"And when you go out in the evening?"

Carly blinked. "You mean on a date?"

He lowered that square chin a fraction of an inch.

"I don't date."

Mitch's eyes narrowed. "You mean you're not seeing anyone at the moment. But that will change."

She hadn't dated since Marlene died and she had no inclination to wade back into the muddy dating waters again anytime soon. But she wasn't admitting that to Mitch and his playmate.

"If I want to go out, I'll hire a babysitter."

"Unnecessary. Ingrid will take over."

"Don't be ridiculous. Even if I went out every night of the week—which I won't—that wouldn't justify a full-time nanny's salary." She turned to the bottled, navel-ringed blonde. "Sorry, Ingrid. Nothing personal. But Rhett just lost his mother, and he's moving into a strange house. That's enough changes for one little guy to make right now."

"He'll adapt," Mitch snarled quietly.

Carly tipped her head back and held his gaze without blinking. "The way I see it, Kincaid, I hold all the cards. I have nothing to gain by moving in here and you have everything to lose if we don't."

Of course, Rhett would lose, too. But his safety was her primary concern. Not even a billion-plus bucks would make her overlook his well-being. She wasn't going to leave him in the care of Mitch's horny, dragon-clawed girlfriend.

She felt a bit unfair for judging the woman by her looks, but after interviewing dozens of day-care providers with Marlene, Carly had learned to tell almost instantly which ones had a rapport with children. Ingrid did not. She was almost as cold and detached as her boss—until she looked at Mitch. Then she looked ready to get XXX-rated hot.

Mitch's nostrils flared and his lips flatlined. He looked angry enough to bend horseshoes with his bare hands or maybe his clenched teeth. "Ingrid, please wait for me in the living room. I'll join you after Ms. Corbin and I have discussed your qualifications."

38-24-34. Oh yeah, those were serious qualifications.

But not for child care.

"I'll show you to your room." Mitch turned and stalked across an Italian marble foyer almost as large as the entire first floor of Carly's house.

He hadn't agreed to her terms, but Carly, curious to see more of the mansion and where Mitch intended to put them, followed him anyway. The staircase rose from the center of the polished flagstone floor like a water fountain arching in opposite directions at the top. Carly's gaze stuck to the flexing muscles of his butt like a fly to flypaper as he climbed.

No way. She couldn't find him attractive. Not after all Marlene had told her. She was merely one athlete admiring another's well-toned physique. *Right?*

Shifting her gaze from the glutei maximi ahead of her, she trailed her host. The walk through the gallery, past antique furniture and paintings that looked as if they belonged in a museum, seemed to take forever. "Good grief, how big is this place?"

"Fifteen thousand square feet," he replied, turning down a long hall. A set of double doors marked the end, but he stopped short of them and pushed open a door on the right. "Your suite."

Carly brushed past him. Her shoulder grazed his chest. She cursed the frisson of goose bumps the small contact caused.

Surprised, she turned a slow circle, taking in the tasteful lavender, white and mint decor that included a curtained four-poster bed, ornate French furniture and plum-colored rugs. The room looked like a decorating magazine snapshot. Perfect down to the last detail. As much as Kincaid seemed to resent her presence, she'd expected to be stuck in a closet somewhere or maybe the servants' quarters.

"Me down," Rhett demanded and squirmed in her arms.

"Not yet, buddy." Not until she'd moved the expensive-looking breakables out of his reach.

She crossed to the bay window and knelt on its cushioned window seat to look into the backyard. Her mouth dropped open. People actually lived like this?

The formal gardens between her window and the opposite side of the U-shaped house looked elaborate enough for a government monument or a movie set, and whoever had designed them had been fond of rulers. All straight lines. Not one single curve. The roses probably even grew square petals.

An expansive tiled patio stretched across the base of the U, complete with a square water fountain and spouting Poseidon statue. The grassy area immediately off the patio contained, of all things, a koi pond. Beyond the fish, rigid rows of shrubs flanked an Olympic-length pool that reached all the way to a seawall, boat dock, yacht and what looked like two hundred feet of waterfront.

"We're going to have to keep Rhett away from all that water."

"I'll order fencing and safety locks immediately."

Crossing to a door, she pushed it open to reveal a luxurious bathroom straight out of a hedonist's fantasies. A glass shower. A tub big enough to accommodate four. A marble-topped vanity as long as a bed. Shaking her head at the opulence, she returned to the bedroom and opened a second door to reveal a closet the size of her bedroom back home. But she didn't see a crib or connecting door to a nursery.

She rejoined Mitch. "Where's Rhett's room?"

He nodded toward the window, indicating the opposite wing of the house. "In the east wing."

"I won't be able to hear him from here."

"That's why we have Ingrid."

"*We* don't have Ingrid. *You* have Ingrid."

His eyes narrowed to green slits. "What are you implying?"

"Your girlfriend is not looking after Rhett."

"She's not my girlfriend."

"Oh please. She almost slipped her hand in your pocket for a quick grope downstairs."

His chin jacked up. He closed the distance between them in three long strides and stared down at her with what would have been intimidating ferocity if she didn't work with professional athletes on a regular basis. She'd become immune to the psyche-out glare.

"I don't keep mistresses in my home."

"But you do keep them. Or in this case, her."

Before he could argue, Rhett launched himself at Mitch, startling Carly so much she almost dropped the imp. Kincaid's only choice was too catch him. Rhett clamped his hands around his half brother's neck and planted a slobbery kiss on his cheek.

The horror in the lord of the manor's eyes made Carly snort with laughter. Okay, so that had been a wet kiss. A little disgust was warranted. She released Rhett's lower half and her nephew shimmied up his brother like a monkey does a tree.

Mitch closed his eyes. The muscles in his jaw knotted—along with every other muscle group she could see. What was going on? He acted as if he couldn't bear to hold the child.

"Take him." He ground out the words.

Confused by his weird behavior, Carly hesitated. Rhett couldn't possibly be more adorable. And he was clean. He didn't even have a dirty diaper.

Mitch thrust Rhett back at her. Frowning, Carly took him. "You want to be his guardian? How are you going to do that when you can't even handle holding him? What is your problem, Kincaid?"

Boy, did she have her work cut out for her in bringing these two together.

Mitch scowled. "I don't have a problem other than a stubborn guest. I'll show you the nursery."

Carly shook her head and stood her ground. "Rhett and I are not sleeping a football field apart. Either you bring his crib in here or I'm staying in the nursery."

"Don't be ridiculous."

Carly held Mitch's gaze. After a moment's standoff, he huffed an aggravated breath, crossed the room to an intercom system imbedded in the wall and punched a button. "Mrs. Duncan, please have the nursery furniture transferred to the blue suite."

Mitch turned and scowled at Carly. "Satisfied?"

"That depends. Let's see the blue room."

He stalked across the hall and threw open the opposite door. Carly followed more slowly, making sure not to brush against him this time when she entered. Mitch made it easy by staying out of Rhett's reach.

Shades of blue from powder to midnight turned the room into a peaceful sanctuary. Like hers, the suite had a connecting bath and a closet large enough to be Rhett's playroom. "It's beautiful, and if I leave the doors open at night, I'll be able to hear him."

A look she couldn't identify flickered in Mitch's eyes. "Fine. Now if you'll hand the b—Rhett—over to Ingrid, we'll have lunch before moving your things inside."

"No Ingrid."

"She is not my lover."

"She wants to be."

A smug smile slanted his lips, and her stomach sank like a wet sandbag. He could charm the birds from the trees with that smile. She hoped he didn't aim it at her very often.

He tilted his head, his green gaze traveled down the length of Carly's body, then slowly returned. Her skin tingled and her nipples tightened in the wake of his inspection. "It disturbs you that she wants me?"

Carly stiffened at his implication that she might be jealous. "There's no accounting for tastes. You can sleep with her and each of the Miami Dolphins cheerleaders solely or en masse for all I care, but I'm not having the woman in charge of Rhett's safety concentrating on getting into your pants when she should be watching him."

The smile vanished. "Ingrid came highly recommended from a business associate."

"Then she won't have trouble finding another job." He opened his mouth—presumably to argue. She held up her hand to cut him off. "Mitch, this one's nonnegotiable."

"Apparently, many things are nonnegotiable with you."

"I'm not afraid to fight for what I want." She had been once, and she'd paid the price ever since.

"Like your sister." His tone made the comment an insult.

Fury, pain and panic hit her like a barrage of arrows. She gritted her teeth and blinked away the sting in her eyes, but she refused to engage in this particular war of words. He couldn't know about Marlene's plan. Her sister hadn't been the type to broadcast her secrets. Not even to her twin. And Carly had no intention of giving Mitch Kincaid ammunition by sharing what she knew.

"Deal or no deal, Kincaid?"

After a few tense moments Mitch nodded once. "No Ingrid."

Carly exhaled. She'd won the battle, but she had a feeling she'd unintentionally declared war against a man her sister had claimed didn't fight fair.

TWO

Carly's plan to turn Mitch into a family man wasn't going to be as easy as she'd hoped. She hadn't expected to have to start with a man who couldn't bear to touch the child.

Tomorrow she'd have to reassess the stages of Mitch's conversion and possibly break the process down into smaller achievable increments. As if she were training an athlete for a marathon she'd set daily and weekly goals toward attaining the ultimate objective by the end of the year. She wanted Mitch to love Rhett as much as she did. Nothing less would do.

She yanked on her nightie and pulled open the bathroom door. Steam wafted into the bedroom from behind her. Glancing at the big four-poster bed, she anticipated sinking into the thick mattress, but first she needed to check on Rhett one last time. She crossed the hall.

This morning, a team of employees had removed the furniture from the blue room and replaced it with obviously new nursery furniture. After lunch, Mitch had surprised her by dismissing them and helping her unload her car himself during Rhett's nap.

So he wasn't a complete jerk and he wasn't afraid of hard work. But not once had she seen him try to connect with Rhett, and that annoyed her like a festering splinter. A child needed the love and support of his family. All of his family. And he needed to know he was loved and that the one in charge would do the right thing. No matter how difficult.

Rhett had been overwound after a day full of changes, but had finally gone out like a light thirty minutes ago. Carly straightened the lightweight blanket covering him and bent to kiss his forehead. She couldn't possibly love him any more if he were her own.

A sound behind her made her straighten and turn. Mitch stood in the open doorway silhouetted by the light she'd left burning in her bedroom.

"He finally settled?" His low rumbling voice raised the hairs on Carly's arms and reminded her she was naked except for her worn thigh-length nightshirt. She hadn't bothered with a robe because she'd thought Mitch would be off in his own wing of the monstrous ten-bedroom house.

Wrapping her arms around her middle, she crossed the lush carpet and stopped in front of him before whispering, "Yes. He's not usually so cranky. Today was a bit much for him, I think."

Mitch's slow head-to-toe appraisal set her pulse aflutter. Dark evening beard shadowed his jaw and upper lip, and his slightly rumpled hair looked as if he'd run his hands through the thick strands a few times. He'd removed his suit coat and tie and rolled back the sleeves of his shirt to reveal muscular forearms dusted with dark whorls.

In a word, he looked sexy. And he smelled great. The crisp aroma of his cologne had faded and a more masculine, more alluring scent had taken its place. Mitch's scent.

Forget it. He's not your type.

"Well…good night." She stepped forward and he moved aside.

"Good night." He turned and walked toward the double doors at the end of the hall. One stood open, revealing the bottom end of a king-size bed covered in a dark green damask spread.

Alarm bells clamored in Carly's head. "That's your room?"

"Yes."

How could she sleep with her door open to listen out for Rhett when she knew Mitch could stroll past at any moment?

Mitch's gaze turned arctic. "And don't bother sleepwalking. My door will be locked."

Anger shrieked through her like steam through a boiling teakettle. Before she could think of an appropriate comeback, Mitch entered his room and shut his door. The lock clicked.

Carly's short nails bit into her palms and fury chewed her insides. Marlene had been too kind in labeling Mitch Kincaid a rat bastard.

So much for sweet dreams.

Laughter pulled Mitch from the dining room to the kitchen. Surprise halted him in the doorway.

Mrs. Duncan had been a fixture at Kincaid Manor since before Mitch's birth, but he'd never heard the woman laugh. He wasn't even sure he'd ever seen her smile.

Making airplane noises, the head housekeeper bent over the brat's high chair with a spoon in her hand and a twinkle in her eyes. *Mrs. Duncan could twinkle?* She caught sight of Mitch and abruptly stopped buzzing. Her amusement vanished and her lined face settled back into a familiar expressionless cast. She snapped upright.

"I'm sorry, sir. I didn't realize you were waiting for your breakfast. I'll bring it right through." She set the spoon and bowl she held in front of Carly.

Mitch's gaze shifted to his unwanted guest. Instead of her usual ponytail, Carly's hair draped her shoulders in a silky smooth curtain of mink brown. The sunlight streaming through the window behind her glinted on a few golden strands.

"Morning, Mitch." She flashed him one of her brick-melting smiles and a shot of adrenaline negated his need for coffee. Apparently, *this* Corbin didn't hold grudges. Or did she merely conceal her vindictiveness better than her sister had?

"Good morning, Carly." She wore another tracksuit—this one in blinding tangerine with white stripes on the sleeves. He focused on her obnoxiously bright clothing in a failed attempt to wipe the image of last night's attire from his mind. Her shapeless, oversize T-shirt had been worn almost to the point of transparency. The shadows of her nipples, navel and the dark curls between her legs had been obvious through the faded fabric.

He'd resented the hell out of his instantaneous response. He didn't like the woman. How could he possibly desire her?

Because you need to get laid.

But not by her.

She had a bowl in front of her and a glass of orange juice. "Della treated me to her secret recipe apple-cinnamon-raisin oatmeal. You should try it."

Della? Who was Della?

"Mr. Kincaid prefers bacon and eggs," Mrs. Duncan said in her usual monotone.

Della was Mrs. Duncan? And Carly was on a first-name basis with her in less than twenty-four hours? As far as he knew, no one in the Kincaid household had ever called the for-midable sixty-something woman by her first name.

Carly grimaced. "They're your arteries. But you'd think after your father's heart attack you'd be more careful."

"I am perfectly healthy, thank you." His cool tone dimmed her smile. "Why aren't you eating in the dining room?"

"Mr. Messy." Her nod indicated the slimy child.

"Which is why we should have kept the nanny. You could have eaten in peace." Yesterday she'd waited until the boy napped to eat lunch.

"Breakfast is one of our favorite times of the day. Isn't it, munchkin?" She tweaked the child's nose—the only clean part of his face as far as Mitch could tell. The brat cackled infectiously, stabbing Mitch with a reminder of other children and another time. An old ache invaded his chest.

"Besides, the view from the breakfast nook is gorgeous. But I told Della that you should add a bird feeder or two to the patio. Rhett loves to watch the birds—especially humming-birds. We'll pick up some feeders this afternoon after church."

She attended church?

Probably to confess her fortune-hunting sins. She might try a different brand of ammunition than her twin, but he knew why she'd been prancing around in her nightshirt last night.

Carly's brown eyes took on a challenging glint. "So…are you going to eat in the dining room by yourself or are you brave enough to join us? Rhett's almost finished. You and your Armani should be safe from soggy cereal bombs."

"I'll join you." If for no other reason than to keep an eye on his unwanted houseguest—the same reason he'd put her in the suite beside his. He chose the chair farthest away from the alleged cereal-bomb thrower.

"Not a morning person, eh?" Carly asked as she scraped the last of her oatmeal from a bowl and tucked it between her pink lips.

"I prefer to gather my thoughts for the upcoming day and read the business section. Are you?"

"Absolutely. On really hot days, we take our run before we eat." She leaned over to wipe the boy's face with a cloth and her jacket and the top she wore beneath it gaped, revealing a glimpse of scalloped white lace on the pale curve of her breast.

The sight hit Mitch with an unexpected surge of hunger—and not for bacon and eggs.

No. He would *not* be attracted to Carly Corbin. Her sister had taken his father for a ride. This twin wasn't going to get the chance to do the same with Mitch. He made a mental note to call one of his usual dates—women who knew good sex was all he'd give them.

"Perhaps one day I'll join you on your run." Again, if only to keep an eye on her. The majority of his neighbors were wealthy and older—prime pickings for attractive gold diggers on the make. Like the Corbin sisters.

"If you can keep up, you'd be welcome. Rhett would love the company."

Another challenge. She seemed to enjoy issuing them. "I can keep up."

Mrs. Duncan placed a plate in front of him. Was that a smirk on her lined face?

"What's with the suit?" Carly asked, recapturing his attention. "Going to church?"

"No. To the office."

"It's Sunday," she enunciated as if he were lacking fifty IQ points.

"I have work to do."

Carly shook her head and made a face at Mrs. Duncan. "A workaholic and a diet disaster. Just like his father."

True, but his spine straightened regardless. "How would you know?"

Sadness shadowed her eyes. "Marlene told me."

"And yet she didn't tell you about the hundred grand she accepted to have an abortion."

Carly glared with enough fire to make a lesser man duck for cover. "If you want to talk trash, then you do it when we're alone. I will not tolerate you making Rhett feel unwanted. And I think you're lying about the money."

"I made the transaction myself. And I have a copy of the check with Marlene's signature on the back."

"I want to see it."

The Corbin women were identical in looks and yet not. Marlene had dressed in designer clothing. Her makeup had been flawless, and he'd never seen one single hair out of place. Beautiful, but hard, he'd concluded within seconds of making her acquaintance. And he hadn't been attracted to her. Nonetheless he'd tried seduction and later threats, but neither had swayed her toward breaking it off with his father. And when he'd finally convinced his father to end the relationship, she'd turned up pregnant a month later.

A calculating woman with an eye out for number one, he'd concluded. He hadn't seen that side of Carly. Yet. But he would. She camouflaged her mercenary streak well. But sooner or later the facade would crack.

Carly sipped her juice. Without the red gloss her twin had worn, Carly's mouth looked softer than Marlene's. Thus far, the only time Carly had shown her hard side was when butting heads with him over the boy. That was to be expected, since the kid was her ticket to Easy Street. Mitch hadn't figured out her MO yet, but she and Marlene were genetically identical twins— one egg separated in the womb. Carly's altruistic pretense had to be exactly that. A pretense to cover a mercenary heart.

And once she realized he was onto her, her mouth would twist the way her sister's had and her eyes would glint like flint. In the meantime, he'd watch Carly Corbin like a hawk does its prey, waiting for the perfect opportunity to swoop in and steal the child from her.

The boy slammed his hands on the high chair tray, startling Mitch. His eggs fell from his fork.

"Man. Man. Man."

Carly righted the sippy cup. "That's Mitch. Your brother."

"Bub. Bub. Bub."

"That's right. Your bubba."

Mitch's spine fused into a rigid line. He opened his mouth to protest he was no one's *bubba,* but the sparkle in Carly's eyes and something about the angle of her chin, dared him. The witch was trying to provoke him, he realized.

Too bad he refused to be her source of entertainment.

He flicked open his newspaper, concentrated on the financial section and tried to ignore the boy's chorus of "Bubbas" and the smirks on Carly's and Mrs. Duncan's faces.

He wasn't going to let Carly disrupt his life. In a matter of days—a month at the most—she'd realize she was fighting a losing battle. And then she'd turn over guardianship of the kid.

Peace and a nanny would return to the Kincaid household the day Carly Corbin moved out.

Carly's body reacted like a Geiger counter nearing radioactive material.

The hairs on her arms rose and her pulse stuttered erratically. By the sound of his step and the scent of his cologne she knew who had entered the living room behind her without looking over her shoulder.

Despite its predominantly white decor, the room wasn't cold or uncomfortable due to the plush rugs on the marble floor, overstuffed upholstery and surprising colorful accents scattered about. She preferred this space to the darker, more masculine den.

"Rhett looks like you," she said, keeping her gaze on the Kincaid family portrait hanging above the mantel. "How old were you when this was painted?"

"Eleven," Mitch replied.

"Everyone looks so happy. The all-American family success story." Her family had been happy...until she'd made an unforgettable mistake.

"Appearances can be deceiving."

That brought her around abruptly. Exhaustion dragged Mitch's features, not surprising since he'd left for work before eight this morning, and it was after 10:00 p.m. now. His suit coat was draped on his forearm and his loosened burgundy tie hung askew.

So much for Sunday being a day of rest. "What do you mean?"

He shook his head. "Nothing. Did you and Rhett get settled in today?"

"We did. Mrs. Duncan and I have babyproofed most of the rooms. So when you notice some of your priceless collectibles missing, I didn't hock them. They've been put away."

As a physical therapist, Carly spent a lot of her day encouraging people to go a little farther than they wanted to go. She saw no reason not to continue that practice with Mitch. "Why is the picture deceptive?"

"Let it go, Carly." If his voice dropped any lower he'd be growling. He turned away.

She reached out and grabbed his bicep to stop him. The muscle bunched beneath her fingers and his heat burned her hand through the thin fabric of his sleeve. "If you expect me to let Rhett live here, then you need to level with me, Mitch. Are there skeletons in the Kincaid closet that I should worry about?"

He stabbed a hand through his hair, effectively dislodging her grasp, and lifted his gaze to the oil painting. "As far as I can remember, my mother wasn't the contented person you see depicted there. She died in a car accident shortly after that portrait was painted. But I was a kid. So what do I know?"

"I'm sorry. Going through your teens without the steadying influence of your mother must have been difficult."

A familiar ache welled in her chest. Her daughter would be twelve now and entering what Carly's mother had always called the testing years. Was her daughter asking the same questions Carly had asked about her birthmother? Did she wonder why she'd been given up and if she was too flawed for even a mother to love? Carly prayed her daughter's adoptive parents were as supportive and loving as Eileen and Dan Corbin had been.

Carly pushed the questions and regrets aside, the way she always did, and focused on the present. But the ache didn't abate. It never did. The pain rested just behind her breastbone like a hole in her heart.

Mitch grunted a nonanswer and headed toward the wet bar built into the cabinetry flanking the fireplace. But instead of liquor, he splashed bottled water over his ice cubes.

"I'm sure you can see why I want to make certain Rhett doesn't suffer from Marlene's absence."

Studying his reflection in the mirror above the marble countertop, she noted the groove in his brow. For a moment, he looked tired and very much like a man who'd just lost his father and had to take over a multi-billion-dollar corporation despite the grief he must dealing with. "Rough day?"

He stared into his glass, then met her reflected gaze. "I've spent the past week reacquainting my brother with KCL. He's been working for our west coast competitor for the past five years. And we had to hire my sister's replacement. Rand and I spent the day training her."

Carly had been disappointed when she'd read in the will that Nadia would be out of state. She'd hoped the female Kincaid would have some maternal instincts and side with Carly on Rhett's care. "Training on Sunday?"

"The cruising industry runs 24/7, three hundred and sixty-five days per year. Good night." He headed for the foyer.

Tonight for the first time since she'd met him, Mitch looked anything but invincible and nothing like the overconfident rat bastard Marlene had described. For some foolish reason, Carly was reluctant to let this approachable mood pass. "Have you had dinner? Mrs. Duncan left a plate for you in the re-frigerator. Want me to heat it up?"

His eyes returned to hers and narrowed suspiciously. "I'm capable of operating a microwave."

His terse reply raised her hackles, but for Rhett's sake, she'd be polite. She had to be if she wanted to make a place for the youngest Kincaid in this family. "I'm sure you can, but I'm offering help and company."

The long stretch of silence spoke volumes. "I could eat."

Carly headed for the kitchen despite the lack of warm fuzzies his reply elicited. And this time she didn't get lost. She'd taken more than a few wrong turns today in the enormous house.

She removed the plate from the refrigerator, slid it into the microwave and punched the buttons. "Your home gym is pretty amazing. Would you mind if I used it?"

"Go ahead."

She leaned back against the counter and observed Mitch. "If you like, I can check your form when you work out to make sure you're not doing yourself any harm."

His shoulders squared. "What are you doing?"

"Heating your dinner? Trying to make conversation? Offering professional advice?"

"Don't."

"Don't what? Don't be polite?"

"Don't try your wiles on me."

Carly's temper ballooned like the plastic wrap covering the plate rotating on the microwave's turntable. She gestured to her tracksuit, which had taken a beating during Rhett's dinner and bath. "That's the second time you've accused me of putting the moves on you. Open your freaking eyes, Kincaid. Am I dressed to seduce you?"

She realized her mistake immediately. Her question invited him to inspect her from her ponytail to her running shoes. He did so slowly and thoroughly, lingering over her breasts and legs before returning to her face. It annoyed her immensely that his appraisal left her breathless and agitated.

"It won't work, Carly. I'm not a sap like my father, nor am I so hard up for a woman that I'll fall into bed with the first attractive female who offers."

His rudeness shocked and infuriated her. If this were a cartoon, steam would shoot from her ears. "Hello! I'm not offering anything except leftovers."

"Precisely." From his tone she didn't think he referred to the leftover orange roasted chicken and vegetables.

The timer beeped. Mitch reached past her and retrieved the plate. She could feel both his warmth and, conversely, the chill emanating from him. He crossed the room and plunked his plate down on the kitchen table. His body language made it clear he didn't want her company.

Carly resisted the urge to stab him with the fork she retrieved from the drawer and settled for slapping the utensil down on the table beside his plate. "If your father was half the conceited jackass you are, then I can't see what Marlene ever saw in him."

"She saw a billionaire sugar daddy and a meal ticket."

Carly glared at him and prepared to blister him with one of the many insults she'd learned from the professional athletes she worked with. But doubt stilled her tongue.

Marlene had confessed in her notebook that she found Everett's fortune quite attractive. But surely her sister had cared about more than the man's finances? And what about the times Marlene had told her she loved Everett? Her sister wouldn't have lied to her, would she?

Yes, she would.

Carly broke eye contact and retrieved the pitcher of iced tea from the fridge. She set it down beside Mitch's plate.

"Go screw yourself, Kincaid. That's the only way a jerk like you will ever have a partner you consider your equal."

With that she pivoted and stomped out of the kitchen, leaving the lord of the manor to his solitary dinner.

She hoped he choked on it.

Three

Kill him with kindness.

As opposed to just killing him—a notion that had entertained Carly far more than it should have for the past few days. Okay, so she couldn't *really* off Mitch Kincaid. But making him run a marathon on a treadmill with no change in scenery could be fun. Or maybe five hundred sit-ups on a cold tile floor...

But none of those would get her closer to her goal of bonding Mitch and Rhett. She sighed and rolled the ball across the emerald lawn to Rhett Wednesday evening.

It had taken her three days to cool off, three days of not seeing the middle Kincaid, of Rhett not spending a single moment with his half brother, for Carly to realize Mitch had deliberately antagonized her Sunday night.

Why?

She didn't think for one minute he honestly believed she was chasing him, because she hadn't flirted even once. Sure, she'd appreciated his physique a time or two. Who wouldn't? But unless he had eyes in the back of his head, he hadn't caught her looking, so that didn't count.

He had to have been trying to avoid Rhett, and since she and Rhett were practically joined at the hip…annoying her meant avoiding his half brother.

She'd decided she'd have to follow through with her plan—regardless of Mitch's irritating comments—if she wanted the males to get to know each other better. With a thirty-some-thing-year age gap between them, Mitch and Rhett would never have the close bond Carly had shared with Marlene. But the brothers had to start somewhere.

A salt-scented breeze blowing in from the water lifted the skirt of the simple peach sundress she'd donned for dinner. She smoothed the fabric back in place. Dresses. Ick. Give her a tracksuit or running shorts and a tank any day. Carly had been the jock in their family. Marlene had been the girly girl.

A wave of sadness swamped her. Carly lifted her chin and inhaled deeply, trying to alleviate the emptiness. The mouth-watering aromas of grilling swordfish with citrus salsa and marinated vegetables filled her nostrils. Her stomach growled with hunger. Mitch would be home soon and they'd have their first family dinner.

She dug her bare toes into the thick grass. So she'd dressed up. Big deal. The evening sun burned down on them, and her outfit would be cooler than pants. If Mitch wanted to make something out of it, fine. Time would prove him wrong. She wasn't looking for a lover, or a sugar daddy or anything remotely resembling either one. Her broken engagement had left her too raw to think about another romantic entanglement.

She caught the ball and rolled it back to Rhett. Rhett needed her. Sure, having someone depend on her for everything both frightened and overwhelmed her, but she wouldn't let down

Rhett or Marlene. Or herself. This time she wouldn't let anyone convince her to take the easy way out. This time she would be the parent she should have been twelve years ago.

The sound of the back door gliding open drew her gaze to the house. Mitch stepped onto the patio. With his eyes narrowed against the setting sun and his hands parked on his hips, he scanned the backyard like a lord surveying his property. He zeroed in on them and her pulse did something wonky. What was up with that?

She touched Rhett's shoulder. "Look who's here."

Rhett beamed and shouted, "Bubba. Ball."

Mitch grimaced and Carly didn't even bother to smother her grin as her nephew chugged forward. Mitch clearly hated the nickname—which is probably why Carly had practiced it with Rhett since she'd picked him up from day care.

"Evening, Mitch."

Mitch's lips flatlined and his attention returned to her. A breeze off the water lifted his glossy dark hair. "Where is Mrs. Duncan?"

"I gave her the day off."

His scowl deepened. "Carly, that wasn't your decision."

"Ball, bubba," Rhett said before hurling the red sphere.

Mitch caught it and tossed it back—gently, Carly was surprised to see. He fisted his hands by his sides. "I won't tolerate you interfering with the household staff."

"Why shouldn't the woman have time off?"

"She has scheduled days off."

"Sorry, but her younger sister didn't conveniently need emergency gallbladder surgery on Della's scheduled day off. Della wanted to be there and I thought she should. They need to spend time together while they can." Because you never knew how much time you had left with a loved one.

The stiffness eased from his rigid face and shoulders. "Why didn't you say her sister was ill?"

"You didn't ask." She transferred the fish and vegetables from the top rack of the grill to a platter, then covered it.

"What is that?"

"Our dinner. We're eating outside. The weather is too gorgeous to be cooped up inside."

"It's eighty-five."

"But the humidity is low for a change and there's a great breeze blowing in off the water. Shed your jacket and you'll be comfortable." She set the platter in the center of the wrought-iron and glass table and pulled the shrimp cocktails from the cooler she'd tucked underneath.

She'd never known there were special bowls or forks to serve the appetizer. This morning when Mrs. Duncan had produced the stemless martini-ish glasses that rested inside crystal globes filled with ice, Carly had had to ask what they were. The special dishes were just one of the many contrasts between the Kincaid's überrich world and her working-class ways. When she had shrimp cocktail, it came on a black plastic deli tray from the grocery store.

"Have a seat and help yourself." She flicked a hand toward a chair.

Mitch laid the folded newspaper he carried beside the plate on the opposite side of the rectangular table from Rhett and hung his suit coat over the back of his chair. "You cooked?"

"Yes. But don't worry. That's parsley on the squash and zucchini, not arsenic. There's wine if you want it."

Mitch lifted a dark eyebrow. "You're not drinking?"

She shook her head. "We're going running later."

He didn't open the bottle, but instead filled his and her water goblets from the insulated pitcher on the table.

She buckled Rhett into his high chair, wiped his hands and then served his diced grilled cheese sandwich. She added a spoonful of green peas and some of the grilled veggies so he could practice his fine motor skills.

Rhett attacked his food as if he hadn't eaten in a week.

Mitch eyed his half brother and then pulled out her chair, showing he did have some manners. "You shouldn't have waited."

She shrugged and sat. "Rhett only looks like he's starving. He had a snack two hours ago. And for him to get a sense of family, we should eat together whenever possible."

Mitch's expression closed like a slamming door.

"No matter how hectic things were when Marlene and I were growing up, my mother insisted on family dinners. It's a great way to unwind and catch up on what everyone else is doing."

Suspicion entered Mitch's eyes. "Carly—"

"Shut up and eat, Mitch, before the ice under your shrimp melts. Contrary to your high opinion of yourself, this is not a date."

Wincing, she reached for her napkin. So much for maintaining peace. She'd just bonked him over the head with the olive branch she'd hoped to extend. But his distrustful glares really rubbed her the wrong way.

"I'm sorry. There's no excuse for me being rude. But it's just dinner. Della already had most of the meal prepared before her sister called. Cooking it was no big deal."

Mitch stared at her in silence as if weighing the truth of her words, and then he nodded and started on his shrimp. Carly dug into hers, savoring the citrus tang of Mrs. Duncan's marinade. She caught herself watching the absurdly sensual sight of Mitch's straight white teeth biting into the shrimp and his lips surrounding the meat.

Get a grip. Kincaid is not on tonight's or any other night's menu. Remember how he treated Marlene?

She polished off her appetizer and reached for the main course. Mitch followed suit, piling large helpings of fish and vegetables on his plate. He devoured his meal almost as ravenously as Rhett had, but with the perfect form of one who'd had etiquette lessons. She wondered who'd taught him the fine art of eating politely. One of his nannies?

"Did you eat lunch today?" she asked to break the silence.

"There wasn't time. Where are your parents now?"

She gave him points for making conversation. "Arizona. Dad needed the drier climate for his health."

"With all your talk of family, why don't you move out there with them?"

"I've thought about it. But my parents' lives are filled with retirement community activities. I'd have to apply for a new license in a different state, and that could mean months without income. My parents can't afford to support us, but they'd feel obligated to try. Add in that children aren't allowed to stay overnight in their complex, and things get even more complicated."

"Leave Rhett with me."

She sighed and wiped her mouth. "Give it up, Mitch. That's not going to happen."

"It could. Say the word and you're a free woman."

She'd been footloose and fancy-free before and she hadn't liked it. How could anyone expect her to go back to normal knowing she'd given up something precious? Twice.

"You act as if caring for Rhett is a burden. It isn't."

"You say that now, but give it time."

"I'll say the same thing next week, next year and ten years from now."

He snorted a sound of disbelief, but she decided not to waste her breath arguing. Talk was cheap. He'd soon see by her actions that she meant what she said.

"You're only twenty-eight. Aren't your parents too young to retire?"

"Mom was forty and Dad forty-five when they adopted Marlene and me." And because Carly had been adopted, she knew exactly what kinds of questions her baby girl would be asking.

Silence returned, broken only by Rhett's babble and the chink of silverware.

"Does Mrs. Duncan need more than one day?"

Surprised, Carly searched Mitch's face. Good to know the rat bastard had a human side after all. "It would be nice if you'd call and offer it. I have her sister's phone number."

"I'll get someone from the temp agency in to cook our meals and oversee the remaining staff if Mrs. Duncan needs more time."

"Oh please. We're adults. We can feed ourselves. I know my way around the kitchen if you don't. And I think your staff can muddle through pushing a vacuum and making beds for a couple of days." His eyes narrowed to slits, pinning her like a butterfly on a collector's board. "What?"

"You intend to work all day and then come home and cook for me. Why?" Suspicion laced his voice.

"For us. And don't take it personally. I'm not after your heart via your stomach. Rhett and I have to eat, too. And I like to cook. I used to prepare all the meals for Marlene and me."

He looked ready to argue, but instead consumed the last bites of his swordfish. He sat back, still wearing the skeptical, guarded expression. "That was good."

"Thank you. And it's healthier than your usual dinners."

His eyebrows slammed down. So much for the truce. "Don't try to change me, Carly. Don't interfere in my life."

"Wouldn't dream of it," she denied and knew she fibbed. By the end of the year she'd have his bachelor lifestyle turned upside down. Priorities changed when a child entered the picture. He'd discover that sooner or later.

He studied her as if she were a puzzle he couldn't figure out—and one he didn't trust.

"Down. Ball," Rhett demanded.

Mitch stood. "I'll clear the table. You get the boy."

Carly blinked. A man in Hugo Boss who wasn't afraid to

do dishes? Nice. Too bad she wasn't looking. "Thanks, but he'd rather play with you."

"No." Swift. Harsh. Unequivocal. Mitch stacked their plates and strode into the house.

Carly stared after him. Mitch Kincaid was going to be a tough nut to crack—even harder than her most difficult client.

But just like she did with her more pigheaded patients, she would find a way to motivate him.

Carly Corbin was a sneaky, devious woman.

Mitch opened the tap in the sink to drown out the squeals of laughter penetrating the kitchen windows. Turning his back on the woman and child racing through the gardens, he bent to load the dishwasher.

Carly was determined to drag him somewhere he would never go again with her home-cooked meals and let's-play-family games. He still had the scars from his last round of playing house. He wouldn't give his heart to a child only to have it ripped out when the mother—or in this case, the guardian—had a change of heart. Once he could guarantee Rhett wouldn't be leaving would be soon enough for Mitch to befriend him. Until then, he'd keep his distance.

Carly had clearly given the idea of moving across the country to be closer to her parents careful consideration. Unless she left the boy behind, that put the terms of the will and everything Mitch held dear in jeopardy.

He had to get custody of his father's little bastard.

Soon.

He closed the dishwasher and straightened. The stillness of the backyard grabbed his attention. He scanned the garden and spotted a splash of peach and Carly's bare legs sprawled on the lawn between the fountain and the koi pond.

Alarm flooded his veins with adrenaline. Had the boy fallen in? Dammit, he'd ordered the gardener to fence the shallow pond and pool, but the custom-made materials hadn't arrived yet.

Or had Carly hurt herself dashing across the grass with her hair and her dress streaming behind her.

Mitch slammed through the back door, leaped from the porch and sprinted past Poseidon and across the grass. He rounded the roses and jerked to a halt.

Rhett lay stretched out on his belly beside Carly with his dark head near hers. Her bare arm encircled the boy's waist.

"Orange. That one's orange," Carly said, pointing at the water.

"Orange. Big," the boy warbled.

"Yes, the orange fish is big. The white one is small."

Mitch's heart jackhammered against his ribs and his lungs burned. Relief over finding them safe segued into awareness of Carly's long legs. Runner's legs. Lean, but muscled. Smooth and tanned. A charge of sexual awareness flooded him and that pissed him off. "What are you doing?"

The duo startled at his harsh tone. Keeping one hand on Rhett's waistband, Carly rolled to her side. "Looking at the fish."

Barefooted and bare-legged, with apparently no concern for the grass clippings clinging to her dress, calves and feet, Carly attracted him far more than was safe. Despite her denials, he knew damned well she was out to hook him. The way her sister had his father. The way countless other women had tried to work their way into the Kincaid beds and coffers.

Sure, Carly was more subtle and she brought a unique angle to the table. She might deny the attraction, but he'd seen the interest in her eyes when she looked at him. Like now. With her sun-streaked hair pooling like silk on the grass, her chin tilted up to expose the long line of her neck and her gaze slowly climbing his body.

Oh yeah, she wanted him.

But even without her mercenary genetics, he couldn't get

involved with her. He'd learned the hard way through both his and his father's affairs that running a business the size of KCL left no room for anything more than temporary liaisons. He'd forget to call, or miss a date, and then there would be hell to pay from the neglected woman. Too much hassle.

He'd stick with women like him who were too committed to their careers to want more than physical satisfaction now and then. The women he called didn't expect romance. They expected hot, sweaty sex. And nothing more. But even that wasn't safe with Carly Corbin.

She rolled to her feet as graceful as a cat and brushed the grass fragments from her clothing. She missed the blade stuck in her hair. Mitch fisted his hands against the urge to reach for it. For her.

"Up. Up. Pig me up," Rhett demanded. Mitch ignored him.

Carly frowned at Mitch, shook her head and bent to lift the boy. Her top gaped as she did, revealing the curves of her breasts and the dusky hint of her nipples. She wasn't wearing a bra. Need kicked Mitch in the gut.

"Want to help me give Rhett his bath?" Carly asked as she straightened.

He forced his gaze from her chest to her face. "No."

But he wouldn't mind bathing Carly, cupping her flesh with soap-slick hands and sinking into her.

Not gonna happen.

He was not like his old man who'd never learned from his mistakes. Mitch thought with the head on his shoulders and not with the one in his pants.

A woman had made a fool of him once.

It wouldn't happen again.

No matter how much he wanted this one.

"Settle him, Carly," Mitch muttered and struggled to ignore Rhett's cries as he paced his room. "C'mon, settle the boy."

Mitch's heart hammered against his ribs and his nerves stretched tight. He didn't want to get involved, but the noise from the blue suite continued to rise.

Where in the hell was Carly?

He yanked open his door and stalked down the hall. Her bedroom door stood open, but the room and bed were empty. Had she gone downstairs? Snuck out of the house for a date?

Bolted like he wanted her to?

At any other time he'd rejoice at the prospect, but not when he was alone in the house with the kid. He forced himself to turn and scan Rhett's darkened room. The glow of the new night-light illuminated the unhappy, red-faced child.

Short arms extended toward Mitch. "Bubba."

"It's okay, kid. Go back to sleep."

Rhett whimpered in response, ripping Mitch in two.

He strode into Carly's room to check the status of her clothes. If they were here, she was coming back. Before he reached the closet another sound registered. Running water. The shower. Relief mingled with disappointment. She hadn't left.

He crossed the plum carpet to the closed bathroom door and lifted his hand to pound on the panel and order her to get her ass out here and take care of the kid. An off-key voice belting out a country ballad stilled his fist and an image of Carly's wet, bare golden skin seized his mind and sent a jolt of arousal through him. The slam of his heart reverberated in his groin.

Down, boy. You can be attracted to any woman but her.

He looked over his shoulder and through the open door at the crying child. Which was the lesser of two evils?

Normally Mitch enjoyed naked women, especially wet naked women, but the genetically identical version of the Machiavellian bitch who'd screwed his father over with the oldest trick in the book was off-limits.

His life would be easier if his feelings for Carly were identical to his feelings for her twin. Marlene had left him cold and not just the day she'd calmly accepted cash to get rid of her baby as easily as she would lunch money. She'd never flipped his switch. She was a liar and a con artist who'd set out to nail herself a rich husband and pulled out all stops to achieve her goal. The boy was better off without Marlene Corbin in his life.

"Mama, Mama," Rhett wailed and Mitch winced. The kid already called Carly Mama. Would Rhett also be better off without Carly? Didn't matter. Carly Corbin's days as Rhett's guardian were numbered.

Being in the same room with Carly when she was undressed and living under his roof could open the door to all kinds of lawsuits and legal complications—if she was looking for a free ride, as he suspected. The last thing he wanted to do was give another Corbin grounds to extort more Kincaid money.

He backed away from the door, heading for the lesser of two evils. The crying child.

Rhett's breath hitched when Mitch entered the room. The boy stood in his crib and held his arms out, opening and closing his tiny hands. "Pig me up."

Mitch fisted his hands by his sides. "Hey, buddy. Carly's in the shower. She'll be here in a few minutes."

The kid's face scrunched up and his bottom lip quivered. Fresh tears oozed from his big brown eyes. Eyes the same shape and color as Carly's. "Up. Up."

Mitch remained a yard from the crib. "You have a bad dream?"

The whimper turned into a cry. The boy grasped the railing and bounced. "Up. Up."

Letting the kid get close even once would be the beginning of nothing good. But he had no choice since Carly wasn't here doing the job she'd committed to do. He shouldn't have let her talk him out of the nanny.

Wishing he could avoid it, but knowing he couldn't, Mitch

gritted his teeth and moved closer. Rhett immediately latched his arms around Mitch's neck, crushing Mitch's windpipe. Or maybe it was the memories choking him. He lifted the sturdy little body and automatically patted the diaper, checking for soggy overload. It felt dry.

The kid hiccupped and burrowed his wet face against Mitch's neck. Mitch awkwardly thumped the narrow little back, and when that didn't settle the boy, he crossed to the rocking chair and sat. Toeing the rocker into motion, Mitch tried to remain detached, tried to shut down the memories. Memories of nights with a colicky child. But he couldn't. His chest tightened with each sway of the rocker.

Soothing nonsense poured from his lips as if it had only been yesterday when he'd performed this same task for another little boy.

A boy he'd planned to adopt and claim as his own.

Rhett felt like Travis, smelled like Travis, cuddled like Travis. Same weight. Same size. Same desperate need for a father's love.

Rhett quieted and grew heavy, telling Mitch he'd drifted back to sleep. But as reluctant as Mitch had been to pick up the boy, now he didn't want to let him go.

He'd missed this. And the only way to ensure he wouldn't have to let Rhett go was to get rid of Carly Corbin.

The sooner the better.

Carly halted outside Rhett's bedroom door and blinked.

As if it weren't shocking enough to find Mitch cradling Rhett and gently stroking his back, a quiet baritone filled the room. Humming? Mitch Kincaid *humming?*

The image didn't fit the arrogant executive she'd seen over the past week and a half.

Eyes closed and with a sad expression on his face, he rested his dark head against the back of the rocker. Rhett sagged on

Mitch's bare chest with his head tucked beneath Mitch's jaw, clearly sound asleep.

Something inside Carly twisted at the sight of the big, strong man gently holding the small boy.

Why was Mitch here? Had he come in on other nights without her knowledge? Was his jerk act just that? An act? Which was the real Mitch Kincaid? The picture in front of her certainly didn't mesh with the description Marlene had provided of Everett's henchman or the emotionless robot Carly had seen so far.

Carly entered the room, and Mitch's eyes flew open.

"Is something wrong?" she whispered.

"He woke up crying. You didn't come." The accusatory tone raised her hackles.

He rose quickly and laid Rhett back in the crib. Carly pried her gaze off the bare, broad V of his back to note the care Mitch took not to jostle the child. He handled Rhett with experienced hands and tucked the blanket around him.

Interesting.

"I didn't hear him. I was showering off the stench of our evening run. I forgot to take the baby monitor into the bathroom with me."

When Mitch turned, the sight of his naked chest made her catch her breath. Oh yeah, he had a fine physique above the low waistband of his pants. Wide shoulders. Muscled arms. Washboard abs. Dark swirls of curls circled his flat nipples and painted a silky line down the center of his lean abdomen.

Dampening her suddenly dry lips, she hoped the lust percolating through her didn't show on her face.

"Don't forget next time." His sandpaper voice sounded harsh in the quiet room. He brushed past her, heading toward the door.

"You've done this before."

Mitch stopped in the hallway and slowly turned. "I told you I knew how to handle kids."

"This is the first evidence I've seen of that. Do you have children of your own who live with their mother?"

"No."

"Then where did you get your experience?"

"Leave it, Carly."

She advanced on him in the dimly lit hall. "You expect me to trust you with Rhett. Tell me why I should."

A nerve in his jaw twitched. "I was engaged to a single parent once."

"What happened?"

"She went back to her famous ex-husband." His blank expression couldn't completely mask the pain in his eyes or the husky edge to his words.

"I'm sorry." Carly reached out and gave his forearm a comforting squeeze. His skin scorched her, but she couldn't seem to pull away.

Mitch's muscles shifted beneath her palm and his chest expanded on a long, slow inhalation. His gaze met hers and desire widened his pupils. The same hunger flooded her veins.

Carly gulped. This could so not happen. Not with *him*.

"What are you doing, Carly?"

Playing with fire, that's what. But she could only shake her head and lower her hand. Too late. Electricity arced between them unbroken.

The dark green gaze dropped from her eyes to her mouth. "Is this what you want?"

Mitch hooked an arm around her waist and yanked her forward. The thin cotton of her sleep shirt and robe weren't nearly enough protection from his searing flesh. Her torso fused to his.

Mitch took her mouth roughly, the initial contact slamming his teeth against hers. She squeaked a protest, but he didn't release her. He merely changed the angle of the kiss.

Every cell in her body screamed with alarm. With arousal.

This wasn't supposed to happen. Mitch Kincaid had hurt and insulted her sister. Carly didn't even like him. How could she when he made no secret of his desire to dump her and keep Rhett locked up like a dog in quarantine?

She had every intention of shoving him away when she dug her fingers into his arm and pressed her free hand against his waist. But the moment his bare, supple skin melded to her palm her body seemed to come up with a different plan. It burned and ached and *needed,* reminding her that she hadn't been with a man in a while. And even then, making love with Sam hadn't felt like this—like a swarm of fireflies taking flight, flickering and sparking nerve endings that had previously lain dormant.

Mitch's lips parted and his tongue traced the outline of her mouth, caressing, stroking. She gasped, and he swept the inside of her bottom lip, tempting her against her will into settling against him and relaxing her jaw. Their tongues touched, intertwined.

She shouldn't be kissing him back. But his flavor filled her mouth and his musky scent invaded her lungs. Dizziness rocked her. She grappled for steady ground.

One hand mapped an upward path along his bicep to grasp his shoulder. The other spread over his back. Hard muscles flexed beneath his smooth skin.

Mitch's big hands raked her back, her waist. He cupped her buttocks and pressed her against his thickening flesh. Her internal muscles clenched and wept in appreciation of the length pressing her belly. A moan snaked up her throat.

He shoved her robe from her shoulders. It snagged at her waist. His frustrated growl filled her mouth. A quick tug and the belt gave way. Her robe parted. His hot hands found her waist through the thin fabric and raked upward. He traced the underside of her breasts with his thumbs and the air thinned.

She ought to protest, but she couldn't seem to put the

words together. She could barely think. All she could do was feel. His heat. His strength. His ravenous mouth. Lust, unlike anything she'd experienced before, rose within her. Her short nails dug into firm tissue and held on.

He palmed her breast and unerringly found her nipple, stroked it, then rolled it between his fingers. A lightning storm of desire shot straight to her core, melting her, making her heart race and her thighs quiver.

A snuffle from the crib penetrated her sensual high and shocked her back to awareness of where she was and with whom.

She ripped herself out of Mitch's arms. Gasping for air, she backed away, righted her clothing and cinched her robe around her waist like a tourniquet.

How could she be turned on by Mitch Kincaid? She knew too much about him. None of it good.

She swiped the back of her hand across her damp and still tingling lips. "That shouldn't have happened."

Mitch's nostrils flared on a sharply indrawn breath. The passion in his eyes turned to frost and his mouth twisted in derision. "Oh, c'mon, Carly. Don't act like it wasn't your plan to soften me with dinner and a sexy sundress. Screwing me is only the next step on your agenda."

"What agenda?" She had one. But it had nothing to do with sex.

"Did you and your sister have a contest going to see who could land the richest sugar daddy?"

Shock and fury and grief ripped through Carly like an explosion. She dug her nails into her palms to keep from slapping his face. "I was engaged, you moron, to an intern with student loans to rival the national debt. Not a sugar daddy. And don't blame that kiss on me. I've done nothing to attract your attention."

"Haven't you? What would you call the curve-hugging clothes, the braless sundress and the hypnotic walk?"

She had a hypnotic walk? "I don't dress suggestively."

"Give me a break. You have a damned good body and you display it like a trophy. Men probably fall at your feet."

Flattering, in an insulting kind of way. But wrong. "Are you deluded?"

"Not deluded enough to fall into your trap. Cast your line somewhere else. Because you're not landing this Kincaid." He stalked toward the stairs.

"If I landed you, Kincaid, I'd throw you back or use you for shark bait. Go to hell, you conceited jerk."

"I've already been there," Mitch growled to the empty foyer. "And you're not taking me back."

He strode down the hall, heading straight to the book-lined study—formerly his father's, but now Mitch's domain. He dragged his father's old Rolodex out of the drawer and flipped through the cards until he found the one he needed. The cool leather chair against his back did nothing to soothe his overheated skin as he punched out the cell phone number.

"Lewis Investigations," a man's voice answered on the second ring despite the late hour.

"Frank, this is Mitch Kincaid."

"Sorry to hear about your father, Mitch. Everett and I went way back."

"That's why I know I can trust you with this job." He briefly summarized the situation, and then said, "I need you to dig up dirt on Carly Corbin. I want anything that could discredit her or prove her an unfit guardian. And I need it yesterday."

The P.I. laughed. "You're definitely Everett's son. I'll get right on it. Any chance you can get me a set of fingerprints?"

He remembered the dinner dishes. "I'll get them tonight and have them couriered to you first thing tomorrow. While you're checking into Carly I want you to look into her sister, too."

"Anything in particular I'm looking for?"

"I want to know what Marlene Corbin did with the hundred grand we paid her. And I want you to see what you can find out about the hit-and-run that killed her three months ago. The police have moved the investigation to the back burner."

Mitch's fingers tightened around the receiver. He had to know the truth, and his father had sworn Frank Lewis was the soul of discretion.

"I need to know if my father was involved in her death."

Four

The rat bastard could kiss.

Carly did *not* want to know that.

She increased her speed, trying to outrun her disturbing thoughts and banish the grogginess left over from a restless night. Rhett cackled in his stroller ahead of her, loving the faster pace and the wind in his face. He pounded the squeaky horn on his toy steering wheel, shattering the stillness of the morning.

Rebound romance.

That's the only way she could explain her reaction to Kincaid's kisses. It had been three months since Sam had dumped her. When he'd learned Carly had been appointed as Rhett's guardian, her fiancé had claimed he wasn't ready for an instant family, and he'd added that he didn't want to raise someone else's brat anyway. Sam had given Carly an ultimatum, him or Rhett.

After the brat comment Carly hadn't had a choice. She couldn't love a man who refused to even try to bond with a child simply because he hadn't genetically contributed to its DNA or one who'd ask her to make that kind of sacrifice a second time. Although to his credit, Sam hadn't known about the daughter she'd given up for adoption at sixteen. She hadn't told him for fear he'd find that decision as unforgivable as her college boyfriend had.

She'd chosen her nephew over fiancé and that had been the end of her engagement. And her sex life.

Okay, so chalk up last night's fiasco to neglected hormones. But still…it was one thing to acknowledge Mitch Kincaid was good-looking and sexy. It was another to have locked lips with him and thought even for one second about jumping his bones.

But she had.

And that's why she'd taken the coward's way out this morning and gone for an early run rather than face the rat ba— Mitch—over breakfast. She couldn't look in his eyes and know he'd made her as antsy as a dog in heat. Not until she had her hormones locked back in their kennel.

Maybe she should go out on one of those dates Mitch had mentioned. She weighed the idea and discarded it. Sex with some guy she picked up in a bar or with one of the blind dates her coworker seemed determined to arrange for her just didn't appeal. She preferred a steady, monogamous relationship with her sex. And love. Or at least exceptionally strong and optimistic like.

The distant scruff of footsteps behind her pulled her out of her funk. Safety wasn't an issue here since the gated community had only one entrance, but company on her run would be surprising. She glanced over her shoulder, but a curve in the road and a lush oleander hedge blocked her view. Funny how many of the mansions were surrounded by the toxic plant. She made a point to keep Rhett's curious fingers out of reach.

If there was one thing she could count on in this very exclusive section of Miami, it was the solitude she needed to get her head together. Rich folks, she'd learned since moving into Kincaid Manor, stayed behind their tall fences. They didn't jog or stroll through the meandering, tree- and shrub-lined streets. The pricey peninsula couldn't be more different from her friendly neighborhood of culs-de-sac and block parties. She knew all of her neighbors.

She jogged in place at a hand-carved wooden Stop sign and waited for a banana-yellow Lamborghini to pass. She waved a greeting, but couldn't see through the darkly tinted windows whether or not the occupant waved back.

The nearing footsteps told her the other runner was gaining on her. She glanced back again. *Mitch*. A nearly naked Mitch. Her heart rate shot up.

He wore skimpy running shorts and shoes. Nothing else. And the view of his torso in the bright sunlight was a hundred times better than it had been in Rhett's shadowy room last night. A fitness model would envy that body, those legs, those abs, and oh, mama, those mile-wide shoulders. There wasn't an ounce of surplus fat on him. Corded muscles wrapped in tight, tanned, glistening skin, bunched and flexed with each long stride and pump of his arms as he closed the distance between them and drew up alongside her.

If not for her tight grip on the stroller handle, Carly would have fallen flat on her face—after tripping over her tongue.

"Good morning, Carly." Like her, he jogged in place. Unlike her, he wasn't winded. Or drooling. His gaze raked over her, lingering on her breasts encased in a sports bra tank before traveling to her shorts and her legs.

So much for avoiding him for a few days. She hoped he'd attribute the heat in her face to exertion and not lust—which had hit her like a hurricane the second she spotted him. His kisses had been that good.

"Morning, Mitch." Carly snapped her attention back to the road and resumed her run. He kept pace beside her.

"Don't let us keep you." *Not exactly subtle, Carly.*

"I've decided to join you and the kid when you run."

Why did she doubt it was for the pleasure of their company? "His name is Rhett."

"Bubba, bubba, bubba," Rhett singsonged.

Mitch shot ahead and turned. Jogging backward, he said, "Mitch. Not bubba. *Mitch.*"

"Mitt. Mitt. Mitt."

"Close enough." Mitch nodded and fell back in line beside her.

They covered a block in silence broken only by the slap of their shoes and the bleats of Rhett's horn. "Did your sister leave a will?"

Carly's steps faltered. "Yes. Why?"

"I'd like to see it."

"I repeat, why?"

"Because anything that concerns Rhett concerns me. I am, after all, his brother. You're only his aunt."

Worry twisted her stomach. The attorney had promised the hastily scribbled will was valid. But he was a small-time attorney and not one of the high-profile types the Kincaids probably kept on retainer. "Half brother. Marlene's will was handwritten, but notarized and completely legal."

"Then you have no reason not to share it."

She couldn't stop him from getting a copy. Cooperating would probably be for the best. "I'll tell my lawyer you want a copy."

"I'd prefer to see the original."

Her nerves snarled tighter. "Why?"

"To make sure the document is valid."

He was going to challenge her right to Rhett. It was all she could do to keep putting one foot in front of the other. "It is."

"Find a renter for your house yet?" he asked before she could get past her panic.

"No."

"Are you comfortable leaving it vacant?"

If his goal was to ruin her run, he'd succeeded. "My neighbors will keep an eye on it for me."

"You trust them that much?"

"I do."

"You might want to consider a security system."

"I can't afford one."

"You could. Just say the word."

"If I moved back home, I wouldn't need a security system." Carly usually ran farther, but she couldn't stomach more of Mitch's company this morning. She took a sharp right at the intersection without warning and headed back toward the manor.

Mitch's steps echoed hers, and he tracked her back toward the house. "Running from something, Carly?"

Yes. You. She glanced at him. "I need to go into work early this morning."

A lone dark eyebrow hiked as if he recognized the lie for what it was. But she didn't care. Mitch wasn't interested in his half brother's well-being. All he cared about was the billions of bucks Rhett represented.

Carly needed to call her attorney and find out if Mitch had any chance at all of stealing her precious nephew. If he did, then renting her house wasn't going to be an issue, because she'd have to sell it and use the equity to pay the legal fees.

Mitch Kincaid seemed determined to screw up hers and Rhett's lives. And Carly was just as determined to stop him.

No matter what the cost.

"Fax coming through," Frank Lewis's voice said through the cell phone line. "You're not going to like it."

Mitch tossed his keys into the porcelain bowl on the credenza. "Why?"

"Because Carlene Corbin is squeaky-clean."

"Nobody's that clean. How far back did you go?"

"Eighteen. Want me to look further? Check for a juvenile record?"

"Yes."

"It'll take some time to crack sealed records."

"I'll wait. What about the other matter?"

"I used my connections to get what the police had on the sister's accident. Nothing of interest so far. No flags on your father."

Mitch exhaled in relief. "Good. Keep looking."

"Everett wasn't Mafia, Mitch."

Mitch entered the study and closed the door. As predicted, the fax machine spewed pages. "No, but we both know you didn't cross him. Marlene Corbin backed Dad into a corner. He would have come out swinging. And he wouldn't plan to lose the fight."

"I hear you. I'm on it. Read the fax. Give me a call if anything rings your chimes."

"Will do. Thanks, Frank." He disconnected, retrieved the report and scanned the pages, noting Carly's University of Florida, Gainesville, education, her steady work history and her broken engagement. Something niggled at him as he settled in his leather desk chair. He reread until he nailed the odd part.

She'd graduated from high school at nineteen when many kids did so at seventeen or eighteen. That wasn't too unusual. Had she missed the age cutoff for entering school? Repeated a grade? He double-checked her birth date. July 9. She hadn't missed the age cutoff. Probably nothing, but he'd get Frank on it.

She'd had a long-term relationship with one man in college, and she'd been engaged until recently to another. What had happened to the college boyfriend and the ex-fiancé?

A knock on the door yanked him away from those intriguing questions. He opened a drawer and shoved the fax inside. "Yes?"

The knob turned and the oak panel opened. Carly filled the gap. She had Rhett on her hip and judging by her purple tracksuit had just returned from work.

"Mitt," the kid screamed and beamed and waved.

A stab of something, probably a hunger pain, jabbed Mitch in the midsection. He jerked a nod. "Hi, kid."

Carly stepped into the study. "Della needed another day. I can have dinner ready in about an hour. Will that work for you?"

"That makes three days off."

"Get over yourself, Kincaid. She's trying to take care of her sister, not going out of her way to inconvenience you. And I told her to take as long as she needed."

He gritted his teeth over Carly interfering with household matters. *Keep your eye on the goal. Get the kid. Get rid of the aunt.* "We'll go out to dinner."

Refusal tightened Carly's features and stung Mitch's pride. Women didn't turn down his invitations. "I just picked up Rhett from day care. Lucy said he was teething and cranky today. I'm not going to leave him with a sitter."

"We'll take him with us."

Carly's brown eyes narrowed suspiciously. "You want to eat out with Mr. Messy even knowing he's likely to be fussy?"

He'd rather have a vasectomy without anesthetic. "We have to eat, Carly. And you've worked all day. You shouldn't have to cook."

Most women would fall all over themselves to be accommodating. Carly deliberated for nearly sixty seconds, and the lack of enthusiasm on her face wasn't flattering.

"Give me ten minutes. And don't make reservations for some swanky place. Make sure it's family-friendly. Rhett will need a high chair." She left, closing the door behind her.

Mitch steepled his fingers and tapped his chin. Earlier today his lawyer had informed him Marlene's will was airtight. Not only had the document been written in her handwriting, the writing of the one-line testament had been witnessed by two bank employees who knew her well.

> I leave everything I hold dear, my possessions, my assets and my beloved son, Rhett, to my sister, Carlene Leah Corbin, because she'll be a better mother to my son than even I could be.

In an overkill move, Marlene had had the thing notarized. Had she taken such drastic moves because she'd feared Everett's rage?

Mitch had never seen his father as livid as he'd been that day in late January when Marlene Corbin had brought her eight-month-old son to the house to meet his daddy. Everett's fury hadn't abated during the month of February while they'd awaited the DNA test results. And then on the first of March Marlene was dead. His father's only comment, "Good riddance," had been heartfelt.

Had his father stooped to murder? Mitch shrugged to ease the knot of tension cramping between his shoulder blades. He'd know soon enough. And then he'd deal with it.

But for now, contesting Marlene's will was out.

He retrieved the fax and resumed reading, but found nothing else of value. True to her word, Carly returned ten minutes later. She'd changed into a short white denim skirt that displayed the length of her legs and a sleeveless wraparound red knit top that clung to her breasts and narrow waist.

She looked good. Good enough to momentarily distract him from his plan. Forcing his head back into the game, Mitch rose and escorted her outside. She headed for her car, he for his.

She stopped in the driveway. "The car seat's in my car."

He eyed the minivan without anticipation and held out his hand for her keys. "I'll drive."

"My car? I don't think so." She turned away and leaned into the backseat to strap the boy in.

Mitch's eyes zeroed in on the curve of her butt, and he almost said to hell with dinner. He didn't like being attracted to his unwanted houseguest. But eating alone wouldn't get him anywhere. After the way she'd kissed him two nights ago, he needed to get her out of the picture. Fast. Or he'd end up no better than his father. Hooked by a Corbin.

Biting back his objections, he pried his gaze from her rear end, rounded the hood and climbed into the front passenger seat. It had been seven days since she'd moved in. He'd expected to see some sign of discontent by now. When would the craving for her single lifestyle kick in? When would she start feeling tied down by her sister's kid?

Waiting for Carly to grow tired of caring for the boy was moving too slowly. He needed faster results.

She settled in the driver's seat, buckled up and turned the key. Mitch checked her ring finger and noted a faint pale indentation he hadn't noticed before. He waited until she'd cleared the guardhouse before asking, "What happened to your engagement?"

Carly braked a little too hard at the stoplight, jolting him forward. He braced a hand on the dash. "It ended. Where are we going?"

"Head toward the bay side of South Beach. Why did your engagement end?"

She shot him a guarded glance. "Sam wasn't ready for a family."

And she came with one. Unless she dumped the kid. "That's a circumstance easily remedied, Carly."

Her fingers strangled the steering wheel and her glare made it clear she'd rather wrap them around his neck. The light turned green and she punched the gas. "Oh for pity's sake. Would you get off that horse? I'm not giving up Rhett."

"You must have loved Sam. You were engaged for two years."

Her throat worked as she swallowed. She kept her eyes straight ahead. "I'm not going to ask how you know that. But, yes, I did. I stopped the day he asked me to walk away from Rhett."

Mitch bit back a curse as another avenue closed. But when faced with a roadblock, he'd learned to search for an alternate route.

If Carly was as squeaky-clean as the P.I. reported, then he'd have to find another way to get custody of the boy. But how could he win her over? How could he gain her trust?

Seduction? The idea shot across his mind like a comet.

He weighed the possibility, and his pulse quickened and his palms tingled the way they did whenever he had a winning plan.

Could he deliberately seduce Carly and win her trust, then stab her in the back by taking the kid?

Guilt punched him a time or two, but he ignored it. It would be nothing more than doing to Carly what her sister had done to his father. Marlene had set up his father, then taken something from him.

Mitch had to carry out his father's last wishes or lose his and his siblings' inheritance. If that meant he had to blur the lines of decency, then so be it. The boy would be well cared for, and no one would be hurt in the long run.

The kiss had proved he and Carly were physically compatible. He studied the curve of her breasts, her narrow waist and the length of her toned legs, and arousal buzzed through his veins.

Sharing her bed wouldn't be a hardship. But how far would he have to go?

As far as it takes.

He'd even marry her if he had to and adopt the child. When the marriage ended, he'd have custody of the kid and Carly would have a healthy bank account.

A win-win situation.

* * *

"He looks just like you, Mitch, except he has Carly's eyes."

Carly opened her mouth to correct the woman Mitch had introduced as a member of his yacht club, but Mitch cut her off.

"Rhett definitely has his mother's eyes."

"Don't tell me Miami's most eligible bachelor is finally going to settle down?" the anorexic, overly tanned, forty-something blonde asked.

Mitch gave her an enigmatic smile and a slight shrug.

Carly wanted to kick him under the table. What was he trying to pull?

To Carly she said, "Kudos, my dear. You have accomplished a miracle."

Carly stiffened at the implication that she'd landed Mitch. Or that she'd even want to. "I—"

"Thanks for stopping by, Sandra," Mitch interrupted. "Tell William I said hello."

"I will. And again, I am sorry about Everett. It's great seeing you, Mitch, and meeting you and your adorable little one, Carly. Ta ta." The skinny body slinked away.

Ta ta? Who said *ta ta* these days? But Carly had bigger fish to fry. "What on earth were you thinking? You let her believe Rhett was yours. And mine."

The idea of having Mitch's baby made her stomach churn.

Mitch glanced at Rhett, who had almost finished smearing and eating his dinner. "You said the kid had a short attention span. Do you really want to waste time explaining this convoluted mess my father and your sister left behind when we could be finishing our meal before he has the meltdown you predicted?"

"No. But—"

"Forget it, Carly. Sandra isn't worth the worry."

"But you lied."

"Replay every word I said. I never lied. She assumed. I

didn't correct her, nor did I confirm her speculations. Give it a rest. The media frenzy my father's death created is just beginning to die down. I'd rather not jump-start it with the kind of scandal his illegitimate child will create. That'll happen soon enough."

Media frenzy. She suppressed a shudder.

She hated that Mitch was right almost as much as she hated that he'd chosen the perfect restaurant and been completely charming and polite throughout the meal. He'd even smiled at Rhett a couple of times.

But he'd been nothing but distrustful and acerbic before tonight, and that made her wary. "Why the chameleon act?"

A dark eyebrow lifted. "I beg your pardon?"

"Why are you being nice?"

"You've stated your case. You're not going to give up the bo—Rhett. That means we will be sharing a roof for the next fifty-plus weeks. No reason why we can't do so amicably."

"I stated my case the day we met. Nothing's changed."

"I thought you'd change your mind. Now I realize you won't. We'll make the best of our alliance." He wiped his mouth and laid his napkin beside his plate. "Would you care for dessert?"

She blinked at the sudden switch in topic. An inkling of suspicion wiggled like an earthworm inside her. Leopards didn't change their spots. Or so the cliché said. And clichés were clichés for a reason. They were usually true.

Mitch had to be up to something. The question was what?

But even more worrisome, Carly had actually enjoyed Mitch's company tonight. She'd better watch herself, because he was still the same rat bastard who'd hurt her sister and had recently threatened Carly's custody of Rhett.

Letting her guard down around Mitch Kincaid wouldn't be a smart move.

Five

Wooing a woman he didn't like but wanted to sleep with was a unique experience for Mitch.

Carly was too smart to fall for the usual bought-without-a-thought generic bouquet or jewelry trinket. Lucky for him, his personal assistant, Marie, knew where to find the right ammo.

Mitch rounded the house with Carlos, the Kincaid Manor groundskeeper, and two large potted plants on hand trucks. Carly looked up from Rhett on his new riding toy. She said something and the kid looked Mitch's way, then abandoned his wheels to scamper over.

The huge grin on the boy's face hit Mitch in the solar plexus with memories of other grins, other kids who'd been happy to see him back in the days when he used to rush home from KCL in time for dinner instead of working until the cleaning crew ran him out of his office. Kids who'd moved from Miami to Los Angeles and out of reach when their father had been traded to a west coast basketball team.

"What's up, little man?" He released the hand truck and extended a hand for a high five, but Rhett bypassed it and twined himself around Mitch's pant leg and stuck like a thorny vine.

Carly followed at a slower pace. Today's tracksuit matched the blue sky above. She'd shed the jacket, and her white tank top hugged the curve of her breasts. Her hair had been released from its usual ponytail to drape her bare shoulders, and a breeze lifted the strands away from her face. How had he never noticed that she didn't wear earrings? Her lobes weren't even pierced, and he found the naked, virgin flesh unusually alluring. Did he even know another woman who didn't have at least one hole in each ear?

Carly nodded to Carlos as she joined them. "What are those?"

"Bud-something. To attract hummingbirds." Odd how tight his throat was this afternoon. He patted the head bumping his thigh.

"Buddleia. That's not what I meant. I know what a butterfly bush is. I have three in my yard. Why do *you* have them?"

"You said the—Rhett liked to watch hummingbirds. These should draw them, since the feeders alone didn't do the trick."

"Up. Up. Pig me up."

Mitch couldn't shake the kid off and he lost a few leg hairs trying. Admitting defeat, he bent and scooped the boy into one arm, and earned himself a slobbery kiss on the chin.

"Mitt."

Mitch swallowed. Hard. He wasn't ready yet to let Rhett squeeze his heart with those stubby little fingers.

Hands on hips, Carly stared at him through narrowed eyes. "Why?"

"I gave you the reason." He passed the kid to Carly and turned to the other man. "Carlos, set one pot on each corner of the patio."

Carly persisted, "And I might believe that was your only motive if you hadn't bought Rhett a wading pool yesterday and the riding toy the day before that."

"The plastic pool is to keep him away from the big pool. And he loves that blue train."

Carly cocked her head. "Have any Greeks in your ancestry?"

"As in, 'Beware of Greeks bearing gifts'?"

"Yes."

"Haven't you ever heard, 'Don't look a gift horse in the mouth'?"

"I also know that one end of the horse bites and the other one kicks. I'm still trying to figure out which end you are. I'll tell Della you're home for dinner. She wasn't expecting you." She turned on her heel and marched through the French doors.

Shot down. Again. He'd known Carly would be a tough nut to crack. He even admired her intelligence in not accepting the gifts at face value because he did have an ulterior motive.

He shoved his hand truck into motion. What would it take to get through to her? And why did it suddenly matter so much?

"Buy you a drink?"

The quietly rumbled question broke the hard-won silence. Carly pivoted away from the crib and jerked a finger to her lips. "Shh."

Mitch leaned against the doorjamb of Rhett's room. Since they'd eaten out together last Friday, Mitch had shown up for breakfast and dinner each of the past seven days. Given Della said Mitch had rarely made it home for evening meals before Carly and Rhett had moved in, Carly had to question the sudden change. And while she was suspicious, she didn't want to rock the boat because dining with him furthered her goal of bonding the brothers. Rhett loved "Mitt's" company.

Unfortunately, so did she.

She joined Mitch in the hall. Once her eyes adjusted to the brighter light, she noticed he'd exchanged his suit for a black polo shirt, a pair of worn jeans that fit him like a designer glove and leather deck shoes. It might be the Fourth of July and a national holiday, but Mitch had gone to work.

"Rough night." The low midnight pitch of his voice made the hairs on her arms lift.

"Rhett's new molar is giving him fits. I gave him Tylenol hoping that'll help him sleep through the night." Rhett had been exceptionally fussy during dinner. Mitch had stuck out the entire miserable hour which had a) earned him points with her, and b) proved they'd made progress. And then her nephew had been nearly impossible to settle for bed.

"A glass of wine might help you unwind enough to sleep. Join me on the patio." Mitch pointed to the baby monitor in her hand. "We'll take that with us."

The wine sounded good, but a voice in her head shouted, "Not wise." She nibbled the inside of her bottom lip in indecision. Just because she'd begun to enjoy their shared meals and verbal sparring, and just because she'd learned to tell the difference between Armani, Brooks Brothers and Hugo Boss, and just because Mitch looked mouthwateringly gorgeous in all three didn't mean she'd do something stupid like fall for him. Thanks to Marlene, she knew too much about him to ever do that.

Which meant she could safely join him for a drink.

"Okay, sure." She hooked the monitor on her waistband and walked beside him down the hall, the stairs and into the kitchen. He snagged a bottle, a couple of glasses and the corkscrew from the counter and tilted his head toward the back door.

Carly opened it and stepped outside. The flagstones radiated remnants of the day's warmth against her bare feet. The patio glowed in the flickering light of the dozen pewter pole torches surrounding the area, and the scents of citronella oil and the sweet aroma of the butterfly bushes mingled in the humid night air.

"You must have been pretty confident I'd join you to light all these."

"I know I needed a drink after dinner. I assumed you would, as well."

She sighed. "You assumed right. Rhett's not usually like that."

"I know." He guided her toward a plushly cushioned seating arrangement where a candle's flame reflected off a small gift-wrapped box resting on the rectangular coffee table.

Carly stared at the package while the man who'd lured her into the moonlight opened and poured the wine. She didn't sit. The setting was far too romantic. Second thoughts crept over her. She shouldn't have come out here with him. Standing awkwardly beside the love seat, she wondered how quickly she could guzzle her wine and make her escape.

He offered a filled goblet. "To two successful weeks as housemates."

She accepted the glass and chinked the rim against his. "May there be fifty more."

For Rhett's sake.

Did she imagine Mitch's eyes narrowing slightly as he drank? He lowered his glass and inclined his head to indicate the gift on the table. "It's for you."

Stalling, she sipped the reddish-colored beverage and shifted on her feet. She'd never been much of a wine drinker, and she certainly wasn't a connoisseur, but this vintage could become a habit.

Wine, moonlight, gifts. Watch it.

"It's not my birthday." Not yet. But soon. And she dreaded waking up Wednesday and knowing Marlene wouldn't be here to share their special day.

"Doesn't matter. Open it." When she made no move to do so he picked up the box, offered it to her and repeated, "Open it, Carly."

Presents meant nothing to him, she reminded herself. So

why did her heart quicken and her body flush over finding a golden-wrapped package for her? Stupid, really.

He had money to burn and he burned it. He'd come home with something for Rhett each day this week. Not that he was spoiling his half brother. Each gift had been something so appropriate and well thought out she'd begun to suspect Mitch might be a decent guy under his expensively tailored wolf's clothing. He'd even bought a car seat for his SUV, claiming that he could get away from the office more easily than she could cancel her appointments if Rhett should ever need an emergency pickup from day care.

She took another healthy swig of the wine, letting the fruity liquid roll around on her tongue before swallowing. She accepted the package, weighed it in her palm and debated the intelligence of accepting a present from a man she had previously considered the enemy. But she wanted to maintain the recent goodwill between them. If the gift was inappropriate, she'd simply refuse to accept it.

She set down her goblet and slipped a fingernail under the tape. Hyperconscious of Mitch's unwavering gaze on her trembling hands, she carefully loosened the foil paper to reveal a square blue velvet box and then flipped open the hinged lid.

Resting on a bed of white velvet, an inch-long golden charm in the shape of a boy hung from a delicate rope chain. Mitch reached out and flipped the charm over. RHETT had been engraved down the center of the back.

Her resistance melted. She could have refused just about anything else. But this…this was perfect. "It's lovely. I— thank you, Mitch."

He took the box from her, removed the necklace and opened the clasp, but instead of walking behind her the way most people would to assist, he stepped closer and raised the ends of the chain to her shoulders.

The warmth of his fingertips brushed her jaw and tunneled beneath her ponytail. She shivered at the featherlight scrape of his short nails on her nape, and then the cool metal settled on her skin.

His palms rested on her shoulders as he studied the jewelry he'd hung around her neck. Electricity flowed from his flesh to hers. "You're good with him."

She shrugged, but the movement didn't dislodge his hands. "It's easy to be."

"Even tonight?"

Carly wrinkled her nose and tilted her head back to look up into that too handsome face. "Tonight wasn't as easy as most, but it's not his fault his gums hurt, and it's not hard to forgive someone when you love them."

Several miles away, the dark sky exploded with color. Seconds later, a muffled series of booms reached her. Fireworks to celebrate the holiday.

Mitch didn't even glance at the light show. He dragged a fingertip down the chain to where the charm rested between her breasts just above the scooped neck of her tank top. Desire arched through her, igniting her skin and tightening her lungs. She tried to tamp down the unexpected and unwanted response, but instead, the memory of how he'd kissed her last week and how he'd touched her made her mouth water and her nipples peak.

Sexual tension hung between them as hot and heavy as the damp night air, and sensation exploded within her like the distant pyrotechnics. The muffled reverberations vibrated along her spine.

Move away, Carly.

But her feet remained planted. Her toes curled on the flagstones. Mitch's grip on her shoulder tightened, and that lone finger trailed back up the chain. He brushed a stray lock of hair out of the way and traced the shape of her ear, fingering the lobe. Carly shuddered. She'd never realized how sensitive her ears could be. Her pulse ba-ba-boomed. Hard. Fast. Insistent.

"You feel it, too," he murmured huskily.

She played stupid, because it was the smart thing to do. "Feel what?"

He lowered his chin and gave her the kind of don't-mess-with-me look that probably sent his employees running for cover. "You know what. The desire. The pull. The connection."

She didn't like knowing she wasn't alone in her insanity. "That doesn't mean we have to act on it."

Another volley of lights and bangs lit the cloudless night sky.

"Why shouldn't we?" His deep voice rippled across her nerve endings, and he lowered his head. His lips feathered over hers, lifted and returned once, twice, each caress as gentle as a butterfly touching down on a blossom.

Carly's muscles locked and her breath lodged in her chest. Awareness ignited below her navel like a lit fuse. She balled her hands against the urge to yank him closer and deepen the kiss.

The big hand on her shoulder shifted to cradle her face and angle her head, and like a mannequin, she let him move her any way he pleased. His mouth opened over hers. He sucked her bottom lip between his. The sharp nip of his teeth sent a bolt of desire through her and surprised a gasp from her.

C'mon, Carly, move away.

And still she couldn't seem to break the connection. Her lips parted and his tongue sought hers. Slick, hot, seductive. She tasted wine and Mitch and a hunger so intense she could barely stand.

Oh, this was a mistake. A big one. No doubt about it.

Mitch's fingers speared through her hair, releasing and discarding her clip, holding her captive. The cool, loosened strands rained down on her shoulders. His other arm banded around her waist, bringing her body into hot, searing contact with his from the knees up. She tried to save herself by leaning back, but that only pressed their pelvises tighter together. His arousal swelled and lengthened against her hip bone, and an answering need swirled inside her.

Oh, mama. Another barrage of booms came across the water and bounced off the stone walls of Kincaid Manor to seemingly pound her from both directions. Or maybe it was her reaction to Mitch hammering her senses.

Getting physically involved with him was wrong on so many levels. But it—*he*—felt so right. His kisses consumed her. His touch inflamed her. Her fingers found his hair, twining in the thick, soft strands. She kissed him back with everything she had. A vibration of approval slid up his throat and down hers to settle low in her belly.

She'd stop in a minute. Before this got out of hand.

But for the moment he made her feel wanted and feminine and desirable in a way that Sam's desertion had stolen from her. Mitch's mouth worked magic on hers. One big hand swept the length of her back and then molded the curve of her bottom.

She finally admitted something her grief over losing Marlene hadn't allowed her to acknowledge. Her broken engagement had battered her ego; Mitch's attention was not only arousing, it was healing to her wounded spirit.

The steam of Mitch's breath on her cheek drew her out of her dark thoughts. She splayed a hand over his pounding heart and lost herself in the baby-soft cotton fabric of his shirt, in the strength of the muscle-packed body against hers and in the flood of his scent, his heat, his flavor.

Boom. Boom. Boom. Her heart echoed the fireworks.

She knew enough about herself to understand this rush of hormones was temporary. As temporary as it was unwise to let herself trust Mitch Kincaid. Once before, she'd allowed herself to get swept away on a whirlwind of desire, and she'd regretted it ever since.

Pulse racing, she reluctantly eased back and wiggled

free of his embrace. From the safer distance of several feet away, she locked gazes with him and took a moment to catch her breath.

His pupils had expanded to almost obliterate the green of his irises, and in the flickering torchlight, dark swipes of color painted his cheekbones. His chest rose and fell as rapidly as hers, and he fisted and released his hands by his side. The hunger on his face sent concussions of want through her. But she resisted throwing herself back into his arms. Barely.

She licked her lips, savoring his taste one last time, and endeavored to shut down this runaway train. "We should forget that ever happened."

His damp lips parted and his eyebrows shot up. "Forget it?"

"It shouldn't have happened, Mitch. Our lives are complicated enough without this." She fluttered a hand to indicate the two of them.

"What's complicated? We share a house, a child and some phenomenal chemistry. Why not share a bed?"

He made it sound so logical. So tempting. "I'm not ready for another relationship."

Mitch's shoulders squared, and his lips compressed. He closed the distance between them, stalking her like a predator does prey. Carly backed up until the wrought-iron chair against her calves stopped her.

"You're the one who forced your way into my house and insinuated yourself into my life."

Before she could escape, his hands lifted and captured her face. He took her mouth roughly, all aggravated, aroused and determined male.

At first, she was too stunned by the barely leashed violence she felt in him to react. And then she flattened her palms against his chest, intending to push him away, but despite the untamed plunder of her mouth, his hands remained gentle on her face. The gentleness got to her. She'd never experienced this kind of pure, unadulterated need. And in that moment of hesitation, the raw hunger of his kiss weakened her resistance.

His hands caressed her face, her hair, her back, her waist. And against caution and common sense, her body responded. Her muscles weakened, her head tipped back allowing him deeper access. Her skin grew hypersensitive to his touch, and her panties moistened. When his thumb found her nipple her breath hitched and arrows of desire hit a target deep inside her.

Instead of shoving him away her fingers fisted in his shirt, then her grip slid upward and clung to the broad beam of his shoulders. She shouldn't be doing this, but at the moment she couldn't remember why and didn't care.

Mitch abruptly released her and set her away almost roughly. Chest heaving, nostrils flaring, he glared at her. "Forget the passion between us if you can, Carly. I sure as hell won't."

And then he stormed inside, leaving Carly alone with her hunger and her doubts and her self-recriminations. A shrill whistle of sound and light split the sky followed by the grand finale of the fireworks exhibition. Carly watched without awe or excitement. Her mind was occupied elsewhere.

What had happened to her vow to keep her distance?

What about Marlene? It seemed disloyal to want the man who'd been so cruel to her sister. And yet Mitch had had Carly clinging and all but begging.

If he'd truly been the untrustworthy rat bastard Marlene described, wouldn't Mitch have taken what he wanted?

Was it possible her sister had exaggerated...or lied?

Six

Forget his kiss? Like hell she would. He wouldn't let her.

Mitch charged downstairs Saturday morning determined to stick to Carly like barnacles on a ship's bottom. If she refused his company, he'd simply insist on spending time with the kid. Where Rhett went, Carly followed.

The sounds of laughter and high-pitched childish gibberish reached him as he neared the kitchen. It had been three and a half years since he'd said goodbye to Travis and Ashley. Would the haunting memories of what he'd lost ever go away? He stopped on the threshold.

The kid spotted him and smiled around a mouthful of food. "Mitt."

A pain clutched Mitch's stomach. *A hunger pain.* He entered the room and paused behind Carly's chair. "Hello, squirt. Mrs. Duncan. Carly."

He rested a hand on Carly's shoulder. She stiffened and her

silky ponytail twitched and swished across his knuckles, but she kept her eyes on her oatmeal. "Morning, Mitch."

"Good morning, sir. I'll have your breakfast in a jiffy."

"Thank you." He circled the table, entering Carly's field of vision and catching a glimpse of desire in her chocolate eyes before she quickly averted her face. His pulse revved in response. "Sleep well?"

Her throat worked as she swallowed. "Yes. Thank you."

"Liar." He lowered his voice so Mrs. Duncan couldn't hear him and earned himself a scowl. The faint circles under Carly's eyes told the truth.

At least he wasn't the only one who'd been miserable. He was still kicking himself for almost losing control last night. He'd never had a problem reining in his hunger before. No meant no. The fact that he'd come so close to overriding Carly's objections and taking what he wanted—what he'd made her want—right there on the patio alarmed him.

Bulldozing over others had been his father's MO. Not Mitch's. Everett Kincaid may have been a brilliant business-man, but he'd been a hurricane in his personal life, leaving a trail of destruction wherever he passed. The Kincaid money broom had always managed to sweep up the debris.

Until Marlene Corbin had come along. And now Mitch had to deal with her twin. Identical DNA. Identical risk.

Still, there was a fine line between seduction and coercion—a line Mitch had no intention of crossing. Morning-after regrets and recriminations were hell to deal with. He'd leave Carly no recourse to cry foul. When she came to him she would do so will-ingly, and not in a passing bout of insane passion. He'd keep this affair, their marriage and their eventual divorce strictly legal.

His father hadn't always cared on which side of the law he walked, but Mitch cared.

"I didn't hear Rhett get up last night," he said to force her to look at him, but paused before adding, "Despite the fireworks."

The flush on her cheeks told him she hadn't missed the double entendre. They'd definitely set off their own personal pyrotechnics. She blinked, hiked her chin and took in his casual clothing. "He slept through the night. You're not going to the office today?"

"I'm spending the entire day with my brother." He lowered himself into the chair directly across from her.

"Will he be around later? I'd like for Rhett to meet Rand."

"I meant Rhett."

Her lips parted and her breasts lifted when she inhaled. Her expression turned guarded. "Rhett and I have plans."

He wouldn't let her shake him off that easily. "Change them."

"I can't."

"Then you'll have company."

"I don't think—"

"To borrow your phrase, Carly, this one's nonnegotiable. You haven't been reticent about your desire for me to spend time with Rhett. I've cleared my schedule for the weekend. He's my priority."

A mix of emotions crossed her face, but the last one, a mischievous twitch of her delectable lips, made him uneasy.

"Okay. We're leaving at eight-thirty." She rose to refill the kid's sippy cup, giving Mitch an opportunity to appreciate the shape of her breasts in a red tank top and her incredible legs below the hem of her blue running shorts.

"You've already had your run?"

"Yes."

"Tomorrow I'll join you."

"We go at six." Her tone implied she hoped that was too early for him.

"I'll be ready."

Mrs. Duncan set his breakfast in front of him. He nodded his thanks, then checked his watch and refocused on Carly.

"If you're going to take a shower before we leave, you'd better get started."

"Rhett hasn't finished eating."

"We'll feed the rug rat."

She looked from him to Mrs. Duncan. "You're sure?"

"Got it covered," Mitch replied before the housekeeper could respond.

Carly looked ready to argue, but instead shrugged. "I won't be long."

She left the kitchen. Mitch looked at Mrs. Duncan. "Do you have a spare apron?"

If his question surprised her, she hid it well. "Yes, sir. I'll get it."

The kid had been fed and hosed off by the time Carly returned with the diaper bag on her shoulder twenty-five minutes later. Her hair draped her shoulders like damp sun-streaked silk, and makeup covered the evidence of her lack of sleep. She'd changed into a lemon-yellow T-shirt and a midthigh-length khaki skirt and white sandals. She looked good. Damned good.

She scooped up Rhett from the living-room floor where Mitch had parked him with a toy truck. "Let me change him and then we can go."

"Done." Mitch never went into any battle without a winning strategy. Diaper duty always scored big points with women.

She stopped in her tracks. "Della changed him?"

"I did. We'll take my car." He led the way to the foyer.

"How old were your fiancée's children?"

Not a conversation he wanted to pursue. "One and four when we moved in together. What's on the agenda for today?"

"And what age when you split?" She ignored his question.

"Two and a half years older. Where are we headed?" He opened the front door and changed the subject.

"Hialeah. Wow. That must have been hard. What were their names?"

He gritted his teeth. "Travis and Ashley. What's in Hialeah?"

"Tina, one of my coworkers, lives there."

The sun shone in a cloudless blue sky. It was early, but the day promised to be a July scorcher. He opened the front and back passenger-side doors and then circled to the driver's side to prevent more questions. By the time Carly strapped Rhett into his new car seat and joined Mitch up front, he had the radio on and the sunroof open. The combination of music and wind noise guaranteed to make conversation difficult.

"Address?"

She recited the info. He typed it into his GPS, which eliminated the need for directions, and set the car in motion. Sure, he'd have to endure a visit with one of Carly's coworkers, but then he'd have her to himself for the rest of the day.

His confidence lasted until he saw half-dozen minivans lining the street and the Mylar balloons attached to the mailbox bearing the street address she'd given him.

"It's a birthday party," he said flatly.

The mischievous twinkle returned to Carly's eyes and the corners of her lips curled up, revealing her enjoyment of his predicament. Her smile had the usual effect of hitting him in the solar plexus.

"For Tina's five-year-old twin sons. Don't say I didn't try to warn you."

Damn. Not the day of seduction he had in mind, but he could roll with the change in plans. The party would last an hour or two, and then he'd be back on schedule. He parked his SUV between two mom-mobiles and tried to conceal his lack of enthusiasm. He'd endured kids' parties before. Hell, he'd planned them. The only guarantees were noise and mess.

Carly ignored the concrete walk leading to the front door of the modest two-story structure and carried Rhett around the side of the house. She pushed open a tall wooden gate, revealing a backyard filled with a couple dozen kids of various ages and half as many moms and set the boy on his feet. Rhett toddled into the melee full steam ahead. Not a shy bone in that boy's stubby body.

Balls of every size, shape and color dotted the patchy lawn and kids raced and swarmed like insects. A wooden swing set with a tree house on one end took up one back corner of the lot. An inflatable bounce castle had been set up in another. Mitch scanned the area for a father, but there wasn't a single male over seven in sight.

"Hey, mister, catch." A football came hurtling toward his head from the left. He caught it one-handed and passed it back.

The gathering of women on the back deck turned in unison. Eyebrows rose, mouths dropped open. Mitch followed Carly across the grass and forced a smile to his lips.

Carly would soon discover that, compliments of his father, Mitch detested being set up to fail.

But he'd have his revenge.

Carly's plan had backfired.

She'd allowed Mitch to horn in on her outing to teach him a lesson. Instead, she'd been the one who'd learned something. For someone she'd believed didn't like children, he'd handled himself and the rambunctious boys very well.

Oh sure, the look of horror on his face when he'd realized they were attending a children's birthday party had been priceless. But his dismay hadn't lasted long.

Within minutes Mitch had charmed the mothers in the group, and then he'd gone to work on the younger set. He'd taken charge of the older boys and organized them into one game right after another for the past ninety minutes, earning him a never-ending stream of accolades from the other women present.

Carly just wanted to go home and get away from the sight of Mitch having fun and the rumble of his voice and his laughter. The combination was doing a number on her concentration. A fact her hostess hadn't missed, if the curious glances were any indication.

Speak of the devil…

Tina plopped down on the picnic bench beside Carly. "You should have told me you were dating again. I would have quit throwing men at you."

Carly looked up from the small pop-up tent where Rhett played beside Tina's two-year-old daughter. Carly had known Tina for six years, and if there was anyone she could trust with the story of Rhett's parentage, it was the coworker who'd taken Carly under her wing on Carly's first day on the job at the sports medicine practice. Tina was ten years older but a hundred years wiser.

"I'm not dating. Mitch is Rhett's half brother."

Tina's blue eyes went wide.

"But keep their relationship to yourself, okay? The press would make a big deal of it. I'm sorry for springing him on you, but he wanted to spend the day with Rhett, and he wouldn't take no for an answer. I tried to call—"

"But one of the twins knocked the phone off the hook and I wasn't carrying my cell phone. It's okay, Carly. Mitch is dessert for those of us who can't have cake and ice cream." Tina glanced over her shoulders to make sure none of the other mothers were within hearing range. "I can't believe it. Rhett's one of the more-money-than-God Kincaids?"

Carly nodded. "I didn't tell you because Marlene asked me to keep it quiet until after Rhett was born and she'd worked things out with Everett. But she died before she and Everett could come to an agreement, and then three months later Everett died. I've been a little crazy trying to sort out everything."

"But you did, right? Renting your house isn't an attempt to clear up a financial mess Marlene left behind, is it? I mean, it was one thing when she moved in and started mooching off you, but—"

"She didn't mooch off me," Carly defended her twin automatically and out of habit. She had to turn away from Tina's give-me-a-break expression. Carly's gaze found Mitch on the far side of the yard. He had the twins and their friends involved in a game of touch football. The man was a work of art, all ropey muscles and athletic grace. A spurt of something wild pulsed through her. She ignored the unwanted feeling and returned her attention to her friend.

"There is no financial mess." Well, other than that missing hundred thousand Mitch claimed he'd given Marlene, but her attorney was looking into that. "The terms of Everett Kincaid's will require Rhett to live in Kincaid Manor for a year if he's to inherit his share of the estate."

"So that's why you were so stingy with your new address."

Carly shrugged. "I don't think I'll be hosting any mothers' mornings out while I live there."

"Mitch invited you to stay?"

Carly grimaced. "Not exactly. He just wanted Rhett."

"Without you? Carly, we both know you'd never give up Rhett. How did Mitch expect to pull that off?"

She hesitated, but after last night's kiss she needed to say the words out loud to remind herself of how low Mitch would go. And Tina knew the truth—the whole ugly truth—of Carly's past. "He offered me money—a *lot* of money—to relinquish guardianship of Rhett."

"The bastard." Tina slapped her fingers over her mouth and glanced at the toddlers in the tent. "He didn't?"

Carly nodded. "Between that and what Marlene told me about him trying to break up her and Everett, I'm afraid to trust him. No matter how charming and sexy he might be."

"He's being charming and sexy?"

"He is now, but in the beginning…" She shook her head and shuddered.

Tina tapped her chin and then a wily smile slid over her

lips. "First, remember your sister tended to be a drama queen. She might have—*probably*—exaggerated. And second, Mitch might be Rhett's kin, but he looks at you like you're the corner piece of cake and he can't wait to dive into all that rich, creamy icing."

Carly jerked around and her gaze slammed into Mitch's. She sucked a sharp breath at the hunger he telecast over the five-year-olds' heads.

"Oh, baby, I want some of that," Tina whimpered.

Cheeks hot, Carly whirled back to her friend. "Stop it."

"Admit it, you want some, too. And when we close up shop in ten minutes you can go home and get some while Rhett naps."

"Didn't you hear a word I said? Besides, even if Marlene exaggerated—and I don't think she did—the last thing I need is a rebound romance. Even if I am tempted." She muttered the last under her breath.

"Honey, you'd have to be dead not to be tempted. And nobody says you have to take an affair seriously." Tina studied her nails with faked nonchalance. "I'd do him just for the memories."

Carly's skin burned like a blowtorch. "Your husband should hear you talk."

"Hey, my husband loves it when I talk dirty." Tina winked and then turned pensive. "Maybe Mitch wants more than just Rhett. Maybe you could have your cake and eat it, too."

"You have got to stop dieting. I can't follow your starvation logic."

"All I'm saying is, why can't you have a few nibbles of Rhett's big brother while you're sharing his house? At the end of the year you'll return to your home and your real life…unless you land yourself a shipping tycoon in the meantime."

"Remind me why we're friends again? Because you're encouraging me to embark on certain disaster."

Tina grasped Carly's hands and squeezed. "No, honey, I'm trying to bring you back to the land of the living. Sam's gone. Good riddance, I might add. And Marlene's gone. Until today, I thought you had, too. This is the first time in months I've seen you excited about anything or anyone besides Rhett. Go for it."

Carly planted her elbows on her knees and her head in her hands. "Tina, that is *so* not the advice I needed to hear."

"You handled the children well today," Carly said as she joined Mitch in the living room just before noon.

"I spent every summer since high school working on Kincaid cruise ships. Corralling and controlling kids was part of the job." He waggled his water glass and raised a dark eyebrow, silently asking if she'd like a drink.

"A glass of Della's lemonade would be great."

He turned to the wet bar to fulfill her request.

"What kinds of jobs?" She placed the baby monitor on the coffee table and sank into the overstuffed sofa cushions. Her sleepless night was catching up with her. She probably should have requested something with caffeine.

"Have you ever been on a cruise?" He passed her the glass, and their fingers touched.

She fought a shiver and shook her head. "Thanks."

Instead of taking the high-backed wing chair he'd been using since she moved in, Mitch sat beside her. His weight tipped the cushion and Carly toward him, and even though their bodies didn't touch, he settled near enough that she could feel the heat radiating off him and smell the potent combination of his cologne mixed with fresh sweat and grass from running around Tina's yard with the boys. Heady stuff. The subsequent squeezing of her stomach had nothing to do with hunger due to the approaching lunch hour.

Her gaze fixed on his muscular legs below the hem of his shorts. A spattering of dark curls covered his tanned skin. She yearned to test the texture, but tightened her grip on her cold glass instead and gulped her drink, hoping the bite of the tart lemonade would shock her hormones back into line.

"There are a variety of activities on board, from day-care-type settings to swimming and rock climbing lessons. When we dock at Crescent Key, KCL's private island, there are scuba lessons, parasailing, kayaking, wind surfing, Jet Ski rentals and an inflatable kids' water park."

"The Kincaids *own* an island?"

"The company does."

She digested that and the slight chill in his voice, and then backtracked to the rest of what he'd said. "So you don't hate children?"

He frowned, leaned back against the cushions and stretched an arm along the sofa behind her. The shift of his body caused his knee to nudge hers. Atoms of awareness coalesced at the contact point. She inched her leg back, but he moved to fill the tiny gap she'd created. Her pulse sped up. "What gave you the impression I did?"

"Besides the snowman act?"

He lifted his water glass and took a sip. "I don't get attached to the ones who are only passing through. I've done that before and I didn't enjoy the aftermath."

"Your fiancée's children?"

If she hadn't been only inches from him, she would have missed his slight flinch. He nodded. Once.

Her heart ached for him. "Do you keep in touch with Travis and Ashley?"

He sat forward, braced his elbows on his knees and studied the contents of his glass. "I tried at first. But it confused them. So I stopped."

He wasn't a heartless bastard after all. He'd done what he thought best for the children. The stiffness of his shoulders and the rigid line of his jaw revealed more than words about the pain he'd suffered. No wonder he'd tried to keep his distance from Rhett.

The fragile shell of her resistance cracked and the need to reach out and offer comfort almost overwhelmed her. "Then you understand why I'll never willingly walk away from Rhett. He wouldn't understand how both his mother and I could leave him."

"He's young. He probably won't remember…her."

Did she imagine that pause? Did Mitch understand how much it still hurt to say her sister's name?

"I hope you're wrong. I hope a child never forgets feeling loved and wanted, even if the ones who loved them are only a part of their lives for a brief time."

She prayed that was the case and that one day her daughter would understand how much love it had taken to make the painful, unselfish decision to relinquish. Because Carly had so desperately wanted to be selfish and keep her. But she'd been sixteen and her baby's father had wanted nothing to do with her or their child. What kind of mother could she have been? She'd had no job and no high-school diploma. What kind of future could she have given her daughter? All the love in the world wasn't enough to put food on the table.

Mitch's green gaze probed hers. He had a way of looking at her that made her feel as if he could see her secrets. She struggled to camouflage her pain.

"What happens when you fall in love again and your future husband, like your ex, doesn't want to raise someone else's kid?"

"Then he won't be my husband. Loving means accepting the entirety of a person. The good and the bad." The men in her life hadn't been able to do that.

"You'll have to find someone who shares your interest in Rhett's future." He paused for several heavy heartbeats. "Someone like me."

Everything inside her went still, but the sudden tinkling of the ice cubes in her glass revealed her hands weren't as steady. "Wh-what are you saying, Mitch?"

He set his glass on the coffee table and then took hers and did the same. "Perhaps we should explore this attraction between us. For Rhett's sake as well as our own. We could have something here, Carly."

He lifted his hand and dragged the back of his knuckles along her cheek. Her reaction to the gentle caress mushroomed through her like an atomic blast.

"I don't think that's a good idea." She dampened her lips, and his eyes tracked the movement.

"Why?"

"Because you tried to persuade my sister not to have Rhett."

His long fingers curved over her shoulder. "As my father's right-hand man, it was my job to carry out his wishes. He asked me to make sure Marlene understood he was too old to raise another child—especially with a woman he didn't love."

Carly winced. "Marlene loved him."

Or at least she'd told Carly she did. And she'd been very convincing.

But what about Marlene's notebook? What about her plan to force Everett to marry her?

"Then I'm sorry for her. His not wanting to share his life or parenthood with her must have hurt." His thumb circled with mesmerizing, breath-snatching effect beneath her clavicle. "Is Rhett down for the count?"

"Yes. I'm glad you were driving so I could keep him awake on the ride home. If he takes a five-minute nap in the car then he won't go back to sleep when we get to his crib, and he'd be seriously cranky by dinnertime." She was babbling, but that was because if she quit talking she'd start moaning.

She couldn't do this again. Another one of his kisses and she'd be a goner.

Get up. Get out of here. At least until you're certain Marlene fibbed about him being a jerk.

Mitch's other hand settled on her opposite shoulder. His long fingers dug into the tense muscles in the back of her neck and massaged with mind- and willpower-melting results. By the time his thumbs traced the sensitive underside of her jaw, her reasons for resisting the intense attraction between them were getting pretty darn fuzzy. Her head and eyelids grew heavy.

"Give us a chance, Carly."

Before she could dredge up an answer from the sludge he'd made of her brain, he leaned forward and kissed her.

Seven

Carly made a decision she was almost certain she'd regret.

She kissed Mitch back.

But she couldn't help herself. Today, this entire week actually, she'd seen a different side of him. One she liked. A lot. One that, when combined with the shocking contents of Marlene's journal, made her wonder if her twin hadn't altered the facts to suit her purposes. It wouldn't have been the first time.

Mitch didn't touch her anywhere except for his lips and the thigh pressed against hers. It wasn't enough. She lifted a hand and cradled his face, loving the prickly warmth in her palm. She stroked his jaw. The slight roughness of his beard abraded her fingertips in a delicious way.

His growl of approval filled her mouth, and the echoes resounded deep inside her. His lips parted and his tongue sought and tangled with hers. The pressure of his mouth increased, tilting her head back for a deeper kiss. She adored his taste, his slick, wet heat, his scent.

But still, he didn't take her into his arms.

Carly moved her other hand to his knee below the hem of his shorts. The crisp curls tickled her palm. She kneaded the hot skin of his thigh and hunger seeped over her like a rising tide, pulling her deeper under his spell.

Mitch's hands flattened over both of hers, halting her movements. He lifted his head. Desire burned in his eyes and darkened his face. His fingers threaded through hers and returned her hands to her lap.

"We need to take this upstairs. But before we do, you need to be damned sure you know where this is headed."

She bit her lip and tasted him. "Where is it headed?"

"I want you, Carly. I think we have a shot at something good together. But I can't make guarantees of forever."

Her heart raced and her palms moistened. Did she want something long-term with him? Maybe. She'd certainly never experienced passion this strong before.

Getting involved again—and so soon—was a gamble. She'd taken several of those in her life and lost everything. But Mitch understood how much walking away from a child hurt. He'd been there. And he'd made the unselfish choice for the children. That fact alone made him more appealing than either of the men she'd thought she'd loved. Surely Mitch could understand and pardon her decision to give her daughter up for adoption?

And then there was Rhett. As Mitch had pointed out, they both had the child's best interest at heart.

She took a deep breath and slowly exhaled. "I'm willing to risk it."

Mitch's nostrils flared. He rose, pulling Carly to her feet. With their fingers still intertwined, he yanked her forward and their bodies slammed together, soft against hard in shocking, exhilarating contact. He pressed a quick, firm kiss on her lips, then released one hand and led her out of the room and into the foyer. He ascended the stairs without haste.

She wanted him to race. To do this before second thoughts overtook her. She hadn't known him long, and it wasn't like her to tumble into bed so quickly, so impetuously.

As if he sensed her encroaching doubts, he stopped on the first landing, backed her against the banister and lowered his head. Hot and hungry and slightly rough, his mouth devoured hers, stealing her breath, her defenses and her doubts.

Her back arched over the rail. The potential danger of falling to the hard marble floor below only intensified the adrenaline rush. She clung to his lean waist.

Just as quickly as he had begun the kiss, he ended it and resumed climbing, but faster this time. His long stride rushed her down the hall—not that she minded—past hers and Rhett's rooms and into Mitch's suite. He shut the doors and backed her against them. She had a brief impression of the bedroom behind him as huge, painted in the palest sage and flooded with sunlight from windows on both the front and back sides of the house.

"Last chance to change your mind." But already his hands reached for the hem of her shirt. The yellow cotton swished over her head in a blur and landed on the floor.

She answered by mimicking his movements and tugging his shirttail up and over his head to reveal those barbell-wide shoulders, the dark hair spattering in a Y across his torso and his amazing, muscle-ripped physique. For a moment she stood motionless, surveying the territory she had revealed. He did the same. His jaw muscles clenched and his pectorals rose on a deep inhalation.

His hands moved to the button and zip of her skirt. The rasp of his knuckles from her navel to her mound weakened her knees and sent a swirl of want to her abdomen. The skirt fell to her ankles, leaving her in a white bra, matching bikini panties and her sandals. For an instant she wished she'd worn something sexier than plain cotton, but the rapid expansion of his pupils smote the thought.

She kicked off her shoes and reached for the waistband of his shorts. The fastening gave way and the khaki fabric dropped down the length of his legs. She had a scant second to appreciate the long, thick bulge tenting his black boxers. The minute his pants hit the floor he kicked them and his shoes aside and swept her into his arms. The radiator warmth of his body pressed her side. She tangled her arms around his neck and scanned the room as his long stride ate up the floor between the entry and his bed.

A sea of glossy hardwood floors surrounded an island-size bed draped in a dark green spread. Matching tall stainless floor lamps arched like palm fronds over each side of the mattress, and pillows piled high against the tall scrolled wooden headboard. She didn't need to see the hardback thriller on the nightstand to know Mitch spent time reading in bed. Something else they had in common.

He set her on her feet and flipped back the covers, revealing sheets in the same sage as the walls. And then his thumbs hooked in his boxers and he bent to shove the silk to his ankles. He straightened, and her lungs and her womb contracted.

Oh, mama! Her fingers curled in anticipation of touching him, stroking him, taking him deep inside. She reached for her prize, but he brushed her hands aside to flick open the front catch of her bra. He caught her breasts as they spilled out, enclosing her sensitive flesh in the warmth of his hands. He thumbed the tips and a moan bubbled in her throat.

Briskly, with sudden impatience, he released her, rushed her bra over her arms and her panties down her legs and then backed her onto the bed. Her bottom bounced on the firm mattress and cool sheets met her back. He turned away briefly, yanked open the bedside drawer, retrieved and swiftly donned a condom and then returned to her. The mattress dipped beneath his weight, and his thighs separated hers. He planted his palms on the pillow beside her head.

She pressed her hands to his chest, halting his descent. She wanted to savor this, to make it last. "Wait. Slow down."

Even his eyebrows went rigid. He squeezed his eyes shut, inhaled. The veins in his throat and one in his temple pulsed wildly. When he lifted his lids she could see he'd reined himself in. As if in slow motion, his elbows bent and he lowered himself, stopping short of full body contact. His lips touched down, hovered and touched hers again, like a hummingbird on a feeder.

His kisses traced her cheekbone, her jaw, the cords of her neck, sipping and laving. His teeth scraped ever so lightly on her skin, and she shivered with need. The mattress quaked beneath her, telecasting the depth with which Mitch fought for control. She slid her hands from the supple skin of his chest to the bunched muscles of his shoulders and then into his soft hair. Cradling his head, she brought his mouth back to hers. His ravenous kiss slayed her. She thought her lungs would burst. The rest of her wasn't far behind.

He lifted his head, stretched out beside her and propped himself up on his elbow. The scalding length of him, of his torso, his erection, his legs, blanketed her from shoulder to ankle. His gaze greedily gorged on her nakedness. His hand stroked and caressed, plucked and glided over her breasts, her waist and her belly, sweeping her into a tornado of sensation. And then his lips followed the same path.

His mouth found her center, and an approaching orgasm coalesced deep inside her. Hunger and passion consumed her, making her forget all about going slow. Her hips arched off the bed. She wound her arms around him, urging him on. "Now."

He lifted his head and leaned back, leaving her hanging on the verge of release. She whimpered in disappointment. He grasped her knee and hiked it over his hip, rolling her to her side, leaving her most intimate parts opened and exposed. His gaze held hers as he kneaded the curve of her bottom and then slipped his hand between them to her slick center.

She loved the dark, passionate look in his eyes, as if he were as close to losing control as her. His fingers slid deep and then withdrew. That single thrust pushed her back to the edge, but left her aching and empty and yearning for more. He cut short her frustrated groan by painting a mind-twisting circular pattern over her flesh. Her lids fluttered closed as intense pleasure arrowed through her. She forced them back open to watch the intense concentration on his face.

Her thoughts, her senses centered on those dexterous digits and on the intense green eyes holding hers captive. Pressure built until it bordered on pain. Once again, he let it subside. Wanting, needing more, she lifted her hips in invitation, pressing against the heel of his hand. "Mitch, please."

His breath hissed. "Not yet."

She was so close her back arched in anticipation and tremors racked her body. She dug her nails into his shoulders and clung, teetering on the brink. She nipped his jaw, his neck, his collarbone because she couldn't reach his mouth. Mitch removed his hand, and she sobbed in frustration. Before she could voice her complaint, he pushed her onto her back and rose above her.

"Now." He took her mouth and her body in duel of simultaneous thrusts. His growl filled her lungs and vibrated to her core.

The shock of his sudden penetration stretched her, filled her and sent a Niagara of release rushing over her. She twisted her mouth free to gasp for breath and held him tight as the cataclysm overtook her to the beat of his hard, deep, rapid thrusts.

He bowed his back, bent and sucked her earlobe between his lips. She'd never felt anything more erotic in her life than the swirl of his tongue combined with the steam of his breath on her neck, the swivel of his hips and the powerful surge of his body into hers. His tempo increased, and her tension renewed. Another climax gathered so swiftly she had no chance of holding back, no chance of prolonging the moment, and then it rained over her like a sudden, violent cloud burst.

Mitch's groan echoed her cry in the big room and then his body collapsed onto hers. Panting for breath, she twined her arms around him and held him close, relishing his weight and the hammering of his heart against hers. She ran her fingertips along his sweat-slicked spine. His shudder made her smile.

She'd had good sex before. She'd even had what she'd considered great sex. Until now. But she'd never experienced anything like this.

Mitch Kincaid had marked her for life.

And she wasn't sure if that was a good thing or merely the promise of another disaster in her future. One far more devastating than any of its predecessors.

Mitch stared at the ceiling and tried to figure out where he'd miscalculated.

Carly was simply another woman he'd slept with. With wealth came women—plenty of women—who'd do whatever a man wanted. A fact his father had taken advantage of too many times to count. Only the last time, it had blown up in his face.

Which brought Mitch back to his present predicament.

He had a plan to execute. Emotion played no part in it.

He wasn't supposed to lose control.

But he had.

He was screwing Carly both literally and figuratively. How twisted did it make him to have enjoyed the process so much that he'd momentarily lost sight of his goal?

Seduce her. Propose. Get custody of Rhett.

His marriage to Carly would be a good one. Short. But good. One he intended to dissolve as soon as the ink dried on the adoption papers.

A twinge of guilt made him want to slide out from under the woman dozing so trustingly on his shoulder and hit the shower. He dismissed the feeling. He wasn't breaking any laws. And in this case, Carly and Rhett would be better off once the dust settled.

Despite Carly's protests, Mitch still believed she'd tire of the mommy game. Not that she'd shown any signs of doing so yet. But she would. He'd bet his share of KCL on it.

Why wouldn't she prefer her freedom when she could have all the benefits of Kincaid money via a generous divorce settlement and none of the obligations?

His mother had done something very similar. She may have stayed in the marriage, but she'd been an indifferent mother at best, one who'd turned their care over to a series of nannies, and Mrs. Duncan, then gone about her life as unfettered by parenthood as possible despite her middle child's attempts to gain her attention.

No. Getting rid of Carly was the right thing to do, and he doubted he'd need whatever Frank Lewis dug up to convince her to move on. If the P.I. found anything.

Carly snuffled in her sleep. Her breath tickled the hair on his chest and the fingers she'd rested just below his navel contracted. The ankle hooked over his calf slid languorously down to his foot and then back up to his knee.

His body tensed and responded as if he hadn't just been sated out of his skull. Would they have time for round two before the rug rat awoke from his nap? Before he could lift his wrist to check his watch, Rhett's cry penetrated the closed door.

Carly stiffened. Eager to escape the awkward postmortem—at least until he got his head screwed on straight—Mitch buried his mouth in the silky, coconut-scented hair next to her ear. "Go back to sleep. I'll get him."

He eased Carly onto the pillow beside him.

"You're sure?" Her drowsy, throaty voice and heavy-lidded eyes hit a bull's-eye on his libido. He wouldn't have to worry about the physical side of their marriage. If today was any indication, the sex would be phenomenal. Not that he intended to cheat, but it was nice to know he wouldn't want to.

"Got it covered." He climbed from the bed and took a good look at her. Once he had his game face back on, he'd take the time to enjoy every inch of her lithe, curvy body. He pulled the sheet over her before he said to hell with the crying kid and took what he wanted. The way he would have done earlier if Carly hadn't slowed him down.

Where in the hell had his restraint gone? The slow seduction he'd planned had taken a NASA rocket out of sight.

Another squawk from the blue room grabbed his attention. He knew from experience the kid started quietly but then opened up to full-throttle screaming.

Mitch yanked on his clothes and strode down the hall.

Rhett stood in his crib, sleepily scrubbing his eyes with his little fists. He spotted Mitch and stretched out his stubby arms. "Mitt. *My* Mitt."

Mitch's heart clenched. Something stuck in his throat. He cleared it. Rhett copied him and then beamed and chortled. Mitch gritted his teeth against a flood of emotion.

Okay, so maybe he was getting attached to the squirt. But that was okay. Soon Rhett would be a permanent member of the Kincaid household.

And Carly would be gone.

He shoved that thought aside and reached for Rhett. The kid latched on with a strangling grip. Mitch pried him loose and shoved a stuffed alligator in the kid's paws. He made quick work of the diaper change and then hefted the kid over his head. Rhett rewarded him with a gurgling laugh.

"What do you say we have lunch, kid?"

He jogged down the stairs, jostling the little baggage, and Rhett giggled. Mitch caught himself grinning back. He marched into the kitchen. Mrs. Duncan turned. Her penciled eyebrows rose and her mouth thinned, reminding Mitch he hadn't bothered to check the mirror. With the way Carly had run her fingers through his hair, he probably looked like an unruly hedge. And then he noticed his polo shirt was wrong-side out. Busted.

"Carly's napping. We need lunch."

"Yes, sir." There was a bite to her words he hadn't heard before. If she'd guessed what went on upstairs, she didn't approve.

Tough. She worked for him. He didn't need her approval.

He strapped Rhett into his high chair and dumped some of the diced fruit and cheese Carly kept in the refrigerator onto the tray and filled the kid's cup. It might have been years since he'd done this routine task for Travis, but his memory hadn't failed.

Mrs. Duncan prepared his meal in silence. She'd never been the talkative type, but this silence screamed disapproval.

"Would you keep an eye on Rhett while I wash up?"

"Yes, sir."

Mitch strode to his study, closed the door and righted his shirt. The red light blinking on the answering machine to his—formerly his father's—private line caught his attention. He rarely used this phone and had intended to have the line disconnected, but hadn't made the call to the utility company yet. He crossed the room and punched the Play button.

"Kincaid, I hit the mother lode on Carly Corbin." Frank Lewis's voice filled the room. Mitch's heart pumped faster, and lava settled in the pit of his stomach. "I need more time to follow up. I'll get back with you when I've filled in the blanks."

What could Carly possibly have in her past to put that note of excitement in the P.I.'s voice?

Part of him wanted to know.

But part of him didn't. And that part concerned him most. Weakness led to defeat. Or so his father always claimed.

He hit the Erase button and then paced into the adjoining

bathroom where he mechanically combed his hair and washed his face. He braced his hands on the counter. The man in the mirror staring back at him looked the same.

But where was the get-the-job-done edge?

He'd wanted dirt on Carly, hadn't he?

So why wasn't he pleased to know he might not have to marry her to get the boy?

Mitch's green gaze crashed into Carly's the minute she entered the kitchen. Her cheeks flushed, and her face wasn't the only part of her warming up. Every area he'd touched made its presence known and his scent still clung to her skin, filling her nose with each breath.

Like a true gentleman he rose and pulled out a chair for her beside a happily babbling, food-stuffing Rhett. She crossed the room, hyperconscious of Mitch's visual caress of her breasts, hips and legs. When his gaze returned to hers the knowledge of the intimacy they'd shared flashed in his eyes. Her pulse tripped wildly and her palms moistened.

But other than that fleeting reaction which passed so quickly she could have imagined it, he offered no cue on how to handle their status change in front of the housekeeper.

"Hi." A crazy shyness stole the rest of her words.

Mitch nodded, but there was no secret smile or even a softening of his stoic features. He didn't lean down to kiss her cheek as she slid into her seat or even touch her shoulder. He returned to his end of the table and picked up the thick toasted sandwich on the table in front of him. He ate with one hand and sorted through the mail stacked beside his plate with the other.

Okay, this was awkward. She'd had morning afters before, but never midday and she'd never shared one with an audience. She wasn't sure how to proceed. She felt as if she'd been dismissed and that stung far more than it should have.

You're falling for him.

Could it be true? Did she more than just like and desire Mitch Kincaid? The leaden sensation in the pit of her stomach delivered the answer.

Desperate for a distraction Carly abruptly diverted her attention to Rhett. She blew him a kiss and received a messy grin in return. As it so often did, her heart swelled with love for this precious child and it ached with sadness that her sister wouldn't be around to see her son grow up. Mitch would, and if Carly had anything to say about it, Rhett's other siblings would also be a part of his life. Because of the terms of the will, he'd have to wait a year to meet his half sister, but that was twelve months during which he could bond with his brothers.

Twelve months in which Carly could get her heart broken. Again.

Was this a rebound romance or something more? Could she and Mitch give Rhett a stable home and maybe even brothers and sisters? Where did they go from here?

Her gaze strayed back to the man at the opposite end of the table. His expressionless face gave no clue. Uneasiness stirred inside her and tension invaded her muscles. Did he expect her to act as if nothing had happened?

Did he regret making love with her? Did the intimacy mean nothing to him? Did he think it meant nothing to her?

Did he think she was easy?

Old taunts and accusations drifted through her mind like ghosts, chilling her, haunting her.

"Is turkey salad okay with you, Carly?" Della's question rescued Carly from her painful past.

"Yes, thank you, Della."

Della brought her a plate. Carly forked a bite of salad into her mouth and glanced at Della. She'd really come to like the housekeeper, but her presence kept Carly from asking the questions burning and churning inside her.

She needed to know the prognosis for this relationship. Good or bad.

One silent minute stretched into five. The only sounds in the room were Rhett's occasional chatter, the crunch of Mitch's teeth biting into his sandwich and the shuffle of papers as he dealt with his correspondence.

Carly's appetite died. She pushed her salad around on her dish and focused her attention on Rhett, but for once her nephew had decided to feed himself relatively neatly and without any assistance from her.

When she couldn't bear the tension any longer she laid down her fork and cleared her throat. "I had a call about my house before I came downstairs."

Mitch's hand stopped halfway to his glass. One dark eyebrow lifted.

"A prospective renter wants to see it this afternoon. I agreed to meet them at three…unless you have other plans."

Hint, hint, big guy. Tell me you want to spend the afternoon together.

"You plan to meet strangers in your house? Alone?"

"They're not strangers. They're a married couple who are good friends with Tina's sister."

He nodded. "Leave the rug rat with me."

The knot of tension between her shoulder blades eased only slightly. She would have preferred he offer to come with her, but she wanted Mitch and Rhett to bond, and this was a step forward. She'd take what she could get, and when she returned from showing her house, she'd corner Mitch and find out exactly what was going on. And then she'd develop a new strategy from what she learned.

"I should only be gone a couple of hours."

"Take your time."

Her gaze searched his. There was a reserve in his eyes that she hadn't seen since the early days in their relationship.

What had changed in the thirty minutes from when he'd left her in his bed until she'd joined him? Because whatever it was, she could feel Mitch pulling back.

Eight

"You ready to tell me what's going on? Or do I need to kick your ass again?"

Mitch flipped a rude hand gesture at Rand while treading water in the deep end of the pool and trying to catch his breath. "You only beat me by two body lengths after ten laps. That's pathetic, considering *I* wasn't on my high school and college swim teams and you were."

Apparently, his brother hadn't slacked off in his training.

"Yeah, yeah, save face any way you can."

Joking with Rand again felt good. It had been a long time. Too long. Once, they'd been close, competitive, too—their father had ensured that—but close. "You're in decent shape for an old man."

"Only two years older than you, brat. And two years wiser."

Shaking his head at Rand's need to get the last word, Mitch swam to the side and, ignoring the ladder a few yards away, hauled himself out of the water. He turned on the stone surround, offered Rand a hand and hoisted him onto the deck.

Rand scooped two towels out of a nearby chair and tossed one to Mitch. "What's up with the unexpected invitation?"

Unexpected because their relationship had been strained since Rand's return to Miami. Mitch hadn't exactly offered his brother an olive branch for stepping up to the plate instead of walking away from the challenge to fill their father's shoes. Maybe he should now that he knew the reason. Rand had left because their father had allegedly slept with the woman his brother loved. A woman currently putting Rand through the wringer, thanks to big brother's portion of the inheritance clause.

"It's good to have you back. I wasn't sure it would be at first, but it's good to be a team again." His brother was holding up his end of KCL and doing a damned fine job of it.

"It's good to be back." Surprise laced Rand's voice. "Now quit stalling. Why am I here?"

"Carly wanted Rhett to meet you." And Mitch wasn't ready for a quiet, intimate evening with his potential bride-to-be. Not until he wrapped his head around the brain-frying sex and the P.I.'s phone call. Mixing business with pleasure had never been an issue for him before. Why did it bother him now?

"Where is Dad's little bastard?"

A sharp rebuke sprang to Mitch's lips. He clamped his jaw shut to contain the words and briskly scrubbed the towel over his body. Not too long ago he'd referred to Rhett the same way, but for some reason he found the words offensive when Rand used them.

"Mrs. Duncan has him. She wanted to do a Web cam chat with her sister, so her sister could see Rhett. You'll meet him at dinner. I'll even let you sit beside him." He barely held his smile in check. His brother had no idea what he was in for.

"Our old guard dog is computer savvy?"

Rand sounded as shocked as Mitch had been. But then Mrs.

Duncan had always remained in the background, more like a fixture of the house than a person. If she'd had personality or interests beyond Kincaid walls, she'd kept them to herself for thirty-plus years.

Until Carly.

Within a week of moving in, Carly had learned the names, hobbies and family history of every Kincaid Manor employee, the neighborhood security guards, the mail carrier and the delivery men, for godsakes. Mitch only knew the names of those whose paychecks he signed or the ones who weren't doing their jobs and needed to be fired. He didn't want or need to know more.

His father hadn't been that way. Everett Kincaid had thrived on knowing every intimate detail about anyone who touched his sphere—primarily so he could use it against them.

"Mrs. Duncan has a top-of-the-line laptop."

"Has she said anything about retiring with the half million Dad left her?"

"She hasn't mentioned it. But she might stick around. She's getting pretty attached to Carly and the little guy."

"Sounds like you are, too."

Deliberately ignoring the first half of that equation, Mitch shrugged. "He's a cute kid. Hard not to like him."

"And the aunt? Any luck getting rid of her?"

Buying time while he debated how much of his plan to reveal, Mitch ambled to the built-in patio bar and plucked a couple of bottles of imported beer out of the minirefrigerator.

Better to keep his idea to himself rather than risk Rand throwing a wrench in his plans. His big brother had always been a rule follower, and while Mitch's plan wasn't illegal, it wasn't exactly kosher, either, even if he believed everyone would end up satisfied in the end.

"Not yet." He offered his brother a drink.

Rand accepted the bottle and popped the cap. "Five weeks

ago you thought this job would be easy, but you haven't sealed the deal. Are you having trouble meeting the Corbin woman's price?"

Mitch took a swig of his beer. The cool liquid did nothing to relieve his parched throat. "I offered her a million to sign over guardianship. She turned me down."

Rand's face hardened. "The bitch wants more?"

Mitch's fingers contracted so tightly it was a miracle the bottle didn't shatter. He reminded himself again that he'd used those same words before he'd gotten to know Carly, back when he'd expected her to be identical to her twin in temperament and greed, as well as looks.

Feigning calm when he was anything but, he eased into a chair and propped his feet on the tabletop. "Carly claims she doesn't want any Kincaid money."

Rand sat in the opposite chair. "You were always a decent judge of character. Either she's not as mercenary as you expected or she's angling for more than cash. Which is it?"

Mitch studied the sweat already condensing on the green glass in the late afternoon heat. A droplet snaked down the side of the neck and over the black label.

As the middle kid, he'd learned to read people pretty well, but his record wasn't flawless. He'd never expected Trish to go back to her cheating ex or Marlene to take the money and run. He sure as hell hadn't expected his father to knock off Marlene Corbin. If he had.

There was always a chance Mitch had the wrong bead on Carly. The future of KCL depended on him being on target. But Carly was…

He didn't even begin to know how to explain Carly Corbin to Rand. She had the bullheaded determination of a Fortune 500 executive, and yet she'd thrown herself in where needed at Kincaid Manor without being asked. Was she selfish or selfless?

"I don't think Carly is as greedy as her sister. She appears more interested in making sure Rhett's future is secure. Once I convince her it is, she'll go." If he was wrong, he'd pay dearly. Especially if he married her. He was counting on her being willing to walk away.

The back door opened. Instead of Mrs. Duncan, Carly waltzed out with a shirtless Rhett on her hip. Mitch nearly fell out of his chair when he saw the amount of skin she had on display. His feet slapped on the tiles and he shot upright. He wanted to wrap his towel around her and conceal her from his brother's close scrutiny.

"Are we too late to join you for a swim?" she called out.

Carly's black bikini wasn't brief by Miami Beach standards, but it framed every curve to full, mouthwatering advantage.

She strolled toward them with a fluid, athletic grace that sent his blood racing for his swim trunks. The woman made her living getting others in shape. She didn't skimp on herself.

Rand whistled under his breath and muttered almost inaudibly, "I'd offer to pull a dad for you, but—"

"No." The word exploded from Mitch's mouth. Their father had stolen more than one woman from Rand. Taking what others wanted—personally and professionally—had been one of Everett Kincaid's favorite sicko games. Mitch had learned early on to hide his emotions and his ambitions.

"I'm glad. Rhett loves the water." Carly had obviously mistaken his no as a response to her question.

Rand rose and extended his hand before Mitch could make introductions. "Rand Kincaid. You must be Carly. And this has to be Rhett. He has Kincaid written all over him."

His brother had turned on the charm and the lady-killer smile. Mitch wanted to clock him with his beer bottle.

"It's nice to meet you, Rand. I've been eager for Rhett to get to know all of his siblings. It's a shame he can't meet Nadia until this year's over."

The handshake lasted too long.

"Mitt," Rhett squealed and dove for Mitch. Mitch caught him, and in the transfer, his forearm brushed Carly's breast. The brief contact sent a jolt of electricity through him. But the best part of the kid's dive was that it severed the handshake.

A tiny hand fisted in Mitch's chest hair. Pain radiated outward and Mitch had to smother a howl. He detached the persistent fingers and pointed to Rand. "Brother."

"Bubba," Rhett replied just as Mitch had hoped he would. This time, it was funny.

Rand grimaced. "Rand. I'm Rand."

"Did you rent your house?" Mitch asked, to draw Carly's brick-melting, mischievous grin away from his brother.

"Yes, the couple signed the lease my attorney prepared. They're moving in Friday. So you're stuck with me for a while."

He ignored the question in her voice. He wouldn't lie and tell her she was welcome here. She wasn't. She was merely a necessary evil. A necessary evil that just happened to light his fuse.

She stared at him and when he remained silent, tension slowly invaded her features. A flush crept up her cheeks and then her chin lifted. Her gaze dropped to Rhett.

"Let's go for a swim, munchkin." Carly reached for Rhett. Her fingernails lightly grazed Mitch's bare chest from his underarm to his nipple as she took the boy. Goose bumps prickled his skin. Deliberate?

Mitch looked into her chocolate-brown eyes and the heat he saw there incinerated him on the spot. Oh yeah, definitely deliberate. What was she trying to pull? The action had been subtle. Rand couldn't have seen it. But Mitch's reaction to her touch and to the memory of how uninhibited Carly had been in bed wasn't going to be as easy to miss. He'd be tenting his trunks if he didn't break her spell.

He wanted her. Now. To hell with his brother—brother*s*, plural. The strength of his craving didn't bode well for his plan to kick her out at the end of the year. But he would. Even if he wasn't right about Carly eventually bailing on mom patrol, Mitch was already married. To his job. It was the only mistress that didn't ask for more than he was willing to give. And the only one that wouldn't betray him.

Carly strolled toward the pool. Mitch's gaze zeroed in on the sway of her delectable butt.

"Nice," his brother said.

Mitch scowled at Rand.

His brother gave him a pitying look.

Damn. He'd invited Rand over for a swim and cocktails because he wasn't in the mood for one of those angsty chats women preferred about what sex really meant. And he knew from Carly's searching glances both at lunch and a minute ago that she had one brewing in her brain.

But instead of his brother being a buffer, Mitch had discovered a possessive streak he hadn't known himself capable of, and he'd played his cards like an amateur.

If he wasn't careful, he could wind up broke.

If his brother smiled at Carly one more time, Rand wasn't going to have any teeth left to smile with.

Mitch set his wineglass on the coffee table and stood. "It's late. Carly and I have to get up early to run before church."

"Church? You?"

He ought to say yes just to wipe the wiseass smirk off his brother's face, but then he'd have to attend the service and Rand would really have something to yank his chain over. Except for weddings and funerals, the Kincaid offspring hadn't seen the inside of a church since their mother's funeral, after she'd nailed their father's favorite sports car to a tree when Mitch was twelve. Their father had always refused to acknowledge a higher power than himself.

"Carly and Rhett go. I have to work."

Rand leaned forward to deposit his glass beside Mitch's, but not fast enough to hide his amusement. "Then I'll get out of your way."

The SOB knew exactly why Mitch wanted him gone. Mitch didn't like being laughed at. He was the CFO of a multibillion-dollar company, respected in his field and damned good at his job. No one laughed at him.

"Thank you for inviting me to dinner, Carly." Rand stood and extended his arm.

Carly unfolded the long legs she'd tucked beneath her in the chair and rose to shake hands. Rand held hers for too damned long. "You're welcome. Please stop by again. I'm so glad to have finally met you."

Mitch ground his teeth. He'd had to compete for his mother's attention and then his father's and then Trish's. He'd be damned if he'd compete for Carly's. She was *his* part of the will fulfillment. Rand could worry about fulfilling the requirements of his own inheritance clause, which, from all reports, wasn't going well.

"I'll show you out."

Rand's lips twitched again and he shook his head. "I know the way."

Mitch stormed to the front door and held it open anyway because Rand wasn't moving fast enough. He waited and tried to rein in the possessive streak burning through him like a lit trail of gunpowder as his brother and Carly ambled toward the foyer at a slug's pace.

What in the hell had happened? When had he lost control of the evening? And why did he care that his brother could make Carly laugh?

He shook with the effort required to restrain his temper and quietly close the door behind Rand.

"I like your brother," Carly said behind him. "He's funny."

The words made Mitch see red. He pivoted. "He's taken."

Carly looked at him strangely. Probably because he'd spit out his reply like chewing tobacco. "He said he lives alone and hasn't bothered to furnish his apartment. He didn't mention being involved with anyone."

"That's because he's on the verge of screwing this inheritance up for all of us. Tara, his personal assistant, is part of it." He advanced on her. "You flirted with him."

Carly parked her fists on her hips, right beside the baby monitor she'd been wearing clipped to the waistband of her low-rider jeans since returning from tucking Rhett into bed an hour ago. Anger slapped her cheeks with color.

"Oh please. You set him up by sitting him next to the kamikaze kid. At least he had a sense of humor about getting bombed. Unlike someone I know."

She charged forward until they were toe to toe. "I didn't flirt. But what if I had? It's not as if you care. For all the warmth you've shown tonight, we could be strangers who met on the street this afternoon, not two people who shared a bed and our bodies ten hours ago."

He'd never liked pushy, temperamental women, but strangely, Carly's anger and aggression aroused him. And he couldn't help but admire that she wasn't intimidated by him. If anything, she leaned into him as if she were trying to bully him. Impossible. He'd been bullied by the best—his father— without success.

"You want warmth? I'll give you warmth." He snaked an arm around her waist and yanked her close. Her body crashed against his, jarring the air from his lungs. He took her mouth almost violently in a kiss that was more combat than caress. Lips and hips ground.

Instead of flinching, Carly gave as good as she got. Her nails dug into his biceps, holding him, not pushing him away.

He grabbed her waist, swung her around and backed her up against the wall beside the front door. She landed with a soft thud and an *oomph*. But she didn't break the kiss. Her palms shifted to cup his face and hold it there.

He forced open her lips and invaded her mouth. Their tongues clashed and dueled, fighting for supremacy. He didn't give an inch in the skirmish, but neither did she. His hands fisted in the fabric of her shirt. He wanted to rip it off. Only their location stopped him. Any of the staff could barge in. Being a Kincaid meant being tabloid fodder. Everyone had a price, and even the most dedicated employee could be bought.

Carly hasn't been bought.

Yes, she has. But by living in luxury instead of with cash.

And still he wanted her. It pissed him off.

Without freeing her mouth, he tangoed her backward down the hall and into his study. One slap slammed the door. A flick of his wrist locked it. He didn't stop until he had her pressed against his desk. Furious with her for the laughs and smiles she'd shared with his brother and even more disgusted with himself for his loss of control, Mitch didn't try to be gentle. He tore her shirt over her head and shoved her jeans down her legs. The monitor landed with a thump. Batteries spilled out and rolled across the rug. He didn't care. Her bra and panties sailed over his shoulder.

But instead of being naked and cowed, Carly attacked. She mimicked his actions, pulling, yanking, popping buttons, and within seconds they were both down to their birthday suits and breathing heavily. His hands chaffed her skin, hurriedly, impatiently, greedily. He wanted to touch all of her. Now.

Her nails raked his chest, his back, his ass. She dug in and pulled him close. Hot skin smelt hot skin. He tasted her naked lobes, her neck, and then bent her over the desk to sample the tight tips of her breasts.

It wasn't enough to sate his savage hunger.

He lifted her onto the dark, glossy surface, pushed her knees apart and stepped between her legs. His muscles clenched in anticipation of sinking deep and then locked in screaming protest. Her slick flesh cradled his erection, tempting him to break every rule ever drilled into his head. "Damn."

"What? Don't stop *now*."

"No condom," he forced between gritted teeth.

"I'm healthy. If you are, then it's okay. I'm on the Pill."

For an unforgivable second he wanted to believe her, to trust her. That infuriated him. Those were probably the same words her sister had used to entrap his father.

"Not good enough."

She whacked his shoulder with an open palm. He barely noticed the sting. "Jerk."

He spewed a four-letter word—one he never used in the presence of a female.

"Please do." The hunger and frustration darkening her eyes slashed right through his restraint. But he didn't see cunning or avarice.

To hell with it. If there were consequences, his attorney would deal with them. Mitch grabbed her hips and yanked her forward, impaling her. A hot, wet inferno enfolded him and his spine caught fire.

He withdrew and slammed home again and again and again, harder and faster with each return. His name rushed across his shoulder in a scalding breath. Her teeth bit into his flesh and her nails scored his back. He'd never come close to experiencing anything like the fierce, animalistic claiming.

Fighting for dominance and control, he forced her back onto the desk. A pen cup fell over. The phone crashed to the floor. He didn't care. He took and took some more—sucking, nipping—and Carly did the same. Her hands and mouth burned over him. They'd both be marked tomorrow.

"Faster." Her heels hooked behind his butt, urging him on. She quivered beneath him. And then her back bowed and her head tilted back, spilling silky hair across the desktop and baring her throat. He sank his teeth into the exposed tendon on the side of her neck, no better than a damned vampire, hungry, so damned hungry for her.

She convulsed beneath him, clenching him with her arms, legs and internal muscles. And he lost it. Shudder after shudder racked him, draining him of everything including his strength.

The arms he had braced on the desk beside her head folded and he collapsed on top of her. His sweat-dampened torso fused to hers and their chests billowed in unison. But as the sweat dried on his skin and his body cooled, so did his fevered brain.

Bowing his head, he silently cursed his stupidity. He'd taken a chance he shouldn't have taken, made the one dumb-assed mistake he'd never made before. Sex without a condom. He couldn't risk the fallout. Couldn't risk her going to ground the way her sister had done, disappearing and showing up fourteen months later with an eight-month-old Kincaid.

He couldn't risk the hell Trish had put him through when she'd become pregnant despite his religious use of protection. The betrayal of finding out the woman he'd worshipped had slept with her ex-husband while she and Mitch were talking marriage had been a living hell. And then he'd had to endure nine agonizing months of wondering if the baby was his or her ex's, and the disappointment of finding out the child wasn't his. Not a good time.

He forced his arms to support him and levered his upper body off the pillow of Carly's breasts. "You'll have to marry me."

She stiffened beneath him. Her legs fell from his thighs and she rose to her elbows. "What?"

"For Rhett's sake." And in case she'd lied about being on the Pill. He wasn't going to wait for the P.I. report or risk her disappearing or face another nine-month wait for a DNA test. He'd push this deal through ASAP. "He needs two parents."

He separated from her physically and attempted to do so

mentally, but the sight of her draped across the desk, of her curves and the damp dark curls between her legs, knocked his willpower sideways. He turned his back, reached for his pants and stepped into them, zipping up before he could repeat his mistake.

He'd never considered having kids before Travis and Ashley had come into his life. After Trish's pregnancy, he'd decided he never would. If there was one thing he'd learned from his relationship with Trish, it was that the mother held all the cards. Even if the baby had been his, Trish would have returned to her ex and Mitch would have been powerless. He might have been granted joint custody. But in majority of the cases the mother was granted primary custody, and the father was turned into a visitor. That was tough on the kids but even tougher on the parent who'd become an outsider in his kid's life.

He wasn't going to be that parent.

And now, thanks to his idiocy and lack of control, more than the Kincaid inheritance was at stake.

Nine

"Are you crazy? You don't get married just because you've had sex."

Carly had once been naive enough to believe otherwise. She'd lost her heart, her virginity and her baby in the process of learning that painful lesson.

She scrambled off the desk, snatched up her shirt and scanned the room for her bra. She didn't see a hint of lace anywhere. Forget it. She stuffed her arms inside her sleeves and towed the fabric over her head.

Mitch's hard, direct stare pinned her in place. "You want to ensure Rhett's future is secure. So do I. This is the best way to do it. We'll marry and adopt him."

Rhett would be her son.

Too good to be true.

Holding her jeans and panties in front of her like a shield, she searched Mitch's face, looking for something—*anything*—to clue her in to his emotional state.

Nada.

And yet she was tempted by his proposal. She liked Mitch more with each exposure and was only a nudge away from falling for him. This evening, watching him verbally spar with his brother had reminded her of what she'd never have with Marlene again. That empty, aching void, one very similar to the one left by giving up her daughter, seemed impossible to fill.

Rebound romance, the voice in her head screamed a now familiar warning.

"Why would you want to marry *me?*"

Mitch finished tucking in his shirt and then fastened his leather belt with much more dexterity than she'd fumbled it open earlier. "We're good together. Explosive."

Amen. She'd never had sex like that before. Wild. Unrestrained. And oh so wonderful. All right, maybe she and Mitch had some pretty powerful chemistry between them.

But marriage?

She couldn't ignore the caution lights illuminating her brain like the Vegas strip. "We've known each other less than three weeks. I don't think it's a good idea, Mitch."

"Besides the timing, give me one good reason why we shouldn't."

Feeling exposed in more ways than one, she stepped into her pants and fastened them.

"Love?" Or lack thereof.

"You've been in love before. How'd that work for you?"

She grimaced. "Not so well."

All three of the men she'd loved had let her down, betrayed her in one way or another and left her. Was it better to go into a relationship with something less fragile than love as the glue to hold it together? With her track record, it was beginning to look that way.

And with the way she felt, wasn't love right around the

corner? But she didn't want a one-sided affair. She wanted to be loved back. Was Mitch Kincaid capable?

He might have started out as a jerk, but she and he shared a strong sense of family. If not, they wouldn't be butting heads over a determination to do the right thing by Rhett. And if she lived here as Mitch's wife and a permanent part of Rhett's up-bringing, she could do her best to ensure her sister's precious son wouldn't be exposed to the world of nannies or turn into some spoiled, rich brat who snorted his life away.

"I like and respect you, Carly, and I admire your dedication to your nephew. It's enough to build on."

Nephew. A reminder that Rhett wasn't hers.

But he could be.

"You said earlier today that you couldn't promise forever," she reminded him.

"I said I couldn't guarantee it. How many marriages starting with that pledge actually last 'til death do us part?"

Less than fifty percent.

We could be a family.

And Carly could give Rhett what her sister had so desperately wanted for him but hadn't been able to achieve—the right to grow up in Kincaid Manor, his father's home.

She was tempted. Very tempted. And not just for Rhett's sake.

Marlene hated Mitch. She'd called him a conniving rat bastard.

But Marlene had called everyone who gave her a hard time names, Carly reminded herself. Her twin had been hot-tempered…and devious, if the notebook was to be believed.

Mitch tried to convince Marlene to abort.

But he'd done so on his father's orders.

Mitch cupped her shoulders, interrupting her private debate. "We could have this—" a nod indicated the desk "—every day for as long as the passion lasts."

Need twisted through her abdomen, wreaking havoc with her reservations. But Mitch had a thing about women having a price. "I'm not looking for a sugar daddy."

"I don't intend to be one."

"I would never abandon Rhett."

"I won't force you to."

Indecision rocked her like a buoy in a tropical storm. "We'd always discuss what's best for him?"

"Absolutely."

"What about brothers and sisters for him sometime in the future? I'd—I'd really like to have a…a baby one day."

Mitch's nostrils flared. "One child at a time. Let's get through the adoption first."

"But you like children?"

He expelled a slow breath. "I like kids."

"And you'd—we'd—be…exclusive?"

"When I make a commitment, I see it through."

Her heart pounded so hard she could barely think. Her resistance wavered.

Do what's best for Rhett.

All she had to do was say yes and Rhett would have a home, family and security, and she'd have the possibility of another baby in her future.

It wouldn't be a storybook marriage, and she wasn't deluded enough to believe she could ever fill the hole in her heart left from relinquishing her daughter. But she wanted a baby and another chance to be the mother she'd always dreamed she could have been. And despite being burned three times, she still wanted a chance at love.

She closed her eyes, inhaled deeply and exhaled slowly, trying to buy calm and time and to gather her courage.

It's the right thing to do.

She met Mitch's gaze. "I'll marry you."

Mitch's fingers contracted, and then he released her. "I'll

have my lawyer draw up a prenup. As soon as it's done and yours has looked it over, we'll do this."

The caution lights flashed. "A prenup?"

"Standard protocol when there's so much inequity in each partner's net worth."

Understandable. If she were him, she'd want one, too. But a small nagging part of her wished he trusted her without legal backup. "You're in a hurry to do this?"

"Why wait?"

"I'd, um…like my parents to be here."

"I'll charter a jet."

"I'll need to see how soon we can reserve the church."

"I'd prefer a private ceremony here."

She'd always dreamed of a church wedding. "But—"

"Your sister has been dead three months, my father just over one. An elaborate ceremony would be inappropriate."

He had a point. "Okay. But I want my preacher to preside."

"A judge will work just as well."

"Not negotiable, Mitch. I want the church's blessing."

His jaw shifted into the stubborn angle with which she'd become so familiar. "If he can do it by the end of the week. I'll make it worth his while to be available."

Her head spun at the speed with which he made life-changing decisions. "I'll talk to him tomorrow after the service. He's not going to be happy about the rush. He usually requires some kind of premarital counseling. Perhaps you'd like to come with me and persuade him to skip that part."

His shoulders stiffened. Mitch's green eyes darkened and drilled into hers. "I'll be there."

Even her preacher had his price.

Carly would become Mrs. Mitch Kincaid Friday evening.

Shocked and a little disillusioned by how easily money had trumped faith and principle this morning, Carly followed

Mitch toward the hundred-foot-long yacht docked at the back of the Kincaid property after church. All it had taken was a generous donation and her pastor had fallen all over himself to accommodate Mitch's wishes. If he'd had other plans for Friday evening, he hadn't mentioned them.

"It's Rhett's nap time. Can't we go boating later?"

"He can sleep on board. I had a nursery set up in one of the cabins while we were out this morning. We have a two o'clock appointment."

"With?"

He paused and turned on the sidewalk. The brisk breeze blowing off the water ruffled his nearly black hair and fluttered the lapels of the navy suit he'd worn to church. She couldn't see his eyes because of his dark sunglasses. "The jeweler."

Her mind shrieked and her feet skidded to a stop. Rings. She hadn't even thought about rings. He was moving too fast. "Can't we drive there?"

"Yes, if we want our engagement to be front-page news tomorrow. I'm trying to avoid having cameras shoved in our faces each time we leave the house."

Front-page news? A shiver racked her despite the ninety-degree heat. She hugged Rhett closer. "That's going to happen?"

"Our marriage will make news. But the attention will pass. Eventually. Lunch is waiting on board."

Carlos, the gardener, and Tomas, a general handyman who helped wherever needed, waited on the dock. Mitch greeted them, stepped on board and turned to offer Carly a hand across the gangplank. The hot seal of their palms quickened her pulse. They'd made love four times in the past twenty-six hours, the most recent just before church this morning, and yet her heart still tripped when he touched her.

From the moment she stepped into the main cabin, she realized the Kincaids took luxury with them wherever they went. She'd been on boats before, but never one as opulent as this. This floating living room with its hardwood floors, white leather sofas and beveled glass and teak tables could have been in anyone's home. China, crystal and a silver ice bucket holding a bottle of something waited on a full-size dining-room table beneath a sparkling chandelier. The plastic high chair looked as out of place as Carly felt.

The engines rumbled to life beneath her feet, but the boat barely rocked as Carlos and Tomas cast off. Mitch led her to the table, took Rhett from her and competently strapped him into the high chair. Mitch had come a long way and no longer froze when Rhett touched him. In fact, he often initiated contact and this morning he'd had Rhett dressed and fed before Carly emerged from the shower. He'd be a good father.

Mitch pulled out her chair. Carly sat. His fingertips dragged along her neckline as he lifted her hair away from the high back of her chair, and she shivered. He bent down and pressed a kiss in the curve of her neck and shoulder and then his teeth grazed her skin. Her breath hitched and heat blossomed in her abdomen.

He straightened, circled to the opposite side of the table and sat directly across from her. She couldn't look away from his handsome face, his tanned skin and his intensely green eyes.

Hers. The possessive statement echoed through her as she briefly shifted her gaze to his mouth. The contrast between his hard jaw and soft lips sent arousal prickling through her. The things he'd done with those lips last night had devastated her inhibitions.

As if he could read her mind, hunger flared in his eyes and arousal darkened his cheekbones. A corresponding flush swept over her. She broke his gaze and focused on Rhett, who was busy examining the dog stamped onto the back of his hand in the church nursery this morning. The church stamped parents and children with the same figure at drop-off time to keep anyone from taking home the wrong child. Both she and Mitch wore blue dogs to match Rhett's.

Bonded by a blue dog. Marked as a family.

Mitch had surprised her by not only allowing himself to be stamped, but also by not washing away the ink as soon as possible.

He'd surprised her in a lot of ways this morning. First, he'd been so attentive at church that anyone watching them would believe this was a real romance. Second, he'd incited very impious thoughts each time his thumbnail grazed her palm or his thigh pressed hers during the sermon. And third, he'd played her preacher like the powerbroker she suspected Mitch Kincaid might be behind his KCL desk.

It bothered her that he believed money could buy anything. But in his experience, it probably had.

She wanted to trust that their marriage would work and wanted to have faith that mutual passion and concern for Rhett would be enough to sustain the relationship. And if she were lucky, love would grow. She was already heading down that path. How could she not? Mitch was tall, dark, handsome, confident, intelligent and fair. His employees respected and trusted him—much more than they had his father, apparently.

And he did nice things. She fingered the boy charm pendant.

Despite the haunting invasion of her sister's warnings that kept seeping into her brain, Carly kept finding more to like about Mitch every day.

Elena, Carlos's wife, entered with a tray. She served Carly and Mitch skewers of large grilled shrimp atop beds of rice and sautéed vegetables. Rhett's plastic plate held his favorite diced foods. Elena left them.

Mitch reached for the bottle and corkscrew. The dark hairs on his wrist beneath his snowy shirt fascinated Carly as he worked the cork free. "After we finish with the jeweler, you need to call your parents. I've arranged for the jet to pick them up Thursday morning and carry them back Sunday. Since we can't leave town until the end of the year unless it's business-related, we won't have a honeymoon."

A honeymoon. Time devoted to nothing but discovering each other's minds and bodies. She hadn't given it a thought, but now that he'd planted the seed she realized she'd love a week of Mitch's undivided attention. Desire made her shift in her seat. "That's okay. I wouldn't want to leave Rhett anyway."

He popped the cork without spilling a drop—the sign of experience—and then filled the flutes with bubbly gold champagne. After wedging the bottle back in the ice, he lifted his flute. "To us. May our marriage be everything we expect it to be."

"To us," she echoed and *tink*ed her rim against his.

The chilled liquid slid down her throat like nectar. "Mmm. You know your wines. I'll grant you that."

Carly found an appetite that had been AWOL since yesterday morning. She set down her glass and attacked her lunch. The shrimp and crisp veggies tasted divine. She'd been too nervous to eat breakfast today. She had no trouble replacing the calories they'd burned now.

"Rand will be my witness. You can invite one of your own or use your parents," Mitch said fifteen minutes later after she'd practically inhaled her meal.

"Only one?"

"The fewer people who are a part of this, the less likely it'll turn into a circus. And unless you intend to quit your job you'll need to warn them at work that they might need to beef up security until the media storm blows over."

"What? No, I'm not going to quit. I love my job."

"Paparazzi enjoy exploiting the rich and famous."

Paparazzi. A warning prickled her skin. "I'm neither."

"You will be."

She chewed over the disturbing news. It wouldn't be the same as before. She wasn't young and naive, and Mitch wasn't going to hang her out to dry to save his own reputation.

Was she making a mistake to bring Rhett into a world where the media watched and waited for fodder?

No. She was giving him what Marlene had wanted—his birthright.

"We'll apply for the marriage license first thing in the morning."

"What about my clients?"

"Reschedule an hour or two. And while you're at it, take Thursday and Friday off."

"Mitch, I can't. People are counting on me."

"Your parents will be here and you have a wedding to plan."

Right again. She mentally pictured her schedule, trying to guess who could be shuffled and who couldn't. "I'll see what I can do."

Rhett finished his lunch and his eyes grew droopy. Carly was glad of the excuse to escape. Mitch showed her below deck to a stateroom as posh as the one in the manor. He'd taken care of every detail from diapers to Rhett's favorite stuffed gator.

She changed Rhett and tucked him into the crib. He immediately went to sleep, taking away her excuse for hiding out. It was almost two o'clock, so she made her way back upstairs.

The engines quieted as she returned to the living area. "Why are we stopping?"

"We have company."

Before she could ask who, she spotted another boat bumping alongside. But it wasn't the harbor patrol, which often stopped boats to check for safety issues. The crew of the other yacht linked the boats, and a distinguished-looking older gentleman wearing a goatee and carrying a briefcase came aboard. Mitch greeted him at the door and gestured for him to enter.

"Carly, this is Mr. Belmonté, our jeweler. He has a selection of rings for you to look over."

Surprised once again, she glanced out the windows on

either side of the room. The closest landmass was at least a mile away. "We're in the middle of the bay."

"It's the best way to ensure privacy," Mitch said as if he shopped in such odd places on a regular basis.

She'd assumed they'd dock at the back door of the jewelry store…or something.

"Good afternoon, Ms. Corbin. I have chosen a number of designs based on Mr. Kincaid's description, but if none of them pleases you I have more back at the shop."

After shaking her hand, Belmonté placed his briefcase on the coffee table and flipped it open. Carly nearly fell over backward. The glittering display of fifty or more rings on black velvet had to be worth bazillions. She couldn't catch her breath, and someone had glued her feet to the floor. Surreal.

Mitch slipped an arm around her waist and guided her to the sofa. Carly collapsed onto the cushion because her legs had started shaking. And then Mitch sat beside her, as close as a postage stamp. The heat of his body seeped into hers.

"Do you see anything you like, sweetheart?"

Sweetheart? Her head swiveled his way. Their gazes collided. "I—I—"

Mitch looked at her steadily. His hand covered the fist she'd curled on her thigh. *He's playing a part.* He'd said everyone had a price. Did he think the jeweler did, too?

Play along. It will be better for Rhett in the long run.

"Which do you prefer? Yellow gold, white gold or platinum?"

Carly turned her attention back to the tray. "They're all so beautiful…and so…" Huge. There couldn't be anything in the tray that cost less than her car. She'd bet some of the pieces cost as much as her house.

She blinked and tried again. "I can't wear anything too large. I work with my hands."

"May I make a suggestion?" The jeweler selected a ring. "This is a flawless three-carat Asscher cut stone. When the platinum bands are added—" he paused to flank the ring with a pair of matching bands "—the stone is protected."

The wedding bands cupped the stone's edges in a swirl of gleaming metal. "It's beautiful."

"Try it on," Mitch urged her. "Here. Let me."

He took the rings from Belmonté, lifted her hand and slid the cool metal down her finger. Warm hands. Cold rings. The contrast overwhelmed her nervous system. But the rings fit as if made for her. A sign? Or a coincidence?

"Like it?" Mitch asked in that low rumble that made her skin tingle.

A knot formed halfway down her throat. Her fingers convulsed around Mitch's. She nodded, and garbled, "Yes."

"We'll take it."

"And your ring, sir?" The jeweler flipped a lever and another velvet layer dropped to cover the solitaires and display a selection of men's rings. "You suggested something simple."

She doubted she could afford anything in the tray, but tradition stated the bride buy the groom's ring. "Mitch—"

"This one." Quick and decisive, the Mitch she'd come to know, selected a wide band and slipped it on.

"Very good choice, sir. Also platinum and it complements Ms. Corbin's ring nicely."

She nudged Mitch's thigh. "Could I speak to you a moment?"

"Certainly. Excuse us." He rose and escorted her toward the bow of the ship. Carly glanced through a doorway and gaped. The kitchen or galley or whatever it was called was roomier than the one in her house. Mitch stopped in a stateroom that put her Kincaid Manor suite to shame.

"I'm not sure I can afford that ring."

"I'm paying for it and the rest of the wedding."

"But the bride is supposed—"

"Supposed to let the groom take care of her."

"But, Mitch—"

His mouth covered hers. He parted her lips and swept the protests from her tongue with his. Leaning closer, he sandwiched her body between inflexible wall and immovable muscle. His strength and his weight held her captive, freeing his hands to caress her waist, her hips and the outsides of her breasts. Overwhelmed by his flavor, his possession, Carly's senses rioted. The strength seeped from her frame until only the thigh he'd wedged between hers held her upright.

By the time he lifted his head, she couldn't find her breath or gather her protests to argue her point. She now knew what kissed into submission meant. In a minute she'd work up a protest over such manhandling.

"Let's get rid of Belmonté," his rough voice scraped over her already heightened senses.

Protesting could wait. "Good idea."

They returned to the salon. Within minutes, the deal was done and Belmonté had left on his boat. Carly stared numbly at the rings weighting her hand like concrete blocks.

She was doing the right thing.

She was certain of it. Almost.

Anxiety gnawed at her stomach, but then Mitch laced his fingers through hers and led her toward the stateroom.

She'd worry about worrying later. Because anything that felt this good had to be right.

Ten

"**B**oons! Boons!"

Rhett's excited squeal drilled Carly's eardrum and jerked her out of her inattentive funk. She looked up and stopped midshuffle.

Helium-filled balloons in every color of the rainbow filled the breakfast nook. "Yes. Balloons."

Rhett kicked and squirmed. She set him down and he scampered across the tile to the curling ribbon streamers tied to the back of the chair Carly always used.

Who? Della? And how had she known it was Carly's birthday? The housekeeper wasn't in the kitchen, but she'd been here because the coffee was on. The scent of Mitch's favorite gourmet brew filled the air.

Mitch stepped up behind her. He didn't make a sound, but Carly's personal Mitch detection system kicked in and she knew he was there before his chest nudged her shoulder and his arm encircled her waist.

He pulled her against him. "Happy birthday."

The balloons were from Mitch? She gasped in surprise and then promptly choked up. Not just because this was a totally unexpected and frivolous gift coming from a no-nonsense man like him, but because she couldn't share it with Marlene. Her sister had loved over-the-top gestures like this.

As if he understood, his arm tightened. He rubbed his smooth, freshly shaven jaw against her temple and his cologne teased her nose. "Nadia says there comes a time in a woman's life when adding more candles to a cake becomes annoying. But she says you can never have too many balloons or flowers. I don't know your favorite color, so I covered the bases."

"Blue. I love blue." Boring, conservative blue. What did that say about her?

"Boons, Mitt. Boons!" Rhett trilled and jumped up and down on the tile by Carly's chair.

"I take it he likes balloons?"

"Oh yes." A crinkling sound caught her attention. She twisted to face Mitch.

He pulled a massive bouquet of long-stemmed roses in every shade from the purest white to the deepest burgundy from behind his back and offered them to her. "Twenty-eight buds for twenty-eight years. But no blue. Sorry."

"They're beautiful, Mitch. Thank you." She accepted them and buried her nose in the fragrant blooms. Marlene would have adored this, too. Carly's indrawn breath stuttered across each rib. She was not going to lose it. Not in front of Mitch. Not in front of Rhett.

"How did you know? About our—my birthday, I mean." She had to force the words through her tight throat.

His gaze shifted briefly to the excited child before returning to hers and then he shrugged. "Tina must have mentioned it."

"Well, thank you. This is a wonderful surprise and a great way to start the day." She forced a smile.

He took the bouquet from her and laid it the on the table and then cupped her face in his warm hands. His thumbs lifted her chin. "You okay?"

No. How was it possible to be so happy and sad simultaneously? She squared her shoulders. "Of course. Why wouldn't I be?"

"Because you're thinking about your sister."

She snatched a breath at his perceptiveness. The fact that he could mention her sister without the usual sneer in his voice doubled her surprise. "How did you know?"

His fingertips grazed her cheek, her neck, and then his palms skimmed down her arms to catch her hands and squeeze. The gesture of comfort and support nearly made her bawl.

"Could be the way you slinked out of my bed this morning and crept back to your room to hole up in the dark instead of letting me be your wake-up call."

Desire burned through her like a blown gas main. Since Sunday, he'd awoken her every morning with his hands and mouth and passion.

At the risk of ruining the mood, she decided to be honest. "Marlene and I usually spent our birthdays together. When we couldn't we talked on the phone early in the morning. This is the first time we w-won't. I—" She paused to swallow an immovable lump. His grip tightened around her fingers. "I didn't expect it to be so h-hard."

Their gazes held and the understanding softening Mitch's eyes made hers sting. "I didn't always like my father, but that doesn't mean I don't miss him every single day or think of things I want to tell him or show him." His gaze shifted over her shoulder to the child still enthralled with the *boons.*

"I'm sorry he missed out on Rhett." Raw grief roughened his voice.

She loved him.

The emotion didn't sneak up on her as it had with her past

loves. It hit like a head-on collision, winding her and making her adrenaline race and her heart thump wildly. In that instant Carly knew without a doubt that she'd fallen *hard* for Mitch Kincaid.

Hoping her discovery wasn't written all over her face, she searched his eyes, looking for reciprocity. But, as usual, Mitch hid his emotions well. That's why the rare glimpses into his head like the revelation about his father meant so much to her.

He blinked, breaking the spell, and then a wicked smile slanted his lips. "Call in sick today. We'll play hooky, hang out at the beach or laze by the pool. Spend the day in bed. We'll do whatever you want."

She was tempted. "I can't. I've already had to shuffle too many patients because of the wedding…and it's better to keep busy, I think."

"I can keep you busy." The sensual promise in his words threatened to hijack her brain on a hormone express train.

"If I didn't have people counting on me to help them get their lives and bodies back together, then I'd jump on your offer…and you." Her face burned. She'd never made such a forward statement before.

His nostrils flared and his chest and pupils expanded. "I like the sound of that. And I'll hold you to it. Tonight."

He brushed a kiss over her lips, a kiss that tasted like a promise. A kiss that upped the stakes.

Because now she not only had to make Mitch love Rhett, she had to make him fall in love with her.

"Where are you racing off to?"

Rand's question cut Mitch off midwhistle. He stopped in the hall outside his brother's office.

Whistle? Had he been whistling? He had. "I'm headed home."

"You've left early every night this week."

"Six isn't early."

"It is for you."

Couldn't argue with facts. He stepped into Rand's—formerly their father's—office. Strange how the anger and resentment he'd experienced upon hearing the terms of the will had faded. But Rand had proved his worth, so maybe not so surprising after all. "I want to have dinner with Carly and Rhett."

And not just because he knew he'd have Carly naked seconds after Rhett crashed for the night. Anticipation kicked his pulse up a notch.

"Didn't you and the kid take Carly to lunch today?"

"I thought she needed the pick-me-up of lunch with Rhett. It's her birthday. Her first without her twin."

Rand's eyes narrowed. His leather chair creaked as he leaned back. "You have a thing for her. Got her in the sack yet?"

"That's none of your business. But, yeah, I have a thing for her. We're getting married Friday night. Be my best man?"

Rand's jaw dropped and his eyebrows shot up. "You're getting married in two days and you haven't mentioned it?"

He'd intended to ask Rand sooner, but they'd spent the past three days in confidential meetings trying to unravel some issues their father had left behind. By the end of each day, Mitch wanted nothing more than to leave the stress of his father's sloppy management behind and go home to the warmth and the laughter that now embodied Kincaid Manor. The current atmosphere was a big change from the meat-locker chill of the past.

"I'm telling you now." He'd delayed informing Rand about the wedding because he knew his brother would want explanations—explanations that would delay his departure.

"Are you out of your mind? What happened to your conviction that Carly is a mercenary bitch identical to her twin in more than looks?"

"I told you I'd misread her."

"You told me you *might* have misread her and that she'd rejected the million-dollar offer to hand over Rhett."

"She also declined the five million I offered in the prenup."

Carly's attorney had nearly had a heart attack at the conference table when Carly had refused to sign until the settlement clause was struck from the document.

Rand's eyes narrowed suspiciously. "Why?"

"She said the money wasn't hers and she didn't want it."

And surprisingly, Mitch believed her. Carly's stubborn insistence had initially shocked the hell out of him, but then he started replaying details in his mind. She'd lived modestly even since moving into the manor, and the house she'd left behind was no showcase. She budgeted her expenses and paid Rhett's day-care bills without asking Mitch to pitch in. In fact, she hadn't asked him for anything that came with a price tag other than fencing around the water features to keep Rhett safe.

Maybe she was the real deal. He'd seen so few altruistic women in his lifetime he probably wouldn't recognize one if she bit him on the ass. Which Carly had. Several times. And he'd liked it.

He wiped off his grin and focused on Rand's scowling face. "Looks like identical DNA doesn't produce identical personalities."

These past few weeks of playing house had made him question his "everybody has a price" mantra. And he'd begun to believe Carly would never tire of Rhett and responsibility, and run.

Rand stared at him as if he'd sprouted horns. "You think marrying her will put a lock on the kid."

He should have known big brother would figure out his plan. "It won't hurt. But that's not why I'm marrying her."

"You telling me you love her?"

Did he love Carly? No. But could he?

"Your silence is screaming, little brother."

Mitch glanced at his watch. A knot of tension snarled at

the base of his skull. "I know what I'm doing. So are you going to be there Friday night at eight or not?"

"I'll be there. But I hope to hell you're not making as big a mistake as Dad did when he became entangled with the other Corbin."

So did Mitch. Because Carly made him want to try something he didn't believe existed—an honest, committed relationship based on something besides his bottom line.

He could get used to this.

Mitch stared at the moonlight dancing on his ceiling and waited for his heart rate to drop back into double digits. But that wasn't going to happen if Carly pressed her lips to his chest one more time.

He tangled his fingers in her hair and tugged her head back. She smiled up at him and tenderness filled him—an emotion that had nothing to do with ringing the bell to start round two of astronomical sex.

This marriage to Carly would be good. And perhaps he wouldn't rush to end it immediately after the adoption went through.

"Thank you for everything you did today, Mitch. It helped…a lot."

"I'm glad." The approval in her eyes made him want to pound his chest like some damned caveman. He settled for pulling her flush against his body and tucking her head into the crook of his shoulder. The air-conditioning kicked on, cooling his sweat-dampened skin.

She took a shuddery breath and tensed against him. "I woke up this morning thinking about Marlene's last moments. That's why I sneaked out. I needed to call the police detective and check the status on the investigation. I need to know the bastard who hit her will be held accountable for what he did."

Mitch fought the tension invading his limbs and robbing

his peace. He couldn't tell Carly he suspected his father had either been driving the car or had paid someone else to take out her sister. "What did the detective say?"

She rolled up onto her elbow. "He says the case has been put on the back burner due to more pressing issues. You're an almighty Kincaid. Can't you light a fire under them? I want someone punished for leaving Marlene to die."

"Carly—"

"Please, Mitch. I don't want your money and I couldn't care less about the Kincaid fortune. But I would really, really like for you to use your influence on this."

He didn't know what to say to her plea. Finding her sister's killer could destroy his family and KCL.

"I'll see what I can do."

But he wouldn't be calling the police.

Carly's parents were due in a matter of hours, and she still hadn't found her missing bra.

Mitch had whisked her straight upstairs to bed after she'd accepted his proposal, and then life had intervened and she hadn't had time to return to the study and search again. Her days had been an exhausting crush of caring for Rhett, working in rescheduled patients, looking for a wedding dress and squeezing in lawyer visits. Her nights had been filled with Mitch.

She plucked at her shirt, fanned her overheated body and expelled a long, slow breath.

She'd expected one of the cleaning ladies to find her bra, and then it would turn up in her laundry. But they hadn't. With her luck, her father would find it. She knew how much he liked libraries, and the Kincaids' book collection was impressive. He'd probably locate her Playtex between Plato and Poe…or wherever Mitch had thrown it.

She headed straight for Mitch's study the minute she

handed Rhett off to Della who had begged to borrow the child for another Web cam chat. The widowed Duncan sisters had declared themselves honorary grandmothers, and with her parents living all the way across the country, Carly couldn't be happier for Rhett to have a makeshift extended family.

The study smelled of lemon polish and eucalyptus. Every surface gleamed—even the desk where she and Mitch had savaged each other five nights ago. Carly scanned the furniture and the tall cherry shelves. Nada.

She dropped to the floor and looked under furniture. No bra. Wait! A white fragment caught her eye. The fax rang as she scrambled to her feet. She ignored it and headed for the floor-length curtains. She whipped back the heavy drapes. Jackpot!

She snatched up her bra and stuffed it in her pocket. The fax spewed pages. There had been a bit of back and forth conversation between her lawyer and Mitch's over the prenuptial agreement and Rhett's adoption. Was this more of the same?

She crossed the room as the last sheet slid onto the tray and lifted the report. Her name jumped out at her from the cover sheet. But this wasn't from an attorney's office. The header said Lewis Investigations, Discreet Private Detective Agency.

A sense of foreboding invaded her, chilled her, and made her hands tremble as she turned to page two.

Kincaid, I promised you a mother lode of info to discredit Carly Corbin as guardian of your father's kid. Here it is. You'll have to consult your attorney to see if Corbin's juvenile records will be admissible in court. If so, then you should have a good shot at gaining sole custody.

Her knees buckled. She sank into the leather chair behind the desk. Mitch didn't want to adopt Rhett and become a family. He wanted to rip her precious nephew right out of her arms. And he was willing to marry her to accomplish his goal.

The gifts, the lovemaking, the proposal had all been ways to win her trust and cover his duplicitous tracks.

Her eyes and throat burned. She blinked and turned the page.

You were right about Carly graduating high school a year later than her twin. Good catch. That clue led to the break I needed.

At age sixteen Carly Corbin had an affair with her twenty-four-year-old volleyball coach. She became pregnant. The coach stated publicly that he wanted nothing to do with Carly or her child—which he doubted was his because Corbin was promiscuous. He accused her of seduction and trying to break up his family. He returned to the wife and kids after receiving no more than a slap on the wrist for screwing an underage kid. His wife not only stood by him, she filed an "Alienation of Affection" suit against C. Corbin, which was later dismissed.

C. Corbin spent six months in a home for unwed mothers and gave the baby up for adoption.

See attached copies of court documents, newspaper articles from Nashville paper, etc.

Carly numbly sifted through the pages and her past came rushing back. She'd been crucified in the papers, deemed the Locker Room Lolita, abandoned by her friends and asked to leave school. She'd disappointed her parents and herself. She'd lost her heart, her innocence and her baby. Her family had moved to another state while she was in the home for girls, to escape the shame she'd caused.

An elephant-size weight settled on her chest. Like every other man she'd fallen for, Mitch had betrayed her. She couldn't believe how much more it hurt this time than the others.

She forced herself to read on.

C. L. Corbin opened an offshore account eighteen months ago with a single one-hundred-thousand-dollar deposit. The beneficiary of that account is Rhett Kincaid Corbin.

She squeezed her eyes shut and groaned. Mitch hadn't lied. Marlene had taken the money to abort Rhett and then not gone through with the procedure.

Questions tumbled like an avalanche through Carly's brain.

Why hadn't Marlene aborted after taking the money? Why had she continued the pregnancy but kept it a secret? Why had she practically gone into seclusion in Carly's house and waited until Rhett was eight months old to introduce him to his father?

Had she felt guilty because she knew taking the money was wrong? Or had she been afraid?

Why had her sister opened the account in Carly's name? It wasn't as if Marlene hadn't pretended to be Carly before, but…this made no sense. If the money was for Rhett, then why not list the account in his name?

"Marlene, what have you done?"

Acid burned a path up her esophagus, but she was determined to finish the last paragraph of the damning report.

I have yet to find evidence linking your father to Marlene Corbin's "accident," but will continue to investigate if you are convinced of his involvement.

Shock stole her breath. Mitch suspected his father had been involved in Marlene's death.

Slowly the gears in her brain turned. That was why he'd silenced her with a kiss last night. He didn't want to discuss Marlene's death or his father's part in it. The Kincaids certainly had enough money to cover up something of this magnitude.

She had to do something. But what?

She heard Mitch's voice in the hall and wanted to run. She couldn't face him now. Not while she felt raw and exposed and too hurt to be logical. But short of diving beneath the desk, escape wasn't possible.

He entered the office with his cell phone to his ear. "I'm getting it now."

And then he spotted her. His gaze dropped to the papers in her hand, then bounced to the now empty fax tray and back to her.

"I'll call you back." He snapped the phone closed. "Carly."

It hurt to look at him. Hurt to know she'd been such a fool. No better than she'd been at a young, naive, stupid sixteen. Now she couldn't use young or naive as excuses.

This time she'd just been stupid. But now she was hurting and angry. She pushed to her feet. "You think your father killed Marlene. How could you keep it from the police? How could you keep that from *me*—especially after last night?"

"There is no proof he's responsible, but I needed to know—for my sake—that he wasn't."

"And if he was?" A tremor overtook her. Not even wrapping her arms around her middle could stop it.

Mitch shoved a hand through his hair. "I don't know. He's already dead, Carly. He can't be held accountable. But if this leaked, the press would take the family and KCL down. People who had nothing to do with Marlene's death would suffer. Nadia, Rand, Rhett and sixty thousand employees."

The way Rhett would suffer if the Kincaids found out Marlene had deliberately trapped their father. Both of them had secrets they'd rather not share. "And you."

"And me."

"Cleaning up Everett's mess is all you care about."

"It's not all I care about, but it is my job."

And she, Marlene and Rhett had been just another cleanup

detail. She understood Mitch's logic for withholding his suspicions, but she didn't like it.

"You could have asked about my past, Mitch. You didn't have to sneak around behind my back."

"I instigated the investigation before I got to know you."

"I don't want to hear your excuses." Because she'd want to believe him. And for her sake, *for Rhett's sake,* that wasn't wise.

"I'm not making excuses. I'm stating facts."

"Hiring a P.I. to smear my reputation shows how low you're willing to go to get what you want. You want Rhett. You don't want me. But I won't be a part of that plan, and I won't let Rhett be raised by a mean bastard who would intentionally hurt others."

Tugging off the engagement ring and placing it on the leather blotter hurt more than it should. "I'm not marrying you. And if you try to take Rhett from me I will go straight to the press with everything. I survived being flayed by them once. I will again.

"I made a youthful mistake of trusting the wrong person. But you, you're deliberately and willfully trying to cover up a possible murder and take a child from the one person who loves him most."

She forced her feet to carry her around the desk. Mitch stood between her and the exit. "Marlene was right. You are a cold, conniving rat bastard."

Mitch didn't even blink. "Carly, you can't take Rhett and leave. We'll—he'll lose everything."

"Maybe you should have thought of that before. Integrity is worth so much more than money. And you apparently have none of one and too much of the other.

"Here's your fax." She shoved the papers into his hand, stepped around him and headed for the door. But she paused in the threshold. Mitch needed to hear the truth, even though he probably wouldn't believe it. No one had. Except Marlene. Carly didn't know why his knowing mattered, but it did. She faced him.

"The newspaper was wrong. Wes seduced me. He convinced me that I had a chance at a college scholarship if I perfected my volleyball skills. At first I only stayed a few minutes after practice. And then we met longer and on weekends. I thought I was in love. And when he kissed me and held me, I thought he was, too." Her voice broke, but she soldiered on.

"I didn't know he was married until I turned up pregnant. He told me then he'd never leave his wife for me and he offered to help me take care of my problem. *My* problem. As if he'd had nothing to do with the baby we'd made. He took my heart, my virginity and my trust, and threw them away as if they meant nothing.

"I had nowhere else to go but to my parents who went to the police. Wes went to the papers."

She sucked in a slow, painful breath. "He told the reporters I was a tramp hell-bent on destroying his marriage and a hazard to all the innocent boys in my school. I denied it, but nobody listened because Marlene…"

She wheezed in another burning lungful of air. She'd loved her sister, but Marlene hadn't always made the best decisions.

"Marlene got into sex early on. But when she slept with a guy, she always pretended to be m-me. I had a reputation for being loose even though I'd never slept with anyone before Wes. So when he said I seduced him, everyone believed it."

Her nails dented the wooden door frame. "I lost everything. My friends. My home. My parents' trust."

A tear burned a trail down her cheek. She swiped it away. Tears solved nothing. She'd cried an ocean of them twelve years ago to no avail.

"But more than that, I lost the right to watch my precious baby girl grow up. I don't know her name. I'll never see her smile or hear her laugh. I won't get to brush her hair or dry her tears. I can't be there if she n-needs me, and I can never tell her how much I loved her even before she was born or how much it hurt to give her away. But it was the right thing to do. So I did it."

A sob clawed its way up in her throat. She swallowed it back. "So, yeah, if you want ammunition to take Rhett away from me, you probably have it. But the man I thought you were, the man I fell in love with, couldn't be that heartless."

He flinched, and that flinch told her what she needed to know. He didn't love her and probably never would.

"Now you know the facts. Tell your private investigator he got it wrong." She bolted down the hall and up the stairs.

Mitch didn't call her back.

Once in her room, she locked the door, backed against it and slid down the wooden surface until her butt hit the floor. She tilted her head back and blinked furiously to keep her tears at bay. When her vision cleared, she saw the wedding dress she'd fallen in love with but couldn't afford hanging from the canopy bed frame. Mitch must have bought it.

But the beautiful hand-beaded silk gown would never be worn. Not by her.

What was she going to do?

Rhett deserved his share of the Kincaid estate now more than ever before. But Carly didn't think she could bear to stay at Kincaid Manor. Mitch's betrayal had demolished her respect for him and for herself.

Worse, his P.I. might be right. Her past might very well cost her the child she adored.

Eleven

A tap on the door froze Carly's muscles and set her heart racing.

She didn't want to talk to Mitch.

"Mama," Rhett's treble penetrated the closed bedroom door.

Rhett. She'd been in such a panic to pack her belongings that she'd left him with Della too long.

Della. Another casualty of Mitch's deviousness. Carly was going to hate losing the older woman's friendship.

"Carly?" Her mother's voice.

And suddenly Carly needed her mother more than she needed anyone. She dumped her armload of clothes on the bed, rushed to the door and flung it open.

How was she going to explain there wouldn't be a wedding?

She didn't have to say a word. Her mother set Rhett down inside the room, closed the door and opened her arms. Carly fell against her and took strength from her hug.

After a few moments, her mother leaned back to look into

Carly's eyes. "Mitch says you're not going to marry him. Tell me what I can do to help you."

The whole story tumbled out in fits and spurts. The will and Rhett's inheritance. Falling in love with Mitch. The P.I.'s report. Getting her heart broken. Again. Her mother waited until Carly ran out of steam.

"First off, Mitch is right. If his father is responsible for Marlene's…end, then a higher power has already dealt out the consequences. That doesn't mean I don't want to know what happened. I won't rest easy until I do.

"Second, you are my daughter. I know you're hurting now, but I also know you have the most generous heart of any woman I've ever met. You're going to make the right decision." She cradled Carly's cheek. The love and approval in her mother's eyes and words brought tears to Carly's eyes.

"Whatever your decision is, your father and I will support you. If you need to leave, we'll help you. But if you want to stay here for Rhett, then your father and I will move to Miami to be your backup."

"But you love your life in Arizona."

"We love you more. And just like we moved to give you a fresh start after you relinquished your baby, we'd move for you again in a heartbeat."

"I thought you moved because I'd embarrassed you."

"No, dear. We told you we left Nashville because we didn't want you to be continually reminded of painful things and because the press wouldn't let you forget. I know you didn't believe us then, but that's the gospel truth. And with the dangerous path Marlene was headed down, it was a good time for us all to start over somewhere else."

Carly's breath snagged. "You knew about Marlene?"

"Of course I did. And your father and I tried to help her, but she wouldn't let us. She derived something from those boys' attention, as inappropriate as it might have been, that we couldn't give her."

"But the home for unwed mothers…I thought you wanted me out of the house and out of your sight. I thought I'd disgusted you."

"Oh, Carly, I'm sorry I didn't communicate my concerns better. I tried, but I was afraid to harp on and sway you into making a choice you'd regret, one you might hate me for later, so perhaps I didn't say enough. Baby, letting you go through that alone was like tearing off a limb, but we did it anyway because we wanted you to have counselors who would help you make a decision *you* could live with. The home promised me their specialists could do that."

Tears streamed hot paths down Carly's cheeks. "They did. And I know in my heart that I did the right thing. I couldn't have been the mother my daughter deserved."

She studied her finger, the one that for a few hours had worn Mitch's ring. "Mom, for Rhett to inherit his share of Everett's estate he has to live here for the rest of the year. I don't know if I can handle that, but I won't abandon him. He deserves this. It's the only thing his father will ever give him. I need to find a way to make it work."

"Why am I not surprised that you would put Rhett's concerns ahead of your own? Running away has never been your style. And I have no doubt that if you choose to stay, you will find a way to manage it. You're strong, Carly. You can handle anything."

Her mother sat silently for a moment and then tilted her head. "Is there a way to share this monstrosity of a house without having to cross paths with Mitch too frequently?"

"Pish! Orange pish. Big," Rhett cried out.

Carly's glanced over to where he knelt on the window seat pointing toward the koi pond. The evening sun glinted off the windows across the yard and an idea took root.

"The nursery is on the opposite side of the house."

Her mother stood and offered a hand. "Then I think we need to see the nursery, don't you? And if it's suitable, then we're going to lay some ground rules for Mr. Kincaid. He's going to learn he can't mess with the Corbins. We are a formidable team."

"I don't need you tonight," Mitch said Friday afternoon from the door of Rand's office, and then immediately turned and left. He didn't want to discuss his aborted plans.

"Whoa," his brother called out and chased him into the hall. "You can't drop a bomb like that and keep walking. You're supposed to get married in a matter of hours. What happened to the wedding? You come to your senses?"

Rand shadowed him past his PA's desk and into his office. "Spill it, Mitch."

"I had Dad's P.I. do a little checking into Carly's past and her sister's death."

"Marie, hold his calls," Rand told Mitch's PA and then shut the office door. "What did he find? She's already married? A black widow? A transvestite?"

Mitch scowled. He wasn't in the mood for Rand's twisted humor.

"There's nothing in Carly's past to change my mind." If anything, he wanted to hunt down an ex-volleyball coach and remove the guy's nuts with a rusty knife.

He'd been his father's axman for years. He should be able to handle this situation without breaking a sweat. He wiped his brow, trying to clear the vision of Carly's pain-filled eyes from his mind. No such luck.

She loved him.

The idea energized him, but at the same time filled him with panic.

"Then what's the problem?"

"She found Frank Lewis's report."

Rand whistled silently. "The guy is thorough and he doesn't pull his punches."

Rand would know. He'd dealt with Frank before moving to California. "No. He doesn't."

"And? C'mon, Mitch, don't make me drag this out of you word by word."

"I also had Frank investigate Marlene Corbin's death. I was concerned that Dad might have had something to do with the hit-and-run that killed her."

Rand swore. Viciously. "You think he did it?"

"Or paid someone to. I have no proof and no reason other than he was more pissed off at Marlene for having Rhett than I've ever seen him about anything before. Not even Nadia's marr—" No need to bring that up. Not speaking about his sister's early and tragic marriage had become a habit. "You know you didn't cross our old man."

"No. Not without repercussions." Rand and their father had a serious load of issues. His brother's part of the will requirement involved one of them. Rand had been forced to return from his self-imposed exile, take over as KCL's CEO and work side by side with the woman their father had stolen from him. The only woman his brother had ever loved, in Mitch's opinion.

He focused on his own problems. "If Dad was involved, I wanted to know before some reporter ambushed us with evidence and used it to take KCL down."

"Understandable. What did Frank find?"

"Nothing to incriminate Dad. But the fact that I'd suspected him and had Carly investigated was enough to send her into orbit."

"Understandable. Wouldn't you have been pissed?"

"Why? I was dealing with facts, not slander."

Rand stared at him with an odd look on his face.

"What?"

"The end justifies the means. You've become Dad."

Mitch reeled back in disgust. "No, the hell I haven't."

Folding his arms, Rand remained silent.

"I didn't break any laws," Mitch defended.

"What about a violation of her privacy? Withholding evidence from the cops?"

"There is no evidence. That's what I'm telling you. Whose side are you on? I'm trying to protect our inheritance and this company."

"We all are, Mitch. But at what cost? Is Dad going to make us stoop to his level to keep what's rightfully ours? And is holding on to Kincaid Cruise Lines worth sacrificing our self-respect?"

Carly had called him a conniving bastard who would intentionally hurt others. Cold, sobering realization crept over him. She was right, and so was Rand.

He'd become his father.

The idea horrified him. He staggered to the window and stared out at the bay thirty stories below. Everett Kincaid had been a mean, bitter SOB. Not openly. He was too clever for that. No, to your face he was charming, caring, and a benevolent CEO of a company voted best to work for five years in a row. He could charm confidential information out of you and you'd never even notice you were handing him the nails to your own coffin.

And then he'd stab you in the back and bury you without hesitation or second thought if it served his purpose.

Mitch did not want to be his father.

"Did she and the kid move out?"

Rand's words yanked him out of an arctic well of discovery. "They've moved into the nursery."

Yesterday afternoon she'd ordered *his* staff to move her and Rhett's belongings, and afterward Carly and Rhett had gone out to dinner with her parents. Last night, his wing of the house had echoed with silence. Silence he'd once relished. Silence that had kept him up most of the night.

This morning, Mrs. Duncan had appointed herself their guard dog. She'd been cold and abrupt—the housekeeper he remembered from the pre-Carly days. He hadn't even caught a glimpse of Carly and Rhett, and damn it, he'd missed the racket and the cereal bombs at breakfast.

"So we're still in this fight to fulfill the terms of the will," Rand said. "I hope to hell Nadia isn't having as tough a time as we are."

"Yeah." Their father's demands might have brought Rand home, but they'd also kicked Nadia out of the only home she'd ever known.

"What are you going to do?"

Mitch looked up and met his brother's gaze. He didn't have it in him to bluff. "I don't know."

Mutiny.

There was no other word to describe the situation at Kincaid Manor this past week, Mitch decided. His entire staff had turned against him and sided with Carly. They spoke to him respectfully and followed his orders, but otherwise stayed out of his way. Mrs. Duncan served his meals in silence.

He'd become an outcast in his own damned home. And he had no one to blame but himself. He'd hurt someone every member of his staff cared about.

Carly and Rhett were within the walls each evening, but managed to completely avoid him. They ate and played in the nursery. If Carly went running, then it wasn't in the gated community. The jogging stroller stayed in the back of her minivan, which led Mitch to believe if she ran she did so elsewhere.

If he wanted to see her, he'd have to hunt her down.

He hiked up the back stairs Thursday evening after dinner. He'd always avoided the nursery. Sealed off from the rest of the house by thick soundproof walls, the place had been his prison as a kid. He, Rand and Nadia had only been allowed out when they were clean and well-behaved. One screwup and back to prison he'd go. He'd learned early on to listen and not draw attention to himself.

The sound of Rhett's squeals and laughter reached him as soon as his feet hit the landing and he caught himself smiling. His step lightened. He quickened his pace and pushed open the nursery door. Carly knelt on the floor beside Rhett in the large main room. Judging by the towel she held, his brother had just finished his bath. There were three bedrooms off this play area, four if you counted the nanny's suite. Which had she chosen for Rhett? For herself?

"Mitt," Rhett screeched. His naked little body streaked across the room.

Mitch dropped to his knees and held open his arms. The boy hit his chest like a torpedo, winding him, making him ache for what he'd thrown away. Mitch hugged him.

Over the top of the fuzzy dark hair, Mitch's eyes sought Carly's. She rose, clutching the towel in front of her. Her damp T-shirt and low-rider jeans clung in all the right places. His pulse drummed out an appreciative beat.

"You'd better diaper him fast unless you want to use a mop." She tossed a disposable diaper in his direction. Mitch caught it, gently tumbled the boy onto the rug. Rhett rewarded him with cackles and wiggles as he taped the diaper on. And then he lifted his little brother and held him tight.

His fool of a father had missed this. And the boy's mother would, too.

Mitch wasn't going to. But how could he convince Carly to let him back into their lives? He stood, holding Rhett against his heart. "You've been avoiding me."

"Rhett has been getting to know his grandparents. They're talking about moving here to be near him."

"They didn't take the jet back to Arizona on Sunday."

She shook her head and her ponytail swayed. "They preferred to get a commercial flight. They flew out this afternoon."

She'd been with her parents all week. That explained why she hadn't been here when he raced home from KCL each night to his silent, solo dinner. He stared at her and tried to prioritize the week's worth of thoughts he'd saved up to tell to her, but settled for, "I'm glad you stayed."

Her chin lifted. "I promised to see this year through for Rhett's sake. He deserves to know his family and to have something from his father besides DNA."

"I agree." Rhett squirmed. Mitch set him down. The child bolted for Mitch's old room and returned with a toy dump truck. He plopped down on the floor and *vroomed* the truck around the rug.

Carly watched him for a moment before turning back to Mitch. "I tried to return the wedding dress. The store wouldn't take it."

"Don't worry about it."

"It was expensive. I hate to see you waste your money. And it's a beautiful dress. Someone needs to wear it."

No, she definitely wasn't mercenary like her sister. How could he have ever believed otherwise?

"I miss your company, Carly. Yours and Rhett's."

Her gasp filled the silence. She blinked and averted her gaze.

"Come back to the other side of the house."

She shook her head again but didn't look at him. "I can't do that. I can't lo—live with a man who'd try to hurt us."

She walked away. The sight gutted him mainly because he knew his actions were the cause of the gulf between them. He wanted to call her back, to haul her back. Into his life. Into his arms. Into his bed. He'd settle for seeing her face across the breakfast table.

He loved her.

The realization crushed his chest and depleted the oxygen in the room. That's why his life had sucked since Carly had returned his ring. The staff hadn't mutinied. Their cold treatment was the same as it had been for years. Ditto the silent tomb of the house. Both were *exactly* the way he used to like them.

But that was before Carly and Rhett had shown him how different, how dynamic life at Kincaid Manor could be.

He missed the controlled chaos. He missed them.

The house and staff hadn't changed. *He* had.

Because of Carly. Because of Rhett.

"Carly." He waited until she cautiously looked at him. "I'm in love with you."

The color drained from her face and her eyes turned guarded. Tense, silent seconds dragged past. She licked her lips and then swallowed as if gulping down nasty medicine. "You're a man who says and does whatever it takes to get what he wants. But that was low, Mitch. Even for you."

A bowie knife under the ribs would hurt less. "I'm not that man anymore."

Disbelief twisted her mouth. "You're not the man you were seven days ago?"

"No."

"Forgive my skepticism. But no thanks to whatever you're offering. We're happy here."

She didn't look happy. She looked as if she wasn't sleeping any better than he was.

"I'll prove I've changed."

A parody of a smile revealed straight, white teeth. It couldn't distract him from the pain in her eyes. Pain he'd inflicted by acting like his father and taking what he wanted without regard to the casualties.

She picked up Rhett. "You do that, Mitch. Now please leave. I need to get Rhett into bed. Good night."

He'd never been one to walk away from a fight, but he

wouldn't get anywhere with Carly tonight. And if he forced the issue, he might run her out of the house. Now that he knew he loved her, he had to come up with a winning strategy.

But before he left, he wanted to remind her of what they'd had. He strolled toward her. Her expression turned wary. He stopped mere inches away and reached out to hug Rhett. If in the process his hand grazed Carly's rib cage and he made her breath catch, too bad. He planted a kiss on the kid's forehead and inhaled his fresh-from-the-bath scent. He caught a whiff of Carly's fragrance, as well. Hunger and need swelled within him. His throat closed up.

He would not lose them, damn it.

"Good night, kid," he choked out before pivoting on his heel and stalking from the nursery. When he reached the bottom of the stairs he sucked air as if he'd just climbed a mountain. His chest ached, reminding him of that video game he and Rand used to play back in their teens. One where the Ninja master punched into some poor sap's chest and ripped out his beating heart. Mitch was that sap.

Winning Carly back seemed impossible. He had to find a way to convince her he'd changed.

But how?

She didn't care about useless trinkets or money. He couldn't buy her love. A first for him, because he'd never met a woman he couldn't buy. Even Trish had liked to be shown affection via a shower of material goods.

Instead of returning to the emptiness of the house, he slipped out the back door, walked down to the waterfront and stared across the bay. The lights of the distant shore and a few passing boats only marginally distracted him, and the waves lapping against the bulkhead did nothing to soothe him.

What could he give Carly that she would never give herself?

An idea shot across his brain. His pulse quickened and his palms tingled. He knew he had a winning plan.

Flipping open his cell phone, he punched Frank Lewis's auto dial. The P.I. answered on the first ring.

"Lewis Investigations."

"Frank, Mitch Kincaid. I have another job for you."

She'd survived. Barely.

Carly leaned against the door she'd closed behind Mitch. She hadn't expected seeing him to hurt so much. But the fact that the old cliché "out of sight, out of mind" hadn't worked with him should have been a clue that getting over him wouldn't be easy.

And when he'd said he'd fallen in love with her, she'd wanted to believe him so badly she'd almost broken down.

"Mitt. My Mitt."

"Yes, munchkin. Your Mitt. Bedtime." She carried Rhett to bed and tucked him in. After a good-night kiss, she retreated to the nanny suite. Restless, she paced the confines of her room. There was no way she could sleep. Not now. She needed a run—a l-o-n-g one. But she couldn't leave Rhett alone.

The week had been both physically and mentally exhausting. Without her parents' help, she wasn't sure she could have endured the dragging time. She'd worked flat out every day, and in the evenings her parents had asked her to show them each of her favorite parts of Miami. In the process of visiting her old haunts, she'd managed to run into her ex-fiancé. Her first one.

Seeing Sam again had been one of those good news–bad news situations. On the positive side, she hadn't experienced even a twinge of jealousy when he'd introduced his new girlfriend. She'd honestly been able to wish them well with no ill will.

On the bad side, she was completely over Sam and not just trying to plug a hole his leaving had caused. That meant her feelings for Mitch weren't a rebound romance.

She blew out a slow breath, crossed to the window and

pushed back the curtains. Her eyes caught a movement down at the dock. Mitch. Those broad shoulders and erect carriage were impossible to mistake. Her heart clenched.

Her love for Mitch was the real deal. And that meant it would be around to haunt her for a very long time.

Twelve

A video conference call was a hell of a lousy way to have a family reunion. But given the terms of his father's will, with him and Rand stuck in Miami unless traveling for work and Nadia in Dallas, Mitch had no choice.

As uptight as he was about what he had to reveal to his siblings, he couldn't help noticing the stress of being exiled from her home and the job she adored was taking a toll on his sister. "You've lost weight, Nadia."

She grimaced into her Web cam. "Most women would take that as a compliment, but I'm not getting that vibe from you. What's going on, Mitch? You didn't have a video-equipped computer system delivered to my door at the crack of dawn so you could nag me about my diet."

He considered and discarded a dozen options for opening the dialogue. "I'm in love with Carly Corbin."

In his peripheral vision, he caught Rand's head whipping in his direction, but kept his focus on his sister.

"Isn't she's our little brother's guardian?" Nadia asked on the wide-screen monitor in front of him.

"Half brother," Rand corrected.

"Yes, Carly is Rhett's guardian."

"Love is a good thing. Why do you look like hell instead of happy to be sharing this news?"

"Because I screwed up." To bring Nadia up to speed he ran through the details, from trying to buy Rhett to his plan to seduce Carly, marry her and divorce her and ended with the investigation and falling in love.

Rand watched and listened without changing expression or saying a word.

Nadia winced a few times. "You've dug yourself a deep hole. How are you going to get out of it?"

He'd lain awake last night trying to come up with an alternative strategy. He'd found none and had finally rolled out of bed before dawn, skipped breakfast and come into KCL to walk the premises.

"Carly is convinced I'll do or say anything to get my hands on my inheritance. The only way I can prove her wrong—" they weren't going to like this "—is by walking away."

Rand bolted upright. "Are you out of your mind?"

Nadia nodded. "I see your point."

"Mitch, you can't make us lose KCL," Rand's carefully level tone all but shouted.

Mitch swiveled his chair toward his brother. "You're the one who said Dad was forcing us to get down on his level to hold on to the company. I don't want to be him, Rand. I don't want to be a cold SOB who uses people and destroys anyone in the way of my quest."

"He's right, Rand. After sitting here for almost six weeks with nothing to do but watch dust motes dance through the air, I'm ready to call it quits."

"What do you mean, nothing to do?" Rand asked. "I shipped you cases of books and videos."

"And I sent the container garden for your deck and a dozen cookbooks and videos and kitchen gadgets. You have time to learn now," Mitch added.

"And they're all great. Thanks. But I can only sit on my butt for so long. You know the will stated I'm not allowed to work, and I'm only allowed out of this building a few hours each day. It's like being in solitary confinement. I'm going crazy. I don't have any neighbors to talk to. The floors below me are commercial offices and the other penthouse apartment is empty."

Mitch detected a trace of hysteria in her voice. "Do you need me to come down there?"

She seemed to gather herself. "Dad is—was—intolerant of weakness, my need to keep busy. My guess is he set me up like this to make me deal with my baggage. I'm dealing. Let's find a solution for you."

"There isn't one."

"Mitch, love is a once-in-a-lifetime thing. Don't throw it away for money or for Dad. Or for us."

His brother shifted in his seat, drawing Mitch's attention. Rand had never been a squirmy one.

"If I do this, we'll lose everything."

"Do it," Rand barked abruptly. "Do what you have to do. To hell with Dad and his games."

"I agree. Mitch, this is your life. We're all smart, educated and experienced. Rand's already proven there are other companies out there that will hire us. We can find one that suits us without the strings attached or the hoops to jump through."

He looked from his brother's stoic, determined face to his sister's. "You wouldn't hate my guts for this? You wouldn't consider me a traitor?"

Rand shook his head. "You, more than any of us, have always taken one for the team. It's time to take what you need."

"He's right, Mitch. It's your turn. Call me as soon as you've done it. The minute you do, I'm out of here."

His siblings' support brought that damned recurring lump back to his throat. If it didn't clear up soon, he'd have to see a doctor. Mitch nodded. "I'll let you know when it's over."

"I can't wait to meet Carly. She has to be great if she's snagged you. Good luck," Nadia said.

"Thanks. But I'll need more than luck."

"You can do this," Carly told herself when she heard Mitch's key turn in the front door. "You've had a broken heart before."

Not like this.

No, she'd never hurt like this. But she had more at stake now. She had to think of Rhett, and for that precious boy's sake she would suck up her hurt feelings and ignore her broken heart and go back to sharing meals with Mitch.

It wouldn't be the most painful thing she'd ever done.

But it would come close.

Her heart beat faster with each tread of Mitch's firm steps across the marble foyer, and then, framed in the living-room archway, he stopped. His eyes found hers and she felt as if she'd caught a twenty-pound medicine ball in the stomach.

"Mitt. My Mitt." Rhett squirmed in her arms. Carly wheezed in a breath and set him down.

Mitch seemed surprised and pleased to find them waiting for him, but neither emotion could hide the stress tightening his features or erase the tired lines bracketing his eyes and mouth.

"Hey, buddy." Mitch knelt, dropped the papers he carried on the floor and swept his brother up into a hug. For precious seconds, he tucked his face into Rhett's baby-fine hair, closed his eyes and held tight.

Carly's heart turned over. Mitch's love for his brother showed plainly on his face.

Mission accomplished.

Anything she might suffer from her time with Mitch would be worth it because Rhett now had another adult in his corner. One Kincaid down. Two to go.

"We missed you at breakfast," she tendered an olive branch.

Mitch lifted his lids and looked directly at Carly. "I went into work early."

"Pig me up."

He scooped up his folders and rose with Rhett in his arms and then strode purposely toward her, not halting until he was only scant inches away. Determination firmed his jaw. "We need to talk."

His body heat and his scent engulfed her. She swallowed and fisted her hands against the need to smooth a hand over the lapel of his charcoal suit that Rhett had bunched and stroke the beard-stubbled line of his jaw.

"Dinner's waiting. Rhett's hungry."

"Eat. Eat. Eat," the imp chanted.

"Mrs. Duncan." Mitch barely raised his voice, but the housekeeper instantly came bustling through the door from the kitchen as if she'd been waiting for his signal. "Would you please feed Rhett and put him to bed? Carly and I will eat later. We'll serve ourselves."

"Yes, sir. My pleasure." Smiling, she took Rhett and returned to the kitchen.

Carly couldn't handle being alone with Mitch. "I don't th—"

He held up a hand to silence her. "We have a lot of ground to cover, beginning with Marlene's death."

Carly barely had time to grasp that info before Mitch continued.

"Frank Lewis located the car that hit Marlene. The driver,

a college kid, admitted he'd been switching CDs and not looking at the road. When he hit Marlene, he panicked and left the scene because he'd had a few beers. When he heard she died, he was afraid to come forward because he knew he'd face jail time. He stashed the car and only recently took it to a shop for repairs. Frank turned the evidence over to the police."

"Thank you. My parents and I needed answers. I'm sorry for the boy, but I'm also glad your father wasn't involved."

"So am I. Not just because of the legal hassle, but because I needed to know he wasn't such an unfeeling bastard that he'd murder someone—the mother of his child, for godsakes—for pissing him off."

He shoved a hand through his hair. Tension radiated from every abrupt, tight movement, but his unwavering gaze held hers. "I've racked my brain to find a way to prove that I love you and that I have no intention of using you to gain custody of Rhett or taking him away from you to get my hands on my inheritance. I'm ashamed to admit that was my original plan. It isn't anymore. I was selfishly thinking of what *I* wanted, what *I* needed, and I never considered who would be hurt in the process. Although I honestly believed you'd tire of playing mommy and want your freedom."

"I would never do that."

"I know that now." He dropped his files on the coffee table and closed his fingers around her upper arms. His warm grasp contrasted with the cold she felt inside.

"I don't want to lose you, Carly. I don't want to go back to being the ice man you so rightly accused me of being, and I don't want to be a heartless SOB like my father."

"Mitch—"

"Hear me out."

She had no choice unless she used her self-defense

training, kneed him in the groin, broke free and ran. But where would she go?

"The only way I can think of to prove that it's *you* I want and not this pile of rocks or a bunch of ships is to renounce my inheritance."

She gasped. That he wanted her more than this estate or the company he lived for made her eyes sting and her heart well with hope. "You can't do that."

He grimaced. "Right. I can't do that. Because I can't selfishly walk away and screw my sister and brothers out of what they deserve. I won't cost them their inheritance."

He released her and picked up the top file. "You'll find the paperwork in here dividing my share of my father's estate between Rhett, Rand and Nadia, but that can't go into effect until this year is over and the terms of the will have been met."

He tried to thrust the documents into her hands, but she refused to accept them. "Take it."

"Mitch, you can't do this. I won't let you."

"I can do whatever the hell I want with my share. It's not against the law to give it away and no one will be hurt."

"*You'll* be hurt."

"If it proves my love for you, I'd happily give it all away."

He loved her. He'd said it before, but this time she believed he meant it. Her heart blipped irregularly.

"This is your legacy, Mitch. Your future. It's the last thing your father gave to you."

"Don't you get it? It doesn't matter. Not without you." Looking frustrated, he tossed the file back on the table and swiped that hand down his face. He paced a few steps away, pivoted and retraced his path. After huffing a deep breath, he picked up the manila envelope and offered it to her.

She kept her hands by her sides. "If that's more of the same, I don't want it."

"It's not. I can't give you your daughter back. I can't erase twelve years of second-guessing your decision. But I can tell you her name, show you her smile and let you hear a recording of her laughter. I can tell you her life story to date."

Carly had never fainted in her life. She came close now. Spots dotted her vision. She staggered back a step and took huge gulps of air. A tremor started in her legs and worked its way upward until her entire body shook.

She stared at the envelope Mitch held, torn between wanting to rip it open and greedily soak up every detail of her daughter's existence and terrified by what she'd discover.

She thrust her arms behind her back.

Mitch frowned. "I thought you'd want this."

Her breath hiccupped three times. "I do. But I—I don't."

She shook her head. "What if I made a mistake? What if she's unhappy or neglected or unloved? How could I live with myself knowing I'd ruined her life?"

"You didn't."

She clung to those words and searched his eyes for the truth. "How do you know?"

"I had Frank Lewis find her."

"I don't think that's legal."

He sighed. "Probably not. But giving her up has haunted you. I wanted to put your mind at ease."

As far as gifts went, this topped the necklace for being the most perfect thing she'd ever received. But she couldn't accept it. She grasped the golden Rhett charm in her fingers and brushed her thumb over the smooth surface.

"You did the right thing, Carly."

"You're sure?" Her eyes burned. She blinked them furiously and focused on Mitch's face instead of the envelope that could answer what felt like a lifetime of questions.

"I'm sure." He backed her toward the chair closest to the fireplace. "Sit."

She did, not because she liked following orders, but

because her knees were ready to buckle. Until her fingernails bit into her triceps she didn't realize she'd wrapped her arms around her chest and hugged herself.

Mitch opened the flap and extracted a single typed page.

She quickly averted her face and covered her eyes. "Wait. Stop. I can't contact her or see her. I would never disrupt her life like that."

"No. You can't and you won't. I had Frank delete any contact information from his records. So even if you wanted to go too far, you couldn't."

She sought Mitch's eyes again. "Just tell me one thing. Is she happy?"

Mitch looked inside the envelope. "Yes. Do you want to see her picture?"

"Yes. *No!*" She wrestled temptation. "No, it's better not to know, better not to search for her in every crowd. I do that enough already without knowing what she looks like."

"Would you like to know her name?"

The push-pull for answers continued. A name wouldn't hurt. She nodded. "Just her first name."

"Her name is Katherine. She goes by Katie."

"Katie." She rolled the name around on her tongue. Her little girl's name was Katie. A sob punched its way up her throat.

"She's not alone, Carly. She has parents who love her and a younger sister who's also adopted."

Maybe Katie's sister would be there for her the way Marlene had always been for Carly. For several moments, she was too choked up to speak. "Thank you."

"Do you want to see the rest?"

It took a minute to find the strength to do the right thing— the right thing for Katie. But she finally shook her head.

"Are you sure?"

"Yes. It's enough to know Katie's happy."

He extracted another sheet from the envelope and offered

it to her. Carly leaned back and squeezed her eyes shut. It wasn't easy when she wanted to know so much.

"It's a list of addresses of the agencies that help connect birth parents with the children they relinquished. I'll help you sign up. And then after Katie's eighteen, if she ever wants to find you, she can."

She opened her eyes and accepted the list. The page rattled in her hand. She hugged it to her chest and blurted, "Burn it."

Mitch stiffened. "The file?"

"Yes. Please, Mitch. I'm strong enough to do the right thing now. I might not always be."

After a moment's hesitation he crossed to the fireplace, extracted a match from the brass holder and struck it into flame. His gaze caught hers, waiting. Carly nodded, and Mitch set the match to the corner of the envelope.

Fire licked upward, consuming secrets best left untold. For Katie's sake.

Mitch dropped the burning pile onto the grate and returned to Carly's side. He knelt by the chair, rested one hand on Carly's knee and the other on her shoulder. Together they watched the last bits of paper curl into ash and the microcassette warp and melt.

When it was over, he cradled her face and wiped her wet cheeks with his thumbs. His eyes met hers, and the love and approval she saw in the deep green depths filled her with hope.

"You did the right thing, Carly," he repeated.

She couldn't hear those words often enough. And whether Mitch meant today or twelve years ago didn't matter. A smoldering ember of happiness flickered to life deep inside her.

"Marry me, Carly. Not for the inheritance. Not for Rhett. Marry me because you've taught me how to do the right thing. And let me love you. Because of you I finally know how."

Air stuttered from her lungs, forced out by the emotions

expanding inside her. She cupped his face and brushed her thumb over his mouth. He kissed the tip.

"You always knew how, Mitch. You've been putting your family first all along. I love you, too. Yes, I'll marry you. For Rhett's sake. But mostly for mine."

Epilogue

Ten months later

"What's that?" Carly asked as she approached the double lounger where Mitch reclined on the back deck of the island villa he'd rented for their honeymoon.

He tossed the envelope on the table and checked out Carly's curves in the tiny bikini he'd bought her this morning. Oh yeah. He wanted some of that.

Her knowing smile reminded him he hadn't answered her question. "It's a letter from my father. The attorney gave it to me before we left Miami. I'll read it later. Right now I have better things to do, like starting our honeymoon off with a bang. Literally. And for that I need you naked."

He winked and reached for the string tying her top at her nape. "This cottage is isolated enough that no one will see if you stay naked for the duration of our stay."

She grinned but swatted his hand away. "I will if you will, but first, the letter. We waited nine months for this honeymoon. I'm sure you're man enough to wait five more minutes."

Her challenge made him smile. The woman did love issuing challenges. Anticipation hummed through his veins. He and Carly had married in her church within two weeks of her accepting his proposal the second time, and he still couldn't get enough of her. The year required by the terms of his father's will had finally ended, and they'd wasted no time in turning Rhett over to his grandparents for some serious spoiling and jumping on a chartered jet. They'd officially kicked off their honeymoon an hour later—in the mile-high club.

He pulled her onto the chair beside him and against his chest before reaching for his father's last words. Part of him didn't want to let the old man intrude on what promised to be one hell of a great week.

Thanks to Carly, Mitch had his head on straight. KCL was thriving under Rand's leadership and Nadia had put her ghosts behind her and was finally happy.

"Mitch, read it. Whatever it says, we'll deal with it. Together."

He took strength from the love-filled brown eyes of the woman he adored more than he ever thought possible and reached for the envelope. His hands trembled as he broke the seal and unfolded the page.

Dear Son,
If you're reading this, then I've kicked it and you've done what I expected of you. You stuck out the year with your little brother. I always could count on you, Mitch. You were my right hand.

It saddened me to see you shut yourself off after you shed that faithless bitch you had the misfortune of hooking up with a few years back. Good riddance to her. She wasn't right for you.

If I played my cards right, being responsible for your brother might have thawed that heart of yours. Children have a way of doing that. Each and every one is a blessing. One that should be shared with someone you love. When you have some of your own, you'll know what I mean, and I hope that day comes while you're still young enough to enjoy them.

I put you in a difficult position with Rhett's momma and for that, I apologize. Marlene swore she loved me, and I think she honestly did. She showed it in a dozen ways. She wanted to be my wife and knew I was old-fashioned enough to want to be married to a woman carrying my child. And while I don't appreciate what she did, I do understand it. But I didn't have any love left in me to give her. Any tender, sappy emotions I might have been capable of died with your mother. And I wasn't about to desecrate her memory by bringing another woman into her house.

But that ended up being a decision I didn't have to make. With Marlene gone, I knew there was only one man who had the tenaciousness to bring the youngest Kincaid into the family if I wasn't around to do it. You.

From everything Marlene told me about her twin, I'm sure the past year hasn't been an easy one for you. From all accounts it sounds like Carly Corbin is as reliable and dedicated to family as you are. I never met her personally, but both Frank Lewis and my attorney tell me she's been a bulldog with that boy since her sister's death. Protective. Possessive. Loves him like a mother. That's all any child needs.

So if you've hooked up with Carly, I take full credit for throwing you two together. If she's made your life a living hell, then it's nothing your ol' man hasn't already done. You're strong enough to survive it.

Take care of Rhett, Mitch, and take care of yourself.

I've never said it to your face, and now it's too late, but I'll tell you anyhow.

I love you, son. You've made me proud.

Your father,

Everett Kincaid

Carly laughed. "He takes credit for hooking us up?"

Mitch shook his head and tossed the letter back onto the table. "That's my father. Take credit for what goes right. Pass the buck when it goes wrong and send someone in— usually me—to do cleanup detail. This time, cleanup detail was pure pleasure."

"He believes Marlene loved him."

Something in Carly's tone sounded off. "There was a doubt?"

Carly sighed. "Yes. I never told you I found her journal after she died. She had a step-by-step plan for marrying your father. She'd always claimed she loved him, but after seeing her pursuit diagramed in detail I wasn't sure. And then there was the money she took to end the pregnancy."

He tucked a silky lock behind Carly's ear. "My guess is she set that up for Rhett because she was afraid of my father. When she told him she was pregnant, he went ballistic. Before he had her thrown off KCL property, he vowed she'd live to regret her actions. And then he sent me to buy her off. She probably believed he'd do something drastic. He was livid enough that I believed he would, too."

"It's sad that we suspected the worst of them."

"But loved them anyway." He stroked a finger along the curve of her breasts. "I like the way this suit accentuates your assets."

"About that…" She blanched, licked her lips and glanced away looking nervous all of a sudden, and nervousness wasn't an emotion his confident wife often displayed.

Alarm prickled along his spine. "Carly?"

She swallowed and then met his gaze. "Your father might be getting his wish."

"What wish?"

"That you experience the, um…joys of parenthood? I'm three weeks late."

A rush of emotions hit him like a freight train. Joy. Excitement. Fear. "You're pregnant?"

Carly's nose crinkled with worry. "Yes. I know we didn't plan this, Mitch, but please…tell me you're okay with it. Because I want this baby and I don't think I could—"

"Okay with it?" he parroted back. Awestruck, he stroked a hand across her flat belly. Wonder filled him until he thought his lungs would burst. "We've made a baby."

"Yes. Probably after I caught Rhett's tummy bug last month. I did the test this morning."

He carefully pulled her on top of him until her knees straddle his hips. He cradled her face in his hands and locked gazes. "I love you, Carly Kincaid, and nothing would make me happier than for you to have our baby."

Mitch pulled her closer and sealed his words with a kiss, because Carly had taught him that actions spoke louder than words.

* * * * *

WED BY DECEPTION

BY
EMILIE ROSE

To Jules (aka Mari Freeman), a truly amazing friend who's been rock solid by my side through the hard stuff. I couldn't have done it without you, girl, and "thanks" is woefully inadequate.

Prologue

"'And last but not least, to my daughter, Nadia…'" Richards, the longtime family attorney paused in reading Everett Kincaid's will and sought Nadia Kincaid's gaze across the long dining-room table.

Every muscle of Nadia's body tugged as taut as a ship's anchor line in a swift current. She and her overbearing—now dead—father had shared a love-hate relationship, and in her opinion, the terms in his twisted will she'd already heard were going to ruin both her older brothers' lives for the next year. She dreaded finding out how dear old Daddy planned to mess with her head.

When Richards realized he had her full attention his eyes returned to the thick document. "'Your work record is commendable and your dedication to Kincaid Cruise Lines can't be faulted…'"

Nadia stiffened even more.

Not good. When her father started with a compliment he always ended with an insult. He liked to lift you up so you had farther to fall when he took you down.

"But your job and your empty-headed friends are all you have. You surround yourself with people who give no thought to the future, who never consider what they would do without their trust funds and never plan beyond their next party."

Nadia winced at the accuracy of his assessment. Her father wouldn't understand that she liked her narcissistic friends because they were too busy worrying about their own neuroses to be interested in hers.

"You're twenty-nine, Nadia. It's past time you grew up, took responsibility for your actions and discovered what you want out of life. With that in mind, I'm pushing you from the nest."

A frisson of alarm crept down her spine. "Pushing me from the nest? What does that mean?"

"'Effective immediately,'" Richards resumed reading, "'you are on an unpaid leave of absence from your position as Director of Shared Services at Kincaid Cruise Lines and you are banned from all KCL properties and Kincaid Manor.'"

Confusion swirled inside her like a riptide. What would she do? Where would she go? With the stroke of his pen her father had taken away her job, her home and any sanctuary she might seek elsewhere. Why?

"'You will reside in my Dallas penthouse for 365 consecutive days.'"

"Daddy owns—*owned*—a Dallas penthouse?"

Richards held up a silencing hand.

"You are not allowed to seek other paid employment or to host parties in the apartment. I expect you to fill your days with a new class of people. And to make sure you're not partying with wastrels every night you must be in the penthouse between the hours of midnight and 6:00 a.m. every night."

Nadia snapped her gaping mouth shut. "Midnight? What am I? Cinderella?"

"'If you fail to fulfill my terms to the letter,'" Richards droned on in his usual monotone, "'then you will lose everything. And so will your brothers.'"

Her brothers. She forced her gaze from the attorney to Mitch beside her then Rand seated farther down the Kincaid Manor dining-room table.

"Can you believe this? He's grounding me and sending me to 'my room,'" her fingers marked quotes in the air, "as if I were a child." She folded her arms and sat back in her chair. "This is ridiculous. I'm not doing it."

"You have no choice," Mitch said quietly, calmly. Typical Mitch. Coolheaded in a crisis. She ought to know as many times as she'd dialed his number.

"Come on, Mitch. I can't give up my job, my home and my friends."

"Yes, you can." Rand leaned forward in his high-backed chair and rested his clenched fists on the table. As the oldest he'd been the one Nadia had always gone to with her troubles—before he'd abandoned her and KCL five years ago without a backward glance.

He held her gaze with his serious hazel eyes. "You heard Richards. If you don't, we lose everything. Mitch and I will help you."

"How? You'll both be stuck here in Miami while I'm banished to Dallas."

"Dallas isn't exactly the Arctic Ocean. We can get supplies in and out." Mitch gave her shoulder a gentle squeeze. He'd been her rock since Rand took off, the one she could count on…no matter what.

"But this is stupid."

Richards cleared his throat. "There's more."

How much worse could it get? Nadia's nails bit into her palms. She took a bracing breath and nodded for the attorney to continue.

"You have been pampered for far too long. Unlike your brothers, you have never even attempted to live in the real world outside Kincaid Manor—not even during college. It's time you learned to take care of yourself, Nadia, because your brothers and I won't always be around to clean up your messes."

Shame burned her face. Okay, so she'd asked for help a few times. Big freakin' deal.

"You will have no maid, no cook and no chauffeur."

Her lungs constricted and her head started to spin. Forget the fact that she'd probably starve, she hadn't had a driver's license before the accident, and she'd had no reason to get one after it. She sprang from the chair before the memories could seize her brain and paced a circuit around the room.

"A car and driving lessons will be provided for you. In addition, you will learn to survive on a monthly stipend of two thousand dollars."

"He's giving me an allowance?" she all but shrieked. She spent more on a single outfit.

"Because you're living rent free, that amount should be more than sufficient to cover your basic needs, pay your utilities, et cetera. A budget should help you understand KCL's employees and client base better."

He didn't think she could live on a budget? Okay, so, no, she'd never had a personal one, but how hard could it be? She was a trained accountant, for pity's sake, and she handled the multimillion-dollar KCL budget on a daily basis.

"This is crazy. Was Daddy out of his mind? Can he do this?"

Richards's bushy eyebrows hiked like thatched cabana roofs above his half-glasses. "One can do whatever one wishes with his or her assets. Your father is not asking you to do anything illegal or immoral. Need I repeat that if you fail, you and your brothers will forfeit your shares of Everett's estate and all of your father's holdings? Kincaid Cruise Lines, Kincaid Manor, each of the properties Everett owned around the globe, as well as his substantial investment portfolio will be sold to Mardi Gras Cruising, KCL's strongest competitor, for one dollar. And you will be left with only your personal funds."

Of which she had none. Thanks to her frenetic attempts to keep her mind and body occupied until she crashed into bed each night from sheer exhaustion, she lived pretty much from paycheck to paycheck.

"No. You don't need to repeat yourself. Dad has made it very clear that if any of us fails, we all lose. Everything. But why Mardi Gras? Dad hated that company with a passion. So do I. Their devious, underhanded, cutthroat tactics have cost us a substantial market share."

Richards shrugged. "Everett didn't share his reasoning on that issue with me."

Rand's fingers drummed the table. "Nadia, as much as I love the idea of Dad rolling over in his grave when Mardi Gras paints its logo on each of KCL's ships, I don't want the bastard to win this time."

Beside her Mitch nodded. "Agreed. We have to fight. It's too big a prize to hand off by default."

She knew very well there were billions at stake. She studied her brothers. Rand might have moved on and made a life for himself elsewhere, but Mitch lived and breathed KCL. Like her, he'd never worked a day for any other company. KCL was his universe, and she couldn't be responsible for taking that from him.

She could see by the resignation on their faces that Rand and Mitch expected her to botch this. That stung. But then what had she ever done for her brothers? They were always doing for her with nothing in return.

She knew what her father was up to. This was another test. Everett Kincaid excelled at testing his children—especially her because she reminded him of his dead wife. He'd always believed Nadia would crack eventually—like her mother had. Why else would he have forced her to endure more than a decade of therapy and now a year of solitary confinement?

But she'd prove him wrong. She'd prove them all wrong.

She would survive a year without her job, her friends and the safety net of her family. What choice did she have? Her brothers had been there for her when her life went so terribly wrong eleven years ago. She owed it to Rand and Mitch to come through for them now.

Her father obviously expected her to be the weakest link. But he'd be disappointed. She wasn't going to fail. She'd show Everett Kincaid his only daughter was made of sterner stuff. Because she hadn't just inherited her daddy's head for business, she'd also inherited his stubborn streak.

She could do this.

No. She *would* do this.

She would simply have to find a way other than submersing herself in work and partying to keep the haunting memories at bay.

Squaring her shoulders, she lifted her chin and locked her quaking knees. "When do I leave?"

One

As silent as a tomb. And after eight weeks of playing Suzy Homemaker, Nadia Kincaid felt as if she'd been buried alive in the luxurious penthouse.

Nice crypt, but still…a crypt.

She didn't even have neighbors as a distraction. The only other apartment in the downtown high-rise had been unoccupied since she'd moved in and the floors below were filled with businesses that didn't appreciate her popping in to visit. Not even when she brought the results of the new cookie recipes she'd tried.

She folded her dust cloth, parked her hands on her hips and stared at the shelves filled with books and videos Rand had sent. She'd promised herself she'd stand on her own two feet in Dallas, and she hadn't wanted to accept her brothers' help, but she also hadn't wanted to starve. So she'd caved and accepted his gifts. With the aid of the tapes and books and cable TV, she'd taught herself to cook. And since cooking was messy, she'd also learned to clean. She'd even managed to master laundry and all those other little things that had always been done for her as a Kincaid heiress. She was proud that she'd only had a few minor mishaps.

So there, Daddy. Two months and I'm still standing. Bet you didn't expect that.

She'd caught up on practically every movie and bestseller released in the past decade and even found a grocery store that delivered to downtown Dallas. Delivery, she'd discovered, was cheaper than taking a taxi to and from the store.

The only challenge she hadn't yet met was the driving lessons. She wasn't ready to get behind the wheel of a car.

Look how much damage she'd done from the passenger seat.

The memory sent her scrambling for a distraction the way it always did when the past slipped from its sealed vault. Whipping her rag back out, she dragged it across the polished granite mantle and focused on her anger toward her father.

He'd underestimated her *again* by giving her this stupid penthouse-sitting, find-herself, real-world job while giving her brothers more meaningful tasks.

Rand had been forced to return to Kincaid Cruise Lines and step into their father's shoes as CEO after a five-year self-imposed exile. Mitch would be playing daddy to their father's illegitimate toddler. But Mitch hadn't been forced to give up his job as the CFO.

She got to watch her nails grow.

But grief underlay her anger like silt at the bottom of a river waiting to be stirred up by a change in current. And her thoughts, like river water, turned murky at the oddest of times. Such as now.

Yes, she was furious with her father for treating her like

an inept child, but she also ached with the knowledge that there would be no more head-butting arguments with him, no more irate confrontations because he'd gone over her head or behind her back and undermined or overridden her decisions at work. There'd be no more fighting over the business section of the paper during breakfasts at Kincaid Manor, no more appropriate-behavior lectures and no more looking up at work or at a society event and knowing he was watching her every move. Watching and waiting for her to screw up and need bailing out.

Three months ago she'd been chaffing at his smothering surveillance and, yes, she admitted grudgingly, over the years she'd done some outrageous things just to get a rise out of him. Now she missed knowing she mattered to someone. Sure, her brothers cared, but they had their own lives and having her disappear for a year was no great loss to them.

But you don't want anyone to get too close. Caring means losing and losing means hurting.

And self-pity is pathetic. Get over yourself.

But she'd swallowed all the domestic goddess junk she could handle. Her brain was atrophying. What else could she do? The will stipulated she couldn't get a job, but she needed more to fill her days than cooking, cleaning and sitting on her butt with a book or movie and waiting for a sound from the hall.

No doubt the security guards and Ella, the neighbor's maid, thought she was stalking them since she rushed out to chat each time she heard the elevator doors open.

She glanced at the window but her own reflection on the darkened glass stared back at her instead of the lush greenery and bright flowers and tomatoes filling the trio of container gardens Mitch had sent her. Her gaze bounced to the grandfather clock. Eleven? Where had the day gone? Without a job to report to every morning and some social event to occupy her evenings time seemed to slip away from her.

Slowly, like a receding ice cap.

She had to find a new hobby, but it would have to wait until morning. And she wasn't going to call anyone else for help. She had to work this one out for herself.

What could she do to fill the hours before even the chance of sleep would come? With the time difference, it was too late to call her brothers and get an update on their romances. Both had fallen in love during her solitary confinement, and Rand and Mitch were well on their way to fulfilling their parts of the inheritance clause. Their happiness only reinforced the fact that she couldn't mess this up. Success or failure now rested solely on her shoulders. Her father and brothers expected her to make a mess of this, but instead she was going to be the one to nail the deal.

She nodded with a whole lot more confidence than she felt and selected a kickboxing workout video. If she did the routine twice, the exercise ought to tire her out.

Trying to work up some enthusiasm, she headed for the DVD player. A muffled thump stopped her. Had it come from the hall? If so, it was far too late for the neighbor's twice-weekly maid, and since security in the building was tighter than the Pentagon, it wasn't likely to be a prowler.

So what was it? Grumpy, aka Gary, the night security guy? He usually covered the Monday night shifts. The guy really didn't like her much. None of the security team did.

But this wasn't Grumpy's usual time. She headed for the foyer and squinted through the peephole.

Across the wide hall a tall, blond guy had his back to her as he shoved a key into the apartment door. His tailored dove-gray suit encased broad shoulders, slim hips and long legs. He carried an ostrich attaché case in his left hand and a Louis Vuitton garment bag sat to the right of his feet.

Her absentee neighbor? Hallelujah. Someone new to talk to. She yanked open the door. The man spun around swiftly as if she'd startled him.

No. It couldn't be. Nadia recoiled, stumbling backward. The doorjamb banged her spine. The pain barely registered. Her heart slammed. Her head spun.

No.

Not Lucas.

Lucas is dead.

But the man in front of her was a dead ringer for her dead husband.

"Nadia?" said an oh, so familiar voice.

Black spots danced in front of her eyes. A cold sweat coated her skin. She gasped for air and clung to the door frame.

"Nadia, are you all right?"

She couldn't move. Couldn't breathe. Couldn't blink. Transfixed, she stared at the apparition wavering in front of her.

"Put your head down."

The briefcase thumped to the floor. A strong hand cupped the back of her neck and forced her chin toward her chest. Her legs folded. She went down hard on her knees. Her forehead pressed the Aubusson rug while her thoughts tumbled out of control.

You've done it. You've finally cracked up. Just like your father expected you to.

When you open your eyes, you'll see a stranger. Not your dead husband. Or maybe nobody at all.

But the firm, warm hand on her nape felt very, very real.

And very familiar.

When the hall around her no longer tilted and whirled she batted that big hand away and eased upright.

Blinking didn't change a thing. The man kneeling beside her still looked like Lucas Stone. His tawny hair was shorter, expensively razor cut instead of the basic barbershop job she remembered. His face was leaner and scored by a few more lines, but those were Lucas's silvery-blue eyes. That was his slightly canted-to-the-right nose and his stubborn square chin.

"Y-you're dead."

The corners of the mouth she'd once loved to kiss turned downward and his eyes narrowed suspiciously. "Not the last time I checked."

"Daddy told me— I missed the memorial service. I— He said you died. From injuries sustained in the wr-wreck."

Scowl deepening, the Lucas look-alike sat back on his haunches. "Kincaid told you I was *dead?*"

Her tongue was as dry as driftwood and about as lifeless. She swallowed and nodded.

"Son of a bitch." He shot to his feet and offered her a hand.

She hesitated, staring at those long fingers, one of which had worn a shiny new gold band the last time she'd seen him— a ring she still kept in her jewelry box at home. Reaching for that imaginary hand would be like buying into this delusion. She rose slowly without assistance and scanned the hall for the guys in white coats. But she saw only the empty private penthouse elevator through its gaping doors.

"This isn't real. You're not real. Tomorrow I'll wake up and—"

The blond illusion followed her into the apartment.

Oh, God. She needed to call her shrink.

You fired him last week, remember?

Oh, yeah. Oops. Big mistake.

"I can't believe your father told you I was dead. What else did he tell you?"

She grappled to make sense of her delirium. "N-nothing."

He stopped a yard away and she caught a whiff of… Kenneth Cole Black?

Did hallucinations have a scent?

Tentatively, she reached out. Her trembling fingertips didn't sink into nothingness. They encountered a firm chest encased in a pale blue silk shirt. She flattened her hand on that make-believe chest beside the navy-and-pewter striped silk tie. The steady thud of a heart bumped against her palm.

Real.

He's not dead.

Lucas isn't dead.

Joy burst through her, warming her, whipping her already racing heart into a wild thrashing rhythm. She was halfway to leaping into his arms and wrapping her legs around him the way she used to but her euphoria sputtered then crashed and burned like a spent firework.

Wait a minute.

She punched his upper arm. The pain radiating from her knuckles definitely wasn't a figment of her imagination. "If you're not dead, that means you dumped me, you jerk."

"You wanted me gone," he countered calmly, evenly.

She gaped. "Are you crazy? I risked disinheritance to marry you. Why would I want you gone?"

"Your father said you regretted your 'little rebellion.' You'd decided slumming wasn't for you, and you were embarrassed by your working-class husband. You demanded a divorce."

Was that true? Had her father lied to Lucas and deliberately separated them? "I did no such thing."

"He also claimed you couldn't stand the sight of me because—" A muscle ticked in Lucas's angular jaw. His eyes filled with sadness, but his gaze didn't waver. "Because I killed our child and with it any feelings you'd ever had for me."

Her eyelids fluttered closed as an arrow of sorrow punctured her heart. Her breath hitched and her throat tightened. She pressed her hand to her stomach—her empty, flat stomach—gathered her courage and looked into the face she'd once adored.

"Lucas, you didn't end our child's life. I did." Saying the words she'd never dared admit to anyone else hurt worse than she'd anticipated.

His face blanched then turned granite hard. "What are you saying? What did you do, Nadia?"

The coldness in his eyes and voice surprised her. Comprehension dawned and the hairs on her arms and the back of her neck rose. "You think I deliberately ended my pregnancy? I would never…" She shook her head at the appalling idea. "I meant I caused our wreck."

The rigidness eased from his shoulders. "I was driving."

He blamed himself? She wouldn't wish that agony on anyone, especially when she knew where the real fault lay. How many times had she cursed herself for trying to seduce her new husband on the way to their honeymoon hotel? How many times had she wished she'd waited ten more minutes to get amorous? Her selfish lack of concern for anyone around them had changed everything. *Everything.*

In seconds she'd gone from holding the world in her hands to realizing what mattered most was something no amount of money could buy and her daddy couldn't fix.

"I had my hand in your pants."

Grief deepened the lines bracketing his mouth. "I missed the stop sign."

"Because I was distracting you." She curled her fingers around his forearm, needing to reassure herself that this wasn't a dream. The muscles flexed taut and hard beneath his sleeve. "Lucas, I was in a coma for a week. If I didn't ask to see you it's because I couldn't."

He searched her face as if seeking the truth, then rage flooded his eyes with shocking swiftness. "The lying, conniving bastard."

"Who?"

"Your father." Lucas expelled the words on a breath filled with pure hatred and his lips flattened into a thin seam.

Everett Kincaid had done a lot of rotten things in his time, and he'd been clear in his intentions to disinherit Nadia if she went through with the wedding. He'd even refused to attend the small ceremony. But after the accident he'd acted as if that threat had never been voiced. She'd believed it was because in almost losing her he'd realized he loved her.

She should have known better. Her father never backed down or admitted he was wrong. He'd seen Lucas as a mistake and, like all her other mistakes, he'd "fixed" it in his own way. The wrong way. She shouldn't be hurt or surprised her father had lied to Lucas and sabotaged her marriage. But she was.

What surprised her even more was that Lucas had let him. She'd thought Lucas was the one man strong enough to stand up to her father. "If you'd loved me, you would have come to see me anyway."

The jaw muscle twitched faster. "I couldn't."

"*Please.* You were the most determined person I'd ever met. I don't believe you couldn't find your way to my hospital room. I was in intensive care hooked up to a billion machines. It's not like I could run and hide."

He broke eye contact for the first time and presented her with his back. His shoulders looked as rigid as a ship's girder and definitely wider than when they'd last been together.

He clenched his fists by his side. "I was paralyzed from the waist down. The doctors told me the odds of me walking again were slim to none."

Her mouth opened, but she couldn't get her vocal cords to work. Her gaze traveled down his broad back. Lucas had been so virile and active. In fact, it had been his incredible body that had initially attracted her attention the summer he'd worked with the Kincaid Manor landscaping crew.

"You must have been terrified over the possibility of being unable to help support your mother and sisters."

Lucas turned and she didn't like the hard, uncompromising look on his face. "Your father said you couldn't handle being saddled with a cripple."

He'd ignored her comment, but she let it pass. She'd never met a man who liked to admit fear or weakness. "And you believed him? You didn't trust that I meant it when I promised 'for better or worse'?"

"You'd been a pampered princess all your life. Did I think you'd want to live in poverty and play nursemaid to a guy who couldn't even piss by himself? No."

She flinched at his crudity and his assessment. Then anger pulsed through her veins. Why did the men in her life always assume she was a useless screwup?

Okay, so maybe she'd made a few silly mistakes, but still… Her father and Lucas had no right to make a decision of this magnitude for her.

"You should have given me the chance to prove myself instead of presuming I'd fail."

She looked him over, trying and failing to imagine him

helpless. From what she could see he was even more muscular and fit than he'd been eleven years ago. And unless she
missed her guess—which was unlikely because she knew
her designers—his suit was Hermès and the shoes, Prada.
Either Lucas wasn't a struggling landscape worker anymore
or he'd come into some serious money. "You're not paralyzed
now."

"Thanks to a series of surgeries and months of rehab."

"And you're here." She waved a hand to indicate the
opulent penthouse level. "Why are you here?"

Did she imagine his hesitation or that he'd shifted his weight
on his feet? "I own the building and I live across the hall."

"You *own* a fifty-story piece of prime real estate in downtown Dallas?" Definitely serious money.

"Yes." The pride and confidence in that single word were
unmistakable. "Why are *you* here?"

"This is—*was*—my father's place."

His eyes narrowed to silvery-blue slits. "My attorney sold
this apartment to an investment company CEO."

"No, my father bought the property under a dummy corporation he sometimes uses." Mitch had done a little digging
after the reading of the will to discover that interesting tidbit.
The question was, why had her father wanted to keep ownership of this place a secret from everyone including Mitch,
his right-hand man?

Lucas snapped to attention and looked annoyed.

Then it hit her. The strength leeched from her legs. She
leaned against the entry table. "My father engineered this."

"Engineered what?"

"This meeting. Dad died. His will requires me to penthouse-sit for a year. He must have known I'd eventually run
into you. Why would he do that?" She paced a circle in the

foyer, sneaking peeks at Lucas every few steps. What had the attorney said? Something about her father realizing he'd made some mistakes that he'd hoped to right. And look how his meddling had brought both Rand and Mitch love.

Surprise stopped her in her tracks. "Unless he's trying to get us back together."

Lucas snorted an unamused sound of disgust. "Not a chance."

"He must be. Daddy buying the apartment across the hall from yours in a building *you* own is too big to be a coincidence."

"Nadia, your father paid me to get out of your life and never contact you again. And he threatened to ruin me and my family if I did. He wouldn't try to hook us up."

Her stomach sank like the *Titanic* and a chill enveloped her like icy water closing over her head. Déjà vu. Buying off people was her father's favorite way to get rid of someone he found undesirable. He'd done it multiple times to both her and her brothers over the years.

"You took money to dump me?"

Lucas swiped his jaw with his hand. A dull flush covered his face. "He claimed that's what you wanted."

"How much?"

"Nadia—"

Her eyes and throat burned. A tremor worked its way outward from the frozen pit of her stomach. "How much did it take to make you forget me, Lucas?"

"I never forgot you. Or our baby."

"How much?" she repeated through clenched teeth.

His jaw shifted. "He covered the cost of my surgeries and rehab, and he offered tuition for my sisters and me to go to the colleges of our choice."

"Give me a number. I want to know *exactly* how much my love was worth to you."

He expelled a harsh breath. "Roughly, two million."

She closed her eyes as a fresh wave of pain, disappointment and betrayal deluged her. Her father hadn't intended this meeting to be a joyful reunion. He'd wanted to make sure she knew that the one man she'd worshipped, the one she'd kept on a pedestal for more than a decade as an icon of perfect love, was no better than the rest of the greedy schmucks who'd leeched off her or taken Everett's payoffs over the years.

Feeling sick, she wrapped her arms around her middle and turned away. Did no one love her more than money?

She'd thought Lucas had.

Wrong.

She'd believed him to be different from the hangers-on of her social circle who were only interested in what being with a Kincaid could get them.

Wrong again.

The knowledge made her feel small, insignificant and unwanted. And it hurt. God, it hurt. She'd loved Lucas enough to leave everything familiar and dear to her to be his wife.

And he'd betrayed her. He'd sold out.

Her father was right. Lucas had been her biggest mistake. And loving him and losing him had almost destroyed her.

"I wish you'd stayed dead." She pressed her fingers to the throb in her left temple and frowned at him. "No, I don't mean that. I just wish I'd never met you again. But let me tell you something, Lucas Stone. Choosing the money over me doesn't make you special or unique. It just makes you one of many and someone I don't want to know."

She had to get rid of him. Her legs shook so badly she barely made it to the front door without collapsing. "Get out."

"Nadia—"

"*Get out.* Before I call security."

"They work for me. They're not going to throw me out." He closed the distance between them and stood toe to toe with her, looming over her. "Don't blame me for your father's machinations."

"This has nothing to do with my father who is—*was*—without question an arrogant, manipulative, interfering ass, and I hope he's roasting in hell at this moment. This is about you. You betrayed me. You chose money over me and you left me alone to grieve for you and our child. Do you know how close I came—"

She clamped down on the words. No, she would never give him that much power over her.

"You're a selfish, sadistic prick, Lucas Stone. And I don't ever want to see you again. Leave."

He stared at her so long she thought she'd have to make good on her threat and call for help. Although who she'd call if building security wouldn't help was uncertain. Maybe her brothers. No. She had to learn to deal with her own issues.

Finally Lucas brushed past her, shattering her heart all over again.

Because losing him to death hadn't hurt nearly as much as knowing he'd willingly left her…

As if she didn't matter.

TWO

Lucas Stone wanted to kill the devious SOB who'd stolen his wife from him. But with Everett Kincaid already dead vengeance was beyond reach.

Or was it?

Kincaid, the bastard, may have been the ax man, but his sons, Rand and Mitch, had been equally convinced that Lucas wasn't good enough for their baby sister. They'd come to the wedding, but they'd made damned sure Lucas knew they were there to support Nadia and not because they approved of him.

Why give up an eleven-year vendetta when he could still have the satisfaction of proving the Kincaids had been wrong to write him off?

The clunk of the turning dead bolt lock jarred him clear down to his marrow. He stared at the door Nadia had slammed in his face. If anything, Nadia the woman was even more beautiful than the girl she'd been. Her hair was still a thick mass of shiny dark waves and her eyes were the same mesmerizing green, but her youthful softness had melted away to reveal exquisite bone structure. The kind of beauty that would never fade. Or so his mother had claimed after meeting her. His family had adored her—right up until she'd allegedly dumped him.

He didn't doubt Nadia's story. The shock and pain in her eyes had been too genuine. And it wasn't as if Kincaid hadn't tried to get rid of Lucas more than once before the wedding. Each time Lucas had been strong enough to resist.

But not that last time. Then he'd been weak. And he'd been afraid he'd become a burden to his already overtaxed mother, and he'd been pissed—seriously pissed—at Nadia and hurt by her apparent betrayal. He'd wanted to strike back in any way he could, and taking Kincaid's money had seemed like the only way available.

What Lucas didn't believe was Nadia's fairy-tale garbage about Kincaid's altruistic motives. If her father had arranged this meeting, it was to rub Lucas's face in what he'd lost not to reunite them.

The question was how had Kincaid discovered Lucas owned this building? Admittedly, KingPin Electronics, the listed property owner, was the most visible of his companies, but he'd intentionally kept his name off the letterhead and executives list. As with most of his companies, he guided his staff through conference calls and orders to his CEOs but rarely made a physical appearance. He kept his face and name out of the press.

His youngest sister called him "the submarine," and he liked the image of always lurking unseen below the surface while he got the job done.

He turned the key he'd left in the lock after Nadia's unexpected appearance, retrieved his bags and entered his apartment. He spent too much time in hotels and it was good to be home. His gaze swept his luxurious living room, each item tangible proof he'd hauled himself and his family out of poverty.

It was amazing how much ambition fury and hatred could generate. Over the past seven years he'd been stealthily stalking his prey, acquiring failing properties, turning them around and selling them at a profit until he had enough cash to ante his way onto Everett Kincaid's playing field. For the past forty months he'd specifically targeted the suppliers Kincaid used, bought them and upped the prices on the products KCL couldn't get elsewhere without a lot of aggravation.

Everett Kincaid had valued cold hard cash over anything and Lucas had been determined to bleed the man's vault dry. Until today, Lucas had also believed Nadia to be as shallow as her father, and he'd planned to make all of the Kincaids pay for treating him like garbage to be cast aside. For once he was glad to be wrong and that his disgust with Nadia all these years had been unjust.

He set down his bags and flipped through the mail piled on the hall table, most of it addressed to Andvari, Inc., which meant his assistant had stopped by the apartment.

The closer Lucas had come to reaching his goal of taking down Kincaid, the greater the need for secrecy, and four years ago he'd created the umbrella company of Andvari. Named for the Norse god who guarded his treasures with a cloak of invisibility, Lucas had made it impossible for anyone to penetrate the smoke screen and discover the true owner of Andvari and each of its multiple subsidiaries.

Or so he'd thought.

How deeply had Kincaid penetrated, and how had he acquired his information? Because without a doubt, as Nadia had said, her father's ownership of the other penthouse couldn't possibly be a coincidence.

He grabbed his suitcase, headed to his bedroom and slung the case onto the mattress. Just because Kincaid had denied him the pleasure of seeing defeat on his face didn't mean Lucas couldn't still have the pleasure of holding all his nemesis had once possessed.

Beginning with Nadia.

Wouldn't it be the ultimate revenge to win back the woman Kincaid had stolen from him?

Love had nothing to do with it. A lifetime of his mother and sisters and himself getting screwed over by that sappy emotion had killed any illusions Lucas had about lust and chemistry and the temporary insanity the combination evoked. Physically, he still wanted his ex-wife. But sex was all he wanted from her.

If there was any justice in this world, that bastard Kincaid would roll over in his grave the day his daughter remarried the man he'd fired and humiliated. It would be an even better day when Lucas Stone became owner of KCL, fired each of the Kincaids and covered each KCL logo with one of his own. And he would.

He didn't expect the job to be easy. But then nothing had been since he'd awoken in that hospital bed unable to feel his legs, see his wife or save his baby.

He whipped his cell phone from his pocket and hit his sister's number on speed dial.

"This better be good, Lucas. I'm in the middle of a hot date. My first in months," Sandi groused in his ear.

He glanced at his watch and grimaced. Almost midnight. "You still want that promotion you've been begging for?"

"Hell, yes. What's the catch?"

"I need time off."

"What's wrong?"

A valid question since he'd lived and breathed work since getting back on his feet. But if he came clean Sandi would get on the next plane to Dallas. "I need a break from the relentless travel."

"I don't believe that for one second."

"You don't have to believe me. Either you want the promotion or you don't."

"I do. I do. Hold on." He heard her muffled voice telling someone she'd be right back then what sounded like swishing sheets. He did not want to know about his sister's sex life.

A full minute later she asked, "What do you need?"

"Take over the Singapore account."

"Are you serious?" She sounded as shocked as she should be. This project was his baby. He'd already put pints of blood and sweat into it, but he should be able to safely hand it over now.

He loosened his tie and shrugged out of his jacket. "Buying up this loan is a big responsibility, but you can handle it. You're ready."

"Why are we incurring the debt?"

"I have my reasons. And I need you to keep any discoveries from Jefferson."

He knew his sister well enough to know the silence meant she was running through all the possible reasons he'd make such an odd request. "It's going to be hard to sign contracts without an attorney present. What gives?"

He wanted to evaluate the Kincaid-Jefferson connection before he went further. Chances were Jefferson had simply sold the apartment to a specific quality of buyer as he'd been instructed. But Lucas didn't want his attorney in on any more confidential dealings until he was sure there hadn't been any greased palms involved. Kincaid had been as crooked as hell and so were many of the people he'd associated with.

"I'd prefer to use another attorney on this one. I'll have someone on board before you fly out to meet with the executive committee."

"It isn't like you to pull a last-minute switcheroo. Why are you?"

He debated refusing to answer, but Sandi deserved the facts. "Jefferson sold Everett Kincaid the Dallas penthouse."

Seconds ticked past then she groaned. "It's Monday. Aren't you supposed to be in Dallas? Please tell me you're not going to get tangled up with the Kincaids again."

He ignored her question. No one knew his ultimate goal was to take down KCL and no one needed to. "I'll have the pertinent files couriered to you tomorrow."

"Didn't Everett Kincaid die a couple of months ago? That means… Lucas, tell me you aren't dealing with that selfish little bitch again."

His teeth clicked together. For the past eleven years they'd all believed Nadia a selfish bitch. He'd have to tell his family the whole story, but not before he verified a few facts. "If you want this promotion, do your job and keep your nose out of my business."

"I don't like this, Lucas. I don't like it at all."

"I don't pay you to like it."

Her ticked-off sniff traveled across the airwaves. "Do you want me to check into Jefferson's dealings?"

"I'll have Terri investigate. If there's a devious, dishonest man around, she knows how to find him."

Understatement of the year. At twenty-four his younger

sister had already married and divorced three of the lying snakes before wising up and turning her loser-seeking talents into a lucrative private detective agency, which Lucas had initially funded. He also employed his sister's firm to run background checks on every employee Andvari considered hiring. Could she have missed something on Jefferson?

"Just tell me the plan so I can prepare for cleanup detail."

"There won't be any cleanup. But if you must know, I'm going to get back everything Everett Kincaid took from me. Starting with my ex-wife."

Every part of the past eleven years had been a lie, Nadia concluded.

Her grief? For naught.

Her father's sympathy? Faked.

His concern for her well-being? Bogus.

Had everything he'd said and done since the accident been a bald-faced lie? Worse, she had believed in his sincerity, which made her a stupid, gullible fool. There must have been clues to his underhanded, twisted machinations. How had she missed them?

And who else was in on the deception? Had her brothers known Lucas was alive and profiting from her pain? Had her shrink?

She slammed the metal rectangular pan onto the granite countertop. The loud twang vibrated her eardrums. She braced her hands on the cool surface and bowed her head. How many people had been secretly snickering at her behind her back all these years?

She would find out. She might be hampered by her location, and her lack of funds, but she would identify each of the Judases before this year in exile ended. She couldn't return to Miami without knowing who she could trust and who she couldn't.

The doorbell peeled.

Glad of the distraction, she pushed off the counter, grabbed her money and hustled to the foyer. She couldn't finish the brownies until the store delivered her walnuts and a new bottle of vanilla. Baking kept her mind from slipping into the deep, dark, bottomless well she'd prefer not to fall into again. She'd spent too much time paddling in the murky depths already.

Who knew when she'd ordered the last batch of groceries that she should have specified the nuts already shelled? She'd never shelled a nut in her before-banished life, and a *Nutcracker* was the ballet she watched at Christmas not a kitchen implement—one of the few this kitchen lacked.

She didn't bother with the peephole since she was expecting her usual delivery guy and she'd told security to send Dan up as soon as he arrived.

But it wasn't Dan on her doorstep. Lucas stood outside looking totally *GQ* in Burberry. She couldn't get over seeing him in a suit instead of the snug T-shirts and jeans or khakis he used to wear.

The little thrill that streaked through her really ticked her off. "What do you want?"

His blue eyes ran over her like heated maple syrup over Belgian waffles, slowly slipping into crevices and beyond and making her hyperconscious of her sleepless night, the makeup she'd slathered on to cover the dark circles beneath her eyes and last season's less than stellar jeans and sleeveless sweater.

He pulled a bag with a familiar logo from behind his back and dangled it from one long finger. "Yours, I believe."

"Yes." She reached for it.

At the last second he snatched it away and sniffed. "Something smells good. What's your cook whipping up for lunch?"

"No cook. Me. Where's Dan?"

"If you mean the kid, I paid him. He's gone." He muscled past her into the apartment, and even though he didn't physically push her aside, his size, scent and presence had the same bulldozer effect of knocking her off balance.

"Come in," she sniped sarcastically. She didn't want him here, the traitor. She offered the folded twenties. "This should be enough to cover the total and the tip."

"I don't need your money. Is that marinara sauce?" He strode toward the kitchen as if he were familiar with the apartment's layout, which as owner of the building he might be. But even more irritating, he acted as if he had every right to venture where he pleased in her space. Which he most certainly did not.

Temper rising, she followed in the trespasser's wake. "Yes. I'm testing a new recipe and I'd like to finish it. So buh-bye."

She'd discovered if she didn't focus one hundred percent on the recipe, she'd mess up something, and sometimes it wasn't salvageable. Or edible. With her new budget she couldn't afford to throw out food—something she would remember next time she went to an overpriced restaurant and left most of her meal on her plate.

It'll be a long time before you hit another trendy restaurant. Forty-three weeks, to be exact.

Not a happy thought. Especially now that *he'd* turned up.

She reached for the bag again and again he eluded her. "May I have my groceries, please?"

"You couldn't cook eleven years ago." His gaze swept the homemade fettuccini waiting to be boiled and the bowl of unfinished brownie batter. He picked up the wooden spoon, stirred the pot then pursed his lips and sampled her sauce.

A territorial urge to growl rumbled through her. "Now I can. Lucas, I'm not interested in playing a childish game of keep-away. Hand over my nuts."

"Invite me to lunch." He scraped a finger along the edge of the brownie batter and licked the thick chocolate from the tip. "Mmm. And dessert."

That was not sexy. *It wasn't.*

She swallowed and closed her eyes against the shower of memories and hormones. Just because he'd had the most talented tongue on five continents didn't mean she wanted to experience his skills again firsthand. How could she ever trust him? She couldn't.

She planted her hands on her hips and scowled. "I don't want your company."

"You have more than enough for two and you know marinara is my favorite."

She'd forgotten. *Liar.* Okay, she hadn't. But she hadn't cooked the sauce for him. She liked it, too. It was the easiest recipe in the book and the only one she'd had all the ingredients for in the apartment. Besides, she'd needed something to go with the pasta she'd made using the machine Mitch had sent. Her brothers kept sending her kitchen gadgets to entertain her. Their help made being independent difficult. But it kept her sane. Catch-22.

"I'm freezing the leftovers for later."

His eyebrows lifted. "You're planning ahead?"

His incredulous tone ticked her off. "Is that so hard to believe?"

"Frankly, yes."

The sad fact was that two and a half months ago he would have been right. She hadn't planned ahead as her father had so unkindly pointed out.

She sighed and pushed back her tangled mop of hair, which only reminded her she would not survive a year without her hairdresser to keep the unruly waves under control. She'd have to find someone local. And cheap.

"Go away, Lucas."

He shrugged and headed back out the door—with her walnuts.

"Hey, hand over my groceries."

"You know the price," he called over his shoulder as he entered the open door of his place. Nadia plowed after him. She didn't bother to close her door because no one could get upstairs without security calling first, which was cool because it meant she didn't have to learn how to work the apartment's electronic security system. She just left it turned off.

"Lucas. Come on." Her steps stuttered to a stop inside his living room. She could see Reunion Tower through the windows on the opposite wall, but the landmark wasn't nearly as interesting as what lay on this side of the glass wall.

His place was even larger than hers. And more luxurious. Turning in place, she ran a quick mental tally of the imported carpets on the Brazilian cherry floor, the café au lait–colored suede sofas and chairs and the beveled glass-topped tables. Pricey. The original art on the walls hadn't come cheaply either. His decor screamed "I'm a success," but in an urban classic way instead of nouveau riche.

Wow. Someone had finally out-Kincaided her father who'd been a firm believer in appearances and accoutrements defining the man.

Lucas's living and dining areas made her want to see the rest of his place. But that wasn't going to happen. She wanted nothing—repeat, *nothing*—to do with Lucas Stone, the mercenary deserter.

"I can't finish my brownies without the ingredients in that bag."

"I like brownies."

She'd remembered his sweet tooth and his love of chocolate chip cookies. That's why she'd chosen to try baking brownies today instead of cookies. Besides, her Sub-Zero freezer was already full of cookie dough that she didn't know what to do with since she could no longer share it with the people downstairs.

She folded her arms. "I don't care."

He erased the distance between them, stopping only inches from her. Her senses went on full alert, but she stood her ground. Not even sheer will could stop her breathing and pulse rates from quickening, her mouth from moistening or her muscles from tensing.

Lucas lifted his hand and stroked her cheek before pushing a lock of hair behind her ear. That simple touch reverberated all the way to the pit of her stomach. Damn him. He knew her middle melted when he played with her earlobe like that. She jerked her head away from that lingering fingertip.

You are not attracted to him. Not anymore. You can't be.

"You care, Nadia. And from what the security team tells me you could use the company."

Heat steamed her face like a ship's boiler. "All I did was drop in downstairs to say hello."

"You made a nuisance of yourself until security escorted you from the premises and banned you from the lower floors."

Sad. But true. "I wasn't after company secrets. I wanted to share my cookies. I can't eat as many as I bake. It's not like I was trying to poison anybody."

"My employees don't need you telling them how to run a more efficient business."

Guilty. So she'd offered a few pointers… Wait a minute. Did he say— "Your employees?"

This time she knew she didn't imagine his hesitation or the slight narrowing of his eyes. "This building houses several of my companies."

"*Companies.* Plural? How many do you own?"

"A few."

Interesting. And vague. Deliberately? Definitely. She could see the guardedness in his baby blues. His evasion piqued her curiosity. Lucas had been ambitious before. But back then his goal had been to eventually own his own landscaping company. He'd been attending college part-time in the evenings earning a degree in horticulture to help him.

She'd have to do a Google search on him as soon as she returned to her apartment and see what she could find.

"I'm good at what I do, Lucas. I could help."

"Get a job."

"I already have a job with KCL. Only Dad's stupid will has forced me to take a leave of absence, and I'm not allowed to—" she made quotation marks in the air with her fingers "—seek other paid employment."

His eyes narrowed. "Why?"

Oh right. As if she'd admit that her father had ordered her to grow up. "It's just his way of tormenting us from the grave. He assigned Rand, Mitch and me tasks we have to complete before we can settle his estate."

"What kinds of tasks?"

"None of your business. My life ceased to be your concern when you sold out."

The flare of his nostrils and compression of his lips told her she'd ticked him off. *Good.*

"What happens if you fail?"

"I'm not going to fail. If you remember, I can be quite persistent when there's something I want." Once upon a time she'd wanted him. But not anymore. "Now please, give me my food."

He kept the bag behind his back. Short of an undignified struggle, which would involve the kind of body contact she wasn't interested in, she couldn't retrieve it.

"Lunch…and dessert, Nadia."

The suggestive pause between the words combined with his deepening voice and the intent in his eyes made her heart thump harder. He wasn't talking about brownies. And her double-dealing hormones wanted to strip naked and dance around the room for him.

But that wasn't ever going to happen again.

"That seductive half smile is wasted on me, Lucas Stone. You've shown your true colors. I have enough backstabbing users in my life already."

Or she had before her father had cut her off from her "friends," none of whom had made an effort to call or visit her in Dallas. Would they even remember her when she returned home? Did she want them to?

"All I want is lunch and a chance to find out if our divorce is valid."

What? Her stomach hit rock bottom. "Why wouldn't it be?"

"If you believed I was dead, then why would you sign divorce papers?"

She winced and wished she could remember what—if anything—she'd signed. "Good point."

"Feed me and we'll talk."

When he put it like that what choice did she have? But first she needed to lock herself in a closet and scream bloody murder.

"Give me a minute." Nadia forced the words through the panic tightening her throat.

She bolted from Lucas's place and back to her own. She really, really didn't want to call Mitch to bail her out of this one, but if anyone could fix this the middle Kincaid—aka Peacemaker—could. She grabbed her cell phone and dialed her brother's direct line.

Her neck prickled. What if Mitch was in on the whole deceitful deal?

"Mitch Kin—"

"Lucas isn't dead," she blurted. "Did you know?"

"What?"

"He lives in the penthouse across the hall from Dad's and he owns this building. Did you know?" she repeated.

"Nadia, calm down. You're not making sense. Are you okay?"

She heard the concern in his voice elicited by the hysteria in her own and struggled to regain her composure before continuing. "I haven't lost my mind. Lucas isn't dead. Dad lied and he paid Lucas two million to dump me and disappear."

"That sorry bastard." She didn't ask whether he referred to her father or Lucas as the bastard. As far as she was concerned the term applied to both men. But her brother's shock and anger sounded genuine, giving her a small measure of relief. Maybe Mitch hadn't betrayed her.

"Mitch, Lucas made a valid point. If I thought he was dead, I wouldn't have signed divorce papers. I certainly don't remember signing anything. I need you to get your hands on whatever paperwork you can find that's related to my marriage, specifically the ending of it, and send me copies of everythi

lawyer licensed to pra

"Don't panic before w

"Don't panic? Are you

rose from the dead."

g. And I'm probably going to need a

ctice in Texas."

e have all the facts."

kidding me? My *husband just*

and plucked the cell phone from Nadia's fingers. S

..., nearly jumped out of her skin and spun around

face her phone snatcher.

Lucas. She hadn't even heard him sneak up behind her

"Hey! Give that back."

He ignored her and pressed her red phone to his ear

the same ear she used to nibble and whisper her most sec

fantasies into. Right before he'd fulfilled each of them

sensual detail. She absolutely deplored the rush of heat th

memory evoked.

"Mitch, this is Lucas Stone. After the accident your fath

told me Nadia insisted on ending our marriage. He had n

sign divorce papers. If Nadia didn't sign the forms or did

know what she was signing, we might still be married."

She couldn't still be married. She *couldn't*.

The strength and fight drained from Nadia's limbs. Sh

staggered to the kitchen and folded, as limp as freshly pressed pasta, into a chair. Parking her elbows on her knees, she plopped her head in her hands.

Lucas had to be wrong. Not just because of the things she'd done to try to forget him, but because she didn't want to be tied to a jerk who'd betray her.

Then there was the truth she'd discovered about her mother after the accident... Those facts changed everything. No matter what her shrink claimed, Nadia couldn't risk marriage. Not with her potentially defective genes.

And that wasn't the only thing that had changed. She pressed a hand over her navel and tried to convince herself that losing her baby had been a good thing given the circumstances. But as always, her pep talk fell flat.

Suddenly, her goal of getting through this year without botching the terms of the will or losing her mind seemed inconsequential. She had worse problems, specifically, the one that had followed her into the kitchen.

She dragged her gaze from his polished Guccis standing toe to toe with her Ralph Lauren sandals, up his sharply creased trousers over his lean hips and flat belly. Straightening, she snatched her phone from his outstretched hand before glaring at him. He'd ended the call without letting her say goodbye to her brother.

"If we're still married, I'll just get another divorce."

His mouth tilted into a see-if-I-care smile. "You're assuming I won't change your mind."

A sound of disgust gurgled in her throat. "Trust me, you can't."

Her unintentional challenge registered in his eyes and she wanted to kick herself for not choosing her words more carefully. She had brothers. She knew better than to throw down a gauntlet that way.

Lucas loomed over her, forcing her to lean way back in the chair and tilt her head to look up at him. His legs brushed her knees and her pulse rattled like a ship's dropping anchor chain. "Do you remember how good it was between us, Nadia?"

Heat blossomed inside her, unfurling like petals opening in the spring sunshine. She pressed her knees together to crush the ache between her legs and fought an urge to squirm in her seat.

How could she still desire him after what he'd done?

The memories of how it had been still haunted her. They hadn't been able to keep their hands off each other. Their passion had overridden everything—especially common sense—which was how she'd ended up pregnant within two months of meeting Lucas.

On her wedding day she'd been so full of joy, hope, excitement and love. They'd made love for the first time as husband and wife in an empty anteroom of his family's church with their guests only yards away because they simply couldn't wait. And despite, or maybe because of their cramped, illicit location it had been the most amazing sex of her life.

She squashed the memory and frowned harder. "That was a long time ago."

His direct gaze held hers. "Letting you go was a mistake. But I wanted you to be happy."

Snorting in disbelief, she shoved the chair backward and stood. "If you're trying to convince me you took that money for *my* benefit, you're wasting your breath. You won't get your hands on another dime of Kincaid money, so don't even think about asking for alimony if we have to redo this."

"I'm not interested in handouts."

"Even though a Kincaid handout bought you *this*." A snap of her wrist indicated his designer clothing.

"What I have now came from my own sweat. Your father's bribe was barely a drop in the bucket."

Two million was barely a drop? How loaded was Lucas?

He set the grocery bag on the counter, shrugged off his suit coat and draped it over the back of a chair. The David Yurman cufflinks he removed and dropped into his pocket were similar to the ones she'd bought Mitch for his birthday last year. He rolled up his sleeves revealing a Cartier Roadster watch on his tanned, hair-dusted wrist.

Oh, yes, Lucas had serious money these days.

But why was he undressing in her kitchen? "What are you doing?"

"Helping you cook."

"I don't need help." Not anymore. Thanks to her downtime in Dallas she'd become a freaking gourmet. But then she'd never done anything by half measures. If she jumped in, she tended to go for the deep end. What was the point in holding back when the things that mattered most could be snatched away in an instant?

"You're going to get my help and my company whether you want it or not." Lucas opened a cabinet door. Apparently not finding whatever it was he was looking for, he searched through another and another until he located her new pasta pot in a lower cabinet.

"You can't just barge in here and take over."

"Looks like I already have."

Daddy, if you weren't dead, I'd kill you for this.

"Then by all means make yourself at home in *my* kitchen." She served the words with a generous side of sarcasm and a mutinous glare.

"Do you have any red wine?"

"I don't drink."

Blue eyes nailed her to the travertine tiles. "That's not what the tabloids say."

Shame crawled up her neck and across her face. So she'd partied a bit over the past few years. But partying alone wasn't fun. It was pathetic. And she'd been alone in Dallas every day and every one of the past fifty-two nights.

"I was trying to forget my *dead* husband and the baby I'd miscarried."

Incredulity filled his eyes and slackened his jaw. "You expect me to believe you've been pining away for me for more than a decade?"

She squared her shoulders and sniffed. "Of course not. I had better things to do."

And if she hadn't, she'd never admit it.

He carried the pot to the sink and hit the faucet lever. While the water flowed he raided her cupboards, found salt and olive oil and poured both into the water without measuring.

She scrambled to her cookbook and scanned the recipe. A teaspoon of salt. Two tablespoons of oil. "How did you know to do that?"

He set the cookware on the burner and turned on the stove. "You've forgotten I grew up helping around the house. I learned how to cook as soon as I could reach the controls on the stove."

How could she ever forget that his loving family had been as warm and welcoming as hers had been cold and reserved? Or that she'd almost become a part of the Stones' tight-knit clan. And thanks to her miserable, meddling father and Lucas's greed she'd lost that chance.

Jerks. Both of them.

"How are your mother and sisters?"

"Fine." He moved to the knife and cutting board she'd left out in preparation for chopping nuts. A quick twist of his wrists tore the bag. He poured walnuts onto the white surface and started chopping quickly and decisively with far more skill than she'd managed to acquire.

Eleven years ago Sandi had been sixteen and Terri thirteen. They'd treated Nadia like the big sister they'd always wanted. And she'd loved it. "They must not think much of me if they believe I walked out on you when you needed me most."

"An accurate assessment. But they'll come around when we tell them the truth."

She'd often wondered why the Stones had never contacted her after the accident. Now she knew. And while she wanted to correct their opinion of her, it wasn't because she intended to allow Lucas back into her life. As soon as she got rid of him today she'd find a way to avoid him until he left town again.

"They don't need to come around."

He barely glanced up. "How many nuts do you need?"

"A cup." She carefully measured a teaspoon of vanilla and turned on the mixer to stir the fragrant liquid into the brownie batter. "Lucas, if we're still married—and I don't think we are because my father wouldn't make that kind of sloppy mistake—we are not staying married."

But her father had made a lot of mistakes recently, a nagging voice reminded her. Big mistakes. Like getting a woman her age pregnant and missing employees embezzling millions from right beneath his nose. Rand and Mitch were handling those messes without her and being excluded irritated her like a bad rash.

She tamped down the accompanying twinge of worry and reminded herself that her marriage *and its dissolution* had happened years ago when Everett Kincaid had still been at the top of his game.

Lucas dumped the nuts into the mixing bowl.

"Hey, you didn't measure. How do you know that's a cup?"

"Experience."

While she'd traveled the globe more times than she could remember before she'd turned eighteen, Lucas had been far more experienced than her in almost every other way eleven years ago, thanks to his less than stable upbringing. The contrast between his simple lifestyle and his savvy attitude had intrigued her.

He's not interesting. He's opportunistic. And don't you forget it.

She scraped the brownie batter into the pan then shoved the rectangle into the preheated oven.

Discovering she'd been living a lie had left her with a lot of questions—questions that had kept her up most of the night. She wanted answers even if it meant tolerating Lucas's company over lunch.

She propped a hip against the kitchen table, aiming for a casual pose when she was anything but relaxed. "What happened to you after the wreck?"

He leaned back against the counter and crossed his ankles. "Your father had me transferred to a Denver rehabilitation facility. He relocated my family and dumped his bribe into a bank account in my name. I studied while I was stuck in that wheelchair. Because of our background and our grades my sisters and I were able to get scholarships and financial aid to cover the majority of our tuition. I invested what was left after the medical bills and made it work for us."

"How?"

"I'm good with numbers." He pushed off the counter and gestured toward the steaming pot. "Water's boiling. Show me what you can do."

A blatant bid to avoid answering, but his tone carried just enough of a challenge to imply doubt in her cooking skills. She'd show him. And she'd get her answers. But first, she reread the last part of the recipe—just to be safe. She'd be darned if she'd have him looking over her shoulder correcting her "mistakes" the way her father always had. She began easing the pasta into the water.

"You took back your maiden name."

The statement made her hand slip. The remainder of the fettuccini plopped into the pot. Her hand shook as she very deliberately set the timer. She wouldn't tell him how numb she'd been after the accident or how little she'd cared what her name was or if anyone ever used it again.

"All my documents were in my maiden name. It was easier not to change everything over."

"The security team says you rarely leave the building. Why is that?"

She turned abruptly. He'd checked up on her? "I don't know anyone in Dallas."

"You know me. I'll show you the city."

"I don't want to go out with you."

"I know the best places to see and to eat."

Her mouth watered at the thought of eating something besides her own cooking or the occasional takeout.

"No, thanks."

"If you do nothing else, you need to see the gardens."

"Gardens are your thing, not mine." *Liar.* Lucas had taught her to appreciate more than run-of-the-mill shop flowers during their time together, and she adored puttering in the container gardens on her patio.

He'd taken her to Fairchild Tropical Garden in Coral Gables on their first date. Not a place to impress a girl, in her opinion, yet he had with his extensive knowledge of the exotic plants growing there. And, yes, okay, the flowers had been pretty and it had been interesting to actually see them in nature instead of in a vase.

Back then Lucas had been all about nature. On their second date he'd taken her to a state park. Initially, she'd been underwhelmed by his choice until they'd paddled around the marshes in a rented canoe talking, flirting and just enjoying each other's company without distractions. He'd shown her a side of nature not even the Audubon calendars could touch. And she'd loved it.

After they'd docked he'd cooked dinner for her on one of the public grills. She'd never had a man other than a paid chef prepare a meal for her before. It's no wonder they'd ended up making love for the first time that night in a campground cabin.

She was a Ritz kind of girl. If anyone had told her the most romantic night of her life would involve sitting on a fallen dead tree, listening to bugs chirp, wine with a twist-off top and dinner served on paper plates, she'd have called them crazy.

Not a memory she needed to wade through right now.

She yanked her thoughts back to the conversation. "It's July and it's hot. I don't want to tramp around outside. Especially with you."

"You never minded the heat before."

The lowered timber of his voice implied more than the temperature outside and rustled up memories of hot, sweaty outdoor sex. And hot, sweaty indoor sex.

She hustled to set the table. "You still like plants? I can't see you making the kind of money you'd need to buy a skyscraper as a landscaper."

"I changed my major from horticulture to business."

"Why?"

His jaw shifted. "Because it wasn't practical to pursue a physically demanding career when I wasn't sure I could do the job."

Her breath hitched at the reminder of his injury.

The timer beeped. She knew from experience that homemade pasta disintegrated if she didn't get it out of the water promptly. Stifling her curiosity about the path he'd chosen, she strained the fettuccini, divided it onto plates then ladled sauce over it and set the dishes on the table. In the confusion of having him there she'd forgotten to steam the asparagus. Too bad. But giving him balanced meals wasn't her job.

She sat at the table, but the delicious aroma wafting up from her plate couldn't tempt her from what she really needed. "How long was it before you could walk again?"

He wound the noodles around the tines of his fork. "Fourteen months."

A long time to be scared. Sympathy softened her anger toward him. Unacceptable. *Don't forget he had your father's money to ease his worries. While you had nothing and no one. You'd lost your baby, your husband and had memories of your mother destroyed.*

"Eat your lunch, Lucas. I have plans this afternoon. And they don't include you."

Nadia opened her door Wednesday morning, bent to pick up her newspapers and froze.

Instantly on alert, she straightened, blinked to clear her

gritty, sleep-deprived eyes and reluctantly lifted her gaze. A dozen feet away *his* door stood open.

"Good morning," Lucas said the moment her gaze collided with his over the top of his newspaper. He sat in a chair that hadn't been in his spacious foyer yesterday with a coffee cup and two more folded papers at his elbow on the credenza. Judging by the way he'd left his door open and angled his chair to face her apartment the man was unabashedly waiting to pounce.

The delicious aroma of her favorite Jamaica Blue Mountain coffee crossed the hall to tease her nose. The rat. Her gourmet brew had been one of the first casualties of her new budget.

Determined to ignore him, she scanned the hall for her newspapers. All three were missing, and not once since she'd moved in had a paper been delivered to his door.

"You stole my papers."

"I'll share them with you over breakfast. C'mon over. We'll eat on the patio." He folded the paper and rose.

Her heart skipped at the sight of his muscled chest outlined to perfection by an Armani crew-neck black T and his long legs encased in low-riding black Prada jeans. The man knew how to dress his assets.

Quit gawking. Her molars clicked together. "I don't want to share my papers or breakfast with you. In fact, I don't ever want to see you again."

"So you said after lunch yesterday." He picked up the other newspapers and strolled deeper into his space.

She debated her options. She could slam her door and ignore him, chase him down and wrestle the papers from him, do as he'd asked or call her brothers and beg them to buy her an airline ticket home.

She sighed. While the last choice appealed the most, it wasn't going to happen. She had to stick this out. Shutting out Lucas literally and figuratively came in a close second, but one of the few things she had going for her in her exile was she finally had the time to stay current in world events by reading the papers cover to cover. She'd already lost touch with her life and her job. She wasn't ready to give up the outside world, and she could only take so much of the news channels' continuous looped coverage and cookie-cutter anchors.

That left options two and three. He was too big to tackle, which meant she had to endure his company. But if he expected her to change into something more attractive than her loose-fitting yoga pants and T-shirt or to put on makeup, then he was out of luck. She nabbed her cell phone from the hall table and padded barefoot across the hall, through his living room and out the glass door. The steamy Dallas heat instantly enveloped her.

His outdoor space, like the part of his apartment she'd seen, was twice the size of hers, and he even had a pool at the far end.

He dropped the papers on the table and faced her. "Why do you have a driving instructor waiting outside for you every day? One you ignore, I might add."

Her gaze snapped from the profusion of brightly colored potted flowers intermingled with odd-looking cacti to him. The security guys must have ratted her out. They'd get no more cookies from her. "None of your business."

"If you lived in Manhattan, I might understand why you don't have a driver's license. But most people in Miami drive. Why don't you?" He pulled out a chair at a glass-topped table set with dishes, a stainless coffee carafe and a heated, covered buffet server and gestured for her to sit.

"What makes you think I don't?" His knuckles brushed her back. She couldn't suppress a shiver. Darn him.

"I checked."

Anger burned a trail under her skin. "You have no right to invade my privacy."

"You live in my building. That gives me the right to do a background check." Leaning over her shoulder and invading her space, he filled a coffee cup for her, then circled the table and sat opposite her.

Okay, maybe he had a point. But she didn't like it. Squelching her irritation she lifted the cup, inhaled the rich aroma and sipped the dark, robust brew. Heaven. She might have to tolerate his company just for his coffee.

He removed the serving dish's lid revealing mushroom omelets, Canadian bacon and baked apples. The cinnamon and brown sugar scent made her mouth water. "Help your-self."

She usually skipped breakfast, but there was no way she'd pass up a meal she hadn't had to prepare and wouldn't have to clean up after. She filled her plate.

He passed her the newspapers and served himself. "You didn't answer my question."

"I never needed a license. I've always had a driver."

"You don't now."

She chewed slowly, trying not to let his statement ruin the delicious buttery taste of the eggs and melt-in-her-mouth bacon. She swallowed. When she, Rand and Mitch were younger a driver had been both a necessity and a security measure. Of course her brothers had rebelled over the restriction and gotten their licenses as soon as legally possible. But she never had because her father had been extremely over-protective. Then after the accident she hadn't even wanted to *ride* in the front seat of a car let alone drive one. Give her the backseat of a Lincoln or a limo any day.

She shoved the thought away and pressed a hand to the gnawing ache in her belly. Lucas might not have died, but her son had. "I guess your spies told you that, too?"

"My *employees* are paid to notice what happens on or around my property. I'll teach you to drive."

Her stomach knotted and her appetite fled. She halted her apple-laden fork an inch from her mouth and lowered the utensil. "No, thank you."

"You were studying for your driver's license exam before our wedding. Why didn't you pursue it?"

"I just didn't, okay."

"If you'd stayed married to me, you would have."

"Moot point. I didn't stay married to you. Your choice, remember?"

His eyes narrowed. He leaned back in his chair. "Are you afraid to drive?"

Her fingers spasmed on the fork. How could he know fear held her back? "Of course not. Don't be silly."

She hoped he missed the crack in her voice.

"You can't let fear rule your life, Nadia."

She couldn't quite meet his eyes and focused on the tip of his nose instead. "It doesn't."

"You claim your father's will requires you to penthouse-sit for a year. What happens if you don't?"

She would have been happy he'd changed the subject had he chosen any subject but *that* one. She abandoned her breakfast. "I'll fail to fulfill my portion of the inheritance clause."

"And then what?"

That her father was willing to give everything he owned

to his enemy rather than his own children was too humiliating to share. "I'll let everyone, but mostly myself, down."

Lucas laced his hands over his waistband. "Have you read your father's purchase agreement?"

She didn't like the sound of that or the intense look in his eyes. "No. Why?"

"Because as owner of this building, I reserve the right to evict any tenant with suitable grounds."

The scant amount of breakfast she'd consumed rolled in her stomach. What constituted *suitable grounds?* She needed to ask her lawyer what would happen if Lucas flexed his legal muscles. Would it set her free…or cost her and her brothers their inheritance?

Could she be held to the terms of the will if the apartment ceased to be available? And could her brothers blame her for aborting her portion of what Rand called the "inheritance curse" if it wasn't her fault? Or could they tie Lucas up long enough with legalese to get through the year?

Part of her hoped Lucas had just handed her an escape clause because she was afraid—very afraid—she wouldn't last another ten months in exile, especially with *him* here. But a small niggling part of her wanted to stay here and prove that she had what it took to stand on her own two feet simply because she was convinced her father and her brothers expected her to fail.

But until she could talk to Richards and find out where she stood she had to stall Lucas. "You can't do that."

"Either you take the driving lessons from me or I make a call to my legal department and you fail your brothers."

"What makes you think you're qualified to teach?"

"I taught both of my sisters."

"They didn't take Drivers' Education like normal people?"

"Our circumstances weren't normal."

Maybe not by his standards, but by hers his family had seemed perfect. Loving. Welcoming. Genuine. Sure, they'd been tight for money and they'd had their squabbles, but the love had been as sure as the sun rising. She hadn't had to wonder what the Stones really wanted from her or if they'd liked her. Every one of them had been an open book.

God, she'd missed them after the accident, but she hadn't had the guts to face them thinking they'd hate her for causing the wreck that had killed Lucas.

Which had turned out to be a total waste of worry on her part, hadn't it? They'd been living high off her daddy's money.

For now, however, what choice did she have but to accede to Lucas's stupid demand? Her cell phone rang before she could acquiesce. Glad for the delay, she snatched it up and checked caller ID. "It's Mitch. I have to take this."

She jumped to her feet and crossed to the far end of the patio and turned her back on Lucas. She stared into the clear water of the pool. "Mitch, what did you find out?"

"I found the divorce petition, but not the final decree. I'll keep looking for that. The petition is signed and looks official."

She exhaled in relief. "I don't remember signing anything related to my marriage, but you know how I was then."

"It was a tough time," Mitch replied. "We understood."

She'd been in a fog for months after the accident, going through the motions and barely functioning. By the time she'd pulled herself together she'd found herself enrolled in accounting classes at Barry University in Miami Shores instead of in New York City studying fashion design the way she'd always dreamed.

Had her father slipped the paperwork by her during that murky period? She hated that she'd been so out of it she didn't even remember. "When did I sign it?"

Papers rustled. "August 13."

Her blood ran cold despite the sultry morning. Mitch went on to rattle off other data from the form, but she barely registered what he said because it didn't matter.

None of it mattered.

Her heart hammered. She wanted to scream, *no,* but her lips moved without making a sound. She gulped air, fighting dizziness and nausea. "M-Mitch, that was four days after my wedding."

"Four days? But you were in a coma for—" Her brother's curses blistered her ear. Apparently Mitch wasn't always cool, calm and collected. That made two of them. "Your signature must have been forged."

Her thoughts exactly.

She tried to calm the horror streaking through her veins, but she was close to hyperventilating. "Does that mean what I think it means?"

"If your signature is invalid, then the document probably is, too, since no one had your power of attorney. I'll get Richards on it immediately. And we'll try to find the rest of the paperwork."

Her thoughts spun out of control as she mentally scrolled through the things she'd done to bury her grief. Things she wasn't proud of. Things a married woman shouldn't do. Because she'd felt dead inside and she'd needed to prove she hadn't died in that crash with her husband and son and because she'd felt she had nothing to lose. Life as she'd known it had ended.

She slowly turned. Her gaze found Lucas's across the patio and she couldn't look away.

"Nadia, don't panic." Mitch's avert-disaster voice didn't have its usual soothing effect.

"What do you mean *don't panic?* I'm still married to Lucas Stone."

Four

Still married.

Lucas couldn't hear Nadia's whispered words, but he could read her lips, see the alarm widening her eyes and the color draining from her cheeks.

He stifled the urge to pump his hand in the air and shout, "Yes!" as he crossed the flagstones. He stopped in front of her close enough for the morning breeze to carry her scent to his nostrils. *Her* scent. Not the pricy perfume she used to dab on interesting places. The memory of seeking out those intimate spots with his lips quickened his pulse. Nadia's fragrance still had the ability to rouse his hormones like nothing else.

She snapped her phone closed and took several deep, measured breaths, drawing his gaze to her breasts.

"Problem?" He kept his tone calm when he wanted to pepper her with questions, starting with what had Everett

Kincaid done wrong? But however his nemesis had screwed up this situation, Lucas wasn't above using it to his advantage.

And then there was the relief that neither of them had married in the interim. Bigamy wasn't pretty. His mother had discovered that firsthand.

Nadia blinked and swallowed and averted her worry-darkened eyes. Very telling. "There appears to be a glitch in the signatures on our divorce paperwork."

The barely detectable quiver in her voice was another giveaway. He knew he'd signed the forms, so his signature wasn't in question. "You didn't sign it."

"Um. I'm…not sure."

The truth was written all over her face. Nadia had never been able to lie worth a damn. Her honesty had been one of the things he'd liked about her…along with her traffic-stopping body, her I'll-try-anything-once sense of adventure and the warmth and openness she'd displayed toward his family. She had never seemed to look down on his mother despite the fact that Lila Stone had had children by three different men and had only been "married" to one of them—Lucas's good-for-nothing already married father who'd climbed into his eighteen-wheeler before Lucas's second birthday and had never come back.

Nadia's family hadn't been as accepting of Lucas. But they'd have to eat that attitude now along with a slice of humble pie when he took KCL from them.

"We're still married. That's what Mitch told you."

Her teeth pinched her bottom lip. "Maybe. He needs to do more research."

A gust blew a strand of long dark hair across her eyes. He lifted a hand and brushed it back, lingering on her soft cheek.

Her breath caught and her pupils expanded to almost obliterate her green irises. The chemistry between them hit him
as hard as ever and it was clearly reciprocated. Getting her
into bed shouldn't be too difficult.

She looked better this morning without the heavy makeup
she'd slathered on her face yesterday. His gaze lowered to
her unpainted lips. "Then by all means, let me kiss my
bride."

He cupped her nape and covered her mouth with his. A
charge of electricity arced through him. He relearned her
softness, and with a sweep of his tongue across her bottom
lip, her taste. For a second she leaned into him before she
jerked out of reach.

Her arms flailed and her eyes widened. He grabbed her
biceps to keep her from tumbling backward into the pool. For
a moment he held her there, off balance and suspended over
the water. Her pleading eyes locked with his, and then he
swung her away from the lip of tile to safer ground.

"Careful."

She struggled to get free, but the flush on her cheeks told
him she wasn't unmoved by the brief kiss.

"Let me go, Lucas. We are not resuming this marriage.
Don't even think about it. My attorney will fix it." The
moment he released her she put several yards between them.

Last time he hadn't had to chase her. Bold as brass, she'd
initiated their first meeting and, yes, he knew it had been to
piss off her father. Lucas had wanted her bad enough not to
care. From that point on all he'd had to do was show up and
let Mother Nature take her course. The attraction had been
that strong. They'd spent every possible minute together.

It didn't look as though Nadia was going to make wooing
her as easy this time around despite the still-strong pull.

"After you finish your breakfast I'll give you your first driving lesson."

"I don't want lessons."

He wasn't letting her off the hook that easily. "What's your job at KCL?"

She frowned as if having trouble following his line of thought. "I'm Director of Shared Services. Why?"

Surprise jolted him and reminded him he should have done his research on their executive board. But he'd had tunnel vision with Everett Kincaid as his target. He'd focused on KCL's data, assets and finances instead of personnel roster because he'd never once considered that Nadia might work for the bastard.

No doubt his finagling with KCL's suppliers through Andvari had been a thorn in Nadia's behind since her position was the one most directly burdened by his upping costs and making it difficult to obtain supplies. He'd have to keep that from her as long as possible or the spit would hit the fan.

"As upper management you know it would be bad PR for Kincaid Cruise Lines if word leaked out that Everett had frauded legal documents and bribed his daughter's husband to disappear."

She stiffened as she registered his implied threat. "You wouldn't do that. You wouldn't smear our names in the press and create a scandal like that."

He wasn't the boy she'd led around by the balls anymore. Life and Everett Kincaid had taught him some hard lessons and toughened him up. "Try me."

"Nadia, loosen your grip on the wheel."

Nadia glared at the man in the passenger seat of the Mercedes. She couldn't do as Lucas ordered. Her entire body

felt locked, her muscles rigid with fear in the leather seats.
And she couldn't stop shaking.

Her mother had died in a car accident. Her baby had died
in a car accident. And until two days ago she'd thought her
husband had, too. Seeing him in the flesh couldn't erase years
of ingrained fear.

Irrational? Maybe. But she couldn't help the emotions
churning through her.

She didn't want to be there. Not in Dallas. Not in this car.
Not with this man—a man who had betrayed her and wasn't
above using leverage to manipulate her.

Shades of your father.

On the other hand, she had to admit this hard-jawed, steely
eyed, bossy, confident version of Lucas was…well, interesting in a way the younger man hadn't been.

Not that she'd ever get entangled with him again. And she
certainly wouldn't give him another opportunity to grind her
heart beneath his John Lobb shoes.

No matter how good he kissed.

The memory sent a flutter of something she wanted nothing
to do with through her. Needing a distraction she scanned the
vast, empty parking lot of the closed facility, hoping security
or the police or somebody would arrive and throw them out.

She swallowed to ease her dry mouth. "We shouldn't be
here. There were posted No Trespassing signs at the gate."

"It's private property. I know the owner."

"And would that owner be you?"

He paused as if considering his answer. "Yes."

"Why is the business closed?"

"You're stalling."

Smart of him to guess that. "And you didn't answer my
question."

"The equipment is being upgraded this week. The plant will reopen on Monday. Start the car."

How hard could it be to turn the key? Impossible apparently since she couldn't relax her white-knuckled grip.

"Nadia, look at me."

She forced her gaze to meet his and found patience instead of irritation in his blue eyes.

"This is no different than driving the bumper cars at the amusement park. You enjoyed that. Didn't you?"

She inhaled slowly, calling upon the memories of happier times to wash over her. She and Lucas had spent a lot of time playing at the things normal people—not heiresses—did. He'd introduced her to a whole different world from the pampered, secluded one she'd grown up in. And he'd helped her fit in. "I did."

"Only this time you don't have to brace yourself because no one is going to bump into you. You have the entire place to yourself. Nothing bad is going to happen."

"Easy for you to say."

"You've driven golf carts. The pedals are the same."

She flexed her cramping fingers. The leather seats grew hot and moist against the backs of her legs.

"Nadia." His patience morphed into inflexible resolve. "We're not leaving until you've driven around the parking lot."

How stupid was it to not be able to drive a dumb car at her age? Definitely a sign of weakness. One she needed to overcome.

Everett Kincaid had abhorred weakness. No wonder he'd hung her out to dry.

"One time around the lot?"

He paused then dipped that stubborn chin. "Once around the entire property and then you can park the car."

One lap. She could do that. She turned the key and the motor purred to life. Her foot weighed as heavy as lead as she transferred it from the brake to the gas pedal. The engine roared, but the car didn't move.

"Put your foot back on the brake and put the car in Drive."

Idiot. But if Lucas thought she was lacking brain cells his even tone didn't show it. In fact, his soothing voice reminded her of the times he'd introduced her to other new things like riding a bicycle, free concerts in the park, making love on a blanket beneath the stars.

Don't go there.

Still trembling, she gritted her teeth and did as he instructed. The car inched forward. Her heart slammed harder, faster. She struggled to keep from hyperventilating.

She would get through this. And then maybe he'd leave her alone.

During her first two months in exile she'd prayed for her neighbor to come home. Now she couldn't wait to get rid of him.

Apparently, there was an upside to loneliness. And as soon as she ditched him she'd enjoy it, revel in it and be grateful for it. Screaming silences and all. No more whining self-pity.

"You're doing fine."

She glanced at him and her gaze snagged on his tender smile—the one that had haunted her dreams for years.

"Eyes on the road, princess."

She jerked her face forward again, but her pulse skittered anew at the old nickname.

"You have forward nailed. When you come around the backside of the building let's raise the bar and practice keeping the car between the lines."

He'd always done that. Encouraged without berating.

Guided rather than ordered. After her father's build-'em-up-to-take-'em-down MO she'd always braced herself after each of Lucas's positive comments eleven years ago. But the negative follow-ups had never come.

She didn't want him to be nice or patient or positive. She wanted him to be an obnoxious ass.

It'd be easier to hate him that way.

Because right now he was making that very, very difficult.

She'd never been more aware of a body in her life.

His or hers.

Nadia backed into the far corner of the elevator, as far from Lucas as she could get. She concentrated on the seam between the doors and tried to tune out the scent of the man standing two yards away. The man currently staring at her.

She sensed that blue gaze as surely as a touch and it made her skin hypersensitive. She could feel so much: the weight of each piece of clothing on her skin, the slight shift of her blouse with each breath she inhaled and exhaled, the tickle of her hair against her cheeks and nape. But along with the awareness and the wariness came a sense of accomplishment.

She'd driven a car.

That didn't mean she wanted to take one out on the road, but still…she'd made progress today that eleven years of therapy hadn't been able to accomplish.

Thanks to Lucas.

Don't go there. He's an opportunistic bastard. Remember?

She couldn't forgive him for choosing money over her, and she couldn't let her bitter feelings toward him soften. But she was in danger of doing both.

Replaying the too cozy dinner she'd just shared with him

at the steak house, the quiet conversation about art and music, movies and books was bad news. He'd put her at ease just as he had on their first date—the only date she'd ever been nervous about in her life. She couldn't dwell on the feeling of success she'd had when she'd mastered his car. Okay, *mastered* might be a slight exaggeration, but her one lap around the parking lot had turned into an hour once she got past her nerves.

And she certainly couldn't recall the good times they'd had together in the past.

She could feel herself weakening. She gave up and let her gaze meet his. The hunger burning in his eyes took her breath away. His gaze dropped to her lips which suddenly seemed dry and hot and swollen. She bit her tongue rather than dampen them.

She wanted him to kiss her. That would be a major mistake. His good-night kisses tended not to end before breakfast. That's how she'd become pregnant the first time. She searched for a diversion. "Thank you for dinner."

"You're welcome. We'll do it again soon."

Not a good idea.

"I'm proud of you, Nadia."

His quietly uttered words sent warmth rushing through her. When had anyone ever told her that? She gathered her wits. "I'm proud of me, too."

"You did very well for your first lesson. Tomorrow will be easier. Be ready at nine."

She winced. "About tomorrow…"

The elevator doors glided open, stilling her words.

Lucas shoved off the wall, but he didn't exit. He came toward her, closing the distance in three long strides. He planted one hand on the wall beside her head.

Her pulse thundered in her ears. She had to break this up. Fast. "Well, okay, thanks again for dinner. I—"

He nudged her chin with his knuckle. She couldn't breathe. God, she wanted him to kiss her. Instead she listened to the voice screaming caution in her brain, ducked beneath his arm and dashed out of the cubicle and to her door.

"I'll see you. Good night."

She hustled into her apartment and shut the door.

Close call. Too close. She had to get control of her hormones before they got her into trouble.

At one minute after six the next morning Nadia eased open her apartment door and peeked out. The hall was empty and Lucas's door was closed.

She had to get out of here.

She stepped over her newspapers rather than bring them in. Let him think she was still sleeping. She quietly closed the door and tiptoed toward the elevator. She'd yet to figure out how her father's minions—whoever they might be—would know if she wasn't inside between midnight and 6:00 a.m. It might be somehow related to the security system that she'd neglected to use even once since moving in. Whatever. She wasn't blowing her assigned task on a technicality.

The elevator opened with a ding. She winced, darted inside and hit the button to close the doors. Her muscles remained stiff with tension all the way down and as she exited the box and crossed the lobby.

"Going out, Ms. Kincaid?" the security guy asked.

She forced a smile and prayed he didn't have a concealed button to buzz his boss in the penthouse. "Yes."

"Would you like a taxi?"

"No, thank you, William."

Hurdle number one. If she wanted to travel under the radar, then she had to master public transportation. But if she could juggle the needs of dozens of ships navigating the globe, she could handle moving one person via a city rail system.

She'd printed a Dallas Area Rapid Transit map from her computer and tucked it into her oversize tote bag along with her laptop. The map and a loosely formed strategy should get her through today and keep her away from this building and its owner.

"You're getting an early start," William said, clearly hunting for information.

And the longer she stayed in the lobby chatting the better chance Lucas had of catching up with her and shadowing her. After yesterday's bonding experience and last night's near-miss kiss she didn't want that.

"Yes. I am."

"Headed anywhere in particular?"

She hadn't been born yesterday. If she told William where she was going, it would probably be relayed upstairs before her feet hit the sidewalk. "I plan to play tourist and see as much of the city as possible. Have a good day."

She plowed through the front doors and headed toward the transit station as quickly as her high-heeled Stella McCartney wedge sandals would take her. She hated liars and fibbing even though telling little white lies was de rigueur in her social circle.

The muggy morning air enveloped her as did the sounds and smells of early rush hour traffic. She was used to the bustle of big cities, but it was different somehow when you had only a general clue how to get where you were going and no driver waiting at the curb to carry your bags or give you directions. Or better yet, to drop you off at the door. She also tended to travel with a posse of friends—or leeches as her father would call them—who knew their way around.

Her plan: find an Internet café and drink coffee until the library's doors opened.

The *library*. She shook her head. Once upon a time she'd have killed time by shopping in Manhattan or Paris or Milan. But not now. Not with her budget and travel restrictions. She needed somewhere free and air-conditioned where she could pass the hours and keep herself too occupied to think about the ecstatic "welcome home" dance her hormones had done when Lucas's lips had touched hers.

She didn't spot anyone following her. Nevertheless, she squeezed into a group of a half dozen other people crossing the street trying to get lost in the crowd.

It might have only been sixty hours since her "dead" husband had risen, but she'd already figured out the Lucas of today wasn't the Lucas of her past. He wasn't going to jump when she crooked her little finger. And she wasn't sure exactly how far he'd go to make her fall in line with his plans. Whatever those were, she wanted no part of them…unless they included a new divorce. And that didn't seem to be on his agenda.

She observed the other commuters until she managed to figure out how to buy a day-pass ticket and then she boarded the train. It was disgusting how reliant she'd become on others for trivial but necessary details in twenty-nine years. Her father was right. She'd had no clue how to survive in the real world.

But she was going to learn.

She wasn't co-dependent at work. On the job she was more than competent. Just look how well she'd done these past three years with that damned Andvari challenging her every step. The company had made her job a living hell by

stealing most of KCL's suppliers. She'd had to bust her butt
to find the goods the cruise line needed at reasonable prices.
Even her father hadn't been able to find fault with the creative
solutions she'd presented to the Andvari problem.

But personally, well, she needed a little more work than a
day at the spa could fix. And that was probably her father's
point in exiling her halfway across the country.

Understanding his motives didn't mean she wasn't still
peeved with him. Seriously she'd-never-forgive-him peeved.

The DART ride passed quickly and mercifully without
incident. She even managed to get off at the right stop. After
coffee and a fruit-yogurt-and-granola parfait she entered the
library as soon as the doors opened. One whiff and she felt
right at home. Nothing smelled like a building full of books.

Back during her college days she'd spent a lot of time
hanging out in the stacks, studying and avoiding her father.

See a pattern here, Nadia? Her shrink's voice echoed in
her head.

Hmm. She avoided the pushy men in her life by hiding out.
Yes, definitely a pattern. One she needed to correct. And she
would. As soon as she was on firmer ground. But for now
she'd continue avoiding Lucas. And if he found her in this
library, then Google said there were twenty-two others in the
Dallas area and all had free Wi-Fi. She'd keep moving and
try to stay one step ahead of him.

Speaking of Google, he'd had her so rattled she'd forgotten to do an Internet search on him.

With the first order of business determined, she found a
quiet table tucked in the back and out of sight of the main
entrance and booted up her laptop. She typed in *Lucas Stone*
and hit Search.

There were several Lucas Stones, but none of them were

hers. Not hers. *Him,* she corrected. She tried a different search engine with the same results, then a third and a fourth. How peculiar. If the man owned businesses, he shouldn't be this hard to find.

She opened her e-mail account and typed in her brother's address. Mitch had resources she lacked. She composed a quick message asking him to check the apartment paperwork for an eviction clause and the will constraints to see if Lucas could indeed boot her out and what the consequences of that would be.

And then she made her last request.

As much as she hated asking for help again, she needed to know exactly who and what she was up against with Lucas Stone.

"You dodged your driving lesson."

Lucas's voice behind her in the apartment hallway made Nadia jump. She hadn't heard him open his door. She kept her back to him and turned her key in the lock. "Sorry. I had things to do."

"You failed to mention your busy schedule last night when I told you to meet me at nine."

Searching her brain for any excuse to get out of another evening in his company, she faced him. He wore faded jeans and a white V-neck T-shirt. Both Diesel. The man had learned how to dress his assets. And he had quite a few of them to display.

Ignore his assets.

"Probably because you ordered me to be ready instead of asking. You should remember that orders give me hives."

Her father had excelled at issuing commands and he'd expected unquestioning compliance. So, yes, she'd stood up to Lucas. Unforgivably rude of her, but given that the alternative of spending the day with him had been much more dangerous to her willpower, she'd decided a little discourtesy was the wiser option.

"You have five minutes to get ready for your lesson."

"Lucas, I'm tired. I've been out all day. I just want dinner and sleep."

"We have reservations after your lesson. You won't have to cook."

Another meal she wouldn't have to prepare. Tempting, but hadn't he heard a word she'd said? "And if I refuse?"

He pulled his cell phone from his back pocket.

He'd call his attorney or the press or…whoever could make her life the most miserable. 'Nuff said.

"It'll take me more than five minutes to get ready."

"Ten."

"Ten minutes? But—"

"Clock's ticking. We're running out of daylight for your lesson." His watch face glinted in the overhead lighting.

"Don't you have anything better to do than harass me?"

"What could be more important than reconnecting with my long-lost wife?"

"I am not your wife."

"Would you like to see the copy of the divorce petition and the final decree I received today? I compared your signatures to the ones from your old letters. The signatures on the legal documents are good copies. But they're not yours."

Just what she was afraid of. Mitch was supposed to be overnighting the paperwork to her so she could verify that fact.

Then Lucas's words registered. *Her letters.*

A flush warmed her from the inside out. He hadn't had Internet access back then so they'd corresponded the old-fashioned paper way. The notes they'd exchanged had been…racy to say the least. Full of fantasies and intent and raw emotion.

She'd kept everything he'd given her. Every letter. Every ticket stub. Every dried, pressed flower. These days the collection was buried in the back of her closet in Miami.

After Lucas's "death" she'd practically set up a shrine in her room for Lucas and their son. Her father had hated that. Now she knew why he'd badgered her so tenaciously to find someone new, rushing her past her grief until she'd struck back by deliberately bringing home the worst possible candidates, one after another, and flaunting them in her father's face until he'd quit nagging her.

But none of those men had ever been able to take Lucas's place or make the numbness go away. And none of them had been able to fill the void caused by the loss of her baby.

Lord, what if she had found someone? What if she'd married him? She shoved away the thought.

"You still have my old letters?" She'd lost count of the number of nights she'd slept with his clutched in her arms.

Memo to self: Throw the crap out.

"I kept them to remind me that some women don't honor their vows."

"But I—"

He held up a hand. "Your father screwed us both. I don't hold you responsible for that. Get moving, Nadia. You only have eight minutes left."

She stomped into her apartment and swung the door shut behind her. A boom jerked her around. Lucas had his palm splayed on the wood. He'd caught the door before it slammed in his face.

"I'll wait inside."

So she wouldn't change her mind and lock him out. Smart man to know the thought had crossed her mind. More than once.

She could argue with him, but what purpose would that serve? He had her with the dual threats of eviction and exposure and he knew it. She marched into her bedroom and locked that door before stripping.

She would not dress up for him. Instead she pulled on last year's black jeans and a lime-green XCVI shirt. The ruched knit top made her breasts look larger. She probably should have had them augmented like everyone else in her Miami circle, but she still had an allergy to hospitals. Couldn't get near one without feeling as if her throat had closed up and she was going to suffocate.

She checked the mirror and finger combed her desperately in-need-of-a-trim-and-highlights hair. Waking up from a coma with a shaved head and tubes coming out of every orifice had not been a pleasant experience. It had gone downhill from there when her father had told her about Lucas and their baby. And then a month later she'd learned the horrifying truth that her mother's death hadn't been an accident nor had it been Mary Elizabeth Kincaid's first attempt at suicide.

Once Nadia had climbed out of her deep pit of grief, she'd vowed to never allow herself to be that vulnerable again. And that meant not opening her heart to a man again—particularly the one in her living room.

Shaking off the memories, she freshened her makeup. She had enough pride that she couldn't go out looking like yesterday's news. She stabbed her feet into a pair of Michael Kors sandals and yanked open her door.

Lucas Stone could force her to spend time with him, but

he couldn't make her forget the hard lessons his disappearance had taught her.

Falling in love with him had been as natural as breathing and the easiest thing she'd ever done in her life.

Losing him had been the hardest. And it had almost driven her to follow in her mother's footsteps.

Five

A bloodcurdling scream to Nadia's right scared the *bejeezus* out of her. She jumped sideways in the semicircular restaurant booth and landed half in Lucas's lap.

She twisted toward the source. A woman in the next booth stared goggle-eyed at the man slumped beside her in his seat, his chest covered in red, his mouth moving soundlessly, his eyes wide and unfocused.

Horrified, Nadia glanced around. What had happened? Had he been shot? She hadn't heard a gun.

She gathered her composure. She'd been trained for disaster back in the days when she worked on KCL's ships, although she'd never had to deal with more than basic first aid. Peeling herself away from the heat of Lucas's body, she tried to slide from the booth to offer assistance. Lucas caught her wrist in a firm grip and held her back.

Heart pounding, she tugged her arm, but Lucas kept her

in her seat. "Let me go. I'm trained in first aid and CPR. I can help."

A smile lifted one corner of his mouth. Why was he smiling when the guy beside them could be dying?

"Nadia, it's a play," he whispered.

The woman at the next table covered her face and began to wail out nonsense, her loud voice echoing throughout the restaurant.

Useless idiot. Do something instead of just screeching.

But the increasingly hysterical woman didn't even try to staunch the bleeding and no one else came forward to help. Nadia snatched up her cloth napkin intent on putting pressure on the wound—wherever it was—and tried to rise again. The clamp on her wrist anchored her.

"Lucas, he needs medical attention. Call 911."

Lucas grabbed her shoulders firmly and forced her to look at him. "It's a play, Nadia. Mystery dinner theater."

She'd heard his low-pitched words, but they didn't make sense. She blinked, trying to comprehend. "What?"

"The victim and his date are both actors. You used to love Broadway. I wanted to surprise you with a show."

He'd surprised her all right. "A play?"

She glanced back over her shoulder to the other people coming onto the scene, their lines projecting to even the farthest table in the room.

A play. And Act I was unfolding right in front of her.

Now that she knew what she was looking at, it was obvious. Good acting, but still acting with the gestures and expressions a little grander than necessary.

Tension drained from her limbs. She felt like an imbecile as she watched the assembled cast go through their lines and hit their marks. Her racing pulse slowed but her face burned.

How many people had seen her try to charge to the rescue? Did everyone in the place except her know they were here for the entertainment?

She wanted to slide down by Lucas's side and hide.

As if he understood, he shifted, draping his arm across her shoulders and pulling her closer on the vinyl seat. He laced the fingers of his opposite hand through hers and rested their linked hands on his thigh. The electrifying warmth of his palm, his shoulder and his leg pressed against hers made her breath catch. And then his scent, his heat and his nearness converted embarrassment into awareness. Her heart skipped anew.

She attempted to pull away. He tightened his hold. She couldn't struggle or make a scene without drawing attention away from the actors who were finally moving en masse toward a stage that an opening curtain revealed.

"How did I miss the signs telling what this was?" she whispered.

He bent closer, his warm breath stirring her hair. "There weren't any posted signs. The place looks just like a regular restaurant."

His mouth brushed her ear as he spoke and then he sucked her earlobe between his lips. The jolt of arousal charging through her wasn't welcome. She wiggled, intent on putting space between them, but his iron grip didn't loosen.

"Be still. Enjoy the show."

What choice did she have?

She focused on the cast, some rising from other tables around them to join the action in front of her. A detective swaggered onto the set. Nadia tried to concentrate on the dialogue, the setting and the story. Anything to keep her mind off the man fused to her side.

She'd always been a huge Broadway fan and often jetted to New York to catch an opening, but she'd never done a dinner theater where the cast actually masqueraded as diners.

When she and Lucas had been dating he hadn't been able to afford Broadway tickets let alone the time off work to go to Manhattan. He'd introduced her to local theater and concerts in the park where more often than not they'd watched from a quilt on the grass. She'd loved the casual performances, but mostly she'd loved watching the entertainment from the vantage point of his arms. She was a little too comfy in those arms right now but another wiggle gained her no breathing room.

She pushed the memories away and immersed herself in the murder mystery until the curtain dropped for intermission. Lucas lifted their joined hands to his lips, jarring her back to the present. The soft brush of his mouth over her knuckles set her heart racing and ignited a flame low in her belly. Their gazes locked in the shadowy theater, and the urge to kiss him hit her hard and fast.

She adored the way he kissed.

"Enjoying the show?" he asked.

She needed to break the spell he'd cast over her before he had the chance to betray her again. But somehow she just couldn't make her body follow orders and instead, she caught herself leaning toward him. "Yes. Thank you for thinking of this."

"You're welcome." He released her hand and brushed back her hair, his knuckles skimming beneath her cheekbone in a caress that made her nerve endings quiver. The reflection of light off the polished crystal of his watch snagged her attention.

Time.

She'd lost track of time.

She bolted upright, grabbed his wrist and turned it so she could see his watch. She'd given up wearing hers weeks ago because awareness of the crawling minutes made the hours drag slower. And she'd had no need to worry about curfew since she didn't go anywhere.

Eleven-thirty. She was going to be late. Adrenaline rushed through her. She dropped his wrist and scooped up her purse. "I have to go."

The detective strolled onto the stage and began his monologue. She hated being rude and walking out in the midst of a performance, but her and her brothers' inheritance depended on it.

"The play's not over."

"I can't stay." She slid out of the booth and hurried toward the exit.

Lucas caught up with her in the lobby, gripped her elbow and pulled her to a stop. His blue eyes searched her face. "Nadia, what's wrong. Are you ill?"

The concern darkening his eyes and straining his face tugged at something deep inside her.

"No. But I…" How much did she want to tell him about her father treating her like a child by grounding her and setting a curfew? None of it. But again, her choices were limited. "Look, just take me home. Or if you want to stay and see the end, I'll take a cab. But I have to go. *Now.*"

"You were enjoying the performance."

"Yes, I was. The show is great. But I have to go."

"I'll drive you home if you level with me."

She hesitated. "Lucas, could we please have this conversation en route? I'll explain. I promise. But, please, get me back to the apartment. And hurry."

He crossed to the maitre d', said a few words and handed the man a couple of folded bills, then he returned to Nadia's side. "Let's go."

Dozens of phrases ran through her head as she hustled to the car. None sounded right, and she still hadn't come up with a suitably edited version of the disaster called her life by the time he'd pulled onto the highway.

He glanced at her. "Start talking."

She sighed. It should have been easy to confess the whole sordid mess in the darkened car, but she couldn't. "I have to be home by midnight."

"Why?"

"It's a condition of my father's will."

"And if you're not?"

"Things could get ugly. Not just for me, but for Rand and Mitch and Rhett."

"I've met Mitch and Rand, but who's Rhett?"

"My half brother. Dad surprised us with an illegitimate one-year-old son."

She had yet to see anything more than e-mailed photos of her baby brother. There hadn't been time to meet him or cuddle him before she left, and thanks to the stupid will she wouldn't get the chance before next June. By then he'd be two, no longer a baby and probably not interested in letting his estranged half sister hold him.

Rhett looked just like a Kincaid. Who would her son have taken after? Would he have been dark-haired and green-eyed like her or blond and blue-eyed like his daddy?

"How could it get ugly?"

Lucas's question hauled her from the deep well of what-might-have-beens. She debated how much to disclose and decided to keep it short. Need to know, as Mitch would say.

"If I don't follow the rules, I'll jeopardize our inheritance. I'm not going to do that."

"This is all about money?"

"No. It's about me coming through for my brothers for once instead of always relying on them." Oops. She'd said too much. She hoped he missed her slipup.

"Relied on them how?"

She winced. "They were there for me after you…died. I wasn't…in good shape. And I owe them this. I have to do my part."

Lucas muttered something that sounded like a curse under his breath. "Your father was a real piece of work."

"No kidding. And the more I learn—" She bit off the words.

"The more you learn…what?"

Lucas had been privy to too many of her rants about her father in the past to be surprised by the secret she'd never disclosed to anyone. Not even her brothers. "The more I wonder whether he loved me or hated me."

"Because you reminded him of your mother."

He remembered. She swallowed, trying to ease the lump in her throat and nodded. He took one hand from the steering wheel, reached across the center console and covered her fist and squeezed reassuringly.

"Hating you is impossible, Nadia. Believe me. I tried."

His words hit her with a punch of choking emotions. The scary part was the feeling was mutual. She couldn't hate Lucas, either. But she had to get over him and move on. Because her memories of the perfect love they'd shared were nothing more than fantasies.

True love didn't come with a price tag.

"We made it with five minutes to spare," Lucas said as Nadia shoved her key into the lock.

"I'm sorry I made you miss the ending of the play."

She opened the door and stepped inside, glancing around and wondering not for the first time if there was a camera or a trip switch or some other 007 gadget to register her comings and goings and whether she was solo or accompanied by a party. Or was her monitoring system something more basic, like her father had bribed the security staff? That would be more Everett Kincaid's style. Her father had always believed everyone had a price. History had shown he was usually right. Take Lucas, for example.

Wouldn't Lucas love knowing his team had sold out to her father? But she wouldn't voice her suspicions, because she wasn't sure what would happen if the reporting on her activities suddenly stopped. Her father's crazy will had left too many strings untied and too many questions unanswered. And all of the clauses were unbreakable, or so her brothers said. They'd each hired teams of lawyers to try to break the will with no luck. She hadn't had the cash to do so.

Now that she was back in her prison away from home, her heart slowed for the first time since she'd raced out of the restaurant. They'd had to detour around a traffic accident and she'd panicked, afraid of being late. She'd never had a problem with deadlines before. In fact, at work she thrived on them. But five minutes to midnight was cutting it too close for her peace of mind.

She turned in the foyer and startled at finding Lucas right on her heels. Close enough to touch if she wanted. And she didn't. Okay, yes, she did. And that wasn't good. Time to finish this before her weak will landed her in trouble.

"Thank you for the driving lesson, the show and dinner."

"We need to get an earlier start tomorrow." He moved forward.

She retreated. Avoiding him was still her number one

priority—especially after the understanding he'd shown tonight both during the driving lesson and when she had to leave the play. His compassion was eroding her defenses.

"Lucas, as much as I appreciate your help, I know you must have to work. Your businesses, whatever they are, can't run by themselves. I'll reengage the car company my father hired and finish the lessons."

And she would. Later. Thanks to Lucas getting her past her initial fear, she believed she'd eventually be able to get a driver's license at some point in the future. But not on busy Dallas roads. Best postpone the whole deal until she returned to Miami.

"Not necessary. I've got you covered." He advanced. The look of intent in his eyes sprouted goose bumps under her skin and doubled her pulse rate. Did he consider this a date and expect the traditional ending?

If so, she had to keep that from happening. She backed deeper into the apartment. "It's late. You need to go. Thank you again. Good night."

"Not yet." He captured her hand, dragged her into the living room and sat on the sofa. He tugged her down beside him. "Tell me what you did after the accident."

She did not want to have this conversation, but apparently giving him the postcard version was the only way to get rid of him. "I went to college. In the summers I worked for KCL."

"Doing what?"

"I worked on Crescent Key."

"The private island the cruise ships use?"

He shifted and his hot, hard thigh pressed hers. His lock on her wrist kept her from escaping. "Yes."

"Doing what?"

She tried to block the memories of being pressed against him without the hindrance of clothing. "I led kayaking and snorkeling excursions or filled in wherever else I was needed."

"Pretty good for a first job."

"Yes. You know Daddy wouldn't let me work before I turned eighteen."

"Nor did you want to."

"Well, no." Having a job had never occurred to her before she'd met Lucas. Why would it? She'd had more money than she could spend. But she'd been prepared to work after they'd married. She'd known Lucas couldn't afford for her not to. But she'd planned to get a job in a chic clothing shop.

Had he leaned closer? She arched her back to escape, but he pulled her forward and lowered his head. His mouth took hers before she could protest or evade him.

The kiss slammed into her like a rogue wave, towing her under in seconds. Under a deluge of memories. Under a somersaulting swirl of sensation. Under the spell he'd always been able to cast over her with no apparent effort. She clutched his upper arms to push him away, but ended up clinging for balance.

He didn't kiss the way he used to. Eleven years ago Lucas's kisses had been passionate, but teasing and tempting, luring her into love play. Tonight he kissed like a man on a mission to destroy each of her reservations.

And he was doing a damned fine job.

Pull away.

The contrast between the softness of his lips and the firm confidence in his possession robbed her of the ability to comply with the simplest of commands.

One arm tightened around her waist, bringing her torso

flush with his hard body. His other hand grazed up her side and her neck to cradle her jaw and tilt her head for deeper penetration. He sucked her bottom lip into his mouth and nipped gently, sending shock waves of arousal through her. The hot, slick, wet sweep of his tongue against hers dragged a hungry whimper from her throat and stirred a whirlpool of want in her midsection.

His taste filled her mouth, his scent her nose, and his big body seemed to surround her, making her feel protected and desired. Just like the old days. She fit against him as if she never should have left.

She'd missed this.

Her heart clamored out an SOS, her muscles weakened and her head spun. She clung to him because she couldn't possibly imagine doing anything else. His five o'clock shadow rasped her chin. Her fingers tightened and relaxed on his biceps like a cat's kneading paws. She couldn't help herself. She needed to touch him.

He shifted, laying her back on the cushions and following her down. His erection lengthened and thickened against her hip. And she wanted him. As much as she'd ever wanted anything. Maybe even more. But she couldn't have him. Not now. Not ever again. Because nothing was the same.

Nothing could ever be the same.

She ripped herself from his arms, sprang to her feet beside the sofa and pressed her fingertips to her mouth. She backed away. She stumbled over something and struggled for balance. Lucas stood and caught her, his grip firm on her elbows. She regained her footing, jerked free and looked down. Her purse. She didn't even remember dropping it beside the sofa.

That was twice she'd almost fallen and he'd had to catch

her. He kept her off balance mentally and physically. She had to be more careful around him or she was going to end up falling again. For him.

One glance at his desire-flushed face and passion-darkened eyes and a fresh wave of hunger swelled inside her. She had to look away and covered the action by bending and snagging the straps of her handbag. She slapped it down on the coffee table, marched for the front door and yanked it open. She focused on his left shoulder as he approached rather than his too-sexy face.

"I can't—I *won't* do this, Lucas. Please leave."

"You want me as much as I do you."

His husky tone made her nipples tighten. "I've learned the hard way that I can't have everything I want. Sometimes what I want isn't good for me."

Silence ticked between them.

"I'll see you in the morning, Nadia. Sleep well."

The second the door closed behind him she sagged in relief that he hadn't argued or tried to change her mind. She wasn't up for that—especially when she'd be fighting herself as much as him. And she wasn't sure who'd win.

But one thing was certain. This marriage was a no-win situation and she had to get out of it. Lucas had taken money to hurt her.

And she was damaged goods.

"Excuse me."

The hushed voice pulled Nadia's attention from the stack of fashion magazines on the library table in front of her early that Friday afternoon.

"Yes?"

A petite salt-and-pepper-haired fiftyish woman stood

beside her. Her glasses hung from a beaded chain around her neck. "Are you Nadia Kincaid?"

Nadia ignored years of ingrained caution and welcomed the interruption because the magazines weren't doing a good job of distracting her from the fact that her brother was getting married today, and she couldn't be there because she couldn't leave Dallas.

Damn you, Daddy.

Rand had promised to figure out a way to stream video of the ceremony through her computer tonight so she could "see" Mitch marry Rhett's aunt—a woman Nadia had never even met.

"Yes. I'm Nadia Kincaid."

"I thought I recognized you from your picture in a tabloid I found this morning."

Nadia fought the urge to shift in her chair. Her cheeks warmed. People were strange. She was no celebrity, but she'd been asked for her autograph before. It was a little weird, a little embarrassing, but it wouldn't cost her anything but time…of which she had a surplus since she was still avoiding Lucas until the last possible moment tonight. "Can I help you?"

"I'm hoping you can. Because you see…" The woman looked over each shoulder and leaned closer. "I read that rag before I recycled it."

Uh-oh. Was she going to get thrown out? And what crazy story had the tabloid "reporters" fabricated this time? She hadn't given them any ammunition to crucify her with lately.

"I'm Mary Branch, the head librarian here. The article says you orchestrated a fund-raiser for premature babies last spring in Miami and raised a record-breaking amount."

Tension relaxed its grip on Nadia's muscles and pride filled her with warmth. "Yes, I did."

She'd donated her time and her expertise at finding unusual, hard-to-get items for the auction because some preterm babies stood a chance. Hers never had.

"Our library fund-raiser chair stepped down unexpectedly this morning. Since I saw you in here yesterday and again today, I'm hoping you'll be in Dallas long enough to give us a few pointers...or whatever expertise you can spare. We're floundering without a leader. It's too late to cancel the event, not that we can afford to. The fund-raiser supports most of our programs throughout the year."

Since finding creative solutions to problems was her thing, Nadia couldn't help but be intrigued. "When is your event?"

"Three weeks."

Three weeks and they were a ship without a captain? Big challenge. "How much is left to be done?"

"I don't know. I have Sue Lynn's notes in my office. I could show them to you. If you're interested in the job, that is."

How many times would her father's stupid last requests come back to bite her? "I'd really love to help you in any way I can. But I can't accept paid employment because I'm on a leave of absence from my other job. However, I can volunteer my time."

"Your generosity warms my heart, honey. It's an absolute miracle to find someone with your expertise at such short notice. Would you like to take a look at those books?"

"Certainly." Nadia rose, a sense of purpose energizing her as she gathered her belongings.

The offer was the answer to her prayers. Helping with the fund-raiser would relieve her boredom and give her a legitimate reason to be out of the apartment and avoid Lucas Stone.

But most of all, it would give her a really good reason to stay in Dallas and something to think about besides her risen-from-the-dead husband—and the very good chance she would fail her brothers.

Six

"I don't care how hard it is to get," Lucas told his lawyer over the phone. "I want a copy of Everett Kincaid's will. Obtain it by any means necessary short of breaking in and stealing it."

A knock on his door surprised him. Nadia. It couldn't be anyone else. Security had buzzed him the minute she'd entered the express elevator. That she was seeking him out this time instead of making him hunt her down accelerated his heart rate and sent anticipation surging through him.

"I have to go. Call me when you have what I need." He disconnected.

Last night's kiss had made him more determined than ever to get his wife back in his bed. She wanted him. He'd tasted it on her lips, felt it in the melting of her body against his and the way her pulse had fluttered beneath his thumb. That's why he'd had her followed this morning. He'd needed to know where she was going and who she was seeing. He didn't play for keeps, but neither did he share his women when he was in a relationship.

He dropped the portable phone on the table, crossed the living room and opened his door. Nadia's flushed cheeks and sparkling eyes took his breath. Her wide, blinding smile nearly knocked him off his feet.

"I have a job."

The library. His behind-the-scenes maneuvering must have paid off. He made an effort to mask his satisfaction. "I thought you said you couldn't work because of the will."

"It's not a paying position. I'm volunteering to help with the library fund-raiser. Their chairwoman quit unexpectedly."

A free 'round-the-world cruise on Mardi Gras's most luxurious ship would do that to some people.

"She left them in the lurch and in a bind. The head librarian recognized me from an article she'd read about an event I chaired in Miami and asked me if I would be interested in taking over as the fund-raising committee chair."

Her obvious happiness hit him in an odd way, one he couldn't explain and didn't want to probe too closely. But somehow her good mood lightened the weight of his day's aggravations, and the excitement radiating from her eased his guilt for having manipulated the situation.

"You like fund-raising?"

He knew she did. He'd read the same article before sending it to the librarian along with the promise of a sizable donation if the library committee found Nadia a place in the group. He hadn't expected them to hand her the top position even though Nadia was well-qualified for it according to his research and the tabloid article.

He'd have had a better chance of forgetting her since the

wreck if those damned tabloids didn't relish reporting on the life of a shipping heiress. But funny how none of them mentioned she apparently worked as hard as she played. Terri's quick report on Nadia had revealed a dedication to her job and to raising money for an assortment of charities. His sister wasn't thrilled to be researching Nadia.

"I'm good at organizing and planning and finding needles in haystacks." Her confident statement and erect carriage reminded him of the old Nadia, the one he'd fallen in love with because she'd honestly believed she could conquer the world and change it.

That self-assured woman hadn't been in evidence since their reunion four days ago. Until now he'd seen no sign of the one who—even though he hadn't realized it was her—had countered his every move from her position as director of shared services when he'd tried to sink Kincaid Cruise Lines via their suppliers. He had to respect that kind of intelligence and determination. When this was over and he'd taken down KCL he'd consider offering her a job.

"The library is lucky to have you."

And he'd be fortunate she'd be occupied during the day because it would give him time he needed to help Sandi finalize Andvari's latest deal. His sister had run into a few snags she couldn't handle alone. Principally, an old-school banker who preferred women stay at home wearing an apron.

"I hope so. But I wanted you to know I'll be MIA for the next three weeks."

Not part of his plan. "Get home each evening in time for your driving lessons."

Her smile faltered. "I don't think I can."

"That's part of our deal, Nadia."

A pleat formed between her eyebrows. "Lucas, this is

important and I'm going to be crunched for time. And tonight I have other things to do. I can't drive with you."

"No reneging allowed."

The corners of her mouth turned down. She folded her arms across her chest and lifted her chin. She hit him with a look that probably quelled those who worked beneath her. "You mean like you did on your marriage vows."

Direct hit. Nadia had developed her claws during their time apart. Interesting. *This* was the woman who'd plagued Andvari. She had a new depth that intrigued him far more than she had as a girl of eighteen.

"We both know why our marriage ended. Your father. But admit it. He was probably right. You couldn't have handled being married to a cripple."

She bristled. If she'd been a cat, she'd be hissing. "You don't know that. Like everyone else, you expected me to fail and you didn't give me a chance to prove you wrong." Her lips flattened and she glanced away as if she regretted her outburst.

"You wouldn't have minded doing without sex? I remember you liking that part of our relationship. Very much."

She'd been insatiable. They both had. In fact, it had occurred to him that she hadn't wanted more from him than the stratospheric sex and the chance to flaunt him in her father's face. And then she'd become pregnant.

She sucked in a sharp breath and her eyes widened. Her cheeks pinked. "You couldn't?"

Now he regretted his words. "Not in the first few months. But that wasn't a priority. Walking again was."

"That must have been scary."

Hell, yes. Everything about that whole damned year had scared him. When he'd been told he'd never walk again, his sisters had been sixteen and thirteen, and his mother had already been working two jobs. She'd counted on his salary from Kincaid Manor to make ends meet. He'd seen himself as a burden his family didn't need and couldn't afford. The only way he could make their lives better instead of worse was to take Kincaid's dirty money.

But he wasn't interested in Nadia's psychoanalysis of his decision.

"Dinner's waiting in the oven. Come in. We'll eat before your lesson."

He reached for her satchel, hooking his fingers beneath the leather strap on her shoulder. She resisted giving it up.

"I told you. There's not going to be a lesson tonight. Mitch is getting married at eight eastern time. Rand is arranging for me to see the ceremony via webcam since I can't be there. I'll be in front of my computer tonight."

"Why can't you be there?"

"I just can't. It's too complicated to explain. Even if it wasn't, it's none of your business."

Another puzzle piece from Kincaid's will, he'd bet, like the midnight curfew, her apartment-sitting and the driving instructor she hadn't used. "Come in and eat. I'll make sure you don't miss the wedding."

He lifted her bag again and this time she let him take it. He set it beside the hall table and led the way to his dining room.

Her green eyes swept the table set for two and narrowed on him as he lit the tall white tapers flanking the low bowl of fragrant, floating gardenias. She hung back by the open frosted-glass pocket doors as if looking for an excuse to bolt.

Her gaze probed his. "What are you expecting from me, Lucas? I've told you I'm not interested in resuming our marriage."

"And I'm not willing to write it off without giving it a shot. We had something good, Nadia. Damned good." Although his expectations of happy ever after no longer deluded him.

Sadness clouded her eyes. She shook her head. "I'm not that girl anymore. I can't ever be again."

"Nor am I that kid. But we are still married." He extracted the plates of cracked and cleaned lobsters from the warming oven, scooped servings of new potatoes and caramelized baby carrots onto each dish then carried them to the table. He returned to fetch the drawn butter and bread basket. "Is lobster still your favorite?"

"Yes." Nadia licked her lips but didn't move from the door. "You cooked?"

"Not this time. Be careful of the plate. It's hot." He pulled out her chair, but she didn't move. "Are you still a chocoholic?"

"Yes."

"Then stick around for the molten chocolate lava cake. If we run short on time, we'll eat it in front of your computer or after the wedding. Maybe I can rig your video to play on the TV so you'll have a bigger screen."

With obvious reluctance she crossed the room and took a seat. He retrieved the champagne and popped the cork behind her back. The noise startled her into turning.

She eyed the bottle warily. "What are you celebrating?"

"Finding you again." It should have been a line, a throw-away meaningless phrase. But it didn't feel like one. And the gravel in his voice hadn't been intentional.

Who was he kidding? He *was* glad to have found her and relieved to know she wasn't the selfish bitch he'd believed her to be. Was it wrong to want her to know that he was more than the white trash Everett Kincaid had accused him of being and that he'd multiplied Kincaid's bribe money many times over?

But he wouldn't reveal that data until he absolutely had to—probably when they applied for a new divorce and had to disclose assets. The knowledge of how much this divorce would cost him made him wish he'd signed the prenup Everett Kincaid had tried to force on him. But Nadia had refused and Lucas had supported her decision rather than cave to her father's demands. Back then they'd believed their love and marriage would last forever. Naive of them.

They would divorce. He wasn't going to fall for her again. Love had no place in his life. Besides, unless he wanted to jeopardize the outcome, he couldn't tell her exactly how far he'd come until he'd accomplished his goal of owning KCL. And then she'd want nothing to do with him.

He poured the champagne and joined her at the table. What she'd told him last night had only whet his appetite for details of her life. "You work for KCL. What happened to your plans to turn the New York fashion industry on its head?"

She appeared to give dipping a chunk of lobster into the drawn butter her rapt attention. "My plans changed. I ended up majoring in accounting."

She'd understated her education. According to Terri, Nadia had an MBA and was a CPA with a bunch of other initials after her name. Dry numbers were a far cry from the creativity he remembered. He knew nothing about fashion except what Nadia had told him years ago and what he'd accidentally learned from his sisters. But he'd seen Nadia's portfolio of drawings when they were dating. She'd had talent.

"It's not what you wanted. You had piles of sketch pads full of clothing designs."

"I grew up and realized the chances of me making it in New York were slim to none."

Plausible, but not true—not when you knew the signs. Nadia's eyes didn't lift above his chin and her fingers twitched on the bread. But he'd let her get away with her fib for now. "Why KCL when you didn't get along with your father?"

She chewed and swallowed. "Why not KCL? It's a financially strong company and repeatedly voted one of the best places to work nationwide."

True. And because of KCL's strength and reputation a straight buyout wouldn't be easy. But he'd found a few weaknesses in Kincaid's finances—specifically the billions Everett had borrowed to finance the five new ships he had on order. Lucas was in the process of buying up those loans.

He applied himself to his dinner. Chamberlain's still had the best lobster in Texas. "So he didn't disinherit you for marrying me?"

"No. I guess he changed his mind after he killed you."

A point in the bastard's favor.

"You have to stay in Dallas, can't get a paying job and must be home by midnight. What other hoops does your father have you jumping through?"

She laid aside her lobster fork. "I don't want to talk about him. He's barely been gone two months. And it's…difficult to discuss his last wishes."

The tone of her voice hinted at anger more than grief which only lengthened the list of questions Lucas had about this whole setup. Something wasn't right in this equation and he wouldn't rest until he figured out what was out of kilter.

He wanted to press for details. He needed to know what he was up against. His focus in recent months had been on the Singapore deal and his recon work on KCL had been done before Everett died. The shift in power could alter his strategy.

But he would have to bide his time. Pushing Nadia too hard and too fast for information could alienate her.

If he'd learned nothing else since his accident, it was that his mother's words were true.

Patience was indeed a virtue.

Waiting for the right moment to strike often meant the difference between taking a loss and making the deal of a lifetime.

Nadia found having a man fiddle with her wiring a strangely intimate experience even from thirty feet away. That could be because she couldn't peel her gaze away from the very nice rear end bent over her entertainment cabinet.

"That should do it," Lucas said as he stepped away from her flat panel television. "We should be able to get the webcam feed on the big screen."

"Thank you. But you don't have to stay. I know how much men hate weddings."

"I'll stay in case you have problems with the connection."

As much as she appreciated that, she'd really rather be alone. She didn't expect the next hour to be easy. Weddings never were for her.

But she'd only done one video conference before and the last time Mitch had sent a team of geeks to Dallas to set it up for her. She'd paid attention to the process, but that had been a two-way feed and this was only a one-way deal. It might be different.

The watch-only format left her feeling a little disconnected, but it was better than nothing. She shook off the negative feelings. "How is it you know all this electronic wizardry?"

"I do a lot of my board meetings via video conferencing."

"Why not in person?"

"Like you, I can't always be there." He activated the TV remote then hit a series of keys on her computer—quite competently she noted. Within seconds a jostling image of a candlelit church sanctuary filled the screen.

Her cell phone rang. Caller ID said Rand. "Hi, big brother."

Rand's face entered the picture. "We're live. Check to see if you're getting the audio and video."

He spoke directly into the camera. His voice came through the phone and then, after a slight delay, through the TV speakers. The echoey feel was slightly disorienting.

"I'm getting picture and sound." Her oldest brother looked happier than she'd ever seen him. There was a smile in his eyes.

"I want you to say hello to someone." Rand reached out and wrestled the camera away from the person holding it and then swung it around, leaving Nadia with a room-spinning, carnival ride sensation.

Tara Anthony, a woman who'd been not only Nadia's father's PA but also Nadia's best friend five years ago smiled into the lens. Tara's cheeks were flushed, her blond curls upswept. Rand and Tara's love affair had been another casualty of their father's manipulations and their reunion had come about as a result of his will requiring them to work together. That circumstance had been the main reason Nadia had jumped to the conclusion that her father was trying to reunite her with Lucas.

Wrong.

Tara put Rand's phone to her ear and waved. An engagement ring winked on her finger.

"Hi, Nadia. I wish you were here, but I'll do my best as camera person to make sure you're as close to the action as you can get."

"Thank you." An ache filled Nadia's stomach and rose like a hot-air balloon to block her throat. She wanted to stand beside her brother when he took his vows the way Rand and Mitch had been there for her. "Why didn't Mitch spring for a professional videographer?"

"Your brothers discussed it and decided not to risk a media circus if news of the wedding leaked out. I'm experienced with a camera, so I volunteered."

"Almost showtime," she heard Rand say.

Nadia sank onto the arm of the sofa, her gaze riveted to the screen as Rand panned the camera away from Tara and over the small gathering of guests.

"Nadia, I'm going to hang up now," Tara said into the phone. "We'll talk later. I want to catch up."

"Okay. Bye, Tara." Nadia closed her phone.

An organ struck a chord and blasted through the TV speakers in surround sound. "There's my cue, Rand," Tara said. "Give me the camera. Go stand by your brother and do your best-man thing."

The picture jiggled as Tara took the camera back. Nadia's eyebrows shot up in surprise. Tara had given an order and Rand, second only to their father on the bossy scale, had followed it. Love must indeed have magical powers.

The camera focused on the closed doors at the back of the church. The music swelled and the doors swung open. Seconds later a dark-haired toddler pelted down the aisle as fast as his little arms and legs would churn. He clutched a small white pillow in his fist.

Rhett. Her little brother.

Nadia hurt as if someone had stabbed an ice pick into her chest. She took a jagged breath. Children always had that effect on her, but this one...this one looked enough like her that he could have been hers. She put a fist to her stomach. Her son would have been ten now.

The camera tracked the galloping child to the front of the church then zoomed in on a kneeling, grinning Mitch. Her brother caught the little boy against his chest and hugged him tightly.

"Good job, buddy," she heard Mitch say. Mitch rose with Rhett in his arms, took the pillow with the glistening wedding bands tied on top and passed it to Rand. Then her big, tough, serious older brother planted a kiss on the fuzzy dark head before handing the boy off to a sixtyish woman Nadia didn't recognize.

The next shot framed both of her brothers, Rand standing beside Mitch. Each of them looked happy and relaxed—so different from their forbidding faces at her wedding. Yes, they'd been there to offer support—or pick up the pieces if she'd changed her mind—but they hadn't been cheerful about it. They'd merely been doing their familial duty. Something her father had refused to do.

Mitch's gaze shifted down the aisle. The camera followed and focused on the slender brunette floating toward him with a blinding smile. Carly, Rhett's aunt and soon to be Nadia's sister-in-law. Nadia recognized the lines of the simple ivory Vera Wang dress. Instead of a veil, a ring of flowers intertwined with pearls circled Carly's head. Her face glowed with love, and when the camera panned back to Mitch, the emotion in his expression punched a sob up Nadia's throat.

She was happy for him. Truly, truly happy. But this was something she'd never have.

Love.

Another wedding.

Children.

Her eyes burned. A tear spilled over and burned a path down her cheek. Blinking furiously, she ducked her head and swiped it away, hoping Lucas didn't see. An arm encircled her shoulders. Startled, she looked up. Lucas's blue eyes trained on her face, offering silent support.

They'd once been that happy couple, the one with so much love in their eyes and their hearts that they hadn't seen anyone in the church but each other.

When she looked at him now, she could see remnants of that man and all she could think was, *what a waste* and *how could I have been so wrong about him?*

Lucas had thrown their love away for money. Sure, her father had contributed to the death of their feelings with his meddling, but if Lucas had truly loved her, he would have refused the money. He would have believed in her and her ability to live the vows she'd spoken. In the end, Lucas Stone was the only one to blame for that final blow of the ax.

She shrugged off his arm, hugged her empty, aching middle and fought back a sob. If she'd been alone, she'd probably be crying like a baby.

Her life would have been so different if, in her moment of selfishness, she hadn't distracted him and caused the accident.

Or would it have been?

Would he have betrayed her anyway? But if they hadn't wrecked, even if he'd eventually dumped her, she would have at least had their son and maybe other children for comfort.

Nadia dragged herself out of the well of what-ifs and forced her gaze back to the TV. Tara zoomed in tight on the bride and groom as they took their vows and exchanged rings.

Nadia pressed her trembling lips so tightly together they grew numb. She thumbed her bare ring finger. She'd refused to remove her wedding band for years. Her father had harangued her about it endlessly. The day she'd decided she would never love again, never marry again was the day she'd finally taken off the plain gold band with hers and Lucas's names engraved inside and shoved it into the back of her jewelry armoire.

And that's where it would stay. Forever.

She would never have it all. Never even attempt it. Because she couldn't trust her judgment and she couldn't risk ending up like her mother and hurting or abandoning those who'd loved her. All she could have was her career, her volunteer work and superficial affairs with men she couldn't love.

Men she couldn't love.

The phrase reverberated through her mind like a cry echoing off the Grand Canyon's walls.

Men like Lucas who were more interested in her money than her heart.

Her pulse quickened. Her skin tingled. The fine hairs on her body rose as excitement raced through her.

Her gaze returned to the man beside her. Her husband. The man who had selfishly taken everything precious to her and crushed it. Her chance for happiness. Her love. And more recently, her confidence in her ability to judge others.

Did she dare take what she needed from him? Could she use her soon-to-be ex for mindless physical pleasure and then walk away at the end of her year in exile?

Walk away. Exactly as he'd done to her.

Taboo.

Wrong.

Tempting. Oh, so very tempting.

Seven

"Ready for your chocolate cake and the rest of the champagne?"

Lucas's voice behind her sent a prickle of awareness down Nadia's spine. He'd left her apartment and returned to his immediately after the ceremony ended. Nadia had continued watching as Tara, acting like a TV reporter, led her through the wedding guests to introduce Nadia to Carly, her new sister-in-law, Carly's parents and finally, Rhett, that adorable, beautiful, perfect little boy.

Ignoring the familiar emptiness, Nadia finished shutting down the computer and turned off the TV. She rose and faced Lucas. He carried a tray holding the cake and ice bucket containing the champagne.

Did she dare follow through with her crazy plan?

What do you have to lose? You've already lost everything.

"I don't want dessert or champagne," she told him.

Lucas's eyes narrowed as he closed the distance between them. He set the tray on the coffee table and studied her for several silent seconds. From the day they'd met he'd been able to sense her moods with uncanny accuracy. Neither her father nor her brothers had ever come close to reading her as well as Lucas had. She could tell from his expanding pupils that he'd picked up on her frame of mind this time, too.

"What do you want, Nadia?" His huskier than usual tone said he already knew.

She took a slow, deep breath and ignored the voice in her head urging caution. "You."

"Why?"

She hadn't expected him to make this hard. He never had in the past. She stepped closer, lifted a hand and flattened her palm on his chest. "Because your kisses excite me and your touch enflames me."

And making love with him might fill the emptiness inside. Temporarily. That was all she could ever hope for.

His heart thumped harder and faster beneath her touch and his chest rose on a slowly indrawn breath. His gaze held hers captive as the seconds ticked past. It had never occurred to her that he might refuse. But his lack of action spoke volumes.

She slid her hand upward to cup his nape. The crisp texture of his hair tickled her fingertips and his hot skin warmed her cold fingers. "I want to make love to you, Lucas, like we used to."

His arm banded around her waist, his hand splaying over her lower back. One tug and her body slammed into his. He was hard. Hot. Solid. She could feel each tensed muscle pressed against hers from his thighs through his shoulders. And still he waited. For what?

She wanted mindless passion. Out-of-control lust. She didn't want time to think, to wonder if this was a mistake.

Rising on her tiptoes, she pressed her mouth to his, opened, closed. She sucked his bottom lip between hers. His breath hissed, but he remained tightly leashed unlike in the past when that last maneuver would have made him putty in her hands.

She repeated the kiss with no better results then nibbled her way along his jaw and nipped his earlobe. Eleven years ago a love bite had always brought him to his knees. But not this time. The growing arousal pressing her belly told her he wasn't indifferent. And yet he still didn't capitulate.

Confused by his control when she was rapidly losing hers, she sank back onto her heels.

Lucas's eyes burned like blue fire, which only fanned the flames in her middle. Oh, yeah, he wanted her. So why was he holding back? "We're too old to neck on the sofa. Which bedroom is yours?"

Adrenaline raced through her then caution finally made itself heard. She wanted to scream in frustration. "The one on the left, but I don't have any condoms. Do you? I wasn't expecting…"

With her stupid midnight curfew she hadn't expected to have a nightlife or any kind of life in Dallas.

"My place. Let's go." He released her and bent to lift the tray. Then he walked away.

Taken aback, she blinked after him. *He'd walked away?*

The Lucas she'd known would have taken her anywhere, any way and as often as she'd wanted. It wasn't that he'd been a pushover, but he'd been a young guy, and she'd learned they tended to think with something besides the head on their shoulders. Admittedly, she'd been known to use that fact shamelessly to get what she'd wanted. But the man in question had never complained.

Apparently, the mature Lucas liked to call the shots. That he didn't make the seduction easy ticked her off a little. But it also excited her. And okay, yes, earned her respect. If she wanted him, she'd have to work for it. A wacko part of her relished the challenge.

She followed him out her open door and through his. Tension twined tighter with each step. Or maybe it was arousal. It had been so long since she'd genuinely felt anything remotely resembling lust that she wasn't sure.

She trailed him down his hall, unbuttoning her shirt on the way and draping it over the hall credenza as she passed. She left her shoes with the shirt and reached for the button on her pants. They fell to the floor. A niggle of doubt over what she'd be revealing hitched her step, but she didn't stop. She kicked off the fabric and kept walking.

She'd bet—she hoped—he'd be so distracted by her black sheer demi-bra and panty set when he turned around that he wouldn't be so in control.

And he wouldn't care about the scar. The scar that told the world she was flawed. Imperfect. Incomplete.

He entered a room ahead of her. She followed and paused in the doorway. His bedroom. She surveyed the wide bed with its curved cognac leather headboard and cream-colored spread, then crossed the carpet to stand beside it. A cluster of lush plants created a small jungle near the wall of windows. Outside the uncurtained glass she spotted a patio with more plants, the corner of the swimming pool and the Dallas skyline in the glow of the setting sun.

He deposited his tray on the dresser and turned. His gaze slammed into hers and then slowly rolled over her from head to toe before returning to the scar. She fought the urge to cover it or dive beneath the comforter. It took colossal effort to remain standing and to breathe. That unsightly blemish defined who she was these days. If it turned him off, then that was his problem. She straightened her spine and squared her shoulders.

Without a word his eyes found hers again. He reached for his shirtsleeves and removed the cufflinks, first one, then the other without looking away. The gold clattered noisily on the dark cherry furniture quickly followed by the *thunk* of his watch. With his eyes on hers he continued disrobing, revealing his chest one button at a time.

His shirt fluttered to the floor and she caught her breath. He'd always had a beautiful body, but now he was more muscled, his shoulders wider, his chest deeper, his rippled belly leaner. His hands went to his belt. The chink of the buckle and slither of leather being pulled from the loops seemed unnaturally loud as did the rasp of the zipper. His pants slid down his legs and he kicked them aside. He stood before her in nothing but black silk boxers. The tented front said more than words. Even if he wasn't saying he wanted her, his body was telling her.

What a difference time made. Instead of a lanky twenty-one-year-old boy, Lucas Stone stood in front of her, definitely all man now—every perfect, delicious inch of him.

Her pulse raced and her mouth dried. Her breath grew short as did her patience. What was he waiting for? She reached for the back hook of her bra.

"No."

The quiet but firm command stilled her fingers. Intrigued by this new side of him, she lowered her arms. The old Lucas would have been all over her by now. Any man would. Despite the scar. She had a darned good body and she worked hard to keep in shape. And she only wore the most flattering lingerie.

He prowled toward her. Finally. But instead of yanking her into his arms he pulled back the covers.

Enough stalling.

She wound an arm around his waist and blindly trailed a finger from between his shoulder blades down his spine—the way he'd always loved. Goose bumps lifted his skin in wake of her touch. And then she hit a ridge of flesh at his waist and stopped in surprise. Her gaze jerked to his. He'd said he had surgeries, but somehow she hadn't processed that information.

She grasped his thick biceps and turned him. Her breath hitched. Two straight scars ran parallel to his spine marring his lower back and disappearing beneath his low-riding boxers. She traced the lines with her fingertips tugging the silk over his hips to reveal the paler skin of his butt and the ends of scar tissue. His underwear slid to his ankles and his taut flanks flexed as he kicked them atop his discarded pants.

The lines had faded to silvery-pink, but seeing the damage done by the surgeon's scalpel made her heart ache. They'd both been permanently marked by their accident. In his case, the doctors had given Lucas back his future, his ability to walk and his ability to live a normal life. In hers, they'd taken away the future she'd dreamed of and an ability most women took for granted and sometimes resented. She bent and pressed her lips to the insult on the otherwise perfect V of his tanned back.

A sharply indrawn breath was her only warning before he pivoted, and in one swift strike encircled her waist, yanked her upright and covered her mouth in a hard kiss. The warmth of his body against hers and his silky hot erection against her belly jarred her heart into a rapid rhythm.

Now that's more like it.

But after that initial hard press his kiss wasn't the same. He didn't simply devour her. He sipped, retreated, teased, tempted and tortured her by withholding what she wanted— his tongue in her mouth, his taste, his body deep inside hers. She arched into him, craving his possession, needing to forget. Her present. Her past. Her defects. She needed to feel feminine and desirable.

The rake of his hands from her thighs over her hips and waist to the sides of her breasts went a long way to fulfilling her quest, but still left her wanting more. She dug her nails into his hair and held him while she licked then nipped his bottom lip. He escaped her and transferred his attention to the pulse hammering in her neck. His teeth grazed her skin and the rasp of his evening beard sent a delicious shiver over her. But she wanted to growl in frustration, pound his shoulders and yell faster, faster, more, more, *more.*

She settled for mapping his body, mentally charting the changes in the shape and feel of him. His buttocks clenched under her palms, his tiny nipples tightened beneath her thumbs. His abdominal muscles contracted under her questing fingertips. She loved the texture of his skin, supple and smooth and scorching.

He slid his hands beneath her bikini panties and cupped her bottom, lifting her off her feet and holding her against him. He had her off balance literally and figuratively. She had to clutch his shoulders to maintain her equilibrium.

His lips parted at last. She met the thrust of his tongue with her own. He tasted the same. But everything else had changed. The sure way he caressed and kissed. The make-her-beg-for-it tempo. The hunger. She'd always wanted him. But not like this. This wanting bordered on pain.

The thought jarred her enough to worry her, then she

brushed her concerns away. She hadn't slept with anyone in a long time. Months? A year? Two? She couldn't even remember the last time she'd had sex. She'd been too busy fighting that damned Andvari.

Pent-up passion. That's all this is.

She wound her legs around his waist, cradled his head in her hands and kissed him again and again. Arching and relaxing her back, she rubbed her center against his thick length. Her desire rose swiftly.

Her panties annoyed her. They were in the way. She wanted to be naked, skin to skin and have him buried inside her. Now. Impatient, she tightened her legs and pressed harder against his rigid flesh.

As if he'd received her message, Lucas flicked her bra open. His hands spread over her shoulder blades. He lowered her onto the bed and followed her down, pinning her between the cool sheets and his burning body. Breaking the kiss, he propped on one straight arm long enough to pull the black bra from her and toss it aside, and then he looked at her.

The hunger in his eyes puckered her nipples and tightened her internal muscles. He cupped her breast, thumbed the tip until she gasped and then he bent to take the opposite one into his mouth. The hot, wet swirl of his tongue combined with the magic of his touch made her back bow and her belly contract. And then he tugged with his lips, his teeth and his fingers. A whimper of want escaped her mouth. His caresses robbed her breath, her sanity and her agenda.

She couldn't remember the last time a man's touch had felt this good. A molten sensation invaded her muscles. She tunneled her fingers into his hair and held him, silently pleading for more. But he abandoned her breasts.

His lips traveled lower. He nuzzled the sensitive undersides before drifting with featherlight whispers across her ribs and then toward her navel. The haze of hunger morphed into a clear chill of tension when she realized where he was headed. She fisted her fingers in his hair and tugged. When that didn't work she dug her heels into the mattress and tried to twist away, but he easily pinned her down.

"Lucas, don't."

"We all have scars, Nadia. Some show. Some don't." His tongue swept down the length of the rippled flesh from her navel to her panties and then back up again to swirl in her belly button.

The move should have repelled her. She hated that scar. Hated what it represented. She never let anyone touch it. Instead, her breath hitched and strangely, she couldn't seem to gather the strength to shove him off. And then he pressed his mouth to her lacy bikinis and his breath steamed right through the thin fabric exactly where she needed his touch the most.

Thoughts of pushing him away vanished under the on-slaught of prurience. She quit struggling and savored the sensation of his chin circling over her flesh with the perfect amount of pressure, the perfect tempo. His fingers edged beneath her elastic leg band at her hip and drifted down toward her center, then away and back again. She groaned and squirmed. He delved deeper, finding her moisture and massaging it in with exquisite thoroughness.

She climbed swiftly. She wanted to whisper words of encouragement, but she couldn't seem to string the phrases together to make her request. All she could do was clutch his hair, the sheets, lift her hips toward his mouth. Release gathered. He eased away from her seconds before she went over the edge. And then he did it again, and again, caressing, arousing and retreating until she thought she'd scream.

"Lucas, please."

He planted a lingering kiss on her hipbone then rolled away and opened a drawer. While he donned the condom she shimmied out of her panties and then lay back, propped on her elbows with one knee bent in what she hoped he'd find an irresistible, inviting pose.

He returned to her, but instead of moving over her and giving her the sexual oblivion she needed, he skimmed her curves with his fingertips, circling each nipple, outlining her waist, her navel and her triangle of curls. Aching and growing more desperate by the second from his teasing sensuality, she writhed beneath him and tried to rise, planning to drag him back down with her. Lucas planted two fingers on her breast-bone and pushed her back down gently, but firmly. The commanding look in his eyes warned her not to argue.

A thrill shot through her. She wasn't used to this man who wouldn't be led or coerced.

Without breaking eye contact he leaned over and kissed her bent knee, then the inside of her thigh. His lips lifted and touched down, each time landing closer to her center, each time making her gasp with a lick or a nip or the rasp of his chin. The prickle of his evening beard on her tender skin excited her unbearably. Her breathing shallowed, quickened, until she was nearly panting. And he knew it. He knew because he watched and noted every hiccup of breath, every quiver, every time she had to bite her lip to keep from crying out.

As if they'd been together like this just yesterday instead of more than a decade ago, he found her pleasure points with unerring accuracy. His tongue flicked over exactly the right spot and orgasm crashed over her with shocking speed. Her eyes slammed shut. His name poured from her lips and her body jerked as her muscles clenched and released over and over.

When the last erotic spasm died he rose to his hands and knees and prowled up her body until he poised above her, his eyes dark with passion and intent. His elbows bent. He took her mouth in a kiss so carnal, so hot and wet and decadent and delicious she could only cling to him. Their tongues tangled and dueled. Their lips alternated between butterfly soft and branding hot. She couldn't get enough of him, of this new version of him.

His fingertips found her entrance, stroked, readied her, and then his blunt tip took their place. She held her breath and waited for him to fill her. And then he did. Languorously. She dug her nails into his buttocks and urged him to hurry, but he wouldn't be rushed. Each long, slow glide in and out filled her with an impatient craving for more.

She lifted her hips, meeting each thrust, and when he released her mouth to suck a sharp breath, she watched his eyes darken as hunger gave them a common goal. She arched upward to nip his shoulder, his neck. His scent filled her nostrils; the slightly salty taste of him pervaded her mouth and his deep thrusts filled her body. Her palms skimmed his back, his buttocks, his waist and chest. The scrape of her nails on his neck made him shudder against her.

She relished the crack in his control. And yet he still didn't speak. The Lucas of her past had been verbal. He'd told her how good she tasted, how good she felt, how hot she made him and how much he loved her. Especially the last one. And she'd been so hungry for those words. Yet despite his silence, his eyes said it all.

For the first time in forever she could feel every sensitized inch of her skin, particularly the parts melding to the heat of his or abraded by the coarse hair on his legs. She felt alive and wanted and desirable and womanly instead of flawed. She banished the sobering thought and focused on the stroke of his hand where they were joined and relished the depth of his penetration.

He filled her, surrounded her, energized her. Her climax built anew, tightening her muscles, stealing her breath, muddling her thoughts. And then it hit. Hard. Fast. Consuming her completely. Sapped, she lay enervated beneath him, so weakened her hands could barely cling to his waist.

His thrusts deepened, quickened and then his groan of completion filled her ears as he shuddered above her. Seconds later muscles went lax and his weight settled on her.

He braced himself above her so that he didn't crush her, but with each of their gasped breaths her breasts kissed his chest.

Making love with Lucas hadn't remotely resembled the mindless sex she'd used in the past to help her forget. No. Making love with him felt good and right.

But was it a mistake?

Did she dare give him a second chance to turn her world upside down?

Eight

Too good.

Are you nuts, man? How in the hell can anyone complain about sex being too good?

Lucas rolled away from Nadia, needing to put both mental and physical distance between them. He had an agenda and he had to stick to it. He couldn't allow making love with Nadia to cloud the issue.

He retreated to the bathroom, disposed of the condom and splashed cold water on his face. He had what he wanted. His wife in his bed. Trusting him. Open to him. A little more persuasion and she'd answer whatever questions he asked, enabling him to get an insider's view on KCL's weaknesses and plan the best attack route.

But getting lost in Nadia's scent, the softness of her skin, the wet heat of her body and her brain-twisting kisses didn't feel like work. It felt good. Too damned good.

No such thing.

Get your head back in the game.

He pushed away from the vanity, pulled on his robe and returned to the bedroom. Nadia, wearing his shirt, sat with her back against the center of the headboard, her long, gorgeous legs bent, ankles tucked beneath her. Her gaze followed him as he crossed to the dresser and retrieved the tray holding the cake and chilling champagne. He joined her on the bed, placing the tray on the mattress between them.

He filled the champagne flutes and offered her one. "Ready for dessert? Sex always gave you an appetite."

She fumbled the glass, nearly dropping it, and averted her face. Was she blushing? Had he ever seen Nadia blush? No. She'd always been bold and aggressive, sure of what she wanted and her entitlement to it. Her take-no-prisoners attitude had been a real turn-on.

But so was this unexpectedly shy side.

"I guess some things never change." Her eyes didn't quite meet his as she picked up a fork, cut into the lava cake and put the small wedge into her mouth.

A crumb clung to her bottom lip. He stifled the urge to lap it up and ate a forkful of the moist chocolaty confection. The rich flavor filled his mouth, erasing what was left of Nadia's taste he noted with a disgustingly sappy hint of regret. He washed it down with a gulp of champagne.

She looked up at him through her lashes. "Why did you take the money, Lucas?"

He sucked in a sharp breath and almost choked on the bubbly beverage. What the hell. What would it hurt to tell her?

"Because I was afraid I'd be a burden to my family. Your father made sure I knew exactly how much debt I was racking up with each day I stayed in the hospital. I was looking at months more of hospital time plus the surgeries. I knew I couldn't afford any of it since I lost my health insurance when your father fired me and the policy from my new job hadn't kicked in yet. But staying for treatment was my only chance to ever walk again.

"My mother and I were barely making ends meet with our combined salaries, and it looked like I'd be unable to work for a long time. Your father's bribe guaranteed we'd keep a roof over our heads and that my sisters would get a good education—something I was no longer sure I could provide."

Nadia's breath shuddered in and then out. Understanding softened her eyes and mouth. "I should have known you weren't thinking of yourself. You always put your family first. Your girls, you called them."

For a brief few months she'd been one of his "girls," and she'd always beamed when he'd told her that.

"Your brothers would do the same for you." A point in Rand and Mitch's favor.

"Yes. They would. That's why I can't let them down this time. There's too much at stake. I have to get it right."

He topped off her glass and then nodded toward her middle. "What happened, Nadia?"

Her sudden stillness told him she knew what he meant. She toyed with the dessert, cut a wedge and mashed it between the tines of her fork, but she didn't eat it. The silence stretched so long he didn't think she'd answer.

"I lost our son and the ability to have other children. They had to take my uterus to stop the bleeding."

Their son. He'd often wondered.

The ache in his chest ambushed him from out of nowhere. Grief? Too late for that. He never wasted energy or emotion on anything he couldn't change.

Before the wedding he and Nadia had discussed having children. A lot of them. They'd both wanted a large family. Nadia had wanted their kids to be close in age so they'd have each other as playmates—something she hadn't had with her brothers who'd been four and six years older. It had been the same for him with Sandi and Terri. Their gender and age differences had kept them from being close.

After Kincaid had fired Lucas for refusing to break it off with Nadia, the bastard had made sure Lucas couldn't get a job with anyone else in the Kincaid's exalted Miami circle. Lucas had finally found a new job with a different landscaping company. The pay hadn't been nearly as good as working for the Kincaids, but there had been room for advancement.

He hadn't known how he was going to support a wife let alone children and help his family, but he'd figured they'd find a way. His mother always had.

"I'm sorry we lost our son." The words sounded as empty as he felt.

She shrugged as if it didn't matter but the tears she blinked away told him it mattered a lot. Then she knocked back half her glass of champagne in one gulp. "I could have had plastic surgery to minimize the scar, but what's the point? They can't put back what they took."

Not even a moron could miss the point that the scar wasn't the issue. He wanted to know the details, but unless things had changed over the years, when Nadia wore that closed expression she wasn't going to talk. He'd have to tease the information out of her slowly or risk closing the door their intimacy had opened. And that open door was critical to his plan.

He decided to try a different path. "Is that why you never married again? Because you couldn't have children?"

"What was the point? No family. No need for a ring. But, no. I didn't marry because I found out after my—our wreck—that my mother was mentally unstable. Her accident was intentional. She drove Daddy's prized sports car straight into a tree and killed herself rather than stay at home and take care of the ones who needed her."

Shock chilled him. "What do you mean she was mentally unstable?"

"My mother was manic depressive or bipolar, if you want to use the most up-to-date term. It's believed to be hereditary, you know? And while the legion of shrinks my father sicced on me over the years swears I don't carry her defective gene, they can't be one hundred percent sure. I'll never marry, never adopt children, and never let anyone depend on me. It's a risk I don't want to take."

The news settled over him, making sense of the crazy stories he'd read about Nadia in the tabloids over the years. She lived as though she had nothing to lose. Because she believed she didn't?

She shifted on the bed, flashing him a glimpse of inner thigh and stirring the scent of their lovemaking in the air. Arousal kicked him hard in the gut. He wanted her again, wanted to saturate himself in her until there were no crevices of need left to fill. And then he'd let her go.

But duty called. He had to leave her in thirty-six hours. Unless… "Come to Singapore with me."

Her chin jerked up. "What?"

"I have to be in Singapore first thing Monday morning to close a deal. The CEO handling the deal I'm closing is a sexist jerk. He refuses to talk to Sandi."

Nadia bit her lip and looked into her glass. "I can't."

"You can work on the fund-raiser from your laptop."

Her gaze met his. She opened her mouth as if to say something, then closed it again. Grimacing, she downed the remainder of her champagne then took a deep breath. "I can't leave Dallas because of my father's stupid will. I have to spend 365 consecutive nights in Daddy's penthouse."

The restriction explained the anger he'd heard in her voice each time she'd spoken about her father. Everett Kincaid had always held too tightly to his baby girl. Eleven years ago Lucas had known that was a mistake and had tried to warn Kincaid he'd lose Nadia if he didn't loosen his grip. That's when Kincaid had fired him.

"And if you don't?"

"I told you before. We lose our inheritance. Daddy gave each of us an assigned task. If any one of us fails, then everything—and I do mean *everything* he owned—will be sold to his enemy for a dollar. Mitch and Rand are well on their way to fulfilling their part. I'm the wild card, the one everyone expects to fall short. That's why I can't mess this up. They're counting on me."

That KCL could be sold out from under him jarred him. He hadn't seen that coming. "His enemy?"

"What kind of father screws his own children like that?" she asked, ignoring his question.

A father like mine. But he didn't say it. He'd never told Nadia about the good-for-nothing bastard who'd knocked up Lila Stone, married her without mentioning he already had a wife and kids then dumped his wife and son without a backward glance. He'd told Nadia his father was gone, and when she'd assumed he meant dead, Lucas hadn't corrected her.

She stabbed the fork into the cake and ate another bite. "I mean it's ridiculous. He took away my job—the one thing I'm good at—and he forced me to give up my friends and my home.

He gave me a curfew and an allowance and took away my maid, cook and driver. He's treating me like a misbehaving thirteen-year-old by grounding me and taking away privileges."

"It's a bit harsh." But not surprising. Dogmatic decrees had been Everett Kincaid's style. The man had been an extreme control freak. It's a wonder any of his children had remained on speaking terms with him. "Who is his enemy?"

She stared at him, blinked and then she smiled and reached for him. Her palm cupped his jaw line. "Let's not talk about my idiot father. Let's make love again. I adore the way you make me feel, Lucas. You help me forget all this crazy will business."

Her hand slid down his neck and over his collarbone, inciting a riot of sensation and short-circuiting his brain. The last thing he wanted to do was lift her wandering fingers from his chest, but he did because there was no way he could focus on his agenda with her touching him. And he needed to know who stood between him and ownership of KCL.

He kissed her fingers, then couldn't resist swirling his tongue around the tips. Her flavor filled his mouth and left him craving more, but he ignored the hunger clawing his insides and settling heavily in his groin. Why was it that no other woman had affected him this way? "If you can't go with me, then give me until Sunday night."

"But the fund-raiser—"

"What did you decide to do about it?" he asked in an attempt to rein in his need.

"We'll have an auction. I need to nail down the prizes this week and get the promotional materials released."

"If you'll spend Saturday and Sunday with me, I'll give you a list of firms and individuals in the Dallas area who will donate."

She tilted her head, giving him a look that started out

curious then turned saucier by the second. "You're sure you can deliver the goods?"

A fresh wave of arousal slammed into his gut. She wasn't just talking about prizes. "Absolutely. I can give you whatever you need."

One corner of her delectable mouth curved upward and sexual mischief sparkled in her green eyes. "I'll hold you to that. I'll bet I can get Rand and Mitch to donate a cruise… assuming the business is still ours when the time comes for the winner to take it."

Which dampened his desire and brought him neatly back to the subject burning a hole in his brain. "I'm sure your father had numerous enemies, but who would he leave his estate to?"

She sighed and pulled away, a sound of disgust rumbling from her throat. "Mardi Gras Cruising."

Shock winded him. He was glad she had her back to him long enough for him to gather his composure. Dozens of thoughts avalanched through his mind. Primarily, the terms of Kincaid's will added to the purchase of the apartment could only mean one thing. Everett Kincaid must have been tracking him all these years. But how? And why?

Lucas was a firm believer in knowing his enemies as well as possible. Had Kincaid practiced the same philosophy? Or was it something more?

He had to find out. "Why Mardi Gras?"

She turned, rolling her eyes. "I don't know. Dad absolutely detested the CEO. They've had a running battle for years because Mardi Gras kept encroaching on our turf by under-bidding us on an assortment of contracts. It really seemed to get under Dad's skin. I can't believe he would rather see the Mardi Gras logo on our ships than have Rand, Mitch and I continue the KCL tradition of running an award-winning organization."

Lucas was well aware Mardi Gras's CEO was an aggressive, cutthroat ass who stayed just this side of legal in his pursuits. That's why he'd hired him. The man was as determined and focused on besting the competition as Lucas. And he was power-hungry. That meant he wasn't about to let slip that many of his decisions came as direct orders from his behind-the-scenes boss.

And then another thought hit Lucas with chilling clarity.

KCL could be his.

All he had to do was get Nadia to leave Dallas.

He weighed the knowledge. But would winning by default give him half the satisfaction as taking KCL by stealth and skill?

And would it be revenge if what he wanted was handed to him by the very man who'd taught him the meaning of defeat?

"Nadia, wake up," a deep voice repeated more urgently this time. Lucas's voice.

Nadia smiled and snuggled deeper into the warmth cocooning her. She fully intended to ignore whoever was trying to rouse her from a dream she hadn't had in almost five years. A dream of Lucas holding her, making love to her. She'd missed that dream.

"Go 'way."

"It's almost midnight."

"Don't care," she mumbled. She knew from experience that when she opened her eyes that would not be Lucas in her bedroom. No matter how much it sounded like him now.

The pillow beneath her shifted, dumping her as it rose. *Pillows rising?* Her fogged brain slowly cleared. She reached out blindly in the darkness. Her fingers encountered supple skin covering a taut backside instead of Egyptian cotton and down.

Oh, man. Who had she slept with this time? Another poor sap who reminded her of her dead husband?

But she hadn't done a Lucas look-alike in...a long time.

And Lucas wasn't dead.

Startled, she popped upright. The lamp clicked on. She winced and shielded her eyes, but not before catching a glimpse of her naked husband beside the bed stepping into his pants. Her body tingled at the memory of how they'd passed the preceding hours.

"Get up. You have to get back to your place."

Her place. *Midnight.* Panic erased the last remnants of grogginess from her brain. She leaped from the bed and scanned the floor. "My clothes. I don't know where I left—"

"You don't have time for your clothes. There are security cameras in the hall. Put this on." He held out his robe.

She checked his clock as she shoved her arms into the black silk sleeves then cinched the belt. Two minutes to midnight. She'd nearly blown it. Her father was right. She truly did need a keeper, and she'd have to be more careful in the future. "I can't believe I almost messed up. Thank you for waking me."

He wore an odd expression on his face, one she didn't have time to decipher.

"C'mon." He grabbed her elbow and hauled her through his apartment, his stride rapid and almost angry. She hustled to keep up, snatching discarded clothing as she raced for the door.

They blasted across the hall and through her unlocked door just as the clock started chiming. She blew out a breath. "We made it, but that was too close for comfort. Coming in?"

She hoped he would. Making love with Lucas had been even better than she remembered. She wasn't sure if that would come back to haunt her, but she'd never know if she didn't pursue this.

Lucas didn't look the least bit interested in round three. He looked tense and maybe even pissed off.

What did he have to be angry about? "Lucas, what's wrong?"

"Good night, Nadia."

She hooked his elbow as he turned away. "The will says I can't host parties. It doesn't say I can't have an overnight guest."

A nerve twitched in his jaw. "Get some sleep. I'll give you an early morning driving lesson and then we'll tour some of the local gardens."

"But—"

He latched his hand around her nape and pulled her forward for a hard and fast kiss. The smooch ended before she could react. "I'll see you in the morning."

He turned away, reentered his apartment and shut the door. The lock clicked.

She sank back on her heels. Well, that had never happened before.

Men didn't throw her out. Was this only a prelude to what she could expect from him in the future? Because she really didn't like the way it made her feel. And that was a bitter pill to swallow because she'd done the same thing too many times to count while trying to forget her dead—her husband.

She'd used men for a few minutes of oblivion, to feel complete and whole, then she'd dumped them. Suddenly, she didn't like the person she'd become very much. Using people was one bad habit she'd have to break.

* * *

"Close your eyes."

Nadia lifted her gaze from the beautiful lily to Lucas's face. "Why?"

"Just do it."

He hadn't been so bossy before. And in the past she would have told him exactly what he could do with that attitude, but learning to deal with her father over the years had made her slightly less prickly.

He shoved his Oakley sunglasses up into his golden hair, revealing the blue eyes she'd fallen head over heels for more than a decade ago—eyes she was in danger of drowning in again today. "You claim you've learned to cook. Let's see how good you are at identifying your ingredients."

He withdrew a white handkerchief from his back jeans pocket and folded it first into a triangle and then into a band which he stretched between his hands.

Her pulse kicked erratically and her mouth dried. "Are you making a blindfold?"

"Yes."

They'd never done kinky sex before, and she wasn't expecting to start now on a Saturday afternoon in the Texas Discovery Gardens with other guests and even children around. On the other hand, if he took her back to the penthouse she'd be more than willing to play whatever games he dished out.

Making love with him last night had made her feel whole for the first time in a long time. She wanted more even though that meant opening herself up for more pain and disappointment, and she'd become very protective of her wounded heart over the years.

"The scent garden behind you was originally developed

for the blind." She started to turn and look, but he caught her elbow and held her in place. "No cheating."

Eleven years ago Lucas had shown her a side of life she never would have experienced inside the Kincaid compound walls. And she'd loved it. She decided to cut him some slack today. They were in a public place. How could it go wrong? "Okay, fine, but no blindfold."

"Don't you trust me, Nadia?"

The multibillion dollar question. Could she ever trust Lucas Stone again? She didn't have the answer. Yet. Yes, she understood his reasons for taking the money. But he'd left her alone to grieve. He couldn't possibly know how close she'd come to— She cut off the thought. She wasn't that wounded woman anymore. She'd come a long way and made a success of her life.

"Fine. Do it."

He stepped behind her. The white fabric fluttered over her head coming to rest over her eyes and the bridge of her nose. His fingers teased her hair as he tied the ends in the back. Goose bumps rose on her arms despite the heat of the day. He might not intend this to be an arousing experience, but the sizzle percolating through her veins was definitely sexual.

Without her sight her senses suddenly seemed sharper. She could feel the warmth radiating off his body, smell the lilies in front of her and the man behind her. She leaned against him, letting him blanket her body with heat. His arms tightened around her waist. His cologne combined with his natural muskiness caused by their hour-long stroll through the gardens on this hot August day filled her nostrils. She licked her lips and tilted her head against his shoulder wanting his taste.

He squeezed her waist then his breath steamed the underside of her jaw a split second before his lips touched down on the pulse quickening in her neck. "Ready?"

For more than blindly sniffing plants. "Sure."

"Good." He gripped her shoulders then turned her around and urged her forward for several yards. His grip tightened, stopping her. His fingertips stroked down her bare arm, arousing a shiver from her. He caught her hand and scraped his nails lightly over her palm then guided her fingers over the pointy leaves of a plant before carrying her hand to her nose.

"Tell me what you smell."

She inhaled. "Rosemary."

"Good. But that was an easy one."

He urged her forward. His tightening grip stopped her after five steps. This time he stroked the tender flesh inside her opposite arm. Desire simmered inside her. His fingers threaded through hers, his palm flattening over the back of her hand, and then he brushed their joined hands over a smooth, cool plant. Together they lifted her hand to her nose.

She inhaled and smelled him and… "Mint."

"Very good." His lips brushed her ear as he whispered the words. His teeth grazed her lobe.

She nearly moaned, but because of the blindfold she didn't know who was around and didn't dare. And just like making love in the church anteroom after their wedding, the idea of getting caught intensified her reaction and filled her with a naughty thrill.

His hips nudged hers forward. She could feel his growing length pressing against her lower back telling her he wasn't unaffected by their little game.

He stopped her again, but instead of gripping her hand, this time his fingers curled around her waist and glided upward.

Under the cover of her arms his thumbs brushed the sides of her breasts. Her breath hitched.

"Reach out and to your left," he ordered in a gravelly tone. His fingers grazed the underside of her breasts stirring an ache low in her belly. "A little more."

Her thoughts exactly. He was only inches from touching her tight nipple. It took every ounce of restraint not to turn in his arms and press her flesh into his palm. Her fingers encountered leaves. She fondled the plant, stroking the fronds the way she wanted to stroke Lucas's skin.

His breath tickled her ear. "What do you smell?"

Him. She smelled him. And sunlight and flowers and she searched her memory to identify the herb. "Thyme."

He grip tightened then released. Her skin cooled without his touch. And then a warm palm cradled her jaw, angled her head and his lips covered hers as softly as a butterfly touching down.

He peeled the blindfold from her eyes. "You have two choices. We can finish the garden tour and go on to the aquarium. Or we can go back to the apartment."

The passion burning in his eyes made her breath hitch. She was falling for him again. Making love with him now would be as good as surrendering to those feelings.

Did she dare risk it?

Did she even have a choice?

He lifted her knuckles to his lips and her stomach somersaulted. No. She didn't have a choice. Because as much as she wanted to hate Lucas for leaving her, she was afraid she was still very much in love with him.

Nine

The black Lincoln limo gleaming beneath a streetlight tempted Nadia more than chocolate when she stepped out of the library late Monday night.

Old habits died hard.

She glanced at her watch, disgusted with herself because she'd lost track of time and stayed later than she should have. But she hadn't wanted to go back to the apartment, which felt emptier now that Lucas had left the building.

She'd have to splurge for a taxi. Once upon a time she would have done so without a second thought. Now it meant she'd have to cut something else out of her budget.

She glared up at the cloud-dotted sky. *Yes, Daddy, I am learning to identify with our largest demographic.*

Turning down the sidewalk, she scanned the streets which were disgustingly empty. It was Monday night. Not much going on in this section of downtown.

"Ms. Kincaid?"

She pivoted quickly. A swarthy man—thirtyish and muscular—in a chauffeur's uniform walked toward her. Years of ingrained caution kicked in. She might choose to live a relatively normal life without bodyguards, but she was still worth billions and kidnapping was a real possibility. Her father had harped on it endlessly—especially after that close call when she was twelve.

Why don't you carry pepper spray like a normal twenty-nine-year-old woman?

"Stop right there," she shouted.

The guy held up both hands and halted three yards away. "I'm Paulo. Mr. Stone asked me to provide your transportation while he's away."

Right. She hadn't been born yesterday. She wasn't getting into a strange car with darkly tinted windows just because the guy knew Lucas's name.

"I don't need a ride. Thank you." She backed toward the library. The doors were locked. Mary, the head librarian, had locked them after letting Nadia out. But she could hammer on the glass and scream until Mary or somebody heard her. And if they didn't come Nadia could run around back to the employee parking lot and hope she could catch Mary before she left. Of course, Nadia would have to leave her Christian Louboutin sandals behind if she wanted to sprint. But thousand-dollar shoes were a small price to pay for safety.

"He said you'd probably refuse and that I should call him if you did." He reached into his pocket and she prepared herself to kick off her shoes and run, but he didn't withdraw a weapon. He held a phone—a six-hundred-dollar phone. She recognized the brand because she owned one just like it. Extending his arm, he walked toward her.

"Stop," she repeated and dug her cell phone out of her bag. She'd call the police if he didn't go away.

"Yes, ma'am. I'll just dial Mr. Stone and put him on speaker for you."

He punched in a series of numbers. She called herself all kinds of fool for not running while he was preoccupied, but his suit was of good quality and it fit as if the limo company had tailored it for him. Only the top-notch places did that. Maybe Lucas had hired a car for her. The idea gave her the warm fuzzies.

"Did you find her?" Lucas's voice said over the speaker and her stomach fluttered.

"Yes, sir. I have Ms. Kincaid here and she reacted exactly as you predicted. We're on speaker phone. Maybe you could tell her I'm legit?"

"Nadia, can you hear me?"

"Yes." She pitched her voice to carry across the distance.

Lucas had been gone less than twenty-four hours and she wanted to talk to him, to tell him about her day and the fund-raising plans. The list of potential contributors he'd given her combined with the names she'd gathered on her own and a day's worth of phone time had garnered more donations than she'd ever hoped for. This fund-raiser could be the best in library history.

"Paulo is at your disposal while I'm gone. I don't want you taking the train."

Part of her was pleased that he'd thought of her. Another teensy part pricked her pride because he'd assumed she would do something foolish. "I'm not dumb enough to ride alone this late at night. I was going to take a taxi."

"Now you don't have to."

She considered arguing. After all, she was trying to stand

on her own two feet and prove she could. Relying on Lucas was no better than relying on Mitch or Rand or her father. But refusing for the sake of principal would be beyond stupid.

"I'll worry less if you use the car especially coming home from the library after dark," Lucas said as if he could read her mind.

Something inside her melted. Lucas was trying to take care of her. He'd done that eleven years ago, too. "You could have told me you were hiring a driver."

"Paulo, turn off the speaker and give Ms. Kincaid the phone, please."

Paulo did as ordered.

Nadia pressed the phone to her ear. "I'm here."

"You had me otherwise occupied before I left and I neglected to get your cell number."

His intimate pitch sent her pulse stuttering irregularly. Her skin warmed even more than the balmy summer night warranted when she recalled exactly how he'd been occupied. He'd spent Saturday night and most of Sunday in her bed. Exploring every inch of her skin and letting her relearn his.

"Thanks for thinking of me, Lucas."

Paulo opened the back door of the limo and she climbed in. The supple leather seats cradled her, a nice change after a long day in the hard, inexpensive office chair the library had found for her to use.

"We made a mess of your place. I've asked Ella to come over and clean up."

Her stomach did another flip. They'd wrecked her bed and then her kitchen when midnight cooking in the nude had turned into sex on the table complete with whipped cream, raspberry jam and chocolate sauce.

Her skin flushed. "I've already cleaned up. But thank you."

"You're sure?"

"I'm sure. My father didn't think I could manage the real-world chores of cooking and cleaning up after myself. I like proving him wrong." Crazier still, she liked seeing the place gleam and knowing it was due to her efforts.

"Everett always underestimated you."

"I know. I'm so much more than just a pretty face." She said the words tongue in cheek and he rewarded her with a chuckle.

"Yes, you are. Think of me when you go to bed tonight."

The low timber of his voice sent a shiver of arousal over her. She angled away from Paulo as he slid into the driver's seat. "I think it's safe to say I'll be doing that."

"And what will you be doing while you're thinking of me?"

Heat rushed through her and pooled low in her belly. "Remembering."

"Will you touch yourself the way I did?"

She struggled to pull a calming breath into her suddenly tight chest. "That's for me to know and you to wonder."

He tsked. "Trust me. I will. I'll see you in a few days and get the details of how you filled your nights. Good night, Nadia."

The call ended abruptly. Disappointed, she stared at the phone, then she composed herself and passed it through the open partition to Paulo. "Thanks."

"Would you like to go home? Or do you need to stop somewhere else first?"

"No. I want to go home. I mean, to the apartment."

And for the first time that was the truth. She'd had an amazing night followed by an even more amazing few days, and she couldn't wait to climb into a tub and savor how much her life had changed. And she wanted to go to sleep on the pillow case she hadn't washed—the one that smelled of Lucas.

Funny. Being stuck in Dallas didn't feel like a death sentence anymore. She hoped that in this case history wasn't about to repeat itself. Because she wasn't sure she'd survive losing him a second time.

Nadia's cell phone vibrated in her pocket Friday morning. *Lucas?*

She snatched it out and angled her back to the door of the tiny office Mary had assigned to her. But the caller ID said Rand instead of Lucas.

"Hi, big brother." She hoped he didn't hear the disappointment in her voice, but his wasn't the baritone she wanted to hear. "Did Mitch's wedding give you and Tara any ideas?"

"Don't worry. When we set a date, you'll be the first to know. I'm not going to let Tara get away this time. Nadia, what can you tell me about Andvari, Inc.?"

He sounded tense. "Why?"

"Because Teckitron, an Andvari subsidiary, just bought up the loans Dad took out to finance the new ships he has on order."

She jerked in surprise. "Why would he have taken out loans? We had the capital. Didn't we?"

"Mitch says Dad had some grand theory about saving money by writing off the finance charges on KCL's taxes and he wouldn't listen to reason. You know how he was when he got an idea. And remember Dad dumped a huge chunk of our ready cash into refurbishing the ships and some of that cash was mismanaged. Mitch and I are still unraveling that mess and auditing the other lines to make sure there isn't more embezzling going on than we already know about. I need everything you can tell me about Andvari."

"Sounds urgent."

"I want to find out who's behind that company. When you add Andvari buying up our suppliers over the past few years to the recent purchase of the bank holding our loans the situation begins to look like more than a coincidence."

"What do you mean?"

"I mean someone has it in for KCL. A personal vendetta. Not surprising since Dad managed to make a few enemies."

She flinched. Rand had never been prone to paranoia or jumping to conclusions. If he was worried, then he had grounds.

Daddy, what have you done?

"I have an Andvari file on my computer. It's woefully incomplete because I just haven't been able to penetrate the Andvari bureaucracy. I'll tell my assistant to e-mail it to you. But good luck with your research. What kind of hole does this leave us in, Rand? Worst-case scenario, if this Teckitron calls the loans we can pay them back. Right?"

The tense silence made the hairs on her body rise. "Given enough time we should be able to raise the capital. But because of the terms of the will we're in an awkward spot financially. Everything's tied up. We can't liquidate any assets or investments.

"To a new creditor we're a high-risk venture because any one of us could blow this thing right out of the water by violating one part of the damned inheritance curse. If that happens, all Kincaid properties are gone and we have no collateral. No one is going to risk billions without collateral.

"God help us when the terms of his will are made public.

The press is going to have a field day. The media furor has barely died down surrounding Dad's death. If the loans being bought up leaks, it'll stir up the hornet's nest again."

Not good. "Get our PR team on it. Have them prepare a statement. If anyone can spin this in a positive direction, they can."

"I'll do it." He paused and the awkward silence had her bracing herself in her stiff-backed chair. "How are you? And what's going on with Stone?"

She raked her hair back from her face and decided to come clean. "I'm in love with him again."

"Nadia—"

"Don't Nadia me. Lucas was as much a victim of Dad's machinations as you and Tara were. Dad was wrong to break you up. Well, he was wrong to break Lucas and me up, too."

"There's a difference. Tara refused Dad's bribe money."

Yes, okay, there was that. Their father had offered Tara an obscene amount of money to be his mistress. She'd not only refused, but also she'd quit her prestigious job as Everett Kincaid's PA and left the company and her friends—including Nadia—behind.

Nadia would be lying if she didn't acknowledge it bothered her that Lucas hadn't been as noble. "He had good reasons for taking the cash."

"Don't wear blinders, Nadia. If he betrayed you once, he'll do it again."

Her stomach churned. "I don't think he will."

"For your sake, I hope you're right. But whatever happens, I've got your back."

A chime sounded announcing an instant message on Nadia's computer an hour after her disturbing phone call from her brother.

Dreading more bad news from Rand, she reluctantly put down the impressive list of prizes she'd accumulated for the library fund-raiser and swiveled the laptop to face her.

LDStone: Working?

Her pulse skipped when she saw the name in the message box at the top left corner of her screen.

Lucas Daniel Stone. She'd named their son after his daddy and called him Daniel. Her eyes burned and her hands trembled as she poised them over the keyboard.

NEKincaid: Yes. How did you get my Messenger ID?

LDStone: I have my ways. And I'd like to show them to you. Preferably in bed. Naked.

Her insides bunched into a hot, smoldering knot of need. He'd been gone a week. A week during which he'd phoned at least once a day and told her in explicit detail what he would be doing to her if he were in Dallas instead of on the opposite side of the globe. This new aggressive side of him turned her on like crazy. It was like having the old Lucas back in a new and improved version. And without the headache of battling her father over him.

LDStone: I'll be home tonight. I'll wear the blindfold this time.

Her breath caught. She plucked at her suddenly sticking Juicy Couture shirt. They'd made use of that blindfold Saturday night and her skin tingled anew at the remembered blind anticipation of his touch.

NEKincaid: I can't wait. She frowned. But I'll probably be late. I'm supposed to meet with the committee tonight to give them a status update. They're a little nervous about having someone new in charge.

LDStone: You'll win them over. I'll be waiting. And when I get you alone...

A throat clearing beside her made her jump. Mary Branch stood by the table with a grin on her lined face.

NEKincaid: I'm not alone now, Nadia typed quickly. Her cheeks burned. Must go.

"Is that Mr. Stone?"

LDStone: Tonight.

Nadia closed her laptop with a snap. "Yes."

"I can't wait to meet him. Having him recommend you to us was such a blessing."

An icy finger of unease traced a path down Nadia's spine. *Coincidences happen.*

"Lucas recommended me for this job?"

"Yes. And what a life saver that was since our chairperson had chosen to quit just hours before his phone call."

That icy finger turned into a cold clenched fist.

You're just letting Rand's phone call rattle you. No one is out to get KCL or you.

But Rand's warning echoed in her head. "If he betrayed you once, he'll do it again."

She took a deep breath. "Is there any chance we can get the committee together before dinner instead of after?"

Because she really needed to talk to Lucas and put her mind at ease.

Nadia knew she'd bowled over the committee with the amount of work she'd achieved in one short week.

But she couldn't care less.

Well, okay, yes, she did care. Her success or failure in Dallas depended on her efforts. Not her father's nepotism or his interventions. No one here would pick up after her if she made a mess of her life. And while that was scary in many respects, it was also strangely liberating and empowering. The possibility of failure didn't terrify her the way it would have just a few weeks ago.

But she wanted—no, *needed*—to see Lucas. Her toe tapped impatiently as the elevator inched toward the fiftieth floor.

Lucas had somehow managed to get her the fund-raiser job, but how and why was still a mystery. Mary must have realized she'd leaked something she shouldn't have because she'd clammed up and refused to offer more information when Nadia pressed her.

Finally the elevator doors opened. Nadia surged forward, but jerked to a halt midstep when she nearly crashed into Lucas's housekeeper entering the cubicle.

"Hi, Ella. Is he home yet?" During her nine-week exile she'd become friendly with the woman.

"Hey, Nadia. He is and he's expecting you. Shall I tell him you're here?"

Nadia shifted her laptop case from one slick palm to the other. She hoped talking to Lucas would make the rolling-rocks feeling in her belly go away. "Could you just let me in? I'll surprise him."

Mischief twinkled in Ella's brown eyes. "I guess I can do that. The caterers have already delivered your meal. The hors d'oeuvres are in the refrigerator and dinner is warming in the oven. Dessert's in the freezer and it looks yummy. I've set the table. Mr. Stone said you'd feed yourselves. Would you like for me to come in and pour the wine?"

Nadia followed Ella back to Lucas's door. "I can handle it. But thank you. I know you want to get home to your boys."

"Before they wreck the place and eat everything that isn't fur-covered and meowing." The housekeeper punctuated the sentence with a smile as she turned the key and pushed the panel open. She stepped aside but didn't follow Nadia in.

Ella had the life Nadia had wanted with Lucas. She had three young sons who ran her ragged with their school and sports activities, and Ella and her husband loved every minute of it.

"If you change your mind about me cleaning your apartment, just tell me or Mr. Stone and I'll pop right over."

"Thanks. I will. But I'm determined to show everyone that I can cook and clean for myself. So far, thanks to that list of tips you gave me that first week, I'm winning."

"I understand."

She couldn't possibly. Because Nadia didn't completely understand the postmortem games her father was playing herself. "Have a great night."

"I will. You, too." Ella waved and headed for the elevator.

Nadia let the door close behind her and dropped her satchel next to Lucas's ostrich case beside the hall table. "Lucas?"

Silence greeted her. She checked the living room then the kitchen. Both were empty. She wandered down the hall toward his bedroom, her heels tapping on the hardwood floors. "Lucas?"

When she reached the door the sound of the shower filled her ears. A smile tugged her lips. She should join him.

But after the day she'd had, she'd rather unwind with a glass of wine first. She'd join him after that if he was still showering. She pivoted and headed for the kitchen. She found the corkscrew, opened the Zinfandel and poured a glass. The cool raspberry-flavored liquid rolled easily over her tongue and down her throat.

The man knows his wines.

She took a few more sips, poured a second glass for Lucas then headed for the bedroom. If she wanted to surprise him, she'd have to lose the noisy shoes. She kicked off her sandals by the hall credenza. After another sip of wine, she set down the glasses, peeled her shirt over her head and tossed it onto the glossy cherry surface. The movement set off an avalanche of mail that had been stacked on the far end of the table.

She jumped forward to catch the cascade, but only ended up scattering the pile far and wide. Kneeling, she collected the letters.

Andvari. The familiar name stopped her mid-reach.

The letter was addressed to D. Stone. Andvari, Inc.

D. Stone. *Daniel.*

With shaking hands she gathered the remainder of the mail and, swallowing the bile burning in her throat, she rose on unsteady legs and flipped through the stack of letters. One after the other was addressed to D. Stone, Andvari, Inc.

She hadn't done an Internet search on Daniel Stone. She'd only looked for Lucas Stone.

Lucas had said he owned "a few" companies. Judging by

the volume of mail, Andvari was apparently one of them. And if Andvari owned Teckitron... As if to prove her point, the only letter that hadn't fallen off the table was from Teckitron's CEO.

She wanted to open it and read it to see if it contained information on the purchase of KCL's loans, but another envelope that had slid farther down the hall caught her attention. She took three shaky steps to retrieve it. Her hand stopped inches short and an arctic chill deluged her. The return address was Mardi Gras Cruising.

Dark spots danced in her vision.

Mardi Gras. The company poised to get everything Everett Kincaid owned.

All of KCL's enemies tied to one man. Lucas Daniel Stone.

She had the proof in her hands that this was exactly what Rand had claimed.

A personal vendetta.

Very personal since her position was the one that suffered the most headaches from Andvari's machinations. She had been the one to slog through sleepless nights and eighteen-hour days to find alternative providers for the supplies their cruise ships needed.

But why? Why would Lucas do this?

Her father may have broken up their marriage, but he'd given Lucas two million dollars. Two million that Lucas had apparently multiplied and used to make a very nice life for himself.

If it had been because he'd believed she'd betrayed him eleven years ago, then why up the stakes now and go after the entire company after he'd discovered the truth?

Why would her husband want to destroy her?

Did he hate her that much?

Ten

The shower door flew open.

Startled, Lucas pivoted and opened his eyes.

"Nadia." He'd missed her. More than he wanted to admit.

She stood outside the glass stall half-dressed and entirely too desirable in a skimpy peach-colored bra, a skinny, short skirt in a darker shade and bare feet. He grinned and opened his arms. "Going to join me?"

"You bastard."

The words brought his gaze back to her face. Her furious face. She flung whatever she held in her hands at him. It took him a second to identify the items raining down.

Letters?

He killed the dual shower heads with a twist of his wrist.

An envelope addressed to Mardi Gras circled the drain.

Damn.

She'd found the stack of mail his assistant had left in the

entry for him—a stack he hadn't dealt with yet because he wanted to shower away the jet lag first and he wasn't expecting Nadia for hours. Ella must have let her in.

"Nadia—"

"Don't you dare 'Nadia' me, you lying son of a bitch."

"I can explain."

"How can you explain making my life a living hell? You started eleven years ago and then repeated the process over and over for the past four years and again this week when your stupid company bought up KCL's loans. Did you ever once think of me or were you in this for your own personal gain the entire time? Or is Rand right? Is this a personal vendetta?"

Rand was on to him, too?

"You are a selfish sadistic prick, Lucas Daniel Stone. And it sickens me that I named my son after you."

Her words hit him like a fist to the gut, winding him, making his head spin. He braced a hand against the cool tiles. She'd named their son after him. Knowing that made the loss more real.

She didn't hang around for him to catch his breath or recover his wits. She spun and stalked out of the bathroom.

Stepping over the wet mail, he grabbed a towel from the rod, hitched it around his hips and took off after her. He caught up with her by his front door. She'd put on her shirt, but hadn't tucked it in. One hand held her briefcase and the other clenched the doorknob in a white-knuckled grip. She yanked the door open.

He slapped a palm against the wood slamming it closed again. "Nadia, let me explain."

Although how he'd make her understand the need to destroy her father, or her family in lieu of Everett, escaped him at the moment.

"Get away from me. I don't ever want to see you again." Pure venom dripped from her words. But the quiver in her voice and her bottom lip called her a liar.

He'd hurt her. The knowledge sliced his chest like a knife. He lifted a hand to her cheek. She flinched out of reach and swung her briefcase at him. He dodged and let his hand drop.

"I wasn't trying to hurt you."

"You've done nothing but hurt me. You show me how good something can be then you take it away. And this time, you deliberately set me up. You made love to me and you made me love you all over again. At the same time you were plotting to take everything important to me away. Again."

She loved him. And she wasn't lying. The bruised look in her eyes confirmed her statement. He sucked a breath through the noose squeezing his throat.

"My *vendetta,* as you call it, was against your father. Not you."

"He's dead! And now, so are my feelings for you."

A lie. She'd screamed the words at a spot past his left shoulder.

She had that closed look on her face. But he had to find a way to keep her here until he could fix this. Because he couldn't let her go. Not yet. "What are you going to do? Run back to Miami and hand it all to me on a platter?"

Her spine snapped straight. Her chin hiked and her eyes found and burned his like lasers. "Bastard."

She had no idea how true that was.

"You're better than that, Nadia. Stronger than that. Show me the guts and the smarts of the woman who outmaneuvered me at every turn when I bought up KCL's suppliers. Show me the fighter inside you. I know she's there." His shoulders were so stiff it's a wonder he didn't dislocate something when he feigned a casual shrug. "Unless you're willing to cost your brothers everything."

The color drained from her face. She vibrated with anger and emotion. A white line circled her tight lips. He wouldn't be surprised if she slugged him. "I hope you burn in hell right next to my father."

"Lying in that hospital bed knowing I'd killed our baby, that my wife didn't want me and that I'd probably never walk again was hell. This is playing the game called life. I play to win and I play fair. If I'd wanted to fight dirty, I would have let you sleep past your midnight curfew the night we made love."

"How magnanimous of you." The pain in her eyes made his gut ache. "I lost everything that day, Lucas. The man I loved. Our child and any chance of ever having another one. A month later I learned my mother chose to kill herself rather than stick around and love me. She left me as if I didn't matter. And you did, too.

"I lost everything important—everything money *couldn't* buy. So don't tell me about hell. Or life. Or fighting. Or playing the damned game. I've survived and I've fought and I've done nothing but play the damned game. Because I had to. Or I'd have ended up like my mother. And trust me, there were days when I seriously considered dying the best option. Because I thought I had nothing to live for."

She choked out a mirthless laugh. "But I forgot. You have no conscience. Knowing I spent the better part of four years wishing I'd died in that car with you would have meant nothing to you. You wanted to know why I didn't go to New York and study fashion design? Because I didn't think it mattered what I studied in college. I didn't intend to live long enough to graduate. I was too busy trying to find the nerve to kill myself."

She yanked the door again. In his shock over her words he let her go.

She crossed the hall, shoved her key in her lock and glared at him over her shoulder. "Stay out of my face and out of my way. Or I will take out a restraining order against you so fast you won't know what hit you. And then I'll go to the press and tell them what a mean, selfish, conniving ass you really are."

Her door slammed in his face and the dead bolt shot home as loud as a gun.

Lucas reeled. He braced himself against the doorjamb.

Nadia had considered suicide.

And if she'd ended her life, it would have been his fault.

Trapped.

Nadia curled in a chair in the corner of her patio as far away from Lucas's apartment as she could get. The heavy night air closed around her. Hot. Humid. Suffocating.

She couldn't leave Dallas.

Her brothers were counting on her. The library was counting on her. She was counting on herself. Running from her problems and calling for someone else to bail her out was no longer an option. Her daddy was right. It was time she grew up.

She picked up her cell phone for about the fiftieth time. She had to make the call, but it was the hardest one she'd ever had to make. Calling her brother to tell him she'd screwed up. Again. She'd been betrayed. Again. Used for what she could give someone. Again. No new territory there.

She'd rehashed every conversation she and Lucas had had, picking each sentence apart and trying to decide if she'd given him any crucial, confidential information that would help him in harming KCL. She didn't know.

Taking a bracing breath, she hit Auto-dial.

"Rand Kincaid." He sounded as if she'd woken him.

How late was it? She didn't have a clue. She tipped her head back. The sky overhead was inky dark and star-studded.

"I-It's Nadia. I'm sorry to call so late."

"What's wrong?" Any trace of grogginess in his voice had vanished.

"You were right. It is a personal vendetta. Lucas is behind Andvari and Teckitron and Mardi Gras."

Rand's curses blistered her ears. In the background she heard Tara asking questions and Rand's muffled response. She couldn't make out the words. "Tell me what you know."

She recapped the afternoon's discoveries. Rand didn't rush her. He let her choke out her words. When she was done she sagged against the wall, out of breath, out of energy.

"Nadia, are you okay? I'll charter a jet tonight—"

"No! We're not blowing this or handing that bastard everything. I'm staying here. You're staying there. We're fighting until the end."

"What do you need me to do?"

"Nothing. Just keep on taking care of business the best way you and Mitch can. I'll be fine."

The questions she'd been asking herself since she'd left Lucas's apartment pounded inside her skull.

"Why would he do it, Rand? Why would Dad threaten to leave everything to a man he paid to get out of my life? Why would he choose Lucas over his own children? He had to know who he was dealing with."

"Dad was twisted. It's impossible to make sense out of his actions. But, yes, this seems more whacked than anything I've seen thus far. He detested Stone. Partly because he thought your husband was a fortune hunter and partly because Dad couldn't stand to lose his stranglehold on you."

She blinked and straightened. "Stranglehold?"

"Dad smothered you, Nadia. You reminded him of Mom. You look like her. Your voice and your laugh sound like hers. And you're as artistic as she was."

Rand would know. He'd been fourteen when their mother died, old enough to remember her. Nadia didn't have as many memories. The few she'd had contradicted each other. Sometimes her mother had adored her. Sometimes Mary Elizabeth Kincaid couldn't seem to stand the sight of her youngest child.

"When those bozos tried to kidnap you when you were twelve, Dad went a little crazy. He didn't like letting you out of his sight after that."

"Don't I know it."

"He loved you probably as much as the old bastard was capable of loving anyone."

She hugged the words close. "You think so? Because it didn't feel like it."

"I know so." Rand cleared his throat. "Are you sure you're...okay?"

She knew exactly what he meant. The uncomfortable hesitation was a dead giveaway. He'd been there too many times for her in the past not to know how fragile she'd been in her grief. "I'm fine. I'm not sad or depressed. I'm fighting mad. And Lucas had better not cross me."

"About Stone..."

She clutched her anger around her like a cloak. "Don't worry about him. Now that I know where I stand with him I know how to handle him."

Brave words and a bald-faced lie. But one hint of vulnerability and one or both of her brothers would be in Dallas. And Lucas, the lying snake, would get everything. She couldn't let that happen.

She would figure this out on her own. No calling in the reinforcements. This was her battle and she'd win it on her turf and her terms.

"You have a hell of a nerve showing up here, Stone," Rand Kincaid growled.

Lucas hadn't expected a warm welcome when he reached Kincaid Cruise Line's Miami offices. He'd expected a fist in his face—*if* he'd gotten past security at the reception desk. Judging by the anger vibrating off the Kincaid brothers as they glared at him across the boardroom table he might get a pair of punches before he left the building.

"How is Nadia?"

It had been a damned long two weeks. She'd refused to open her door when he'd knocked and wouldn't speak to him when they passed in the hall. She'd refused the gourmet meals and flowers he'd had delivered.

"None of your goddamned business." Mitch bit out the words.

"The bodyguard is unnecessary. I'm not going to hurt her." One of these turkeys had hired a mountain-size goon to keep him away from her. Nadia never left the apartment without the knuckle-dragger by her side to run interference.

It frustrated him that she lived yards away and couldn't have been more unreachable if she'd been on another continent.

"What do you want?" Rand barked.

"To broker a deal."

The terse curse and redundant hand gesture from the

oldest Kincaid didn't surprise him. Lucas knew his single-minded selfish need for revenge had hurt Nadia deeply. Her brothers wouldn't, and shouldn't, forget that. If she were his sister, he wouldn't.

He hadn't expected making amends and finding a solution or forgiveness to come easily. It had taken him ten days of meetings with a legal team and business advisors to find a potential way around the mess of Everett Kincaid's last wishes.

Neither of the Kincaids invited him to sit.

"My understanding is that if the terms of your father's will aren't met, Mardi Gras cruising becomes the owner of everything he possessed. Correct?"

Rand planted his fists on the table and leaned across aggressively. "How do you know that?"

"Nadia told me part of it. The rest I discovered when I read a copy of Everett's will."

"Son of a bitch," Mitch snarled. "How did you get a copy? It's not public record yet."

"I believe your father's favorite phrase was 'Everyone has a price and a weakness…look hard enough you'll find them.' Everett exploited my weakness and found my price. I was wrong to take his payoff and abandon Nadia. I hurt her. There's no getting around that. My reasons for taking the money don't matter. I make no excuses for being a stupid, greedy coward."

Their raised eyebrows told him he'd shocked them.

"My vendetta was with your father, but as Nadia pointed out, he's gone. It's time to end this. I want to sell Mardi Gras to KCL."

Identical Kincaid chins jacked up. Lucas had Mitch's and Rand's undivided attention. Taking advantage of their stunned silence, he laid his briefcase on the table, popped the locks and withdrew a sheaf of documents. He slid the stack across the wide table and focused on Mitch's eyes—eyes the same green as Nadia's.

"I've had my attorney draw up the sales contract."

"Why?" Rand asked, his tone guarded and suspicious.

"Because if Kincaid Cruise Line owns Mardi Gras Cruising then no matter how this year ends and whether or not the three of you fulfill the terms of Everett's will, KCL and every other property Everett owned will remain in Kincaid hands."

"You're saying if we forfeited, we'd be forfeiting to ourselves. That's twisted logic," Rand said as he flipped through the pages. "But it might work. We'd have to have our attorneys and accountants go over this."

"Of course."

Shaking his head Mitch stepped back from reading over his brother's shoulder. "We can't do it. We don't have the ready cash—as you no doubt know since your company bought off KCL's loans. This is an empty gesture. And if you call the loans, then we're in worse shape than when we started."

"I'm not calling the loans, although I admit that was my initial plan. The terms will remain exactly as stated in the original loan documentation. As for whether or not you can afford the deal…I don't believe you've seen my asking price. Page fifty. Last paragraph."

Pages rustled. Seconds later Rand pinned him with an incredulous stare. "Are you out of your mind?"

"Your father would have sold his entire estate to Mardi Gras—to *me*—for one dollar. It's only fair I match his price."

He'd lose billions. But he'd recover. Because as two long weeks without Nadia had taught him, some things were worth more than money.

Mitch's eyes narrowed to slits. "What's the catch?"

Lucas smiled, because of course there was a catch. There was always a catch when a deal sounded too good to be true.

"Call off the goon. I want to talk to Nadia."

Mitch bristled. "She doesn't want to talk to you."

"That's the deal. I talk to her tonight at the library fundraiser or the offer is off the table. Take it or leave it."

Mitch still looked ready to punch him, but Rand eyed him with a new respect. "You have one night. After that if she wants nothing to do with you, then you'd better back off."

"Deal." He extended his hand across the table.

Eleven

"You're cutting it close, Cinderella."

Nadia jumped and spun around, nearly falling off her Dolce & Gabbana heels and onto her last year's Badgley Mischka-gowned butt. "Lucas, go away. I don't have time for you now."

She'd been avoiding him for two weeks. Her crazy schedule planning the fund-raiser had helped.

When she'd spotted him in the crowd tonight she'd wanted to run and hide. It hurt to look at him in his black tux and know she'd loved and trusted him twice and each time he'd chosen money over her. But instead of running, she'd simply done her job as MC. Staying onstage had made avoiding him easy.

She scanned the street. Where was the car and driver she'd hired for the night? If she didn't find them soon, she'd have to take a cab…or not. The event had ended fifteen minutes ago and apparently all the taxis had been taken.

"I sent your henchman and your car away," he said as if reading her mind.

"What? You had no right. I need that car. Or is this another ploy to steal my father's estate?"

"Your brothers haven't told you." A statement not a question.

"Told me what?"

"That we talked today."

"You talked to Mitch and Rand? About what?"

He shook his head, an ironic smile twisting his lips. "I'll get you back to your place before midnight. But you'll have to trust me, Nadia."

"Like that's worked so well for me thus far."

"Trust me," he repeated and held her gaze.

She looked into his blue, sincere-looking eyes and called herself an idiot for not telling him to go to hell. She obviously had no judgment where he was concerned. But she didn't run from her problems anymore. She might as well get this confrontation over with.

"Fine. Where's your car?"

He reached for her elbow. She dodged him. He shrugged. "Follow me."

He strolled back toward the building with no apparent haste. After a second she hustled after him. "Lucas, I have to go. I don't have time to hang around here."

"Our ride is on the roof."

"The roof." She stopped.

"The helipad, to be more precise." He opened the glass door and waited for her.

"You flew here in a helicopter?"

"I was out of town today and my flight was delayed. I came here directly from the concourse. There's a helipad on my— our—building."

Car? Helicopter? What did it matter as long as she made it home by midnight? And no matter the mode of transportation, his company would make it an uncomfortable ride. "Let's go."

He led her to the elevator and up to the top floor where they had to depart the cubicle and climb a short flight of stairs. "How did you get permission for this?"

"I made a donation." He shoved open the door to the roof and, sure enough, a small blue-and-white helicopter waited.

"Just like you made a donation to get me the chairperson job."

He looked at her in surprise.

"Did you think I wouldn't find out when I started tallying our take? Money's all that matters to you, isn't it? You're just like my father. The end justifies the means and the bottom line is all that counts."

That stopped him in his tracks. He looked at her. "In my quest for revenge against your father I became so obsessed with humiliating him the way he had me that I became just like him. But I'm not anymore."

She rolled her eyes. "Right. It's so humiliating to take two million dollars."

"He made me beg, dammit," he snapped, then looked away, wiping a hand across his jaw as if he regretted his words. His gaze met hers again. "Everett made sure I knew I was a liability. To you. To my family. He even mentioned getting the police to charge me with involuntary manslaughter in the death of our child. That meant legal fees and possibly jail time. Before he was done with me I was pleading with him to help me."

That sounded like her manipulative father. And okay, yes, she could see how that might sting a man's pride. But to deliberately set out to destroy her family's business…? "Just take me home, Lucas."

He helped her climb aboard—not an easy feat in her long form-fitted gown and heels. His knuckles brushed her belly as he assisted her with her seat belt and her heart jolted with each contact.

Within minutes they were soaring above the Dallas skyline. She'd flown in everything from ultralight planes to jumbo jets, but this helicopter was one of the plushest aircraft she'd ever ridden in. The well-insulated passenger compartment was relatively quiet. The seats were deep and supple leather, the paneling real wood grain.

The jingle of keys pulled her attention back to Lucas. He dangled a pair of keys bearing the Mercedes emblem from his fingers.

"What's that?"

"A gift for you. Congratulations on passing your driving test and getting your license."

She pulled in a shaky breath but ignored the keys. "How did you know?"

"Because I care enough to check. I'm proud of you, Nadia. That took guts."

Her heart hitched and her eyes burned. "Don't. Don't feed me any more lines or lies."

"I'm not."

The cadence of the rotors changed. Nadia used the excuse to break his gaze and look out the window. She hated that she wanted to believe him. She spotted their building and checked her watch. Twenty minutes to spare. Lucas hadn't lied about getting her home on time.

Her stomach lurched as the craft descended then gently bounced on the pad. The motor whined down. Lucas opened

the door and handed her out. His palm burned against hers
and he refused to release her despite her tug. Her pulse ricocheted wildly as his fingers laced through hers. He said something she couldn't hear to the pilot then guided her toward a
door set into the wall.

Moments later she stood in front of her door.

"Invite me in."

She ought to say no. She was exhausted and emotionally
wobbly. The past two weeks had been hell. But since he'd
given her a ride… "It's been a long day. You can come in for
a few minutes."

He followed her into the living room, his eyes scanning
the place as if he expected someone to be waiting.

"Do you want a glass of wine or something?" *Some
hostess you are. Talk about a rude and abrupt tone…*

He shoved his hands into his jacket pockets. "No. I want
to apologize for underestimating you eleven years ago. The
truth is, it wasn't you who I thought would fail. It was me.
I felt like less than a man. I expected you to reject me so I
rejected you first. I was trying to salvage what little pride
I had left."

His honesty took her breath. "You were afraid."

His lips compressed then seconds later he nodded. "Terrified. But not half as scared as I was when you told me
you'd contemplated suicide. Nadia—"

His voice cracked. He swallowed and blinked. His jaw
muscles bunched as if he were gritting his teeth. "I couldn't
have lived with that on my conscience."

"I had help. Professional help. And my family."

"You should have had me."

"That would have been nice. We could have helped each
other through the tough times."

"You don't ever think about—" He stopped as if he couldn't bear to say the words. She understood his reaction. Most people had the same aversion to the dark side of depression.

"No. Those dark days are over. The doctors believe my issue was a combination of grief and postpartum depression. But I'm okay now. Really okay."

He lifted a hand and stroked her cheek. She felt his touch deep in her belly, but couldn't find the strength to pull away.

"Nadia, I can't go back and undo what I've done wrong. But I will swear to you that I will never underestimate you again. And I will never deliberately make a choice that will hurt you. Give us a second chance. I need you in my life."

The words dredged deeply. A part of her heart yearned to try. But another part held back. Unable to speak past the lump in her throat, she shook her head and moved out of reach.

"My need for revenge is over. I let KCL become symbolic of the pride I surrendered when I took your father's money. I was ashamed. I knew what I'd done was wrong and that I was a coward for not facing you and taking your rejection like a man. I somehow convinced myself while I was battling to get back on my feet that conquering KCL and your father, by humiliating him the way he had me, I could somehow restore the faith I'd lost in myself."

She bit her lip to hold back a hiccup of sympathy. "My father hurt a lot of people."

"He hurt you. I can't forgive him for that."

"But why is he threatening to give you everything if we don't jump through his hoops?"

"I have no idea. The only thing I can guess is that he's been tracking me, monitoring my progress. Maybe he's rewarding me for becoming exactly like the man I despised." He captured her shoulders in his hands. "But I'm not that man anymore. I love you, Nadia. I'm not sure I ever stopped."

She gasped at the swell of emotion his words evoked.

"I love your determination, your persistence, your try-anything-once attitude. But I'm hoping you'll try me. Twice. Give me a second chance to make this right. To make us right."

Her thoughts tumbled like river rocks, rolling over and over noisily. Did she dare trust him again? She wasn't the girl she'd been and could never have the life they'd planned.

Her cell phone rang. She ignored it. But it rang again and again and again.

"Answer it."

She glanced at the caller ID. "It's Rand. I'll call him back."

"Answer it," he repeated more insistently.

"What?" she practically barked into the phone.

"Are you with Stone?"

She blinked. "Yes. Why?"

"Give the man a dollar and tell him he has a deal."

"What?"

"Just do it, Nadia. He'll explain." Rand hung up on her.

She stared at the phone. "That was weird. He said, 'Give the man a dollar and tell him he has a deal.' What does that mean?"

A smile slid across Lucas's sexy lips. "Need to borrow a dollar?"

"I have a dollar. But why would I give it to you?"

He held out his hand, palm up.

Grunting in frustration, Nadia dug a dollar out of her evening bag and slapped it into his hand. Hard.

He tucked it into his pant pocket. "I flew to Miami today to broker a deal with your brothers."

Suspicious, she narrowed her eyes. "What kind of deal?"

"KCL now owns Mardi Gras Cruising or will as soon as the paperwork is signed and notarized."

"What?"

"KCL bought Mardi Gras for one dollar—the price your father put on his holdings. When the deal is closed you can get out of this apartment and go anywhere you want. You'll be free instead of trapped here for a year."

"I don't understand. Why would you sell your company at a multibillion-dollar loss? What's in it for you?" None of this made sense. Just two weeks ago Lucas had been trying to destroy KCL.

"What's that old cliché? When you love someone you let them go? You won't be bound by the terms of your father's will because if you forfeit, everything will be handed over to Mardi Gras, which you Kincaids will already own. So you'll be giving it to yourselves."

The convoluted logic almost made sense. "Is that legal?"

"According to the best legal minds I could buy, yes. And I'm sure your brothers had their attorneys go through the purchase agreement with a fine-tooth comb, too, before agreeing."

"You sold your company for a dollar so I could have my freedom?"

"I want you to be happy, Nadia. With or without me. That's all I ever wanted. Even when I walked away eleven years ago that was my goal."

Her vision clouded. She blinked to clear the tears and a hot trail burned down her cheek. "I'll stay in Dallas for the full year because Daddy expected me to fail. I need to prove to him and to myself that I can take whatever life dishes out."

"Now that's the attitude of the woman who's given Andvari hell for the past forty months."

"I'm not the girl you fell in love with eleven years ago, Lucas. I can't give you the family you want. I can't have children."

"We don't have to make babies to be happy together."

"I don't even know if I want to risk adopting. The doctors tell me I don't carry my mother's trait for bipolar disorder. But what if they're wrong? What if I end up ill?"

"You said I never gave you a chance to prove your love for me by telling you I was paralyzed. Works both ways, princess. You're not giving me a chance to prove mine, either. Nadia, I will love you even if you end up like your mother. And if you need it, then I will take care of you and keep you safe to the best of my ability." He cradled her face in his palms. "I love you. Let me prove it."

And then his lips touched hers in the gentlest kiss they'd ever shared. When he lifted his head she looked into his eyes and saw the emotion to mirror his words. Her heart swelled and tears of happiness clogged her throat.

She covered his hands with hers. "I want to take that chance. With you. Only with you."

"Marry me."

She gave him a patient look. "I'm already married to you."

"Marry me again. But this time we'll meet at the altar as equals."

"I never considered you less than my equal, Lucas. But if it's important to you, then, yes, I'll marry you again."

Epilogue

Nadia sat behind her desk at KCL and sighed in satisfaction. It was good to be home and back on the job.

Her year in exile had flown by—thanks to Lucas's company—and life was good.

No, better than good because she had it all this time. A husband who adored her. A job she loved. And family. His and hers.

She glanced at the card that had been tucked in the massive flower arrangement from Lucas's mother and sisters.

Party at 7:00 to celebrate your first day back on the job.
Be ready to boogie Stone-style. Martinis on us.
Lucas's Girls

"Ms. Kinc—Mrs. Stone, your husband is here," her assistant said over the intercom.

"Send him in, Ann." She rose, circled her desk to meet him halfway.

Lucas strode through the door, looking powerful and gorgeous as always, this time in her favorite black Armani suit. His blond hair gleamed, but it was the way his eyes lit up when he saw her that made her heart flip-flop. Not once in the past nine months had she had any reason to doubt his love or his loyalty.

He covered the carpet in long strides and didn't stop until his arms surrounded her and his lips covered hers. She adored his kisses. The devouring ones, the gentle ones, the tempting ones, but she especially liked this kind—the kind that promised more than kisses later.

He lifted his head. "Good first day back?"

"Absolutely." When he kissed her breathless that way he couldn't expect long-winded answers. He was lucky to get more than one syllable.

"Ready for this?" The sun glinted off his wedding band—the one she'd given him years ago—as he reached into his coat pocket and withdrew an envelope.

The final words from her father. Her heart stumbled.

Each of her brothers had received letters from her father soon after completing their portions of the yearlong inheritance clause. It stood to reason she'd get one, too. Lucas had volunteered to pick hers up from Richards's office on his way back from the final inspection of the property he'd purchased to house all of his businesses in Miami. Mardi Gras would fall under the KCL umbrella, but his other companies would be housed near enough that she and he could slip away for lunches together.

"Would you rather do this at home?" he asked.

She shook her head. "No. I want to read Dad's words here

where I can still feel his presence. He may have broken us up, but he also brought us back together. And I'd have to be in serious denial not to admit that we're both stronger people for difficulties we went through and the time we spent apart."

"Agreed. But I still resent being robbed of eleven years with you." He offered her an envelope, which left one in his hand.

"He left me two letters?"

He shook his head, a frown puckering his brow. "Your father left one for me."

"That's odd. I don't think anyone else outside the family received a last missive."

"Who goes first?" he asked.

"Me. I need answers." She led him to what she called her oasis, a seating nook in the corner of her office. Lucas had helped her build a minigarden when she'd moved in over the weekend. She had blooming orchids mixed in with the emerald-green tropical plants and fragrant gardenias. She kicked off her Versace heels and sat on the love seat. Lucas settled beside her, hooking his arm around her shoulder and tugging her close.

Nadia's hands trembled as she opened the flap and withdrew the folded pages. She took a deep breath and flattened the pages in her lap so that Lucas could read along with her.

Nadia,

If you're reading this, then you have passed the final test your old man is going to throw at you, and I'm probably exactly where you've told me to go a hundred times. Roasting in hell. I'm not saying I didn't deserve the verbal fireballs when you threw them. I held you too tight.

My only excuse—well, I have two of them. First, your mother, my darling Mary Elizabeth, made me promise to take care of her little angel. (Almost blew that one, didn't I?) I think she knew she wouldn't be around to do the job. But don't ever doubt she loved you. She just couldn't fight her demons. And God help me, I couldn't fight them for her even though I tried.

Second, you reminded me of your mother in so many ways. Your laugh. Your smile. Your zest for life and your artistic talent. Although you're mentally much stronger than she ever was. I barely survived losing her. I didn't think I'd survive losing you, too. But I almost did lose you. And it was my own stupid fault.

In protecting you from life's lows, I also robbed you of life's highs. I can't help believing if I'd given you the wedding your mother would have wanted you to have complete with chauffeurs and horse-drawn carriages, then you wouldn't have lost my first grandson. And you wouldn't have hit rock bottom. That guilt ate away at me every blessed day. And I made things worse by getting rid of Stone.

I was wrong about him, Nadia. And you know how much it sticks in my craw to admit to being wrong. But I shouldn't have tried to play God. He loved you and I had no right to take that from you. But I did. I shamelessly kicked the man when he was down and bleeding. Literally. When I look back on my life, that is not one of my finer moments and it is my biggest regret. In trying to make your life easier, I robbed you of the love of your life and denied you the chance to experience what I had with your mother. As much as losing her hurt me, I would do it all again to relive the days I had with her.

Sending you to Dallas where you'd run into Stone may have been too little too late. But I had to try. And I hate like hell that I won't be around to see the outcome.

If nothing else, I hope this year on your own has shown you your inner strength. You always were a fighter. The only Kincaid who fought as hard and tough as me. That's why seeing you so down after the accident gutted me. And, yes, I pushed you around and hit your hot buttons just to get a rise out of you. But it beat the hell out of watching you go through the motions without caring what happened. (Boy, did you make me pay for hitting your buttons.)

If this letter finds Stone by your side, then I wish the two of you years of happiness and joy, and I take credit for fixing my biggest mistake and getting you back together. If he's not with you, then he's not the man I thought he was and he's not worthy of you. Screw him.

But you're a stubborn cuss, just like your old man. If he's not there and you want him, I'll hand you one last weapon. You're still married to him. The divorce paperwork was forged. I've left a letter with Richards saying so. Again, my intentions were good but maybe my methods weren't the best. If either you or he had wanted to marry again, I'd have had a hell of a mess on my hands. But I figured since that kind of love only comes once in a lifetime, I was pretty safe.

Two pieces of advice to you, Nadia... First, remember if you don't believe in yourself no one else will. I hope this year gave you that confidence. And second, live life to the fullest—the good and the bad—before you run out of time and all you have are regrets for what you didn't do and things you didn't say. Like I did.

I never told you I loved you. Now I'll never get the chance except in cold, dry words typed on paper. Too little. Too late.

I love you, baby girl. And I am so damned proud of you. Your mother would have been, too. You are easily the best thing Mary Elizabeth and I ever did together and the best parts of both of us combined.

> Your father,
> Everett Kincaid

Nadia blinked furiously to clear her vision. A blur of white passed in front of her eyes. Lucas's handkerchief. She'd become quite fond of those little white monogrammed squares and the games they played with them over the past months.

She accepted it and blotted her wet face. "My mother and father loved me. You can't know how many times I wondered."

Lucas's arm tightened around her. "I told you it was impossible not to love you, princess."

"But Daddy didn't explain that clause concerning Mardi Gras. Why would he choose you over his own children?"

"Maybe my letter has the answer." He opened the envelope and withdrew a single sheet.

> Stone,
> I wronged each of my children. But I wronged you even more. And in doing so, I almost lost my daughter.
> Ironic, isn't it? In trying to crush you I almost destroyed the person who meant the world to me, my baby girl, the spitting image of my Mary Elizabeth and the apple of her mother's eye.

I've followed your progress over the years. I guess I was hoping you'd prove I'd done the right thing in getting rid of your ass. But you didn't. You made me eat crow every time I turned around. Not my favorite diet, I'll tell you.

Stone, you have more chutzpah than me. Honest to God, I don't know another person I can say that to. Your ambition and intelligence remind me of myself at your age. But you're smarter, more patient. And since your good-for-nothing father (yes, I know about the bastard) isn't around to say it, let me say it. You are one hell of a man. Remember, it's not who your daddy is that matters. It's who you are that counts.

In putting your family first (hell yes, I know why you took my money), you showed me my mistake in tearing you and Nadia apart. But I was stubborn. I stuck to my guns. And then you multiplied *my* money and turned around and used it against me. Damnation, man, that takes balls. My hat is off to you.

I have no doubt that if I hadn't been watching you like a hawk you would have eventually launched a sneak attack on KCL and taken us down. I've made enough mistakes to give you footholds. You're good. Since I wasn't going to be around to see it happen I decided I'd reward you for your cunning. But I won't deny I'm hoping my kids have enough of me in them to spike your guns.

Gotta love a good fair fight.

If you learned the terms of my will (and I'm sure you did), you know how easily you could have won by cheating. If you're reading this, then you played straight. I gave you a second chance to choose between my money and my daughter. You did the right thing. I have to respect a man whose moral code is strong enough to keep him from taking the easy road.

I didn't play fair with you last time, Stone, and for that I apologize. You'll notice I did this time. I didn't give my family advance warning of your identity and your intent. To the victor goes the spoils and all that crap.

I sure did love watching you and Nadia sparring with that Andvari mess. Proved to me once and for all that the two of you were evenly matched. Good God, that girl has what my daddy called gumption. Stuck it to you, didn't she? It was a pure joy to watch the two of you dancing around the ring.

I wish I could be around to see how this battle ends, because I'll bet it's going to be one hell of a show.

Take care of my daughter, Stone. Love her and any children you might adopt until your last breath. If you don't, I'm going to come back and haunt your ass.

Respectfully yours,
Everett Kincaid

The last line of the letter startled a burst of laughter from Nadia. She blotted more tears, but she was smiling. "That sounds exactly like my father."

"He knew it was me the entire time."

Only one line of the letter bothered her. "He thinks we're going to adopt."

"Princess, I'm happy with just you."

"We always wanted a family. You'd be such a good father."

"Then we'll get goldfish or dogs."

She took a deep breath, rolling the words she'd been privately thinking around in her head. "I—I think I'd like to raise children with you."

His sharp breath told him she'd surprised him.

She worried her bottom lip with her teeth. "Maybe we could hire a surrogate to carry your baby. Or check into adoption."

He stroked her cheek with a gentle hand, but it was the love in his eyes that cocooned her. "We'll do whatever you want. But remember, as long as I have you I have all I need."

* * * * *

A sneaky peek at next month...

By Request

RELIVE THE ROMANCE WITH THE BEST OF THE BEST

My wish list for next month's titles...

In stores from 18th October 2013:

☐ In the Italian's Bed – Carol Marinelli, Margaret Mayo & Catherine George

☐ Passionate Affairs – Kate Hardy, Nicola Marsh & Natalie Anderson

3 stories in each book - only £5.99!

In stores from 1st November 2013:

☐ The Illegitimate Heirs: Luke, Zach and Jake – Kathie DeNosky

☐ Bride Under the Mistletoe – Susan Meier, Cara Colter & Jessica Hart

Available at WHSmith, Tesco, Asda, Eason, Amazon and Apple

Just can't wait?

Special Offers

Every month we put together collections and longer reads written by your favourite authors.

Here are some of next month's highlights— and don't miss our fabulous discount online!

On sale 1st November   On sale 1st November   On sale 18th October

Save 20%
on all Special Releases

Come home this Christmas to Fiona Harper

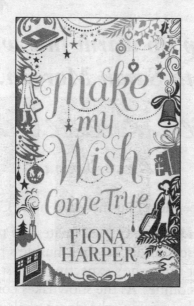

From the author of *Kiss Me Under the Mistletoe* comes a Christmas tale of family and fun. Two sisters are ready to swap their Christmases—the busy super-mum, Juliet, getting the chance to escape it all on an exotic Christmas getaway, whilst her glamorous work-obsessed sister, Gemma, is plunged headfirst into the family Christmas she always thought she'd hate.

www.millsandboon.co.uk

3/MB442

Wrap up warm this winter with Sarah Morgan…

Sleigh Bells in the Snow

Kayla Green loves business and hates Christmas.

So when Jackson O'Neil invites her to Snow Crystal Resort to discuss their business proposal… the last thing she's expecting is to stay for Christmas dinner. As the snowflakes continue to fall, will the woman who doesn't believe in the magic of Christmas finally fall under its spell…?

4th October

www.millsandboon.co.uk/sarahmorgan

1013/MB435

She's loved and lost — will she ever learn to open her heart again?

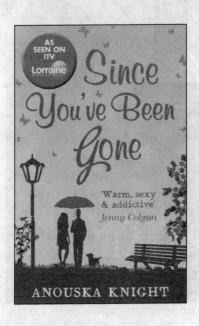

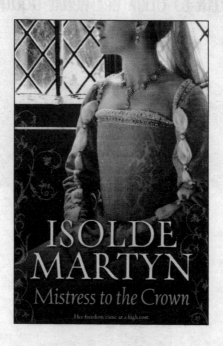

Meet The Sullivans...

Over 1 million books sold worldwide!

Stay tuned for more from **The Sullivans** in 2014

Available from:

www.millsandboon.co.uk

The World of Mills & Boon®

There's a Mills & Boon® series that's perfect for you. We publish ten series and, with new titles every month, you never have to wait long for your favourite to come along.

Blaze.
Scorching hot, sexy reads
4 new stories every month

By Request
Relive the romance with the best of the best
9 new stories every month

Cherish™
Romance to melt the heart every time
12 new stories every month

Desire™
Passionate and dramatic love stories
8 new stories every month